LAY DOWN YOUR WEARY TUNE

LAY DOWN YOUR WEARY TUNE

W. B. Belcher

OTHER PRESS

NEW YORK

Lyrics on page 305 from "I Ain't Got No Home," words and music by
Woody Guthrie. WGP/TRO-© Copyright 1961 (Renewed), 1963 (Renewed)
Woody Guthrie Publications, Inc., & Ludlow Music, Inc., New York, NY,
administered by Ludlow Music, Inc. Used by permission.

Production Editor: Yvonne E. Cárdenas
Text Designer: Julie Fry
This book was set in Dante and Trade Gothic
by Alpha Design & Composition of Pittsfield, NH

1 3 5 7 9 10 8 6 4 2

Library of Congress Cataloging-in-Publication Data

Belcher, W. B. (William B.)
Lay down your weary tune / by W. B. Belcher.
pages cm
ISBN 978-1-59051-746-8 (pbk. original) — ISBN 978-1-59051-747-5
(e-book) 1. Ghostwriters—Fiction. 2. Folk musicians—Fiction.
3. Secrets—Fiction. I. Title.
PS3602.E433L39 2016
813'.6—dc23
2015016956

Publisher's Note:
This is a work of fiction. Names, characters, places, and incidents either are the
product of the author's imagination or are used fictitiously, and any resemblance
to actual persons, living or dead, events, or locales is entirely coincidental.

For Kate,
from start to finish

*Sometimes people carry to such perfection
the mask they have assumed that in due course
they actually become the person they seem.*

W. SOMERSET MAUGHAM
THE MOON AND SIXPENCE

· INTRO ·

When little Sammy Sweet fished a waterlogged wool cap out of the river, Trooper Mark Calvin, of the New York State Police, said it was "definitive" proof that Eli had drowned. Case closed. Time to get on with our lives. But three days later, in the hollow behind the paper mill, Sammy snagged Eli's bruised leather satchel from the murmuring backwash. A half mile upstream from Eli's last known location, the discovery was fodder for a new round of conspiracy theories, conjectures, and what-if scenarios. To further infuriate the troopers, the bag's limp, deformed body wore a small bullet hole just above its clasp. Members of the trolling media, busybodies, and Galesville's newfound tourists all voiced the same question from the same village sidewalks and gas pumps and barstools: "What the hell happened to Eli Page?"

Some of them believed his disappearance was an elaborate hoax, a ploy to sell records—Eli, after all, was known for this trickery and sleight of hand almost as much as he was known for his music. Almost. But no one wanted to be duped. Even Hal Holland, the editor of the local paper, who once swore up and down that he saw a body plummet into the swollen Battenkill, backpedaled when word about the satchel spread through town. Now he tells everyone who will listen that it was just his mind playing tricks on him. Me? I'm not sure what to believe.

It's been two months, nineteen days, and twenty-one hours since Eli was last seen, walking alongside the road in a wild summer storm. Several witnesses reported that he was stumbling, unfazed by the headlights, detached from all earthly endeavors.

The river went over its banks that night. The town flooded, as it's prone to do when the heavens break open. After the water receded, the villagers put aside their differences and worked with a common purpose: Find the lost man. We employed bloodhounds to catch his scent, sifted through every inch of the Battenkill from Galesville to Easton, swept the land from the village proper to the fairgrounds. Found nothing. No sign of him. The national media grew restless. With their awkward satellite trucks, they reported on the search while peddling Eli's legacy, prompted by obituaries written well before Eli Page disappeared. Seven weeks in, attention spans fizzled, the bloodhounds caught a new case, volunteers dwindled, and I was left wondering how it could have ended the way it did.

Time marches on and we all wait for some sort of revelation. We look for miracles in the small things. We look for answers in wool caps and leather satchels, but answers are hard to come by these days.

So here I am, slumped over the harvest table in the dining room of Eli's farmhouse, a house that has been a port in the most frustrating and beautiful storm of my life, and I'm determined to write it all down, to contribute in some small way to our collective understanding of Eli Page, and maybe, just maybe, provide a note of truth to a composition famously built on lies.

Despite all that has happened, it is still his house—if I were to crack it open, it would sing, like a music box, a song for Eli. But that's no easy task. Even though it feels as though I've been here, in this old farmhouse, for much longer, I've been in Galesville for only seven months. Yet in that span, so much has changed that cannot be reversed. I wish I'd done things differently. I wish, as most people do at some point, that I knew then what I know now, but it doesn't work that way for a reason. After the fighting, after the flood, after the search, after it all, I sit in his chair, drink from his cup, and type this on his Underwood.

"Listen," he'd say if he were around. "Stop thinkin' and just listen."

Between inhale and exhale, the world on the other side of the window dials up its volume. Everything is music. The birds pass their song from bough to bough, from wire to rooftop, and the wind rustles the brittle leaves like the soft rattle of a snare drum. Somewhere a church bell rings, a woman laughs, a baby cries, a dog howls, a fish jumps out of the water. And somewhere Eli Page is singing the blues, and people like me can feel their lives ripping apart at the seams.

· FIRST ·

The first time I met him, he was nothing but a sleek silhouette, thin as a tongue depressor, and I was too enamored to peek behind the veil. Obscured by the stage dark, he was faceless, the shadow of everyman, but I knew his name, his songs, his story even before he uttered a word. Or at least I thought I did.

It was early 2001, and I was working, as I tended to do on Friday nights, at the university's Performing Arts Center. The PAC. As far as work-study programs can be ranked on a scale from 1 to 10 (1 = utterly depressing; 10 = mildly enjoyable), my job as a stagehand was a consistent 8 because, and only because, of one spectacular perk—a free wing-side pass to all road shows, plays, and concerts. "A Night with Eli Page" would be my last gig as a stagehand, but it was worth the trouble.

The call was fifteen minutes. Behind the curtain, the overhead lights buzzed with anticipation and the air reeked of burning dust. My supervisor, Alice the Impaler, scurried center stage to triple-check the equipment, the temperature of the bottled water, the angle of the stool.

Alice was a senior with rose-colored tips in her hair, hair that always smelled of stale coffee, an aspiring actress–turned–reluctant stage manager. I was a sophomore who asked too many questions. After her thorough review of backstage, she stopped flitting around for a moment and stared at me as if I was to blame for the weather, Eli Page's absence, and her failed love life.

"Everything will work out," I said, breaking the silence.

"Really?" she replied, her neck muscles tight, bulging out of her collar. "Our goddamned musician went for a walk and we've got a full house. So forgive me for not sharing your blind optimism. I've got shit to do."

"He'll be back...any minute now."

"Bet your life on it?"

I paused, just for the briefest of moments, before answering. "Yeah. Sure. It'll work out."

"Great. Problem solved." Alice pushed the button on her headset receiver, and her voice burst through the static: "Listen up, everyone. Jack's sure the talent will be here any minute now. 'It'll work out,' he says. No need to panic. Good thing Jack's here to teach us a thing or two about the virtue of patience. Be sure to thank him."

A chorus of acknowledgments echoed through my headset. "Thank you, Jack." Even the freshman in charge of the push brooms mumbled "Praise Jack" under his breath with the venom of the oft-maligned.

"Now it's on you, and I will tear you a new one if he doesn't show." Alice was a half foot shorter than I was, but I froze when she took my measure, and I swear her eyeballs jiggled inside their sockets when she spoke. "Keep your headset on," she added as she bolted across the stage, the beam of her flashlight cutting a path through the darkness.

I did as I was told.

Truth was, it happened all the time. Performers arrived late, drunk, discombobulated. We'd skip the sound check and walk-through. No big deal. I'd pull the curtain when I was told to, move stuff around on cue, and close the velour when Alice said, "Curtains . . . go." We always managed to survive. Okay, yes, this night was extraordinary. It was more than a passing show. The trustees, mostly baby boomers who'd spent their formative years listening to Eli Page's protest songs, slipped and slid their way to the PAC to relive their rebellious youth, if only for an hour or two. They sat in the red-roped front rows, and Alice was all too aware of their presence. To ratchet up the stress, the concert had sold out weeks in advance, so she was faced with twelve hundred cold and stubborn souls who came to catch a glimpse of a true counterculture icon. If he didn't reappear, it could very well turn into a riot (or so said Christopher, our house manager and part-time soothsayer).

Five minutes to curtain. Alice's voice buzzed on the headset to alert everyone that "Mr. Page" was "MIA" and we would hold the curtain until "plan B" announced itself.

"Still grinning, Jack?" One last quip before she clicked off.

Eli Page was known for his miraculous disappearing and reappearing acts. Famously, after he hit it big in the '60s, he secluded himself in the southern Berkshires for nearly two years, refusing contact with all but a few close friends. Then again in 1974, he disappeared for months only to reemerge in Europe for the start of a comeback tour. Alice's anxiety wasn't unfounded, but everyone knew the risk. It was all part of the larger mystery of Eli Page.

Stage left was my station. My walkway, which was marked with glow tape, stretched along the rail from the proscenium to the fire door at the rear of the building. Within the folds of the curtain, I inhaled dust and fire retardants until I was dizzy. To clear my head, I paced upstage and downstage, downstage and upstage. Behind the scrim and masking sat a pile of platforms labeled BYE, BYE, BIRDIE, stacks of recycled two-by-fours, and paint buckets filled with carriage bolts and drywall screws. Thirty hemp ropes were locked along the rail, each numbered and held tight by a red lever and ring. Behind the ropes, bricks were slotted into place to counterbalance the scenery hanging precariously above the performers' heads. As if the constant reminder by the technical director and stage manager to stay within the glow tape wasn't enough, signs were posted on every surface. DANGER! SHUT THE DOOR!! DON'T TOUCH!!! My favorite sign declared RED MEANS SERIOUS in bold black ink. Under those three words, someone had scribbled, R U F-ING KIDDING ME? in red marker, followed by a hastily drawn hangman with x'ed-out eyes.

The winter storm beat against the loading door.

In Alice's absence, I took a closer look at Eli Page's guitar. What harm would it do to finger a couple chords? No one would know. But I was interrupted by the *thud-swish* of the fire door. As I retreated to my post, I glimpsed the figure of a man in the doorway. Slender. Almost feral.

While the exterior light shaded his face, it simultaneously lit a dance of snow specks in the air above his head, creating a ghostly halo in the void.

The building shivered.

Everything went dark when the door slammed shut. My eyes charged and readjusted in the flux of light. A slow scuff of boots on the stage floor made its way through the darkness as the figure moved toward me. I aimed my flashlight on the ground in front of the scuffing and scraping, and Eli Page stepped into the pool of light.

"There's no turnin' back now." His voice crackled as if he'd swallowed fire. "I shoulda known better. I shoulda kept on walkin'."

"Mr. Page?"

"Yeah, yeah. That's right. That's me." He brushed the snow off his shoulders and continued in my direction. My stomach lodged itself at the base of my throat, cutting off all air. The muscles in my back tightened until I was ramrod straight up and down.

"Everyone's looking for you," I said.

"Shit. Is it that time already?"

"Actually, you were supposed to go on fifteen minutes ago."

"Well, I guess you could say I've never been the punctual type," he said, a smirk lifting his bony cheeks, hard cut in the downlight. He tossed his coat onto a pile of platforms.

"I should let my stage manager know."

"Why ruin the fun?" He squinted to see the stage setup. "Who are you, anyway? Least you can do is give me a name before you blow the whistle."

"Who am I?"

"You must call yourself somethin'. Bob. Bill. Henry. Scratch. Thaddeus. Tell me it's Thad. Unfortunate name, but it's got an interesting sound. Punches off the tongue like a drumbeat."

"Jack Wyeth."

"Wyeth?" He paused, cocked his head. "Where're you from?"

"Nowhere special."

He nodded as he repeated "Thad, Thad, Thad," jerking his chin forward, spitting out the name like bullets. Before I could convince him to stay put, he was at center, lifting the guitar from its silver stand.

I glanced at the glow tape at my feet, thought twice, and then joined him in the shallow spotlight that fell from a single gelled Leko—an early-evening tint that made his face roll with grays and blues. For the first time, I could see the pale fire of his eyes.

"Well, John Wyeth of nowhere special, I'm Elijah Page." He stuck out his hand. I tried not to appear too eager to take it, but I quickly relented.

"Jack," I corrected him as we shook. "It's Jack Wyeth."

"All right, Jack. Tell me—what brought you to this institution of geniuses?"

"Studying. Music, writing, history. A little of everything, I guess."

"Sounds like you need a map."

"I play." I pointed to his guitar. "Or try to. And I write some for the *Daily Collegian*."

"Well, let's hope we don't lose you to the dark side when you've got that sturdy piece of paper in your hands."

"No. That won't happen."

"Sure. You've got good intentions." He hung his head and massaged the back of his neck. Even with the stage light at a minimum, the ice in his hair melted fast, dripping tiny beads of water onto the guitar's body. "You've all got good intentions, right?"

I nodded.

He continued: "Make sure what you're doin' means somethin'. Don't just tear people apart unless it means somethin'. Tell me that makes sense."

"It does. Very much."

Static shocked my ear and Alice's jagged voice said, "Christopher has made a decision." With my hand to my earpiece, I walked back to my post. Eli followed close behind, leaning in to hear the words spilling out of the headset. "We'll give it until eight twenty-five, and then Christopher will alert the chancellor." I placed my hand on the button to respond. Eli looked at me and shook his head ever so slightly. I pulled my hand away.

"Who's Christopher?" Eli asked, his voice mockingly effete and nasal.

"House manager."

His smile widened, showing his crooked incisors. So many questions filled my head, but they all came to a standstill in the bottlenecked expressway between my brain and my mouth. The more I thought of them, the more I reconsidered their premises and sent them on a detour—they were meaningless questions, questions that any fan would pose. Although I don't remember it, I must've made a decision to remain silent, for the reward of kinship was far more important to me than knowing about his favorite city or his favorite song.

"Thad," he said again. "'The Terrible Death of Thaddeus Miles'—how's that for a song title?"

I laughed. Embarrassed, I removed my face from the light.

"Now that you're loose, son, here's the plan," he said.

Eli was in his late fifties then, and he was touring incessantly. He performed 150 times a year, give or take; the university was merely one stop of a never-ending show. Even so, he was full of energy. A whirlwind, a puckish rogue in black, he smelled of whiskey and woodsmoke, and although I was unnerved at first, he had a kind, warm disposition that quickly put me at ease. His shoulders slumped, and I wondered if that was his natural posture or if the constant weight of the guitar—even if minuscule—somehow made him start to fold in on himself.

As he voiced his plan, laying out a set of tasks for me to complete, we were interrupted by a loud crash, metal on concrete, which originated from upstage. Eli grabbed the flashlight from my hand and crouched behind a stack of platforms. A fraction of a second later, Alice barreled through the undersized doorframe that led to the greenroom.

We both paused in our tracks when the crowd went silent. After the audience resumed their laughter and conversation, Alice continued her approach. As she did, I spotted the empty guitar stand and realized that Eli had taken his instrument with him.

I jumped forward to cut Alice off. "Are you okay?" I asked, expertly blocking her view.

"Some moron put the music stands in the middle of the stairs," she said. "It's not where they live." Suddenly, her focus shifted. She pointed to the bolts strewn across the floor. "Did you knock this bucket over? Someone could break an ankle. What the hell are you doing outside the green zone anyway?"

"Sorry. I was checking on the noise. Wanted to make sure no one was hurt."

She glared at me. "Get back to where you belong." The earpiece crackled. Two seconds later, Alice vanished.

Eli reappeared with his guitar in his grip. His grin had doubled in size. Inclined to follow his plan simply because he told me to do so, I asked, "Okay, what's next?" Truthfully, back then, he was a magnet, a born leader, a persuasive man in a rather small frame, and he could disarm you with a wink. He strapped the guitar to his torso and rolled his head back and forth in a brief exercise.

At twenty-five past eight, the crowd began to stomp in rhythm and chant, "Eli, Eli, Eli." I peeked around the curtain and saw Chancellor Cross, a rare guest in the PAC, step onto the stage, lift his finger to his mouth, and shush the crowd. A tall man with a sweeping comb-over and a red bow tie, he raised his hands above his head in Nixonian fashion, and the crowd leveled. When he brought his arms down, his bony shoulders sliced holes in his suit jacket. In a very diplomatic, calming tone, he said, "Well, ladies and gents, we have a bit of a delay due to the ice. Nothing to worry about, but if you would kindly take your seats, remain patient and respectful, I'm sure our guest will arrive—"

That was my cue. I jumped straight up and tugged on the rope as hard and fast as I could. The curtain swooshed toward the wings, kicking dust up in its wake, until it crashed against both sides of the proscenium. The chains chimed above my head. The swift action revealed the small shape of a man on the outskirts of the stage lighting. The crowd rose to their feet and burst into a roar of laughter and cheer—half for Page, half for the chancellor who, while spinning around, nearly fell into the first row.

Eli Page beat on his guitar with the force of a hundred fists. It was so loud and jarring that it vibrated my teeth. I half expected the guitar to explode in his grasp or, at least, crumble into a thousand pieces. The chancellor slid back into his seat as Eli belted out "The Ballad of the Listless Gambler."

> *He was tone-deaf two times over*
> *But that hardly slowed him down*
> *His love of the whiskey river*
> *Cast him from every flop in town*
>
> *Oh, that poor listless gambler*
> *Should've quit when two bills ahead*
> *But they took his cards right from him*
> *And tossed him in the riverbed.*

Over the headset, there was a piercing static and then I heard, "Kill the house lights. Kill them now. Go to sound cue three," and then, "What the fuck is going on here?"

The speakers were hot, and every person in the building except Chancellor Cross was on their feet, on their toes, leaning forward to feel the music.

Eli Page had been strumming his guitar for the public for decades. Everyone had heard his voice. Hell, half of the guitar-slung student population—myself included—covered his songs in Nell's Beans or the Black Sheep. Yet none of that noise could match the electricity and excitement that overtook the crowd, the theater, the whole damn campus during that live show. There was a sense, no matter how ridiculous it may seem now, that I was watching the most important and remarkable ninety minutes of music there ever was and ever would be. "The Passion of Saint Eli"—that's the title of the review I wrote for the *Collegian*. The gist was that his talent was much more than music; he shed light on universal desires, fears, anxieties. He spoke about being alive in an insane world, and he gathered all the pieces of the human entanglement with God and country and failed relations and mixed them with lust and longing, a whole spectrum of shared experiences.

We all cheered when he began "Upcountry Blues" as an encore. It was a sullen song, one of my favorites for sentimental reasons—a song my father was fond of before he took off. As the song progressed to the third verse, the crowd grew eerily silent. I peered around the curtain to make sure they were still breathing. And, honestly, at the same time, I had to bite the inside of my cheek to stop the tears from welling up. Eli offered no reprieve. Instead, he transitioned into "Goodnight Irene," urging everyone to sing along with the chorus, even though he chose

Lead Belly's haunting lyrics over the softer touch of the Weavers.

Irene good night, Irene good night
Good night Irene, good night Irene,
I'll get you in my dreams.

When finished, Eli merely nodded to the audience—which stood in applause—and remained anchored to the stage floor until I pulled the curtain shut.

That was that. It was over. Applause shifted to laughter and inane conversation, boots dragging on the aisle rug, seats springing up. As the crowd scampered out into the ice storm, Eli took a deep breath, lifted the guitar strap off his shoulder, and gently laid his instrument down into its battered case. Squatting beside the coffin, he brought his hands to his face and rubbed his palms against his eyes and temples. As he popped up, I looked away and pretended I was busy securing the area. After a moment, he approached.

"That was fun."

"How can they do that?" I asked, astonished at the crowd's ability to pick up and move on. "How can they just tune out and go home like nothing happened?"

"They listened. They were entertained. That's enough," he said.

"Is it?" Not for me, I thought. Not at that moment.

"It is."

We shook hands. His fingers were vibrating, but, at the same time, he seemed deflated, defeated. Maybe he was drained after the performance. Or maybe he wanted to keep playing. Maybe he had no desire to get back on that bus to drink and pass out and end up in Rochester or Philadelphia or wherever the next morning.

"Let me give you some advice," he said. "Don't worry about them. Get yourself right. If you've got somethin' to say, get to work and say it. If not, find somethin' better to do with your life, 'cause you don't want this"—he motioned to the stage—"unless it's the only thing that calls." With those parting words, he trudged upstage and opened the door. A moment later, he was gone, absorbed by the icescape.

Chancellor Cross and three important-looking men in overcoats—trustees, I assumed—pushed their way through the curtain.

"Where is he, young man?" the chancellor asked. I pointed to the door and watched them go, knowing that Eli was long gone.

The headset squawked in my ear: "Great work, everyone. Jack, go fuck yourself."

John Allen Wyeth is the name on my birth certificate, but everyone called me Bird until I left Stockton, Massachusetts in 1999. Officially, as the story goes, I was nicknamed after a family friend and guardian angel, Floyd "Bird" Brown, who saved my father's life by yanking him out of the Housatonic River in the middle of a nor'easter. Maybe that qualified him for naming rights; I'm not so sure. According to my mother, she resisted the name until I was cut out of the womb at thirty-three weeks. Four pounds on the button, I donned the plum-red hue of a newly hatched robin. "You chirped nonstop for the first three days of your precious life," she said on more than one occasion, "then you just shut down like your vocal chords were broke or something, and you've barely made a peep since." After I left for college, I tried to reinvent myself, whatever that means. Now I answer only to Jack.

The original John Wyeth, my father, disappeared the day before my fifth birthday. After his so-called brush with death, he knocked up my mother, sold his Telecaster, and filled out an application for the tower shift at the mill. Once the adrenaline faded, he took off to find something more exhilarating—raising a kid was just another job, another shackle, another link in the chain that was pulling him under. Some people are just not cut out for the flimsy art of parenthood. That's the way I see it, and that's all I'm going to say on the subject. For now.

My childhood in Stockton was a tug-of-war between fact and fiction. The town was built around a failing paper mill, yet everyone pretended it was a wonderland of opportunity—they existed on a potent cocktail of faith and pride that I never could grasp. The young men, high school heroes, grew old, tore their ACLs in pickup games or threw their backs out on the racquetball court. They would hope their eight-year-olds could throw harder, run faster, and be better; they were always searching for the next hero. All the while, they'd punch in at the mill, forty-five years would slip away, and they'd get cancer and die. It's been that way for more than a century. Most Stocktonians let it take its course, but not my mother. "This town sucks you in and rattles you around like a penny caught in God's vacuum cleaner," she used to say. At fifteen, I was offered a summer job mowing the lawns at Clark & Co. When I told her, she charged at me with a shovel in her grip. Swinging it in the air, inches from my nose, she yelled, "If you go anywhere near that mill, I will knock you on your ass!" Consequently, I turned down the job and started a lovely career as a busboy. My mother was always on the lookout for greatness. Her love for my father blossomed out of her desire for extraordinariness, and that desire transferred to me when he departed. It was the fiction of great expectations.

For many, Stockton was enough. Casey, my best friend, dreaded leaving for college. Stockton was his home, and he was one of its favorite sons. "Why?" I asked. "Why would anyone want to stay? Please explain it to me." With a smile and a shimmer in his pale brown eyes, he fondly recalled how everyone chanted his name as he closed out a perfect game. He described the marathons of H-O-R-S-E he and his older brothers played in the driveway until well past midnight. He obsessed about the time he felt up Liz McKernon on the shores of Clark Pond. And he visited his grandfather's grave at the Hill Street Cemetery whenever the leaves turned red. For those reasons and many more, it would always be his home.

Not me. I'd been trying to escape for as long as I could remember. Shortly after my father left, I hopped on my hand-me-down Huffy, training wheels attached, and attempted to pedal my way out. As I rode by the reservoir on the edge of town, a powder blue station wagon swerved off the road. The driver rolled open her window and screamed, "I know your mother, young man, and I'm going to race down this road and tell her what you're doing!" Then she sped off, kicking rocks into my spokes. I picked up my bike, spun it around, and pedaled as fast as I could. Pumping the wheels and panting up the hills, I nearly made it home before I saw my mother flying out of the front yard with a wooden spoon raised over her head.

The second time I tried to leave, I was thirteen. My friend Joey swiped some cash from his mother's purse, and together we hiked up an off-season road, hoping it was a shortcut to the train station in Pittsfield. When the sun fell behind the mountains, we were still trying to make sense of where we had been and where we were going. The darkness became disorienting, so we abandoned our journey and followed the mill's flashing red lights home to Stockton. A police cruiser stopped us at the town line. "You boys have a death wish?" the cop asked. Under his breath, he called us "a bag of idiots." We knew it was dangerous, but it didn't matter. We just wanted to get out. Joey succeeded, in a way—the cop brought him home to find his mother asleep on the couch, their collie licking a white powder off the coffee table. Joey was shipped to a foster home. I never saw him again.

Needless to say, the summer after my seventeenth birthday, I packed up and left for college. As I stuffed my bags into the belly of a Peter Pan bus, my mother grabbed me by the scruff of the neck, bowed our heads, and said, "God hates the happy middle. So, if you want to be a screw-up, be an extraordinary screw-up, live low, and deal with the consequences. But I'd suggest that you use the many gifts that you were given, live on high, and make me proud." Then she released me, wiped the holy tears from her eyes, and walked away with her chin in the air. I wish I could say that her words inspired me, but that'd be ridiculous. After lugging my stuff into the dorm, I got high with my new roommate, a want-to-be jazz guitarist, and forgot that Mary Wyeth ever cared enough to pass along a bit of hackneyed wisdom.

Sometimes I wonder if I was born restless, or if it was the by-product of my mother's grand scheme. Whatever the reason, I couldn't stay in one place. Not for long. After I met Eli Page, I began to feel as if I was out of my body, looking down at myself, searching for meaning, trying to live up to her expectations and Eli Page's advice. "If you've got somethin' to say, get to work and say it." Heeding those words, I dropped out of school, lived in and out of my car, booked gigs whenever and wherever I could, and started a blog as a companion of sorts to my nomadic existence. Within a few years, I'd driven through Boston, Providence, Brooklyn, Buffalo, Nashville, Wichita, Louisville, Memphis, New Orleans, and dozens of small college towns with names like Ames and Paint Lick and Wilkes-Barre. Skilled at unplugged cover songs, I lulled the coffee crowd into a strange brew of contentment and confusion with "Play with Fire" and "Maggie's Farm" and "I Ain't Marching Anymore." On more than a few occasions, raucous audience members shouted "tree hugger" or "hippie" or "stoner." Some asked aloud, "Who the hell is marching?" If I had to pick the most infuriating response, it would be the old standby: "Hey, dude, 1965 called, and they want their music back." (It's amazing how many times I've heard that exact phrase, word for word.) As I rambled from town to town, I picked up some freelance writing gigs, placing five hundred words here and there about musicians who'd fallen by the wayside; I busked on street corners and bus stops; I fell in and out of love; and I questioned the purpose of it all.

Eventually, I landed in New Haven and found work for a start-up alt weekly that quickly and predictably fell apart. I was unhinged, burnt out, lonely. No desire to begin again or begin at all. I couldn't pay my rent. Not that it was a surprise to anyone (except my landlord). I was a chronicler of music that had faded beyond nostalgia into irrelevance. No one was listening. Everyone was worried about anthrax in white envelopes, snipers on the highways, airplanes falling from the sky; they were thinking about wars in caves, paint-by-number terror charts, and economic hijinks. While some overcompensated by planting magnetic ribbons on every square inch of their SUVs, others, like myself, seized up, gave in. I stopped acting like I had anything to say. What was the point? We were all lost anyway.

About that time, I met a girl named Melanie at a costume party at Yale. She was a honey-eyed actress with a sharp tongue and sexy voice. I was the paid entertainment (currency = beer). Decked out like an early '60s housewife, complete with a white apron and a checkered blue dress, she crossed the room, grabbed my arm above the elbow, and said, "Are you going to kiss me or stand there holding your guitar for another half hour?" So I kissed her. That's how it started. I found a day job, and after seven months of saving, I bought a ring. How crazy is that? I told myself that it was time to settle down, time to leave the music behind. I planned this whole other life around Melanie, but the job, the relationship, and my sanity all imploded soon after I staked my ground. Mistakes were made. A lot of mistakes. So one frostbitten New England morning, after I'd paid my debt, I packed all that was left into my Chevy Celebrity, that aging workhorse, and sped north to Saratoga Springs, New York.

Recap: At thirty years old, I was a never-was musician and sometimes music journalist who slept on a foldout couch in my best friend's basement and played cover songs on the street corner for a few dollars a week. Nearly ten years after "A Night with Eli Page," all that was left of my little life-altering moment was a distorted memory, a few blog posts, and a faded article in the *Daily Collegian*.

That was until I received a strange phone call in March of 2010.

As I stood outside Caffè Lena — an old folk club that had presented Eli Page, Bob Dylan, Dave Van Ronk, the Reverend Gary Davis, and you name it back in the day — and scrounged in my pockets for coffee money, my cell phone buzzed. I flipped it open, and a soft, tender voice asked, "Will you hold for Mr. Gettleson?"

"Who's Mr. Gettleson?"

"Hold please," she said.

And I did. Had nothing better to do. I stepped out of line, and I held for twelve minutes, resisting the urge to hang up the whole time. Finally, Barry Gettleson jumped on the other end. He introduced himself as Eli's manager and friend. He said that he'd had a hell of a time trying to track me down, but he was sure glad he did. Then he mentioned my blog, some of my old projects at *American Songwriter* and *Sing Out!*, a mutual friend in Woodstock. It was all very confusing. "Eli digs your stuff," he said. "His response to the idea is tepid at best. It'll be a challenge." "Legacy," "perspective," "posterity"—those were all words he threw around, but I wasn't following his line of thought.

"Stop," I said. "I don't understand. What do you want with me?"

"I've got a project," he answered. "Something that you won't be able to resist."

The basketball's airy bounce caught my ear before Casey dribbled into the light. The rest of his neighborhood was dark except for the flickering of TV screens in bedroom windows. Nothing good ever came from these midnight displays of athletic prowess.

He jumped and released the ball. *Clank.* As I watched it sail left toward the front lawn, I locked stares with Denise, his wife, who was leaning on the porch rail with a full glass of white wine in one hand and a rolled-up *Saratoga Living* in the other. I waved. She stood up straight, spun around on her toes, and entered the house.

Casey and I were friends because our mothers were friends once upon a time. They were both abandoned wives raising hyperactive boys, and they took turns feeding us proper meals, bandaging our wounds, and putting us to work. He was the closest thing I had to a brother. When I arrived in Saratoga with little warning, he took me in without hesitation, but three and a half months later, it was clear I'd overstayed my welcome.

"Can I ask you something?"

"What if I say no?" Casey kept his eyes firmly fixed on the rim. "Will you leave me alone?" He sprinted to the hoop and put the ball in.

"Probably not."

"Yeah, I didn't think so."

"Denise wants me out, right?"

"Let's keep Denise out of it," he said. The ball banked off the backboard and fell softly through the worn net.

"If she wants me out, I'll get out. I understand," I said. It was easy enough to see that I was a source of tension in his marriage, but if you ask me, the strings were too tight to begin with. Casey had been pushing Denise to have another kid. He was impatient. After law school, they'd decided to have two children, spaced four years apart. It was a rational plan, made by two rational people, and I knew it would never work. "Actually," I said, "I might be packing up a bit sooner than I thought."

For the first time since I returned from the Caffè, Casey stopped toying with the basketball and looked at me. I told him about the phone call. Even though he'd deny it, I saw a smile twitch beneath his chiseled face. He'd hoped that fate would intervene, and his prayers were answered. That's what the twitch said to me, anyway.

"What did this Gettleson guy say?" Casey asked as he passed me the ball.

"It's complicated."

"You'll have to do better than that." He was outright giddy at his stroke of luck. "Come on," he shouted. "Shoot the ball!"

Casey was a winner, the very model of success, a bright star in an otherwise dull universe. As his best friend, my failures were intensified by his successes. That dynamic continued even after our lives diverged and Stockton was far behind us. In high school, he collected girlfriends and varsity records; I collected rejections and bootleg CDs. His jump shot led us to consecutive state championships, and his golden arm struck out more hapless souls than any other pitcher in county history. He aced every class with a smile and a wink, from kindergarten to Rensselaer to law school. "It was all a breeze," he said when he was recognized by *The Business Review* as an up-and-comer in the burgeoning field of intellectual property law. Before he was twenty-eight, he was married to a beautiful, brilliant Cornell grad and fellow law school success story, had a son, a stately house in a ritzy Saratoga neighborhood, and a Lexus that repelled mud. His annual salary was more than I'd make in my lifetime. He was exceptional; he was extraordinary. I was his charity case.

I shot the ball from fifteen feet, and it dropped in with a satisfying *snap*.

"What do you have to do?" He picked it up.

"Persuade Eli Page to let me . . . tell his story, I guess."

"So you'd be his biographer?"

"It's a ghostwriting gig. I'd do most of the writing, but it would be uncredited. They'd be his memoirs, his stories."

"As long as it pays, it doesn't really make any difference," he said matter-of-factly. Casey was nothing if not practical. "The guy's a live wire, right?"

"He mostly keeps to himself."

"So he's a recluse. What's the hold up?"

"Well, he hasn't signed off on the deal. It sounds like he needs some arm-twisting."

"Twist away. That's right in your wheelhouse, my man."

"Twisting?"

"No, jackass. Writing about has-been folk musicians."

Was it? I wondered. I didn't know what, if anything, was in my wheelhouse. If the offer had come five years earlier, I might've shared Casey's optimism. Now I was motivated mostly by anxiety and caffeine. Gettleson's plan was desperate. I knew that from the start, but it wasn't the desperation that bothered me. I was worried more about my own inability to write, to communicate. The last two years, give or take, I'd reached down deep inside of myself and tried to pull out something worthwhile. What I found was sludge. No decent songs. No decent stories. Hardly a decent blog post. Just sludge. All of a sudden, I'm thrown in that sludge and told to swim (and to convince Eli Page to swim alongside me).

"From what I've heard at the Caffè, he's not doing well."

"Not well how?"

"I guess he's not always..." I searched for the right word. "Lucid."

"Wow. Sounds like a hoot."

"I'm sure it's all exaggerated," I added, mostly for my own benefit.

"What did you tell the man?"

"I said I'd think about it, call him back."

"Come on! Don't flake out on me." Casey's shoulders straightened.

"Shoot the ball," I said.

He threw it up without looking and it hit the back of the rim. "Am I missing something? This is the opportunity you've been tiptoeing toward. The second chance you're always going on about."

Casey wasn't crazy. I was waiting for my second chance, but I knew that second chance is just another way of saying last chance, final chance, do or die.

His bad shot bounced into my hands. I dribbled in place.

"Don't get me wrong," he continued. "The blog thing was a win for a while—people actually read it and that's a plus. And you're one hell of a musician. No one is taking either of those away from you. But sooner or later, you've got to drop all the baggage and let yourself go make a living, right? Step up to the line and be counted."

"If you say so."

"Don't you want some of this?" he asked while motioning to the vinyl-sided landscape that surrounded him. Casey was trying to be helpful, but the daily come-to-Jesus lecture was maddening. "It's not pretty out there," he added.

"Thanks for enlightening me."

"Frat buddy of mine from RPI has three degrees and a clean record, and he still can't find work. This falls right into your lap and you wishy-wash your way over here like you've got options. It's almost upsetting."

"I'll probably do it," I confessed.

"Good. Then maybe you can move on."

"I *have* moved on."

"Come on. Try to get by me," he challenged.

I played along. He forearmed me, pushed me, forced me to use my weak hand. I glanced up at the hoop, and he slapped the ball from my grip. With the tenacity of a second-string point guard, I recovered and blew by him, but he fouled me hard, sending me to the ground in a pile of flesh and bone. It hurt. A lot. The most irritating side effect of the exchange was that it worked. It got my blood moving; it made me think; it knocked the decision loose.

I got to my feet and checked the ball. After a half-hearted jab step, I drove to the basket, stopped dead, and faded away from Casey's flailing arms. The ball soared out of his reach and into the basket with a swish.

"No question," he said, short of breath. "You've got to go. I'm sick of this poor-Jack crap."

Casey wanted me to be like him so that he could understand me. He couldn't grasp the fact that I didn't care about new cars or granite countertops; I didn't aspire to possess a fifty-one-inch plasma 1080p or a shiny espresso machine or some Patagonia European goose down jacket that I'd never wear. I was looking for something else, something harder to come by.

"I'm kicking you out. Go do something productive with your life."

He picked up the ball and tossed it into the garage. Before I could catch my breath and protest, he disappeared. A few seconds later, the garage light went off and I stood alone in the cool dark night.

Casey made good on that promise too—he did throw me out. But before he had a chance to lug my bags to the sidewalk with the trash bins, I phoned Barry Gettleson and told him I was his man.

Seven miles east of Saratoga Springs and casa de Casey, the traffic thins, the population dwindles, and the blurry backdrop of so many Saratoga picture windows slides into focus. Ornate Victorian homes give way to horse pastures and apple orchards with rotting fences; horse pastures and apple orchards give way to dairy farms and nameless hamlets and acres of rolling green land. East of the Hudson, life looks inward, trees lean toward New England's practicality, and simple living is the prevailing philosophy.

"Pull it together," I said to myself as I crossed the county line, drawing closer and closer to Eli Page's hideaway. The early afternoon sun warmed the inside of my Chevy. Neither the wind whistling through the cabin nor the road humming beneath my tires could dull my apprehension.

The night before, I'd scribbled Gettleson's directions on a Xanax-labeled scratchpad, which I'd stolen from Casey's kitchen counter. A day later, they read like bad song lyrics:

"Go east on 29, take a right on 61 / follow road as it twists up the hill / at Galesville's single light, take a right and a right / to cross a red covered bridge at the Battenkill." I sang to myself, "at the single, solitary light, take a right, take a right, take a right."

My phone vibrated against my thigh. I pulled the car into the driveway of a nearby farm stand, dug the cell from my jeans pocket, and tried to figure out who was on the other side. The "212" gave it away.

"Where are you?" Gettleson asked.

"Still on Route 29," I said, quickly scanning my surroundings. Across the road there was a large wooden sign whose red-and-blue carnival tent logo read WELCOME TO THE WASHINGTON COUNTY FAIR—AN AGRICULTURAL TRADITION FOR OVER A CENTURY. I told him as much.

"Good," he said. "Listen. He should know you're coming, but take it slow. We're going to have to ease into this. Get me?"

"Is there something you're not saying?"

"No, no, no. Everything's fine. This is just a heads-up. Listen, I've got a meeting. I'll give you a call in a couple days to see how things stand. Okay. Great. You're a champ."

The line went dead before I could ask him to clarify "ease into this."

I stuffed my phone back into my pocket, sat up in my seat, and gazed at the empty fairgrounds. Out there, behind acres of chain-link fence, were barns and bleachers and dirt tracks, an ancient red caboose, old farm machinery whose metal claws tore into the earth, and even a bandstand. No doubt the grounds would burst to life in a few months. I imagined the midway lit up, the barns full of livestock, screams and laughter coming from the Ferris wheel or the Tilt-A-Whirl. Finally, I swung back out onto the road only to find myself behind a tractor caked in mud (I hoped). The machine, which was three times the height of my car, slowed the traffic to a crawl. A few miles later, when the tractor was well behind me, I turned onto County 61 and caught back up with the Battenkill.

Galesville
Historic District
Est. 1801

The sign's reflective gold lettering flickered in the sunlight. "You'd never know it was there unless you knew it was there, if you get my drift," Gettleson had said. I finally understood what he'd meant. Hidden on a county route, Galesville, which straddles New York and Vermont, remains invisible until a few hundred feet after the welcome sign, when a chrome diner, a Stewart's Shop, and a cemetery all come into view.

As I coasted through the village, I couldn't help but be drawn to the old IGA grocery store, its brick slathered with bright white paint and half covered by a tarp. A woman stood in front of the whitewash. A paint roller dangled from her hand, and she stared at the wall as if she was figuring out a puzzle. Distracted, I nearly clipped a police cruiser in the breakdown lane, where a state trooper was busy scolding a group of high schoolers in a busted Ford Taurus. I tapped the brakes and swerved around the vehicles. My errant driving caught the trooper's attention, and he shot me a deadly look. Up ahead, a single, solitary traffic light blinked yellow. Caution. Slow down. At that moment, I knew that Galesville was a place I'd learn to love and hate in equal measure.

CROSS AT YOUR OWN RISK. A metal sign carrying those five words of warning was tacked above the mouth of the covered bridge, just high enough to be illegible until I was a split second from entering. My car thrummed along the wood planks, beating the inside of the structure. Once on the other side, River Bend Farm revealed itself. Set back behind a stacked stone fence and wrought-iron gate, it was impossible to miss, even if its facade wasn't exactly warm or welcoming.

I parked in front of its carriage barn and stepped out to take a look around. The house, the land, the outbuildings were all overrun. Untamed. Deteriorating with force and urgency. The bones appeared solidish, but even I, who knew very little about historic preservation (or maintenance) and who, let's be honest, am controlled by little fictions, knew that the structures needed aid. The house had withstood two hundred years, two hundred winters, but its paint had submitted long ago, its enormous chimney was disintegrating, and its trim was chipped and rotted. Faith alone could not keep it upright for much longer.

Attached to the house through a one-level post-and-beam mudroom, the carriage barn and its elaborate cupola, shiny slate roof, and jocular weathervane were all evidence of New England's charm a stone's throw from New England's border. A half century younger than the main house, give or take, it too was desperate for attention.

I knocked on the front door and waited. No answer. I tried three more times, but there was still no movement as far as I could tell. Peering through a side window, I found no sign of Eli Page, or anyone, for that matter, but instead of calling Gettleson, which would've been the practical thing to do, I peeked around back.

Behind the house stood a few abandoned barns that leaned dangerously into the earth, a dilapidated silo, and a blue tractor that looked as if it had been lifted from a recent archaeological dig. Everything was worn down, faded.

"Hello," I yelled. "Anyone out there?"

No sound. No movement.

Convinced I had the time wrong, I retreated to the car to find my phone, but before I could dial Gettleson, the front door creaked opened. After a few seconds, a shaggy mess of a man stepped out. Feet shoulder width apart, the man stood as if to balance himself like a boxer poised to launch a haymaker in my general direction. A welterweight, but a boxer nonetheless. His glare hit me like the wave of heat from a bonfire.

"What'd'ya want?" he asked.

"I'm Jack Wyeth. Barry Gettleson sent me."

"Who?"

"Barry. Gettleson." As if those words triggered a call to action, a giant dog emerged from behind the man and blitzed me. The enormous creature, a mutt monster with a black-and-tan coat, attempted to jump and greet me, but he barely made it off the ground. I recoiled. The dog sniffed my hand and then nudged its head against my hip so hard that it knocked me into the side of the Chevy.

"A little help," I pleaded with the old man. He continued staring at me. So, at a loss, I reached for the dog's head and tried to push it aside. It didn't budge. The tail whipped the rear fender with a *thump, thump, brush, thump*. All the while, the thing panted like an asthmatic dragon, and I wondered how quickly it might wear itself out.

"Tig," the man finally called. "Get inside." The dog looked up at me, disappointed, and then turned its head and slowly, painfully obeyed the command. "Figured you for a no-show," he said.

"Well, I'm here. I made it."

"Ain't that my luck?" The man wore dusty jeans and a corduroy jacket like Eli Page was known to do, his shoulders slumped like Eli Page's, and he was a wiry five foot nine like Eli Page, but sometimes denial is as blinding as a flashbulb. A long gray beard hid his chin, and I struggled to see his eyes, his most recognizable feature, as they were masked beneath age and skin. All things considered, I was forced to concede that yes, yes, it was Eli. Nevertheless, this wasn't the Eli Page I'd met ten years earlier. He wasn't the smirking Eli Page from his album head shots or the four covers of *Rolling Stone* or the old Joe Alper photos from Caffè Lena. Once, in an old record shop, I found a print of a young Page, leaning against a stage door, ankles crossed, sucking the cold air through his harmonica. For years, the picture was tacked to the bulletin board above my desk. That guy and this guy were not one and the same.

"What was it again?" he asked. "John Wyeth?"

"Jack. Jack Wyeth. Barry Gettleson said you—"

"Follow me," he instructed.

Time takes its toll, I thought, as I entered the house. Page had shadows under his baggy eyes as if he was perpetually hungover. He needed a cutman. Up close, he looked even more like a stringy old boxer who had just retired with a 50–50–0 record or an old actor preparing to howl on the heath. His existence had wrinkled him to the core.

Eli Page's famous "breakdown" and vanishing act was well known and still talked about in hangouts like Caffè Lena, but here's the wrap-up: Five years ago, Eli disappeared from the scene and resurfaced in this quiet upstate village, refusing contact with the outside world. Everything else is hearsay. People love gossip almost as much as they hate the truth, but both pale in comparison to the comeback story—they're happy to see their heroes knocked to the pavement only to get back up, bloodied but alive. It's an American tradition. Everyone loves that tale, but standing there, I felt that Page's story was in its final round, begging for the bell to ring. Something over the last decade had jostled him, spun him, and helped him spiral blindly toward oblivion. Book or no book, I wasn't sure resurrection was possible, but then again, I wasn't sure he was looking to roll back the stone.

"Go lie down," Eli barked at the dog. The mutt didn't move. "Tig. Lie down. Now." The dog eyeballed me as he collapsed on top of his understuffed pillow. Eli threw a milk bone in the animal's general direction. It skipped its way to the dog's snout. Tig stretched his neck and captured the treat, expending as little energy as possible.

"Tig. That's an unusual name," I said. "Is it short for something?"

"Short for El Tigre," he answered.

"Really?"

"No. The name came with the dog."

When we reached the front room, I was drawn to the large fireplace, surrounded by raised wood paneling from chair rail to baseboard. What remained uncovered was a pale yellow plaster like the faded pages of an old paperback. In the dark corners, small fissures cracked diagonally across the surface. Not unlike the exterior of the house, the meticulous craftsmanship was fighting back the signs of age—and losing. A braided rug covered much of the wide pine floor. On top of it, a leather sofa and a plush armchair were set for seating, except that the armchair served as a de facto bookshelf for dated magazines, newspapers, volumes of poetry. Eli Page fit his surroundings like an actor fits the stage scenery. The room was uniquely his even in its fakery, but there was one glaring, unforgivable flaw: There was no guitar in sight.

He relaxed into the folds of the sofa. I stood by the armchair and waited for direction. Across from me, there was a closed door, and to the right of the door, an empty television cabinet was stuck in the corner like a weeping fig. Its lacquered top was layered with dust, but a prominent outline remained.

"What happened over there?" I asked, pointing to the unit.

"Tossed it out the window," he said.

"Nothing worth watching?"

"Gave me a headache."

He wasn't going to make it easy. I lifted the newspapers from the armchair, placed them gently on the rug, and sat down across from him.

"Mr. Page." Panic burned in my chest. I cleared my throat and repeated, "Mr. Page." He stared as if he were seeing me for the first time. I didn't know what to say, so I said his name again. He blinked, and the expression on his face shifted from worry to impatience. "Are you okay?" He blinked again. One more time: "Mr. Page."

"Eli. Call me Eli," he said firmly.

"Eli. Sorry. Should we talk about the book?"

He propped a cushion between his thin frame and the arm of the sofa. His old joints crunched as he adjusted. After a failed attempt to cross his legs, he merely placed his calf on the opposite knee. His corduroy jacket was so small that his hairy forearms stuck out when he put his elbow on the sofa's arm and rested his cheek in the palm of his hand. I mirrored his position as best I could, all the while yearning for the Eli Page I met years ago, full of vigor and humor, playful and alive, the Eli I thought I knew. For a fleeting moment, I worried that he could see that memory reflected in my eyes. I looked away.

"Ease into this," Gettleson had advised, but what did that mean?

"I guess we should talk about the arrangement," I said. The words vibrated in the air between us for a moment before dispersing.

"Can you use an axe?" Eli asked.

"What do you mean?"

"To split wood? Done work like that before?"

"Sure." Sweat tickled my sideburns. The room was unnaturally warm. "Why do you ask?"

"It's good to know how to use an axe."

"Okay."

"Not 'okay.' It's important. Where would we be without it?"

"I think there's a misunderstanding," I interrupted. "I'm here to help you...with your book...as a ghost-writer...if you'll let me."

"You're here because I invited you," he said.

"True." I nodded. "As a writer." I tried to sit up, but the slope of the armchair's seat cushion encouraged bad posture. "But, yes, to answer your question—I've used an axe on a few occasions."

"Good. If you're gonna tell the story, you gotta know it'll be a bloody mess."

There, at that moment, beyond the chaotic beard and wrinkles, I recognized the Eli Page of my imagination—the shape-shifter, the charlatan, the prophet. At one time or another he was a young, wiry folk singer with an electric smile; a protest poet, touring the university circuit to discuss the crossroads of music and civil rights; a labor rights organizer; and an old bluesman, the elder statesman of the American music scene. These images were stacked before me, waiting to be chopped down. Each of them carried a splinter of truth and no more. I knew that it was essential to look him in the eyes and say something new, something honest. The problem—I didn't have any idea who he really was, which brought me to an unfortunate conclusion.

"Maybe I'm not the right man for the job," I said.

"Givin' up already? Might be a new record." He looked at his naked wrist.

"You're probably better off with someone *close* to you," I continued. "Someone who knows you. I was told—"

"Forget what you were told, Jack. Nothin' is what it is until I say it is," he said.

"Okay." I squeezed the back of my aching neck.

"I know what I want." He exhaled those words like a threat. "But whatever plans Barry's got you executin', they're a waste of time. My time and yours. I don't need a babysitter. And I don't need a showboater."

"Maybe I should leave." I stood up.

"Don't be an idiot. Sit down," he said, remaining on the sofa. "You wanna know somethin'? It's not chance that brought us here. I remember you. No way you'd make it through that door otherwise. What was it—2000, 2001? Somethin' like that. I remember you. I'm not senile."

"I didn't say—"

He ran his hand through his beard, clawing at his jaw-line. "You're new to this type of thing, right?"

"How do you mean?" I sat back down.

"Ghostwriting? 'Cause you're new, I'll give you a break. But it goes like this—I talk, when I want to talk; you listen. Eventually that listenin' leads to writing, the writing leads to a book, and we're all happy as termites in a woodpile."

"Okay." I nodded. "Gettleson said you read my blog."

"Blog. A stupid word," he said. "He printed out a few chapters."

"Posts." I corrected him and immediately regretted it.

"I don't give a damn what you call them, but they were okay. Liked the interview you did with Bromberg. That one wasn't half bad. Anyway, I asked Barry to look you up. I had my reasons. And I liked that you play and you seem to care about the music. Runs in your blood. Ain't that right?"

I nodded, confused.

"You wouldn't try to sell me out, would you? Maybe this whole setup is a little unusual, but I don't do things the way they want me to."

"Yeah, I know that much."

Eli cocked his head to the side and stared at me.

"Do you have any family?" he asked.

"Maybe. Somewhere." I shrugged.

"Is that right?"

"Unless you know something I don't."

"No one to hold your hand when times get tough?"

"Guess not."

"What's your story, then?"

"I don't know that I have one."

"We both know that's not true." Eli tipped his head, directing me to the stack of newspapers on the floor. On top of the pile was a red folder labeled WYETH, JOHN.

"What's that?" The question rushed out. Suddenly, I was very conscious of my breathing.

"Barry can be very thorough when he wants to be."

I was sure that the red folder at my feet contained info on my parents, my post-drop-out wanderings, and my more recent screw-ups. Why, armed with the red folder of truth, would Eli Page even waste his time with me? That, in my mind, was a valid question but one I didn't dare ask. In a matter of minutes, he had thoroughly wrecked my confidence and flipped this whole process on its head. Once a trickster, always a trickster.

"What's your plan?" he asked.

"I'm just trying to get back on my feet, find something meaningful to do."

"Aren't we all," he muttered. Then he took a long breath, raised his chin, and stared at the ceiling. My hands shook. I waited for him to call me out. It was inevitable. *Phony. Poseur. Get out of my sight.* Suddenly, I was cold at my core. Ice cubes in the abdomen. He tugged on his jacket sleeve and sank back into the cushions. "Let me put it another way—what do you want outta life?"

"I take it day by day."

"To what end?"

"I play guitar, write, try to contribute. Like you did. I want to be a part of something bigger than myself. Most of all, I just want to be free. I'm searching—"

"What a line of bullshit," he interrupted. "Why the hell should you write my story if you can't find your own? Tell me that."

"I guess I'm sort of hoping this is where my story begins," I answered.

A smile surfaced beneath his beard. Suddenly, he leaned forward and then propelled himself to his feet. I followed his lead. He reached his hand out. I shook it, utterly confused.

"One more thing," he said, holding on to my hand and not letting go. "Do you have any experience painting houses?"

"No. Not really."

"Good. 'Cause I don't need a corner-cutter." Finally, he released his grip. "You'll stay in the carriage barn. I don't want you to come for a couple days and take off. I'm countin' on you to stick around. I need work done. You need time. We can help each other."

"What about the book? Can we—?"

"Let me get the keys." Eli exited into the hall.

"Can we at least discuss the deadline?" I spoke loudly so my voice would travel around corners. A moment later, he returned with a key chain.

"I have three rules. One—don't blab about me to the outside world. Tell them everything they want to know about you; leave me out of it. And, yes, people will ask. Two—don't disturb my routine. That's very important. Three—respect my privacy throughout the house. I'm not used to having a stranger lurking around. It's off-limits. If I catch you snoopin' around, me and you are gonna have problems."

"Mr. Gettleson had something else in mind."

"Forget whatever Barry told you. He's a schemer. Listen to me."

"What about the deadline? I think—"

"It looks like," he interrupted yet again, "your car is packed full of junk."

My eyes fell to the ground.

"If you've got somewhere else to be, I'll understand, but it looks to me that you're at the end of the line, son. I'm offerin' you a chance to do something meaningful. It's my opinion that it's in your best interest to step up and take it."

In the mudroom, a pile of wood, split and stacked, leaned against the rear wall. Eli steadied his weight on the stack as he bent down to pick up a leather bag and a flat cap from the floor. I stood by the door to the carriage barn, wondering what I'd gotten myself mixed up in.

"I eat breakfast at six," he said, slowly straightening himself, sighing as he did.

"A bit early for my blood."

"Tig likes to get his exercise before the day breaks."

I laughed at the line, but he didn't join in. The last time I saw the dog, he was splayed out on the living-room rug, huffing, panting, gasping for air. Exercise? That old dog didn't look like he had the stamina to lift his head, let alone get pumped for a predawn jog.

"The silver one opens the barn," he said, placing a key chain in my hand. It held half a dozen keys, every single one of them silver. "Holler if there's a problem. Otherwise, I'll see you in the mornin'. Unless I don't." Even though it was barely four thirty in the afternoon, I accepted his instructions without debate. He turned and left, taking his bag and hat with him.

After I tried a few, I found the right key, unlocked the door, and climbed the stairs. The upper floor of the barn was not what I expected. Narrow, rectangular windows allowed sunlight in one side in the morning and the other in the late afternoon, but the roof slanted downward at a steep pitch to the knee walls, which left minimal headroom except for a four-foot-wide path along the centerline. It was stuffy, stagnant, as if it hadn't been open in years. The smell of dry wood and heat and stale bedclothes reminded me of my mother's attic.

When I was a kid, the attic served as my own personal library of song. A few weeks after my father disentangled himself from family life, I climbed the ladder in my footed pajamas, pulled his prized record collection from a foot-locker, and studied every single sleeve as if each one held a clue to my existence. The dusty yellow of Bob Dylan's *The Times They Are A-Changin'*, the burnt orange of Robert Johnson's *King of the Delta Blues Singers*, the blue block lettering on Ramblin' Jack Elliott's self-titled album, the red banner above a copper-colored Woody in *Woody Guthrie Sings Folk Songs*—I committed the jackets to memory. I lifted the player out of its storage space and plugged it into an exposed outlet. Eli Page's *Up Country* (cover: black-and-beige close-up of Eli's wide, penetrating eyes) was the first record I slipped onto the turntable. I dropped the needle and upped the volume to ten—half to muffle my mother's sobs and half to summon my father back home: a terrific failure on both accounts.

One true thing I knew about my father, one thing that cannot be denied, was that he was a musician's musician, an obsessive fan, a listen-to-this-and-it-will-change-your-world type of guy. He craved new material, and he cherished the old. The addiction surrounded him like a fog. He'd lie flat on the living room floor with "Highway 61 Revisited" cranked up so loud that the glassware shivered in the kitchen sink. I listened to his records every afternoon until my mother, a few weeks later, said, "He's not coming back, Bird. He's left us to rot." At first, I didn't believe it—he'd never leave the music behind. But months fell away, and I was forced to accept that he was gone. Part of me blamed Eli Page and Bob Dylan and Phil Ochs for all that had happened in my short life (a part of me still does), but what good is blame if the blamed are not around to be thrashed? After summer sizzled and the attic air reached 108 degrees, I returned the records to the footlocker and buried them beneath a frayed wedding quilt.

Later, as a teenager, the records were a connection, a ghostly bond between absent father and angsty son. I was summoned to those exposed joists again, and I thumbed through the same locker and uncovered that same *Up Country* album. In many ways, Eli Page was always in my life, standing in the attic, with his wild eyes and his windswept hair, patiently waiting for me to listen up. The protest songs, the roots, the Irish folk, the acoustic blues—they were all caged in the dark playlist of my mind. It was as if my DNA was built around two guitar strings he twisted together. Teetering on the edge of adulthood, I found that his music was my music, an echo of my voice trapped in an empty room. It wasn't the low twang of the guitar or the rapid strumming or the skillful finger-picking that tugged at me; it was the whispery slide of the finger flesh along the strings. That noise, for I have no better word for it, which marked the end of one chord and the beginning of another, offered a sense of authenticity; somehow it signaled both emptiness and an end to emptiness. In it, the belief that music could lead to truth, to reconciliation, to some sort of closure.

But that was a long time ago. A decade and a half later, I wasn't nearly that naïve.

After I lugged my duffel bags to the barn and laid them on the bed and stacked my notebook, phone, and wallet on a flat-top desk and moved the misfit furniture around the room and contemplated my strange predicament yet again, I was beat. In the fading daylight, I imagined Eli, as a young man, sitting at a desk like the one in the carriage barn, scribbling lyrics that transformed the rain on the windowpane into shooting stars or soaring missiles. In a Greenwich Village walk-up with scuffed walls and tin ceilings, music pounded the street below and a brutally naked brunette stood in the light of the oversize windows facing MacDougal. No doubt that his imaginary apartment, like my new carriage barn living quarters, was built for daydreams, reflection, creative pursuits. In my haze, I began to worry that I'd agreed to something uncommon, something unbound, something that could, for all intents and purposes, lead to my ruin (or, I suppose, glory).

Seated at the desk, I scratched some of my initial observations into my notebook, but it was like taking inventory — all surface, no depth. At first, I blamed it on the pen and paper. I couldn't remember the last time I wrote in a wide-ruled pad. Even if my laptop hadn't died a violent, virus-ridden death in Casey's basement, River Bend would've rendered it half useless. There was no Wi-Fi or broadband; there was barely electricity. Instead, this was a house for contemplation.

Surrounded by built-in shelves, the east window offered a cushioned seat. I lifted the dusty pillow to reveal a set of thin brass hinges. The box was empty except for a single artist's brush. Half the diameter of a pencil, the tool was tiny and well used; the words AMERICAN PAINTER were hidden under a smattering of dried green and blue paint. I opened the window a fraction, fell into the bed, and listened to the water wash steadily downstream. Like a thousand voices in an anxious crowd, the river's noise swelled and shrank and swelled again. It lulled me to sleep.

When I woke many hours later, the memory of my mother's attic lingered behind my eyelids. I grabbed my phone from the desk and looked at the time: 6:17 A.M. Zero bars, zero messages. After stretching and splashing water on my face, I stumbled into Eli's kitchen. He wasn't there, but a bowl of soggy cereal sat on the table, a spoon wet with milk to its side.

Outside, the sun was starting to dry the wet grass. I walked around the house and found Eli on the front step.

Blurry-eyed and trancelike, he sat with his arms folded tight to his body, his back curved. He looked like a frail and beaten tramp, a hobo who had fallen out of the train car. At his feet, I spied a newspaper, wrapped in its plastic.

"Why're you creepin'?" he asked.

"Sorry. I didn't want to disturb you."

He grunted as he got to his feet. "Too late."

"Is that today's paper?"

"I just missed the little bastard." He bent down and picked up the plastic-wrapped package from the step. "I'm tempted to lock the damn gate. That way he can't get in here."

"Why don't you?"

"How'd I ever receive visitors?" I waited for him to wink or nudge me with his elbow, but he didn't. "You look like you want to ask me something," he said.

"Should I?"

"Just don't ask anything stupid."

I wished I had something to write on, but I knew, even then, that my contract with Eli was different; he didn't want a reporter, a journalist—he wanted to talk to someone the way he'd talk to a friend. I'd have to ease in.

"How long have you owned this land?" I asked.

"Five, six years. It was empty for a long time. Fallin' down."

"But you always planned to move here? To Galesville, I mean."

"I don't plan on much."

"Then why this place? Why this town?"

Eli gazed off, across the water, with the same pensive intensity he once held when he was locked in song, even in front of tens of thousands.

"Why not?"

"Is there something about Galesville—?"

"I thought you were gonna ask me about the paper or breakfast or something like that," he said. "I'm not prepared for a serious discussion."

I backed off, wondering if I'd misconstrued his invitation or if he'd changed his mind after my first question. Both were probably true.

We stood shoulder to shoulder facing the street. Without looking in my direction, he put the paper in front of me, wanting me to take it from him. I did. The headline read: "No New Leads. Police Ask for Public's Help."

"Tell you what. I'll give you a hundred bucks if you can hit the paperboy with this thing next time he rolls around, another fifty if you can knock him off his bike."

I smiled but stopped when I realized he was being serious.

"He's a good kid. I think. But I've told him three damn times that I don't want this thing. I don't care if I've got four months left on my account."

"He keeps it up?"

"Says he has to. I should lock the gate."

The roar of a truck engine startled the crows in the lawn. A black Dodge Ram raced down River Bend Road before downshifting and slowing at Eli's gate. It crept along the pavement, eventually pausing in the middle of the road. It must be someone Eli knew, I thought, but Eli showed no signs of recognition or worry or curiosity. In fact, he turned his back on the street. The truck punched the gas and sped westward, over the hill, out of view.

"I gotta lock the gate," he said again.

"Does that happen a lot?"

He shook his head in such a way that I didn't know if he answered yes or no.

"If my cereal's soggy, I'm gonna sue the publisher," he mumbled as he toddled toward the house.

The next morning I stood outside, anxiously awaiting the paperboy, but the kid never showed.

Within a few days, everything around me burst with a new life. The bark on the locust trees no longer looked like dead skin. Alive, their wild zigzag limbs stretched out in chaotic patterns that raked the cloudy sky. The river sparkled. The hills were lush and green. Even the house's weathered exterior had shrugged off its dull, lifeless coat and dashed wholeheartedly toward summer.

Eli, on the other hand, sank farther and farther into some self-prescribed hibernation. Since our discussion about what to do with rogue paperboys, I had spoken to him on only a handful of occasions, each more meaningless than the last.

One morning, while looking out the carriage barn window, I observed him at work. In the early light, he lifted rocks from the south field and dropped them into piles beside the barn. At first I dismissed it, but even after I showered, dressed, and made coffee in the kitchen, Eli continued to dig and lift and haul and collect the rocks. By midmorning, his three piles were waist high. Balanced and artful in their own way, they were stone cairns, monuments of some unknown significance. I abandoned my coffee to go help.

"What're you up to?" I asked as I brushed by his shoulder.

"Who are you?"

"Who am I?" Taken aback, I barely managed to get those words out.

"Name, please?"

"Jack. Wyeth."

"Yes. Of course you are. Don't be stupid."

"Are you okay?" I asked, wondering if he'd truly forgotten about me. (It would've explained a lot.) Then I reached down, picked up a rock, and cradled it like a football between my forearm and ribs. "Need some help?"

"Do what you want," he said.

"What are these for?" I heaved the rock into the air. It crashed against the pile, rolled, and settled in the grass. Eli didn't answer. "Fence? Foundation?" I asked.

"No."

"Do you have a use for them?"

"No use."

"Then what's the purpose?"

"Unearthing them's the purpose," he said, his breathing labored. Dirt and sweat smudged around his temples and under his eyes, which made him look like some sort of crazed grave robber. Pausing to catch his breath, he stared out over the pockmarked field.

"If you say so." I backed off.

With my sleeves up to my elbows, I collected the rocks he had unloosed and lugged them across the yard. Earlier, as I watched Eli from the window, I noted the care he took as he stacked the rocks on the heaps. Instead of launching stones like a shot-putter, he'd balanced them on each other until an odd sort of symmetry appeared—one pile resembled an apiary, while another took the shape of a miniature round tower. There was art in the labor.

From the far corner of Eli's open land, I carried exposed rocks the size of cannonballs to their staging area. Pain shot up and down my back from belt to neck. I stopped to stretch. That's when I realized Eli had disappeared. He must've quit as I was dragging my aching body to the far end of the field for the umpteenth time. Later, in the living room, after I'd showered and applied a large dose of Icy Hot to my flesh, I asked him why he'd left without a word. "The job was done," he answered. "What was there to say?"

I was too exhausted to bite my tongue.

"Why don't you let me know when you want to stop dicking around?"

"I didn't ask for your help," he responded.

"Is this a game?"

"I don't know. Is it?"

"You could've given me a heads-up, out of courtesy."

He snorted, stood, and left the room.

For several days after our little tête-à-tête, Eli retreated into his routine, which involved some type of physical labor (or long walk) in the morning, lunch, reading, nap, afternoon work, and evening reflection interspersed with food and scotch. Night after night in the living room, he was wordless. At the time, it was like I was enduring the world's longest silent treatment, and my attempts to spark a discussion only made things worse. When his glass was empty, he'd thrust himself out of his chair and walk away as if I didn't exist. One particularly silent night, Tig thumped over to me and laid his head on my thighs. I petted him and knew just how he felt.

Frustrated, I wandered around the yard until I found service, and I called Casey only to be redirected to his voice mail. My rambling message contained gems like "second chances are overrated" and "it's true—Eli Page is unhinged." Despite my earlier basketball-induced conversation with Casey, I wasn't convinced that I'd earned a second chance, and I wasn't convinced Eli Page could grant me one, even if I had. So, once again, I was left to observe, to be Eli's audience of one.

That night, when I set out to write, I found myself lost in daydreams. Eli's songs ran through my head and I pretended that I wrote them, pretended that it was me in front of the crowd in Newport, pretended that Casey and others admired me, respected me, recognized my talent. And then I started to shake. Uncontrollably. Almost violently. It was exhausting to believe, even in my fog, that I could connect only behind a mask. When the lights were out or when I was bored, there was nothing left to do but imagine. So I set out to imagine a day, an hour, a minute where real, uninhibited connections could exist between two people. Without pretense. Without deception. I didn't know if it was truly possible.

A couple days later, while I sat in the kitchen waiting for my tea to cool, a white van pulled into the driveway. I rushed to the window and found a teenager, barely driving age, on the front step. He carried a cardboard box and that droopy-eyed look of boredom that only a teen can pull off in earnest. I swung the door open before he had the chance to knock.

"Who are you?" he asked.

"A friend of Eli's."

"Where's the old man?"

"Gone," I said.

"Dead?"

"No," I answered. The glee in his voice surprised me more than the word "dead." Why would he suppose Eli was dead? And, equally puzzling, why would he be so happy about it? "He's busy."

"Too bad. Here's his order," the boy said. "I was told to leave it." With each word he tried to make himself appear taller.

"Order?"

"Groceries. From the IGA. Dude, get with the program."

"Fine. I'll take it." He placed the box in my arms. It was heavier than I anticipated. My legs bent to accommodate the weight. The boy went back to the truck and grabbed another box, which he placed on the front step.

"You know," he said, "he can't get away with it forever. He's not that smart. Just saying."

"What's he getting away with?"

"We both know what's real. He's gonna get caught."

"I don't know what you're talking about."

"Sure. Whatever you gotta tell yourself." He winked. Before I could piece together another question, he turned and walked back to his van.

I stood in the doorway, arms full, and watched his van puff blue smoke into the air before eventually disappearing into the covered bridge. (I'd later learn that the boy's name was James. He was an arrogant little snot, but I welcomed the brief distraction his deliveries provided.)

In the kitchen, I unpacked cans of soup, a glass bottle of milk, boxes of bland cereals with names like Heart Healthy and Triple Bran, bags of celery and carrots, and four quarts of blueberries. Hidden under the berries were boxes of vitamins and supplements—men's multi; fish oil; vitamins D, C, and B_{12}; Huperzine A; and vinpocetine. After the groceries were shelved, I grabbed my notebook, went outside, and sat on the step.

Again, I tried to write, but I was distracted by James's comments. What was he getting at? What was Eli mixed up in? I needed to get out. It had been less than two weeks, but it felt like a month. Apart from the season's ebb and flow, the wind and mud, I was disconnected from the world beyond Eli's property. There was a sense of comfort in my seclusion, but also the smell of mildew and rot. River Bend was starting to wear on me. So I made up my mind to go into town as soon as possible.

Music was eerily absent from Eli's house—no television theme songs or radio sugar pop, no guitars strumming or harmonicas wailing, no evidence of the extraordinary life left behind. Even my own six-string had been incarcerated, locked in its case, and hidden from sight. When I agreed to Gettleson's plan, I'd envisioned Eli Page holed up in a custom home studio, picking his guitar, writing new work. Yeah, I was intrigued by the apocryphal stash of unreleased songs, but forgetting that, I was certain that music, even in its most generic form, would be present. Omnipresent. But this was not *Music from Big Pink*. Eli's house was a temple to the art of silence, which, to my surprise, made me nervous. I'd grown accustomed to the sound track of my life, the backing track that consisted of acoustic strumming on street corners, brakes squealing, buses accelerating. If someone had told me that Eli Page had banished music from his life, I would've called him a liar and a fool, but that was exactly what he'd done.

Music was in exile and I was stir-crazy.

One morning, while Eli was out on his walk, I entered the covered bridge, which was both an amplifier and a crossing. Inside, it smelled like a woodshop. The water shushed beneath its planks. I felt like I was floating, drifting in an ark, lost at sea. When I exited on the village side, I was charmed by a fledgling pianist. Most likely a child at practice. As I continued down the road, I found the student and teacher seated together behind a small window of a yellow house. Pausing for a moment, I listened as the young girl pounded "The Entertainer" on the keys, fumbling through its ragtime repetitions. A wave of heat washed over my body, initiated not by the music itself but by the introduction of music in relation to my monastic weeks of stillness and silence. The music was a gift, a reminder of the pleasures of the symphonic world.

Did Eli truly appreciate what he had given up? Did he ever think about the life that existed beyond River Bend?

It was a courageous act in some way, an act of dedication. Not unlike a priest reporting for duty or a soldier giving himself over to a higher power, maybe Eli had made a decision to search for something greater than himself, something unattainable. Or maybe that was just wishful thinking.

Light cascaded over the pavement; the road shimmered. Eli had separated himself just far enough away, where he was both apart from and a part of Galesville. His stone walls, his wrought iron, his trees, and his red bridge were instruments of isolation, warning outsiders to keep away or else. But at the same time, he had chosen to live within arm's reach of a community. There was no denying it. He could've easily inhabited some mountaintop cabin, miles from civilization, but instead he chose a farmhouse just beyond Galesville's center. Why? The contradiction was meaningful. It had to be.

On uneven slate sidewalks, splintered and cracked from years of wear, I continued toward the heart of the village. The budding treetops swayed. Brave new foliage filtered the morning sun. The neighborhood was bright, beautiful, awash in spring greens.

By the look of it, nearly everyone was outside cleaning, gardening, or walking their dogs. A young man with two Great Danes—one black with white spots, one white with black spots—smiled meekly at me as he was yanked across the road. An elderly gentleman in a sweater vest raked last year's leaves in his front lawn, seemingly one at a time. When I got close to his property, he paused, stared, and waited for me to pass.

Two massive brick churches with dull red-, blue-, and green-slated spires stood tall on Church Street. These places of worship were probably, along with the colonials on the street, some of the village's original structures. In my reverie, I imagined hundreds singing "The Old Rugged Cross" and "Shall We Gather at the River" from their pews, eyes closed, swaying side to side in unison like passengers on a ship at sea. The buildings were worn, for sure, but their craftsmanship was still awe-inspiring even if protective panels clouded their stained glass and tinted it yellow like dandelion wine. On the Methodist's roof, there were dozens of empty pockets where slate used to hang, which made me wonder how the spires were maintained and if slate had rained down on an unsuspecting funeral or wedding party at one time. My eyes were drawn up the spires into the blue spring sky, empty save for the faint trail of a jet long gone.

Dead flowers, broken branches, and wet leaves were piled along the perimeter of the village park. A chain saw revved in the distance. Across the street, a mangy terrier licked mud from the sidewalk. Hanging from light posts surrounding the park were blue banners with white letters that read THE GALESVILLE COMMONS. Armed with my notebook and a pen, I made my way to a large wooden gazebo near the center of the commons.

A young boy screamed, "You're dead. You're so dead." Another responded, "I bet you a million dollars I can hit it." Over my shoulder, I saw them chucking clumps of mud first at each other and then at a No Parking sign. One sprinted toward me, all the while yelling, "The gazebo is base! The gazebo is base!"

As I sat down on the gazebo's steps, a mud pie whizzed by my head.

"Sorry, mister." They ran off before I could say anything.

To my left, beyond the retreating boys, a few women stuck their hands and shovels in the dirt. Actively, quietly, they brought the plant beds back to life, raked and bagged dead leaves, and wheeled away the detritus. The woman with the wheelbarrow, years younger than her fellow gardeners, glanced at me as she filled the tray with weeds and dead flowers. I tried to play it cool, but I could tell that she was watching me, which only made my actions self-conscious and awkward. I feigned interest in my notebook.

This is what I wrote: "Galesville possesses a simple, rational layout, one that stems outward from a New England–style green or commons area. Main Street runs west to east, along the south end of the commons. It connects the convenience store and IGA to the old business district, which houses a dozen village shops along a beautified streetscape. Beyond the village shops on the south end are the old mills and the Battenkill River." Stilted, mechanical prose. I couldn't focus.

Every few sentences, I looked up to see if the woman was still there, still studying me. I caught her sideways glance a couple times. From what I could tell, she was around my age, give or take, with long brown hair pulled back in ponytail, and a mischievous demeanor.

After I gathered the courage to introduce myself, I stood up, stepped out of the gazebo, and promptly slipped on a mud pie that had been splattered by my feet. I reached for the railing to catch myself. No luck. My arms swung wildly; the notebook left my fingertips. I tried to brace my fall. Instead, I crash-landed on my back and tailbone. The impact punched the wind from my lungs and sent a bolt of pain along my lower spine.

No one was watching, I told myself, from the ground. No one saw a thing. I sat up as fast as I could, inhaling, gulping the air. My back ached and my chest burned.

As if the whole situation wasn't embarrassing enough, the woman abandoned her wheelbarrow and rushed toward me. I closed my eyes, hoping I'd disappear. At the very least, I wished she'd let my lungs refill before asking if I was hurt.

"Are you okay?" she asked as she reached my side.

I held up my hand as if to signal that I just needed a minute. Although I couldn't speak, I managed to croak "fine" in between a few breaths.

"Are you sure? That was quite the pratfall, Buster Keaton. What'd you trip on?"

Still not able to answer, I pointed to the clumps of mud on the slate path leading to the gazebo.

"I should've guessed." She reached out a hand and helped me up. Once I made it to my feet, I brushed the grass and dirt from my back. "Are you sure you're not broken?"

I nodded before adding, "Wind. Knocked. Out."

"Oh. That makes sense. I was beginning to worry."

"No need. I'm fine," I said, slowly regaining my ability to talk. As I did, I looked over my shoulder to see the mud on the seat of my pants. "But I definitely bruised my tailbone."

A sly smile cut across the woman's face. Both her plum sweater and her dark jeans were worn and frayed. Scuffed-toed work boots peeked out from under denim cuffs. Amused, she bit her lip and choked back a laugh. "I'm sorry," she said. "I laugh when old ladies fall over too. Just ask them." She pointed to her fellow gardeners, who were only passingly aware of what had transpired. "It's all fun and games until they bust a hip. Your hips, on the other hand, seem to be working. Even if the 'tailbone' isn't one hundred percent."

I tried to find something witty to say, but I was too slow and too embarrassed and too strained to come up with anything. Her smile faded, but I saw the amusement linger in her eyes. Bruised, I turned my interest toward my lost notebook.

"It's over there to your left," she said.

"Sorry?"

"The book you tossed in the air. It's to the left." She crossed in front of me and plunged her arm into the boxwood shrub. A second later, her arm reappeared, unscathed. She raised my notebook over her head in triumph like a preacher holding a Bible closer to heaven.

My breathing was back to normal.

For a few seconds, I locked stares with her, and I saw something warm, something honest in her face. I also saw something I hadn't seen in a while. I don't know what to name it exactly. Self-possession? Fearlessness? Pride? Her eyes were an imperfect green like a glass bottle when emptied of its wine. Soft lines lived beside those eyes. I couldn't look away.

Probably freaked out by my staring, she looked down at my notebook.

"This machine kills fascists," she said.

"What?"

"Your sticker." She lifted the notebook so that I could see its cover. I'd forgotten that I'd stuck the Guthrie line on the front. "How's that working out for you?"

"Not sure. Don't see any fascists around at the moment, but you never know."

"Some are pretty outspoken. Others tend to lurk."

"Exactly. That's why I sleep with one eye open."

"Well, at least you sleep," she said. "Here you go." She handed the notebook back to me. Her fingers were splattered with dried white paint. Maybe it was the smile or the way she cocked her head or the confidence, but for whatever reason, I thought she'd snatch the book back just as I reached for it, and I was disappointed when she didn't.

"I've always been partial to 'this machine surrounds hate and forces it to surrender.' But maybe that's just me."

"Can't argue with Pete Seeger."

"A national treasure."

"I think they're waiting for you," I said, tipping my head toward the gardening crew. The wheelbarrow was full, and they focused their collective attention on us.

"I should get going. They'll need my help." She looked me over again. "Plus I'd say you're back to top form."

"Just sore."

"Try not to trip on anything else on your way out," she said. I couldn't tell if she was joking or not. Before walking away, she brushed a leaf from my shoulder.

"Thanks again," I said.

"Don't mention it, Jack."

In that moment, I was confused, dumbstruck, completely incapable of asking any questions, let alone the most obvious—how did she know my name? I didn't say a word.

"See you around," she added, over her shoulder.

Just like that, she went her way and I went mine.

For nearly two hours, I sat in the kitchen and waited, but it wasn't until well after one o'clock that Eli and Tig finally returned home. Six or seven hours had come and gone. The dog's tongue hung from his mouth as he made his way to the pillow bed and collapsed. Eli's shoulders slumped. He dropped his satchel by the door. Then he trudged through the kitchen, boots muddy.

"That must've been one hell of a hike," I said.

Eli lifted his gaze to meet mine. I peered at him, offering as stern a look as I could muster. Then he chucked the rolled-up newspaper at me.

"Good-for-nothing paperboy," he said.

"Is the offer still good?" I asked. I bent down and picked up the paper.

"What offer?" In and out of the kitchen, Eli set up and took down piles of books, papers, random objects. Still, even as he busied himself, he moved in slow motion. Half time. Quarter time. It was painful to watch.

"The hundred dollars. You said if I knocked him off his bike, you'd pay up."

"Don't be stupid. Does it look like I have time for stupid?"

"We were just talking about this," I insisted, "a couple weeks ago." As I stared into his eyes, I wasn't sure Eli recalled our earlier discussion. "Never mind. Forget it."

At that moment, I couldn't help but wonder what conversations Eli remembered, if any. Gettleson had alluded to these lapses, but I now saw how the book project could be derailed before it even made it onto the tracks. I stood straight and asked the question I'd been waiting to ask: "Where'd you go? At least tell me that."

"Nowhere."

"I want to know," I said to him.

"No. You don't wanna know," he answered.

"You don't even register what I'm talking about, do you?"

"Does it matter?" Eli removed a pot from a cabinet, filled it with tap water, and placed it on the stovetop. As he bent over the cutting board, he halved a few potatoes, pausing every few minutes to stretch.

"Yes. It does. It does matter," I said.

Most mornings Eli would be long gone before I woke, and I wouldn't see him until around lunch. On those rare mornings he stayed close, I'd wake to find him hammering damaged fence, stacking split wood, or attempting to rehabilitate one of the many failing barns on his land. As long as I could keep tabs on him, my mind was at ease, but when he was missing, I was a supernova of curiosity.

"Are you bored?" he asked as he diced the potato with a heavy knife.

"No. It's not about boredom."

"Then why are you whining?"

"I'm trying to understand how this is going to work."

"That's your first mistake."

The knife *thunk-thunked* against the cutting board.

Eli dropped the potatoes into boiling water. He was a decent cook, but I began to suspect that he used food as a shield. Apple-glazed pork, pecan-encrusted chicken, roast salmon with leeks—it took patience to cook those meals, and I was learning that, despite my first impression, Eli Page had a tremendous amount of patience. Yet just when I thought I was starting to acquire some sort of understanding of Eli's zigging, he'd zag. For example, after the salmon, we dined on frozen pizza and canned beef stew for three days. Conveniently, on the nights I was likely to ask questions, he armed himself with recipe books, spices, and a sharp knife.

"Read the paper and shut up." Eli dropped a cabbage onto the chopping block and brought his knife down hard through its core. The two halves rolled in opposite directions.

On page four of the *Galesville Mirror* was a weekly column by Hal Holland, titled "Rearview Mirror." Its folksy, old-timey tone was reinforced by the column's typeface—an antiqued Americana. As Eli shredded the cabbage, offering an underlying beat to my lunch, I sank into Holland's language—specifically, his use of the majestic plural. The royal "we" made me feel like an insider and outsider all at once. "We remember the good old days, when we listened to stories on the radio and they taught us something about how to be with each other," it read.

"On weekends, we sat on the porch and struck up conversations with passing neighbors. We helped each other out. It was our nature, for we were taught to be polite. We lived, loved, played, and prayed together. We fought wars together and honored our heroes when they came back dead or alive. We believed in our town, our country. Yes, we were proud. Yes, we were blind. But can you blame us?" We. After I finished the column, I refolded the paper and flipped it over to see the *Mirror's* headline: "Vandal Strikes for Third Time This Month." I scanned the opening paragraphs of the article. Same pattern. No new leads. No new information. From what I could discern, Galesville had experienced a rash of vandalism, burglary, and suspected arson since the ice had thawed, and no one knew what to make of it.

"Did you see this?" I asked Eli, placing the paper back on the counter in front of him. "Looks like someone trashed the Historical Society this time—smashed all the windows and set the files and cabinets on fire."

"Not surprised. The whole world's gone crazy."

"Why would someone do that?"

Eli shrugged. "Make yourself useful and get me two bowls from that room over there," he directed.

"The dining room?"

"Yeah. That's what I said."

The hutch was empty except for a few candlesticks, an assortment of linen, and a white ironstone soup tureen. "Where?" I asked.

"I might've packed them away." He pointed to the harvest table and two half-filled cardboard boxes. The bigger box was full of leather-bound books with familiar names on the bindings—William Butler Yeats, Dylan Thomas, W. H. Auden. A Post-it note was attached to the top flap of each box. In tiny, compact handwriting it read JENNY LEE. I found the bowls in the adjacent box under a lace tablecloth.

"Are you getting rid of this stuff?" I asked, careful not to seem too invested.

"I don't need it anymore."

"The books or the bowls?" I asked.

"The clutter adds to my confusion. Everything'll end up at Belanger's. It's for the best."

"Belanger's?"

"Yeah, it's an antiques barn," he answered before pushing a helping of colcannon in front of me. The steam warmed my chin. I stretched, unable to get comfortable. Eli's mood had shifted considerably. He was downright amicable; therefore, I made up my mind to eat my lunch and ask him, flatly, when we should start his book project.

"It's been a few weeks now," I said.

"A few weeks since—?"

"Since I moved in. We're on deadline." My mouth was full of potatoes.

"Whose deadline?"

"The editor wants something . . . to show we're moving ahead . . . I need to give Gettleson an outline and maybe a couple dozen pages," I said. It was a lie—I had no contact with the editor; in fact, I didn't even know who the editor was or what house had paid for the book. I spoke only with Gettleson, and he hadn't called in days.

"Give 'em somethin', then," he answered without skipping a beat.

"I don't have anything. You need to work with me. Give me an hour or two."

"Make somethin' up. Can't be hard. Everyone else does it." He continued chewing. It began to rain softly. In the spaces between our words, I could hear the soft drops wash over the windows.

"Give me something to start with. Anything."

"I can't," he said, suddenly serious.

"Why?"

"I need help." The plea was quiet, red faced. I leaned forward so much that the back legs of my chair lifted off the ground.

"Tell me what to do." Safe to say I was stunned by his sudden vulnerability, his sincerity.

"I need you to . . . do something for me." He grabbed the newspaper from the counter. "Before you start, you gotta go to town and pick up a few things." He scribbled in the paper's margins with a pencil and then handed it back to me. I unfolded it just enough to read the list and then placed it in my pocket.

"You want me to paint the house?"

"Yup. It needs a fresh coat. I'll leave you some money. Should help with your boredom."

"I'm not bored. I'm just looking for a little cooperation. They're not the same thing."

"You sure about that?"

I couldn't help but meet his smirk with my own. "Fine.

I'll do it," I said. "In exchange for two uninterrupted hours of your time."

"That's not the deal," he said.

"That's my deal. Two hours as payment."

He mulled it over. "After the house is painted. And no half-assing it."

"Okay."

"All right."

"Fine. I'll get started first thing."

Eli stirred his food in small circles. Unhappy with the negotiation, he didn't eat another bite, but I didn't care—it wasn't as if I was pleased to be painting his house. But I *was* happy that he had started talking to me again. Plus, the colcannon was pretty damn good.

I searched the carriage barn for jumper cables. The morning after my negotiation with Eli, my car refused to turn over. If I didn't know better, I'd swear Eli had sabotaged my Chevy.

The first floor of the barn was clean, cold. Empty metal shelves lined the walls. A blue tarp covered a lump in the center of the space. Like a magician (or a used-car salesman), I yanked the tarp away to reveal a '66 Mustang, its navy paint dulled, its tires flat. The doors were locked. Peering through the driver's-side window, I saw an orange distributor cap on top of a rag in the passenger seat.

No cables or ordinary wrenches lived in the barn. All I found was a set of tools from an earlier century—augers and rasps, flathead screwdrivers with wooden handles, coffee cans filled with nails and bolts, and brown rusted

C-clamps. No crescent. No Leatherman. No luck. I trudged out of the barn with nothing but a vintage vise grip to show for my effort. So thoroughly deflated, I didn't even realize that Eli had company until I looked up and spotted an old Blazer in the driveway.

"Eat something, for crying out loud. You don't want to lose your rosy complexion." A woman exited the house, hugging a box of books to her chest. When she saw me standing there with a rusted vise grip in my hand, she paused for a moment, tilted her head as if she was trying to interpret an abstract painting, and smiled.

Eli disappeared into the entryway. The door slammed shut behind him.

I tossed the vise grips in the grass and offered to give her a hand.

"Don't you dare," she said. "I got it." As she brushed by me, I recognized her from the commons, and I felt like an idiot. "How's your ass? Still bruised?" she asked as she lifted the box into the back of her truck, sliding it beside a chest of drawers and a battered Hudson River School–inspired painting that, at least when I left the house after breakfast, had hung in Eli's living room. Then she turned to face me, eyebrows raised.

"Honestly, it's really freaking sore."

"I bet it is."

"So you're Jenny Lee?"

"That'd be me," she said. Then she gestured to the open hood of my car. "Let me guess—you failed auto shop in high school?"

"The battery is dead."

"That's not so bad. You need a jump? I might have some cables." She walked over to take a look at the car's engine.

"Doubt it will help. It's got no juice at all."

"That's no good," she said while removing the metal support and dropping the hood. It slammed shut.

"I'm Jack, by the way, but you already knew that."

"Another good guess," she said. "Eli's told me all about you. Sorry I didn't introduce myself earlier — I thought I'd give you some time to recover."

"Thoughtful of you." I was stuck on the fact that Eli was talking about me behind my back. What was he saying? What impression did Jenny Lee already have of me? "The whole scene on the commons, it wasn't my most graceful moment." I rubbed my lower back.

"Where're you headed?"

"I was going to the hardware store, but—"

"Get in." She nodded toward the passenger side. "Eli mentioned you might need a ride."

Her statement seemed to confirm my original suspicion about Eli and the battery. I let it go and hopped in the Blazer. Despite its age, the blue-and-white body was clean and shiny as a newly purchased Matchbox replica.

"Thanks for helping me out," I said.

"Don't mention it. I like collecting favors. Just remember that you owe me."

She turned the key, and the full-throated rumble sounded more like a boat than a street-legal truck. As she drove across the bridge and down Church Street, I glanced over at her and saw that sly, mischievous smile on her lips, the same smile that she held at the commons. It was if she was waiting for me to finish a lame joke.

"How old is this thing?" I asked, patting the dash.

"Nineteen seventy-five. Lucky if it gets a mile and a half a gallon," she said. "Ivory took care of it, though. Used it for pickups and drop-offs. Not much else. He can't drive these days, so it's up to me."

"Ivory?"

"Ivory Belanger."

"From the antiques barn?" I felt like I was shouting over the engine noise.

"Right. Sorry," she said. "Everyone knows everyone else around here. It's not often we get newbies in town." She glanced at me. "Ivory's my boss. You should come by, meet him, and check it out sometime."

"Sure. Where is it?"

"It's that one," she said, pointing to an old barn on the hillside, shaded by trees. "You can't miss it."

"So Eli's giving all of his stuff to an antiques store?"

"You can say that. It's much more than an antiques store. I think you'll be surprised." She kept her eyes on the road. "It's a town landmark. One of the few reasons that people come into Galesville."

"I'll check it out."

"You better. I know where you live." She downshifted. The truck bucked and roared. "Speaking of. Tell me something, Jack. Why is it that you're here?"

"How do you mean? I thought Eli told you—"

"I heard his version. I'm asking about yours."

"It was an offer I couldn't resist," I said, remembering Gettleson's declaration. "But I can safely say that I didn't know what I was getting into."

"Well, he doesn't have much left. If you use him, exploit him, hurt him in any way, I will make your life a living hell. Understood?"

"Yeah. Completely." I took a deep breath. "Can I ask why you care so much?"

"I've got a lot at stake here, a lot of time in," she said. "And I don't need you coming around and messing it up."

"That's not my intention."

"Good. Galesville Hardware," she announced, hitting the curb as she pulled into a parking space. "I'll drop off my stuff and come back 'round to get you. Shouldn't be too long."

"You don't have to —"

"It's no problem," she said, finally meeting my eyes. "Really."

"Okay." I opened the door and stepped out. "Thanks, again."

"Don't go anywhere until I get back."

"Where am I going to go?"

An old-fashioned bell rigged above the door chimed as I entered. Inside, the store was yellow like harvest wheat under lazy fluorescent lights. Rows of white aluminum shelves were organized like stacks in a library and marked on the end caps. Electric. Plumbing. Hardware. Lawn.

As I stepped forward, the worn wood floor creaked so ferociously that I thought it might snap under the stress. I pulled Eli's list from my back pocket and began searching for supplies.

Two older men stood along the back wall. Above them, big red letters shouted PAINT, but they were obviously perusing chain saws, brush hogs, and Weedwackers. Dressed in muddied Carhartt jackets and well-worn jeans, their body types couldn't have been more different. The tall, thin one had a sharp, pointy nose and stood nearly a foot higher than his friend, a plump, scarlet-faced man with round glasses. Benjamin Franklin and the Tin Man. The taller one gesticulated wildly as the chain saw in his grip swung from side to side, an extension of his arm. His friend shook his head and waved his finger.

"Damn you, Chuck. You're just dead wrong on this subject."

"I don't see how."

"It's about everyone contributing."

"Lies. It's about tyranny."

"You mean to tell me—" The chain saw connected with a pile of boxes, knocking them to the floor. The men were unfazed. "You mean to tell me that you believe in that bullshit."

"I don't trust that we know what's really going on."

"Do we ever?"

"No one elected you—"

"Well, maybe they should've."

The short man snorted.

"What? What's so funny?"

Embarrassed, I focused on my list. I didn't know where to begin since the paint wasn't in the Paint section. After glancing down the aisles, I went to the counter for help.

The clerk leaned on her elbows to view cable news on a tiny television stuck between the fax machine and the lost-and-found box. Her blond hair was pulled back into a messy ponytail, leaving her bangs to fall in front of her face. A nametag on the counter, which I assumed belonged to her, said NIKKI. She remained crouched over, but after I spoke, she lifted her head just enough to look over her shoulder at me, and I saw that she was older than I first thought, probably early thirties, and I had the sense from her demeanor that she'd worked at the store for a decade or more.

"Yup," she said.

"I need paint."

"Okay." She swiveled around in her chair and looked me over. "Paint's in Plumbing," she said. "Back of the aisle, to the left."

At the far end of the store, directly opposite the sign for Paint above the two men, who were still arguing, was the Plumbing section. While I gathered the items on Eli's list, the argument escalated and carried across the store.

"What about the break-ins? What's your theory?"

"Drug addicts."

"That's stupid. I'll tell you who it is."

"Go ahead."

"That musician. He's trouble."

I stopped sorting through the brushes and leaned in to better eavesdrop.

"Why on earth would he bother—?"

"Maybe he didn't like what was in those files."

"That's hogwash. Honestly, do you think he's capable?"

"Ask the police. Why are they keeping an eye on him if he's so goddamned innocent? Answer me that."

"Because they're just as idiotic as you are."

"You'll see. You'll be eating crow before the second cut."

One of them sighed like a jetliner coming in for a landing, and then, all of a sudden, they stopped talking. The tall man threw the door open and stormed out. Nikki didn't look up from the television. It was as if it happened every day; she didn't seem to care. A few seconds later, the short man went to the register, paid, and left.

"Did you find everything?" the woman asked as I approached the counter.

"I think so."

"What's the project?"

"I'm painting a house," I answered. "Out on River Bend Road."

"You're gonna need a lot more paint."

"Well, that makes this the first of many trips."

She scanned my items. All except for one can of primer, which I still held in my grip. As she reached for its handle, I flinched and dropped the can. The impact against the wood floor cracked the seal, and a slim stream of gray primer leaked onto the floor. She grabbed a handful of rags from underneath the counter. "Not many homes out there on River Bend," she said.

"I'm staying with a friend." Together we wiped up the paint; it left a gray streak on the floor. "Eli Page."

"Oh," she said, pausing before carrying on, hoping I didn't notice. "That's cool. Is he as crazy as everyone says? I mean, I've seen him around, and I've heard some stories." She stood up and tossed the dirty rags into the trash.

"What kind of stories?"

"Lots of things. He's a drunk. He's catatonic. The usual. The kids around here think he's a ghost, but they think everyone's a ghost. Most people just think he's a weirdo. Sorry. That's insensitive. Unstable. That's what they say. They see him walking around with that dog. Never says a word. It's a bit strange."

"I guess."

"You name it, he's to blame. He's the boogeyman in this town."

"It's just gossip," I said, feeling the need to defend Eli's image. Why? I don't know. If he wasn't concerned about his image, why should I be? In fact, he was fighting against his image since he arrived. It might've been better if I'd just kept my mouth shut.

"You're probably right."

"I'm with Eli all the time," I lied. "He keeps to himself. Nothing to worry about."

"Tell me, does he still play his guitar?" she asked.

"No. Not that I've seen."

"Too bad. I always wanted to go to one of those barn concerts. It was the thing to do before it all blew up."

"What do you mean?"

"Well, you know," she continued. Clearly I didn't. "You're with the guy all the time. Why don't you ask him?"

The bell above the door chimed, and a man, decked

out in his Sunday best, entered like he owned the place. The clerk slid back behind the counter. Her shoulders slumped and her arms seemed to pull themselves in.

"What's the good word, my sweet Nikki?" the man asked without a hint of self-consciousness.

"Same as always," she answered.

"Come on. Lighten up." The man had the same arrogant pitch to his voice that Casey had, used the same inflection, and walked in the same self-assured way (crotch first, everything else second). If attitude were genetic, they would've been brothers.

He leaned against the counter, and I noticed a bulky black pager on his belt. Nikki kept her gaze on the register.

"Are you still mad?" he asked. "How many times do I have to explain? I didn't really lose my temper. That's not me. It's just for show. Part of the job."

She didn't answer. Instead, she grabbed my cash and made change.

I felt the man glare at me, and my hands began to shake.

"Sorry about the mess."

"No problem," she said as I left. "Good luck."

Using a paint bucket as a stool, I sat down and waited for my ride.

Behind me, the door swung open and the man with the pager exited like an errant gust of wind. He paused to stare at me before he strutted away, muttering something to himself, whipping up dust in his wake.

Ten minutes turned into fifteen, and I began to worry

that Jenny had forgotten about me. At first impression, she was a puzzle, but I was attracted to her indifference, her distance, and what I perceived as a comfort in her own skin. It didn't hurt that these were all traits that Melanie, my ex, didn't possess. I'd been in Galesville for a few weeks, and I was amazed just how much I craved this social interaction without even knowing it. The kicker: I'd learned more about Eli (or people's perception of Eli) in my brief venture into the village than I'd learned the whole damn time in his house. We may die alone, but we live among men—isn't that the saying?

I stood up when I saw the Blazer coming down Main Street. She had removed the hardtop so that it looked more like a small-bed truck than an SUV, but it was instantly recognizable. She double-parked in front, holding up traffic. I placed the supplies neatly in the back, hurried around, and jumped into the passenger seat. Beside me, in between me and Jenny, was a new car battery.

"Stopped at NAPA," she said. "It was on the way."

"You didn't have to do that."

"No big deal. Kathy owed me a favor. Call it a welcoming gift." She glanced over at me, eyes wide.

As she drove, I feigned interest in the homes, the scenery, the commons. It was all an attempt to steal a look or three or nine at Jenny. When I did, I noticed that she had a scar on her upper cheek, a crescent moon behind her eye, barely visible. She caught me looking.

"Car accident," she said. "Windshield. I got lucky."

"Sorry."

"For what? It wasn't your fault."

Uncomfortable, I changed the subject. "They were talking about Eli in there," I said.

"Who were?"

"Two older guys in the store."

"It happens." She shrugged, but I saw her shoulders tense up and her jaw set.

Before I knew it, we were crossing the covered bridge and entering River Bend. Jenny pulled into the driveway and parked by the carriage barn. Eli and Tig sat on the front step. Jenny honked, neither of them acknowledged the noise. In fact, neither of them moved. I jumped out and unloaded the supplies.

"Thanks for the ride and the battery. I owe you."

"Don't forget. Two favors now. They add up quickly."

"I'll try to keep count."

"Listen. I'm glad you're here," she said. "I know he wants to be left alone, but it's good to have someone. Just in case."

Was I Eli's *someone*? I looked back at the step and he was gone.

"In case of what?" I asked.

She smiled as she drove away, kicking up spring dirt and mud behind her.

"We all hide. Behind masks. Behind curtains. Behind others," Eli said, more or less. "Every single one of us plays our part." His words were slurred, and my brain was slow to translate. "Hopeless actors—all of us."

"I'll drink to both sound and fury." My face was hot, my head was heavy. With my glass at eye level, I swirled the scotch, coaxing the ice to melt and drown the Johnnie Walker. Each sip smoldered in my chest cavity, boring a hole to my heart.

"Look at you." He pointed at me, arm outstretched. "Who'd'ya think you are?"

"You are who you say you are."

"That's the problem." He lifted the black-labeled bottle and poured himself another drink. Black Label was the only liquid allowed in the living room. It was his go-to, and he drank it as if he were trying to burn off what remained of his voice and hasten his transformation into broken-down bluesman, pining for lost times.

I put a roof on my glass with my palm. The fire was too much. The inside of my nose tingled. Harnessing some bravery, I stood up, blinked away the tears, and stumbled into the wall. The room hula-hooped. I propped myself up and placed my forehead on the cool plaster, which offered some relief.

"Look at you. Crooked. Crippled. Can't even hold your whiskey." Eli's words tripped off his tongue, but his sentences, his responses were short, choppy waves lapping against the shore.

"Get to the point already."

"Tell me what you're hiding," he demanded.

"I'm not the one with the secrets. There's not a lot of mystery here." I banged on my chest with my open hand.

"Let's be real. You're hidin' behind somethin'. Those jeans, that mussed-up hair—that's your mask, that's your role."

"The role of Jack Wyeth as played by Jack Wyeth," I said as I clenched my teeth.

"Exactly. My point."

"Oh no, no, no. I'm honestly me. Why is it so damn hard, man, to trust? People should be real. They should show themselves," I said. In my haze, I could feel my blood pump down my limbs and back up again.

We were drunk enough to embarrass the dog. Tig glared at me with his big, sleepy eyes and then planted his face into his pillow. I imagined a drunk, lonely Eli, before my arrival, sizing him up and tearing him down. *Look at you,* he would've said, *with your tail between your legs and your perfect wiry coat. So trendy. So nonchalant. Let's be honest, dog. Let's stop playin' games.* He was right—everyone has an image he wants to project. What bothered me, in my gloomy confusion, was that his argument was hypocritical. Eli Page was an image-making savant—so much so that no one knew who he actually was under all his masks. But still he was *known.* His true thoughts, feelings, beliefs expressed through his music. He was an enigma, authentically contrived, as real as the next guy.

Across from me, I zeroed in on a door and wondered if it was just storage or if there was another room on the first floor. Maybe it was the scotch, but something didn't add up. "What the hell is behind that door?" I asked, or thought I asked. When Eli didn't offer a response, I wondered if I'd even said the words aloud.

The spinning room was a ship spiraling down the drain. Leaving the door for a sober moment, I closed my eyes and tried to recapture my equilibrium in the dark. No use. When I opened them, I found myself staring at Eli. He downed the last drops of his drink and glared menacingly at the bottom.

"What's your problem?" he said. For a moment, I thought he was conversing with the glass. "Your face is fucked," he added.

"Tell me something," I said, "about Jenny Lee."

"Ha!"

"What?"

"Forget it."

"Why?"

"She's got her secrets," he answered. "Just like the rest of us." Then he stood up and stumbled out of the living room as if I was a figment of his imagination, an apparition, an afterthought. What could I do but totter to my carriage barn suite, whack my forehead on the slanted ceiling, and fall facedown on the bed? Tomorrow was another day. Another chance to peel away the mask. Another failure waiting to begin.

But I was too tired to sleep. A sour lump sat in my stomach. The room expanded and contracted like an overworked, undershaped heart while Eli's words burned hot in my memory. I demanded honesty of others, but was I being honest with myself? Did it matter? I didn't say anything at the time, but Eli's insistence brought to mind a line from one of his early songs: *Day by day it all fades away, leaving us with nothing but a life in disarray.*

Late the next morning, it was back to housepainting. Since my trip to the hardware store, I'd spent my free mornings chipping away paint peels. Flecks of dry latex and slivers of siding were in my ears, in my hair, down my shirt. My eyes were always itchy. Those were my grievances on a normal day—add to that my head-pounding misery, and it didn't make for a pleasant start.

It's never a good idea to stand on an extension ladder and burn in the sun while nursing a hangover. It was Eli's fault, damn it. He poured the drinks. Again and again and again, he tested my resolve. He made it his purpose to get and keep me drunk until well past midnight. Maybe he was trying to bond, although he rambled about masks and role playing and dishonesty. Still, those late-night hours were the most significant time we spent together. I couldn't just give that up.

The spiteful, raging sun pounded me with its fists. My skin sizzled. I dunked my brush into the can, and with wide, sloppy strokes, I slapped on some more red paint, which spread like crushed cranberry against the thirsty wood.

I was about to hang it up for the day when I noticed a small untouched patch about six feet to my left. As I stepped a rung higher, the old aluminum extension flexed and vibrated. Before I had time to react, my knees were pushed up against the top of the ladder and my thighs were pressed against the house. I had to paint that goddamn spot as fast as I could and get down. So I stretched my arm out, dipped the brush in the can that dangled from the side of the ladder, and made myself as long as I could as I reached for the void. The ladder shuddered. My whole body contracted, tried to pull itself into a fetal position. The ladder shifted to my left and I went with it, dropping the brush as I reached out for something, anything, to stop the fall. When I bumped into the window molding, I gripped the wood with all my strength—my knuckles went as white as I imagined my face looked.

My options were limited. Could I jump and, if I could, would it be any better than falling? Could I ride the ladder down like I'd seen in the movies? Could I shatter the second-story window and climb in? The ladder shook as it tried to shrug me off. Best-case scenario: broken bones, cuts, bruises.

Pinned to the molding, I tried to look through the second-floor window. Was that Eli's bedroom? Twisting my neck to get a better look only made my balance worse, but I was willing to risk the injury. From up high, I imagined the layout of the house, the bedrooms stacked on top of the living room, dining room, and kitchen. Something was off. The square footage didn't add up. Where did the two shaded windows below me, on the first floor, lead?

Someone coughed.

"Hello?"

"That's one hell of a situation you have there." The voice wrapped around me.

I clung to the ladder. "Can't...turn...around."

"Need some help?"

My hangover said his question was moronic, but I wasn't in a position to call him on it, whoever he was. "This piece of molding is the only thing keeping me up."

"You're Jack?" he asked. "Jack Wyeth?"

"Yeah, that's me." Puzzled, I tried again to see over my shoulder, but only an annoying shadow was visible.

I knew at once that this was the type of guy who hung in your blind spot on the highway and then pounded his horn when you shifted lanes.

"My girl told me you were visiting?"

"Your girl? Who says that?" I muttered under my breath.

"Are you related to Elijah Page?" The familiar tones of his voice bugged me. There was contempt somewhere in those drawn-out notes. I answered no and waited for his help.

"Friend?"

"Painter," I said.

"A live-in painter? Must be a city thing." He laughed.

I began to think he was never going to help. "I'm not from the city," I said.

"Well, you're not from here, and that's all that matters."

"Who am I talking to?"

"Mark Calvin. Folks call me Cal."

"Well, Mark Calvin, can you give me a hand before I break my neck?"

No answer. He let my request linger before he hit me with the next round.

"Where's Elijah Page?"

It was a good question, but I had no idea.

"I'll answer all your questions if you help me down," I blurted out, trying to blunt the sharp-tongued and unfriendly phrases that were scrolling through my head.

"Is that a promise?" the man asked.

"Sure."

I felt the ladder stabilize as he grabbed hold of the rails. My knees strengthened; the vibrations stopped. I took the first step with caution, not convinced that this stranger wouldn't dump me to the ground. After the fourth step, I balanced myself and quickly descended.

On solid footing, I turned to face Mark Calvin while I rubbed the knots in my neck, and I was shocked to see his neatly pressed uniform. Folks call me Cal was a New York state trooper equipped with all the goodies—gun, cuffs, wide-brimmed hat, overbearing confidence. His eyes were glazed over by the spring sun. Good thing his sunglasses were in his shirt pocket, I thought, because I would've burst out laughing if they were on his face.

"Thanks for the help," I said. He raised his chin, and at that moment, I realized where I'd heard the voice before—the hardware store. He was the guy with the pager. Still arrogant, he was somehow a different man in the confines of his uniform; it was as if his clothes didn't quite fit or as if he was trying too hard to appear straight, intimidating, muscular.

"Who are you and what are you doing here?" he asked.

"Is Eli in trouble?"

He raised his eyebrows and ogled me as if I were trying to sell him insurance. "One could say that," he said. "If he knew what was good for him, he'd turn himself in."

"For what?"

"You never answered—"

"Jack Wyeth. Nice to meet you." I extended my hand. To him, it didn't exist.

"What are you doing here?" he repeated.

"At the moment? Trying not to vomit."

I don't know why I felt I had something to hide, but Cal made me nervous. Truthfully, I had a healthy distrust of uniforms. They made me anxious in the best of situations.

"I asked you a serious question."

"And I answered."

His jawline sharpened.

"Look," I continued, "I'm just here helping out Eli. Nothing noteworthy about it."

"I'll be the judge of that."

"Okay."

"You said you'd answer my questions."

"Within reason," I said.

"That wasn't the deal."

"I don't like to lie to strangers, but better sore feelings than broken bones."

Mark Calvin placed his hands on his belt. "One more time," he said.

"Nope. I've got nothing to say."

"I should've left you up there," he remarked, and started off. He strutted down the driveway like the king rooster, paused, and then turned around. "Jenny says hi, by the way."

"Jenny?"

"That's what I said." He cleared his throat and lowered his voice. Shaking his head, he lifted his cheek, gathered his thoughts, and continued: "Jenny. Jenny Lee Flynn. She's the one who told me about your... existence. I don't like to be in the dark. Remember that. It will do you good."

No matter how hard I tried, I couldn't hide my disappointment. What was Jenny doing with this guy?

"What's your problem?" I asked.

"I don't have a problem with you. Not yet. Just a simple request—tell me where Eli Page is at this very moment. That's all."

"As I already said, I have no idea."

"Not good enough."

"So what did Jenny say exactly?"

He grinned, knowing that he'd gotten to me. I attempted a smile, but I'm sure it came out crooked and full of vinegar.

"Unless you want an ass-whooping, I'd wipe that wiseass smile off your face," he warned.

"Sir. Yes, sir." My head throbbed.

"She was confused. Didn't understand why Page needs you around. Me neither."

"Well, that makes three of us," I said under my breath.

"What?"

"Forget it." I retracted the ladder.

"It doesn't have to be like this. Just tell me where Page is."

We were twenty yards apart and shouting at one another. The volume of our voices grew after each pause and each step.

"I can't."

"Can't or won't? I helped you off the ladder."

"I appreciate it, but I don't know where he is."

"If that's your story—"

"Do me a favor, will you? Tell Jenny I said hi back."

His eyes narrowed. "When he returns, tell him that he can't avoid me forever. I need satisfactory answers. This little game he plays, being aloof or above it all, is going to bite him in the ass soon enough."

"I'll pass it along."

He scuffed his boots on the driveway and left. I knew then that he'd be back, but I had no idea it would end the way it did.

I tossed the brush into a can of paint thinner and walked to the hose to wash up. My hangover had faded into a persistent, dull nagging. It was almost noon, and I couldn't help but wonder where Eli was, what he was doing, and why it was secret.

The siren from the cop car blared and bounced off the house as Trooper Calvin drove away. As much as I hate to admit it, it scared the living hell out of me.

What I knew: the door was locked. What I needed to do: walk away. What I did: rush the door, slam my dropped shoulder into the hardwood, and bounce off like a crash test dummy. Twice. Then I kicked, punched, and pushed at it until I was winded and sore. It didn't budge. Bruised, I leaned my back on the wood and slid into a sitting position. Nothing to be done. No safety pins, paper clips, letter openers, or credit cards could disengage the lock. And, yes, I even thought about yanking the pins from the hinges, but the hinges were hidden inside. The room was a vault.

It felt good to bang the back of my head against the solid, unmovable surface of the door. So good that I did it again and again until my head began to throb. I tapped it one last time for good measure and something dropped from above, caught my peripheral vision, and pinged like a tuning fork against the wood floor. A shiny shard of metal, a silver key. It rested beside me, mocking me with its two eyeholes. It must've lived on the casing all along. I bounced to my feet, placed the key in the lock, and finally opened the door.

Stacks of books, boxes of records, old posters and play-bills, letters and photographs—the room was the lost city of Eli Page. I thumbed through the vinyl-jammed crates: Woody Guthrie, Thelonious Monk, Roy Orbison, Cream, Muddy Waters, Johnny Cash, Ramblin' Jack, the Weavers, the Yardbirds, Howlin' Wolf. Blue Note and Folkways and Columbia. An ancient Circle of Sound record player lived on top of a boxy steamer trunk. The Zenith's cylindrical wood-encased speakers sat off to the side like time cap-sules. Seven, no, eight cases were wedged between the crates and an oak rolltop desk. I pulled one from the set, opened it, and unleashed a worn-down Gibson J-50, which I immediately recognized from many photos of Eli at the Bitter End and Gerde's Folk City.

Framed gig posters from the '60s and '70s were stacked next to an unframed canvas, an oil painting of Eli at the Troubadour. These pieces of history formed his legacy— his past, present, and future—and something in me cried out that I was supposed to be the go-between, the media-tor, the translator.

The desire to organize the entire room from top to bot-tom, to catalog each piece came on like a fever. I finally had a bead on Eli. For all of his posturing, all his minimizing, all of his denial, he still kept this hidden room. Maybe that old Eli Page wasn't as dead as he wanted me to believe.

I sat down in a wooden swivel chair by the rolltop and envisaged Eli plucking memories from the images that dangled all around him. If the synapses didn't fire, he had backed up the hard drive. This was his memory bank. This was his collage. This was his safety-deposit box. And it was my all-access pass.

I lifted a picture of Eli from the desk. In a disaster of an apartment, not much bigger than the carriage barn bedroom, Eli, hidden under a small Irish cap and a wispy beard, sat on a tattered couch, his ankle slung across his opposite knee, his head cocked down to the right, his eyes pointed upward in the opposite direction. He stared at the camera as if he was about to devour it. Maybe it wasn't hunger in his eyes, maybe he was just drunk or stoned, but, nevertheless, the photo and the room unleashed a new energy, a new round of questioning, a renewed motivation.

The room's air was musky, stagnant. It had been shut up too long. Surrounded by piles and piles of artifacts, a treasure trove, I knew that I still needed Eli to open up, to acknowledge this past, to provide context to these artifacts if nothing else. My new plan, as it emerged, was this — in the mornings, while Eli was away, I'd explore; in the evenings I'd carry on as if nothing had changed. Using these two tracks, an A-side and a B-side, maybe, just maybe, I could make the project go.

I ran my hand over the contents of the desk. A stack of letters, bound together by two elastic bands, sat on the desk blotter. My fingers tightened on the brittle, yellowed envelopes. The thwack of the storm door jolted me from my makeshift research. Eli was home early. I slipped the letters in my waistband and left the room in a hurry.

After I locked the door and returned the key to the woodwork, I crossed the living room in three giant steps, plopped down in the armchair, and took a newspaper from a pile beside the sofa. Never in my life had I moved with such swift efficiency, and I'm not afraid to admit that I was somewhat proud of my reaction.

Eli poked his head into the room. "What're you doing?" he asked.

"Nothing. Reading." Beads of sweat slid down my face. My stomach churned. I wiped my brow with the back of my hand.

"The light's terrible in here. You should be more careful with your eyes."

He flipped the light switch on and went into the kitchen.

On my way to the carriage barn, the corners of the letters jabbed at my lower back. I was certain that the stack would fall out, splash across the floor, and expose my betrayal. When I was safe inside my room, I set the letters on the bedside table. Looking back, I think I knew, even then, that those letters contained something worth noting, but I didn't know just how much they would impact the next two months. How could I?

Carefully, I slid the rubber bands off, unfolded the paper, and scanned their shape, size, and characteristics. All of the worn envelopes were postmarked 1975.

Discolored and wrinkled, they must've been balled up and restraightened again and again. Some of the words were smudged, unreadable, blacked out from years of thumb rubbing. Whole lines were obscured. All in all, there were eight letters, penned by the same hand on the same lined notepaper and signed with the same initials—H.M.

February 23
My Sweet Eli,

Where are you? What are you doing at this very moment? Let me see, it must be after three in the morning in London. I imagine you sunk into some scratchy bed in some smoke-filled hotel room, the guitar laid next to you (in my place), strung-out little girls hanging outside your door, crying, "Eli! Eli! Are you in there?" How'd I do? Am I close? Of course I am. I accept how things are, but it doesn't keep my mind from drifting into these little bouts of fancy. I'm just being honest. Yes, and jealous. But mostly honest. When have I ever strayed from that?

It's late here, for me at least, but I can't sleep. Every time I close my eyes, I hear your voice like a thousand larks on my windowsill. No, nightingales. It's going to take some time to adjust. That's all. That's what I keep telling myself. I'm lonely, but we made the right decision. Wasn't it the right thing to do? It was. Don't be silly. We have time.

I went to the spot today. To tell you the truth, it was a struggle to get up and down. My feet were swollen and sore when I got home. Everyone was furious with me. I probably should've told them where I was going, but I'm not used to the attention now that you're away. I know it's not like me, but the majority of my waking life is filled with these types of thoughts. When did I become so wrapped up in you? So be it.

My hopes for you:

1. I hope you're excited, and you're enjoying London.

2. I hope you are keeping your nose clean.

3. I hope you will send me word as soon as you can so that I can think clearly and stop ███████████████

██

██

For example.

I miss you. That's how I know it was right. Or close to it. What is right anyways?

Yours, H.M.

———

March 12

My Dear, Sweet Eli,

My daily life is a farce. I swear it's like <u>Laugh-In</u> meets <u>The Bald Soprano</u>. People won't let me do anything. Ma says it's for my own good, but how can it be for my own good if I'm always annoyed and angry? Does that make sense? That can't be good, right? I know you'll understand. You're the only one who hears me. We speak the same language. Sometimes, when I'm talking, it's like they're hearing Italian (or nothing at all). They nod and brush my hair like I'm a doll in need of an attitude adjustment. And I'll tell you what—the word "uncomfortable" has a new meaning. That's neither up nor down, but it's true. I wish you could see me. No. I take that back. Better to remember what I looked like before it all began. There's so much to tell, but I'm too sleepy to keep at it. Please write. Soon.

H.M.

———

April 4

Elijah,

This is getting ridiculous. I promised myself I wouldn't spiral into self-pity like some soap starlet, but I was never good at keeping promises. You know that. It's something we share. I feel better when I write, though. That's something. It's almost as if I'm talking to you. Even if it's one-sided. I heard you were ██████ ████████████████ Is that true? I hope not. Life can spin out of control in the blink of an eye. Don't let it.

Did I mention I miss you? I miss a lot. I'm full of misses like sitting next to you, your hands on my skin, the grass between my toes, the wind in my hair, the sound of your voice when you sing. Well, that one is easy enough to solve... Everything else fades in and out, but I can still hear you. I was going to write about longing, for you, for your touch, but it just sounds stupid. We weren't cut out to give or receive sappy love letters. It's not our style. Forget what I have said. It's stupid, selfish.

My back aches. There's nothing to be done about it, but it keeps me awake. I wish I could take something for the pain or to help me sleep, but I'm not allowed. Ma even took my books away. Proof that words are dangerous. And my boots. Boots and books. Quite the statement.

How's the tour so far? I read there was a riot in London. You are definitely to blame! You've rotted their minds! I read too that you have a file. A file?! I don't know whether to laugh or cry at that. Ma threatened to call the authorities if you even tried to call. She would do that, wouldn't she? FBI. No, I shouldn't kid around about that. They're probably listening in.

I can only imagine the hotels, the people, the fun you're having. I hope you're getting used to it all again. Don't get frustrated or overwhelmed when they crowd your space. They love you. They're glad you're back. Most of them, anyway. Remember that. They've come to see you. You tell the truth. Even more so now. Don't forget that your music helps them, makes them feel something other than depressed and strung out. Your voice is meaningful. You always had that gift.

I am lonely without you, my troubled Eli, but I hope you are driving them crazy. Get some sleep. Stop inciting riots.

Yours, H.M.

———

May 2

Sweet, Sweet Eli,

It's been a week since my last letter, but it's felt like months. They won't let me do much here. Even putting pen to paper is frowned upon. I want to scream because I ache all over and they won't leave me alone, but it wouldn't do any good. Actually, let me see. (Screaming.) Didn't work.

I read about you today in the paper. Again. It said the crowds are huge. People are excited you're back on tour. The paper said that you're going to Paris next week. Is that true? You're probably there already. I wish I could be with you. Take your time, for me. Remember all the details so that you can tell me. Someday we'll go together and you'll show me around. Then we can pretend we were together for it all. We can change the story to suit our needs.

Well, this has to be quick since I hear Ma making noise in the hall. I'm sorry if I sound out of it. It's this strange medicine they keep pumping into me and their rules. Always with the rules. If I could, I'd leave in a second and come find you. Tell Barry to bring you back to me soon.

I hope you're well on the other side of the world. That's what it feels like.

Please write. Or better yet, send me a postcard from Paris.

Yours, H.M.

———

May 20

Eli,

Me again. I haven't heard from you at all. When did I send my first letter? February or March, I think. Are you getting any of them? I can't be sure. I know that you must be busy. As luck would have it, I have all the time in the world to write and wait for word from you. Funny. Ma heard your new song on the radio. She said it was catchy, but she didn't get it. "Too wordy." She prefers James Taylor. That made me laugh. Laughing hurts, though.

How am I feeling? I'm feeling okay, really. I shouldn't complain. Things could be worse. To be honest, I get frustrated. I'm feeling really weak and bored with all this rest, but I do as I'm told. They must know what they're talking about, right? ████████████████

████████████████

Are you getting these? Or are you too busy to write? I understand if you are, but please just send me a note so I know you haven't forgotten. I'm joking. I know you haven't.

My handwriting is getting worse, I've just noticed. Legible or not, it helps me to think of you reading my scribbles and ramblings even if you don't have time to ramble back.

Got to go. They're coming in for my daily poking and prodding.

Yours, H.M.

———

May 31
Eli,

The phone in the room rang last night, and I thought it was you. Please call or write me. Please. A simple note to let me know if you are getting these.

I warn you now that I'm going to whine. Just for a moment. My ribs feel like I've been kicked by a horse. (I was kicked by a horse when I was 11. Did you know that? I do know what it feels like.) They have me in some stupid position and I'm not allowed to move. I feel like I don't have to be here at all, like they could do it without me. I know that sounds silly, but I have no say. Ma is always telling me to be quiet and listen. Be quiet and listen, be quiet and listen, be patient and listen to the doctor. If she only knew how close I am to screaming...or grabbing her by the perm and tossing her out the window. She says everything is fine, it's all normal. Easy for them to say. I can tell when people are lying to me. I could always tell when you were lying. Remember that.

I don't know what to say to you. I feel completely put to pasture. I feel like I'm disappearing. Where am I in all this? What say do I have? My body is doing things without my permission. My head spins and my thoughts are out of control. Emotions I didn't even know I had take over and I say things that don't even make sense.

I made Ma cry the other day. I didn't even feel sorry afterward.

Please don't think I'm trying to make you feel guilty. That's not my intention. But this is hard. I can't lie about that.

Yours, H.M.

———

June 4

Eli,

I've come to the conclusion that you are not getting these. Why else would I not hear from you?

Yours, H.M.

June 29

Eli,

I can't write anymore. This will be my last letter. I haven't heard from you in over four months. I doubt that you are getting these. I feel like I'm putting these letters in a bottle and throwing them into the sea, hoping that they'll drift across the Atlantic and find you. Am I crazy? Do you care?

They say I need to focus. You're a distraction. Letter writing is a distraction. The doctor said to forget about you. If I could move, I would've slapped him. He's an arrogant know-it-all anyways. He'd deserve it. He keeps telling me I'm doing things the wrong way. Like he'd know better.

It's day to day here. I think I'm doing okay, but Ma won't look at me. She's mad, and I can't remember what I did to make her so upset.

Anyway, I need to concentrate. I feel like unless I stop and focus I'll disappear completely. It's hard, but I'm doing it whether I like it or not.

Please believe me that I don't blame you for this or for not writing. I thought you should know that. I don't have any delusions. Maybe you've decided this is not what you want. I knew it was a possibility all along. I'm not sure it's possible to have both things. So, if that is why you are not writing me . . . don't worry. Live your life, but send me word. It will make things easier. This is hard. Too hard for one person. I suppose that will change. I suppose I'm just whining.

I can smell you and I can taste you, but it is not enough. I need to know you are there, somewhere, even at a distance. If it weren't for the radio and the occasional newspaper article, I'd be lost. So send word. Just two words or one if you can spare the time. One word? Can you send one word?

Do you know what I thought about last night? For some odd reason, I thought about when we went to the fair last summer. You tried and tried to win a necklace for me until I convinced you that I didn't need it. We sat under the tent and ate funnel cake. The powder stuck to your shirt and it began to rain. I remember everybody rushing into the tent as we sat together and waited out the downpour. And we made a decision. Those memories help more than you can imagine. I am nothing but memories and hope, hope and memories ███████████████████████████ I'm scared, Eli. I'm more scared than you know.

That's all. My last letter. Return soon.

I love you always. H.M.

My lips were dry from reading and rereading the words aloud. A metallic taste sat on my tongue. I folded the letters along their well-worn creases and rested them on my bed.

Eli's tour through Europe was well documented in any number of biographies, films, and essays, but from my fragile recollection, no one with the initials H.M. had ever been mentioned. Not even in a footnote. What had happened in 1975? That was the big question that no one had ever asked.

My phone vibrated in my hand. I answered without checking the number.

"Please hold for Mr. Gettleson," the secretary said.

Barry Gettleson had called three times in as many days, and I'd successfully been out of range each time, sending his secretary directly to voice mail. He'd finally caught me with the faintest of signals.

"Update me." His voice burst through my phone's static.

"I'm making progress."

"Progress? What does that mean?"

"You know more than I do about the way he works. I'm trying to establish a relationship."

"Does he buy what you're selling?"

"I'm winning him over." The lies came easy when Gettleson was the recipient.

"Good. Send me what you got."

"Well, I have notes, sketches. It needs shaping," I said.

"Jack, don't screw with me."

"I'm not."

"You waste my time, you waste my life. You get my drift?" His voice popped in and out as if he was fiddling with the phone. "Did I or did I not take care of you?"

"It's not about the money. You told me to ease in."

"Weeks ago. That's an eon, man. Life moves fast."

"I understand," I said. "You need pages."

"Exactly. Don't disappoint."

"I'll send something."

Again, Gettleson faded out. I heard the ghost of a conversation in the background but couldn't piece it together.

"Enough about business," he said. "Tell me about his state of mind."

"What do you want to know?"

"Is it partly cloudy or partly sunny, if you know what I mean?"

"Mostly cloudy. Chance of silence," I said.

He exhaled into the phone. It occurred to me that I was playing Gettleson's game, mirroring his demeanor, giving him the person he wanted. My head ached.

"Time is not on your side," he said.

"Don't I know it."

"Well," he continued, "shape it, model it, massage it. Throw in a happy ending on the house. Whatever you've got to do, do it. Send me something soon."

"Yeah. Okay."

"Don't make me call back at the end of the week to hound you. I would hate for our conversations to take an unpleasant turn."

"I said I'd get you something. I will."

"Think about this — what the hell would your life look like if you weren't doing what you're doing? You understand? Don't get sucked in."

He hung up.

Sucked in? What did he mean by that? As I sat on the front step, I lingered on Gettleson's statement or warning or whatever it was. Yes, if I weren't in Galesville, I'd be fighting with Casey, avoiding Denise's cold stares, and busking on street corners. Eventually I'd find my way at Caffè Lena, that little hole-in-the-wall that Eli Page frequented back in the '60s and '70s.

My admiration for all the musicians, young and old, established and emerging, who still come out to play, to tell stories, to say something cannot be understated. Maybe it's because every one of them shares something with Eli Page—his influence was as potent as the musty smell in the room. Guitarists steal finger-picking, singers strain their voices to sound more like him, and many performers even stare off over the heads of the audience, pretending to be lost in thought. His legacy, and the legacy of so many others, is carried forward in places like Lena's.

Apparently I missed the Caffè more than I thought. I missed its entrance, which was shellacked with old images of wandering troubadours who'd floated in and out of the coffeehouse since 1960. I missed the brick walls, the uneven floors, the heat of the lights. I missed the laughter, the sing-alongs, the stories. Inevitably, someone would recall seeing a young Pete Seeger step onto the smoke-filled stage or John Hammond or Kate McGarrigle or that stormy winter night (in '63 or '64) when Eli Page had refused to sing, instead performing a Beckett-inspired mime act with Lena's help from the house. I missed all those musicians who refused to give up, not allow themselves to believe that, perhaps, the time for folk music had come and gone.

Of course, I admit that on some nights it felt like we were all merely going through the motions, as if revisiting the folk scene would conjure the chutzpah of an earlier era, one long since removed from our consciousness. Rather than commenting on current struggles or fully comprehending the intent, newbies would cover a song from 1968 and make it sterile, indifferent, and uptight. They'd say, "Dylan can't sing," and they'd recite, "Oh,

Mama, can this really be the end" as if it was a lecture on the history of Mobile. Me? Well, I'd do a mean imitation of Page or Woody, but I knew that these covers were merely shadows. The audience would politely applaud and pretend that it all mattered, and then they'd go home and watch *American Idol*. Worse yet, during a cover, my voice would crack and the illusion would disappear. There were ups and downs, and we all yearned for those performances that would burn hot in the memory, but they were few and far between. It was hard to believe that any of us could make a dent in the universe.

Caffè Lena aside, the simple fact was that if I wasn't in Galesville at that moment, I would've been dialing Melanie's number to ask her what she wanted, to ask her to forget everything that happened, to ask her to redeem me. But in Galesville, I wasn't the same restless and malleable person. I was a different Jack Wyeth altogether. It wasn't reinvention; it was as if I was getting closer to touching the image in the mirror.

All of that was running through my mind as I was standing on the front step, peeling an orange, waiting for Jenny to stop by for another pickup. She arrived before noon.

"So," she said, hands on her hips, "is this how you spend your days?"

"Well, some have greatness thrust upon them; others paint their houses."

"It doesn't look so bad."

"Thanks, I guess." I offered her a slice of my orange. She declined with that crafty smile, roguish and reassuring at the same time. "I'll be done soon enough."

Without pause, Jenny walked into the house and came out with a box in her arms. She always knew where to go. She never hesitated. "Is this all he left?"

"As far as I know." I tossed the last of the orange slices into my mouth and followed her to the Blazer. She placed the box next to a crate of old bottles and a couple of broken chairs.

My lips and hands were sticky from the fruit, and I was suddenly self-conscious of the volume of my chewing. I swallowed.

"I met your boyfriend the other day," I said, figuring I'd throw it out there.

"What the hell are you talking about?"

"Mark Calvin, state trooper."

"He's not my boyfriend," she said, but I could tell that the words stung.

"According to him, you're his *girl*."

"I'm not anyone's *girl*."

"So, just for clarification, you're not together?"

She crossed her arms and leaned back to size me up. "No, we're not, but it's complicated." Her smile was gone. "Most things are." Our banter was no longer playful. I had crossed some invisible line. "As much as I'd love to stick around and chat about this bullshit, I've got to get back." She jumped into the driver's seat and slammed the door.

"I'm sorry for bringing it up."

"Next time," she said, measuring each word, "if you have a question, just ask."

She shifted into reverse and drove out of the gate onto River Bend Road. As the truck vanished, I found myself thinking about Mark Calvin, Jenny Lee, and the world of information I didn't know and probably never would.

Just then, Eli and Tig appeared on the road. Tig wobbled slowly, deliberately toward home. Like a child, Eli jumped and splashed in yesterday's puddles. It was a thing of beauty.

I filled the kettle with tap water. Intrigued by the hiss of the splash against the aluminum sink, I twisted the faucet on and off, on and off, on and off, creating a percussive backbeat.

Already released from its plastic raincoat, the *Mirror* was unfolded and neatly laid out on the counter. In his small, compact writing, Eli had scribbled in the margins.

In the beginning there was nothing.
God said let there be light.
There was still nothing, but
Now we could see it better.

Was he sending me a message or was he passing the time by doodling on the newsprint? Leave it to Eli, I thought, to find some existential amusement to occupy his breakfast time.

I flipped through the paper, looking for an update about the break-ins, vandalism, and subsequent investigation. Without TV, email, or the Internet to steal my time, the *Mirror* was one of my only connections to the little town carrying on just beyond River Bend, a town I was yet to fully comprehend, but the outlet was flawed, narrow, incomplete.

Every Thursday, without fail, its eight flimsy gray pages arrived on Eli's doorstep by the hands of that pesky paperboy. Taken together, the paper presented a kaleidoscopic view of Galesville and its neighboring communities. No stories of national significance. Instead, local color and hometown pride filled its columns. It delivered even the driest information with the inadvertent humor of false humility. The "Town Crier" section overflowed with minutes from council meetings, school announcements, and notices of church services. The obits, where the recently departed enjoyed a detailed retelling of their lives and accomplishments, offered insight into the town's history and politics. Pages four and five contained letters to the editor and semiregular columns by village raconteurs. The content of the letters ranged from hearty congratulations for "getting it right" to broad, misguided musings on patriotism to rants about village taxes and service agreements.

In the few weeks since my arrival, the headlines had grown bolder. Tensions were high. Questions about trespass, breaking and entering, theft, and vandalism arose, and outside influences (such as Eli Page) were often blamed. At times, the *Mirror*'s inside/outside approach bordered on xenophobia. Living ten, fifteen, twenty years in Galesville didn't make you a local; that label was reserved for founding families and blood ties. In a sense, we were all carpetbaggers.

I flipped the paper over. On the back page, staring at me, slightly out-of-focus, crooked and cross-legged, stood Jenny. She held a paintbrush in her hand. The photo was taken in front of the IGA building. Its caption read: "Local artist, Jenny Lee Flynn, paints new village mural."

The teapot whistled. I ignored it as I quickly thumbed through the thin pages to find more information or an accompanying article, but there was nothing. The black-and-white photo existed as a single, solitary beacon in a sea of local copy. The pot rattled on the stovetop. I turned the burner off and let it cool. My interest in tea had evaporated. Folded twice, I jammed the *Mirror* into my back pocket, and I went down to the river.

The Battenkill raced around the rocks, splashed along the bank, and forced chunks of dirt and mud and grass to give way. The water's pace fluctuated wildly whenever there was a storm, and over an inch of rain had fallen the previous night. I crouched at the river's edge and stuck my hand in the water to feel its muscle and weight tug at my fingers. There was beauty in it, but there was also panic. Ever-present, always rushing forward, the river collected questions but offered few answers. When I spoke, my confessions were washed downstream. So I spoke to it about Jenny, about my wishes, my fears, my frustrations.

I hadn't slept well the night before. After a string of storms, it was so humid that I twisted in my sheets for hours. In the morning breeze, the same dread that kept me from a sound sleep cooled me. What it was exactly, I wasn't sure. If I had to describe it, I'd call it a deep and growing fear of my own limitations. As a man, as a musician, as a fiancé, as a "ghostwriter," as a son—had I failed at them all? Maybe failure was my biggest success.

I removed the paper from my pocket and reexamined the photograph. Then I folded it into the shape of a boat, the way my father had shown me when I was still less than three feet tall. I set the boat on the river, made a wish, and sent it downstream. Maybe it would find its way to Jenny. Stranger things have happened. It sailed away, skimming along the top of the water before it finally sank under its own weight.

Locals refer to the largest building in town as Middle Block. Once a grand hotel that bustled with activity, the massive (by Galesville standards) four-story structure was celebrated for its tall clock tower, which rose from its center like an overexcited exclamation point. In 1978, in a last-ditch effort to save the historic building from ruin, the town consolidated all of its offices and administrative services in Middle Block.

I followed the arrows up a concrete ramp, wondering if I'd happen upon Eli safely tucked away in the library. Over the previous two days, I'd upgraded my search for Eli with frequent trips into town. Like a true detective, I asked around, but no one ever saw him. Where would he go to spend an entire morning? I asked myself. In between the stacks was as good a guess as any.

The Galesville Library was built into the guts of the hotel's high-ceilinged lobby and grand ballroom. On the ground floor, the shelves bumped into ornate moldings while special collections gathered dust in the second-floor audience boxes, accessible only by a spiral staircase. The revamped front of the building overlooked the south side of the commons at Church and Main. Its tall windows let light into an immense open space with reference materials and computer terminals.

"Can we help you with something?" Two women stood behind the counter. The one who spoke had pale lips and a long face. She stood straight up and down and glared with a dead-eyed boldness that was disconcerting. The other woman, just as tall and stringy, bent over and thumbed through books on a red rolling cart.

I asked about Eli.

"We haven't seen Mr. Page in months," the bold woman said. "Sorry." The other woman glanced up from the cart, but she didn't open her mouth.

"I figured I'd give it a shot." I should've known better.

"Can we help you with something else?"

"Is it all right if I check my email?"

"Do you have a library card?"

"No. I'm new here."

"Would've never guessed," she said as she reached below the counter and lifted out two sheets of paper. "Fill these out, please. First one is for a card. Second one states the rules of conduct for Internet usage."

I scribbled my information into the appropriate boxes of the application, pausing only to ponder my address. After a moment, I listed it as 10 River Bend Road. A few minutes later, they printed me a shiny library card, extending full lending rights and privileges to "Jack Wuelk." Close enough.

In the grand old ballroom, I logged on to an old desktop, complete with a huge monitor and clunky beige keyboard, poured over my email, and surfed the dross. After writing a brief message to Casey, I deleted a whole bunch of spam, refreshed my online profiles, and pruned my carefully constructed Internet life, which in my absence had been dismantled e-brick by e-brick. Too much time had passed. My digital family had moved on. A Galesville-induced isolation had fractured my social networks, which bothered me much less than I thought it would. In an inauthentic century, I was tired of chasing my own persona.

Before my allotted thirty minutes were up, I checked a few trusted discussion boards for references to Eli Page in 1974 and 1975 as well as his European tour, commonly referred to as his Comeback Tour (even though there have been two subsequent comeback tours). For good measure, I ran "H.M." and "H + M" along with Eli's name and the dates of the letters through a few search engines. Nothing turned up.

I logged off, leaned back in my chair, and watched people walk by the window: a young man bumping a stroller over the uneven sidewalk, a lunchtime jogger zipping through the commons, a stocky old woman attempting to saw off her neighbor's errant tree branches. No clue that they were being spied on, unaware that they were players in the unfolding scenes of my life, they carried on. They were not self-conscious. They did not spin lies. No need. As far as they were concerned, they were alone. As close to honest as could be found.

Just then, as if my unconscious had conjured her, Jenny wandered by the window. Peaceful, uninhibited, she swung her arms playfully as she looked up at the treetops. A black-and-gray newsboy hat with a small brim shielded her eyes, but I spotted her right away.

Abandoning the computer, I jumped up and ran toward the exit.

"Sir!" One of the librarians commanded without raising her voice. "There is no running in the library." She pointed to a sign above the counter that said as much in comic-sans font.

"Sorry," I said as I slowed to a power walk.

"If you do find Mr. Page, remind him that he has an overdue book," she added. "We don't want to have to get nasty."

I pushed through the door, ran down the ramp, and burst out onto Main Street. No trace of Jenny. Just me, Jack Wyeth (or Wuelk, if you prefer), standing on the sidewalk, mouth open, scruffy chin in hand while the librarians looked on and chuckled silently behind the glass.

The day after the paint dried, I sat on the step, anxiously awaiting Eli's return. Behind me, his newly painted house was slick and clean, its earlier drabness masked by a new red skin. Unblemished. My wrists and finger bones ached from squeezing the brush handles for hours on end, but I'd finished in good time.

Off in the distance, high on the road leading away from the village, man and dog appeared. Where were they coming from? Had they crossed into Vermont? There was nothing over there for miles. Slowly, methodically, they approached. I stood up, watching them as they lumbered forward as if it were the last stretch in a marathon. Ten minutes later, Eli entered the drive with Tig close behind.

"How was your morning?" I asked, blocking the entrance.

"Quiet."

"Where did you go?"

"Where we always go." He was still a master at answering questions without providing an actual answer—it was his second-best talent.

"Did you see the house?"

Impatient, Tig huffed. Then he nudged my leg aside and made his way to the water bowl.

"No. Is it done?" Eli asked, without looking up. As soon as I took my eyes off him, he slid around me and entered the house. I followed, knowing that I'd just been outsmarted which, I admit, stung a bit. He tossed his satchel to the floor and leaned his cane against the wall.

Replenished, Tig breathed on my hand before sauntering off to his pillow like a world-weary traveler. His paws left mud prints on the wood planks from the door to his water bowl to his bed.

"Finished this morning, and I think it looks pretty good."

"I'll take a closer look tomorrow." He entered the living room, dropped down on the sofa, and closed his eyes. That was my cue to leave him alone. Only I couldn't do that. Not after I'd busted my ass to finish the house.

"I did what I agreed to do," I said. "It's time to pay up."

"Pay up?" he asked, eyes still shut tight.

"We had a deal. You gave me your word."

"I don't know what you're talkin' about."

"We had an agreement."

Wide-eyed, he sat upright in his seat. "You think you're smarter than me? That you can wind me up in circles and point me where you want me to go? Do you think you can just bend and twist me until you get what you want? Is that what you think?"

The air in the room was motionless, humid. I had mentally prepared for his rebuttal, but I didn't anticipate the bewildered look, the complete unknowing.

"A deal is a deal."

"I wouldn't've agreed to something so stupid," he said, his voice rising and filling the corners of the room. "What do I get in this so-called deal?"

"A painted house. That was the exchange—the paint for two hours of your time."

Then, suddenly, as if he had some vague recollection of the deal, he was quiet. He caught his breath, unfurled his eyebrows, and stared at me. "It's not a good time."

"Okay. What about tomorrow?"

"No. That won't work."

"When exactly would be a good time? You tell me."

Eli leaned into the cushions, tipped his head back, and sighed. Tig lifted his eyes and ears to check on us.

"What I am I supposed to do," I asked, "if you bail on the deal?"

He shrugged, damn him.

My head was full of bees. I felt my face burn as loud as the buzz in my skull. Eli turned my thoughts inside out, my reason into blindness. I muttered curses to myself and scratched and clawed at my own neck. Although it seemed real enough, I wasn't certain; I suspected he might be screwing with me, playing senile to avoid paying on his debt. The moments of confusion were always so convenient.

"You're the one with the book deal. If you don't want to do it, just say the word," I said. No response. Eli's face was at rest. "It's your legacy we're talking about, not mine."

At this point, I wasn't sure he was even hearing me. I left the house to get some air.

Outside, the river roared with a shocking intensity. This, I thought, this was what Gettleson meant when he said that Eli was out of sorts, when he advised me to take it slow, ease into it. But "out of sorts" didn't cut it. Eli was in and out of time and space.

I dug my cell phone out of my pocket.

"Mr. Gettleson's office. How may I help you?" The secretary's voice was as soft and sweet as a lullaby. "Hello? How can I help you?" I hung up and looked back through the living-room window.

Eli was no longer on the sofa. Instead he was sifting through piles of mail, newspapers, and magazines. He moved from the drop-leaf table on the far side of the living room to the dining room, and he grabbed the papers from the dining room and deposited them on a growing pile next to the fireplace.

I reentered the house.

"What're you doing?" I asked.

"What the hell does it look like? Organizing. This place's a mess."

Ten minutes prior, Eli had been half asleep, swallowed in the cushions, swatting at me with his eyes closed. Now he was up, bounding around, moving piles across the room like some unhinged postmaster. The air went out of my chest. Dizzy, I placed my hand to my forehead and closed my eyes. Even the darkness behind my eyelids spun. My shoulders slumped and my knees loosened. I needed to calm down.

"Where do we go from here?" I asked in the most neutral tone I could muster.

"We? There's no we. There's only me. It's only ever been me."

Eli lifted a stack of magazines and tossed it into the air. One by one the glossies crashed to the floor beside my feet. "Everybody wants a piece. They watch me, they wait for me to crack, they run through the yard, they stand at the window. They all want a piece."

"Who are you talking about?"

"Don't play dumb," he said, lips tight, eyes narrowed. "All you keep askin' about is a deal, a stupid book. Sit down and answer questions, Eli. Answer questions about an Eli Page that no longer exists, a dead man, a man full of worms, a man that never existed in the first place. You're no different than they are."

"Calm down."

"Fuck you," he said. "Go away."

Tig yipped in his sleep.

"I think you've lost your . . . your clarity . . ."

"I haven't lost a goddamn thing. Who the fuck do you think you are? Who are you to say I'm losin' anything. Are you a doctor? Do you have a PhD in clarity?"

"Maybe you should see a doctor."

"Maybe you should shut your goddamn mouth."

"I didn't mean . . . I'm trying to help . . ."

"No. Go away. I don't need your help."

"Trust me," I said, but it was too late. He swung at me repeatedly, but he was too far away, too slow, too old. I moved out of the way.

Trust is intangible, of course. I'd tried to establish trust, but it wasn't enough to combat illness on the field of battle, if it was indeed illness. I was beginning to doubt my own sanity. Eli was inside his own head, categorizing his own regrets, conversing with ghosts that he wouldn't introduce to me. Not now. Maybe not ever. I was nauseous. The pile making, the depressive silence, the vanishing act, the bouts of rage — they were all signs of trouble. This man was losing his goddamned mind, and I, being the ultra-intuitive person I was, didn't have a clue what to do to help. Or he was playing me. Both were equally plausible and equally unnerving.

Eli fell back into his seat, reached for his bottle, and poured the scotch into his glass.

If I knew one thing for certain it was that the drinking exacerbated the confusion, but he'd rather subdue his unconscious and struggle through the nettles of his own memories (real or not) than give up his Johnnie Walker. Scotch or no scotch, he had zero plans to sit beside me and recount his life.

He tossed the drink down his gullet and filled his glass again.

"I tried once to make a go of it," he said when he caught me staring at him. "But I fucked it up. I made bad decisions. A lotta bad decisions." He scratched his beard. "I wish I could go back and fix it all, but I can't. There's nothin' I can do about it now except live with the consequences."

"Is that why you're here?"

"I am where I am."

"Eli." I decided to go all out. "I can help you."

"How's that?"

"We can start with your story. It might help to say it aloud."

"People have been telling my story for me for years, for decades, without me saying a word. Why ruin the fun?"

I understood for the first time that *I* was supposed to be the truth teller. Eli preached about the masks people wear and the lies they tell, but he was no different. He hid himself from the world. My job was to strip away his mask and show what he was unwilling (or unable) to show on his own.

Eli stood up, wobbled, and fell back down again.

"You okay?"

"If you want to help, you can get me upstairs."

He stood as best he could, and I wrapped my arm around his back to steady him. Then we slowly climbed the stairs to the mysterious second floor.

The hallway's red floral wallpaper curled at the seams. The planks below my feet were scratched and faded. Lugging Eli's frame with me, I made my way to his bedroom by picking the first door on the right, which happened to be the only door that was open.

I lifted Eli into his bed and covered him with a dark red patchwork quilt.

He was out cold.

Before running back downstairs, I took the opportunity to look around.

His bedroom walls were muted. The honey-brown floor looked like it had been beaten with a chain—there were knots missing in the wood, cracks between the boards, and a visible slope. There were also Post-it notes on every item. The bed, the side tables, the trunk, the lamps, the clock—all labeled. A white stone bowl on the bureau, which held a few dollars in spare change, boasted two sticky notes on its lip—one read "bowl" and the other "change." Everything seemed to gravitate toward the window, as if the river, which ran in clear view, had some magnetic pull. A sticky on the window had one word on it: "Hardscrabble." I shut the curtains.

Out in the hall, I hurried to the next door down, wrapped my hands around its wooden knob, and popped it opened. It was hollow, empty. From what I could tell in the dark, its pine floorboards were painted gray, its walls whitewashed, its plaster ceiling brown and bubbled from years of water damage. Blackout shades were drawn. The plaster around the wood trim was cracked and broken, the lath exposed like a bloodless wound. I left it alone.

I crossed the hall and turned the knob to the next room, expecting to find another empty, misused, strung-out space. Instead, I discovered an actual bedroom. I flipped on the overhead light. Brass bed, braided rug, a white quilt on the mattress, a simple dresser, a small desk, the room had been occupied at some point. It smelled like talcum powder and rubber. Above the dresser was a dirt-brown stain, an outline against the whitewashed backdrop, which was punctuated by a hole in its center. Sure enough, when I opened the closet, I found an empty frame—a void where the mirror belonged. Preserved within the closet: a wooden easel, a tackle box of art supplies, and a dozen blank canvases.

I stood in the center of the room, paralyzed with curiosity until I heard Eli call out. It took me a moment to realize Eli was talking in his sleep. It was mostly nonsense, but it was enough to derail the snooping.

I turned off the light and shut the door, careful to leave everything exactly as I found it.

Perched on the hill that overlooked the village, Belanger's Barn was never far out of sight. From a distance, it was a solid, untoppable rural monument surrounded by strange sculptures and fields, but up close, the oxblood red barn teetered on a pile of old stones.

Wooden signs directed me to a dirt parking lot. I stepped out and immediately was surrounded by wrought-iron weather vanes; fountains, stained green from ancient trickles of water; cast-off pieces of fence; brass bed frames. I followed the narrow pathway leading in, casting an eye toward the field of statues—animals, saints, cherubs. It was an acid trip, a dream, a carnival of curiosities.

Inside the barn, Ivory Belanger, an old man with a pointy gray beard that stretched from his bony chin to his concave stomach, sat on a stool, his curved back like a boomerang poised upright. With a book on his lap and a ribbon in his hand, he was in some sort of trance, absent from the physical world, humming Johnny Cash's "That Old Wheel." His skinny legs dangled, dangerously twisting around the middle rung. I waited for him to greet me, but he kept humming his tune.

A stuffed moose stood at the foot of the stairs, surrounded by cow skulls and long horns. Next to the giant animal I felt small, insignificant. I reached out and touched its antlers.

"Break it. Buy it," Ivory Belanger warned, acknowledging my presence without looking in my direction. "That's our policy."

"Sorry." I slid my hands into my pockets.

"Leave him alone, Ivory." Jenny's voice reverberated through the barn.

The old man grunted.

"Where are you?" I asked, trying to find her among the objects. Finally, I turned my head to see her descending the wide staircase with an urn of some sort in her grasp.

"You know, it's about time you visited," she said.

"Better late than never."

"Is that so?"

"In most cases."

"Well, come on, then." She brushed by my shoulder to set the urn beside Ivory. "Let me show you around."

She led me through the belly of the barn, beyond antique furniture of all shapes and sizes to toy chests filled with porcelain dolls with cracked heads to a room that housed a wolf's head, old street signs, and rows of glass bottles. I breathed in the dusty air. There was purpose to the madness, but I began to feel claustrophobic.

"It's a work in progress."

"Where do you get it all?" I asked.

"Estates and auctions."

"You're a hoarder."

"No, no, no. I'm a connoisseur, an artiste." Jenny smiled.

"Of nostalgia?"

"Something deeper. Something more connected to who we are at our core. It may just look like ordinary junk, but for me, it's about shared memory. Symbols, icons—that's how we make sense of the world. Do you know what I'm saying?"

I nodded. Her enthusiasm was plain to see.

"Sorry. I don't mean to blather."

"What's with the old man? He wouldn't even look at me."

"Ivory? Well, he's legally blind, but don't let that fool you. He has the locations of important items committed to memory."

"Is that so?"

Now I wasn't sure if Jenny was pulling my leg. Everyone is a trickster.

I will give her this—each room we entered did evoke some connection, some feeling in me, even if I couldn't put my finger on what it was.

We continued through a small room that had old toys and metal lunch boxes.

"How's the book coming?" she asked.

"Fine," I lied.

Jenny tucked her hands into her tiny sweater pockets.

"I'm sure he's got a lot of stories to tell," she said, keeping her eyes pointed toward the floor as we headed to the second floor.

"He just won't share them with me," I said, a few steps behind. I wanted so much to tell her about the letters, but I feared it would only get me in trouble. She was protective of Eli in a way that I didn't understand.

"Give it time," she advised. "It's not easy."

Upstairs, Jenny guided me through a room full of chairs, dozens hanging in the air above our heads. The next room contained type press trays, old street signs, paint-chipped wooden doors, tin cans, and Depression glass. Finally, we entered a large room filled with desks and sofas and bookshelves stuffed with an eclectic assortment of books. If Belanger's was modeled after the inside of a madman's head, we were standing in the brain, a museum of nerves.

"Most of Eli's donations find a home here," she said. "It's good stuff, but I'd love to have more folk memorabilia or even one of his guitars. Too bad he's gotten rid of all that."

I stared up at the thick hand-hewn beams above the wooden bookshelves. At first, Eli's threat of minimizing his life seemed like a bluff, but in the library, among his things, the thinning down of his life was real. Still, there was something about the abandonment of his history that felt deceptive, hypocritical, especially since I knew there were things he had stashed away. Jenny was right—it was a museum of lost or abandoned memories, a history of looking. Interestingly, it was also history for the taking. Something you could buy, bring home, and reuse.

"I'd get lost in here," I said.

"We've lost a few kids, but they more or less had it coming." She shrugged before tucking a few rebellious strands of her hair behind her ear. "Besides, I'm just getting started," she said. "You think it's full now, just wait. I've got big plans."

"What more do you need?"

"There's so much more to the story. The fun part is that I never know how the story will unfold until I find the objects—their discovery feeds the narrative."

"That's interesting. But whose story is it? That's what I want to know."

"Galesville's, of course."

She described how she built each room, placing objects in relation to one another, anticipating how visitors might enter and which way they might walk. As we talked, it became clear to me that while Eli was an artist in retreat, removing objects from his consciousness, pushing them into self-storage, out of the way. Jenny, on the other hand, was a curator forging ahead, collecting trinkets and idols and symbols and rearranging them to build a new story. Despite the obvious similarities between Belanger's Barn and Eli's locked room, the results were diametrically opposed. Jenny forced order upon chaos; Eli was chaos.

Their discovery feeds the narrative. I replayed that line in my head, committing it to memory. It was the perfect summation of my ghostwriting gig, except that the discovery portion had been slow going until I found the key to the study.

I realized at that moment that my initial impression of Jenny was too limiting. There was a savvy creativity behind the mask, a know-how, a worldliness. As much as the barn was a way station for curiosities, it was also a living art installation, every inch of it designed to tell a story.

She watched this realization come over me. Her eyes searching, intent on knowing what I was thinking. Suddenly I wanted to embrace her, to kiss her eyelids. She must've sensed the desire, because she took a step back. To distance myself, I walked around, reading the titles, looking at the other objects in the room.

"How did you get into this? Did you go to school?"

"I did do a semester and a half at UVM."

"Why'd you leave Burlington?"

"Long story." Those two words were lonely and sorrowful, as if she expected to feel better after uttering them and was gravely disappointed.

"Did you study art?"

"That was the plan. Is it that obvious?"

"I had a little help—I saw your picture in the *Mirror*."

"Oh, no. I was hoping it would go unnoticed," she said, attempting to hide her reddening cheeks. She was flirting with pride; she just couldn't commit to the act. "Is it too much to ask you to forget you ever saw that photo?"

"What's the mural's all about?"

"Oh, God, that's an even longer story."

She told me about a grant she received, and she detailed her plan for the mural and how she was worried about its unveiling. Even though she remained nonchalant and self-deprecating, her demeanor changed. It evolved into something more comfortable, more pensive, more real, as if she were becoming more confident by the minute, more trusting of me.

"I'm sure it'll be amazing."

She let the compliment stand, which in itself was a small victory.

Behind Jenny, in the stacks of leather-bound books, I saw a completed set of colorful paperbacks from the Great Books Foundation and an early edition of *Portnoy's Complaint*, stuck between Marilynne Robinson's *Housekeeping* and Norman Rush's *Mating*. The book jackets reminded me of my father's record sleeves.

"Speaking of the paper, what do you think about what's going on around town?" I asked as I reviewed the book spines.

"I don't know. It's odd. That type of stuff doesn't happen in Galesville."

"You know they're looking at Eli for it, especially your friend Cal."

"It's mostly talk."

"Even so—I wish Eli would just tell me where he goes every day."

"He gets in his own way," she said. "Sometimes you've got to sneak up on him."

Then, as if on cue, she held up a finger as if to say *wait here* and walked out of the room. With Jenny gone, I took a closer look at an old set of maps, which hung from chains. I zeroed in on the Battenkill and watched it descend from Vermont and cross into New York. Jenny returned with a black case, the size of a hardcover book.

"A gift," she said. "Saved from an uncertain fate." The edges of the case were battered and scraped. She laid it softly in my hands, and the material felt rough. I flipped the lock and it popped open. Inside were three vintage Hohner harmonicas.

"Pretty cool, right? They were Eli's," she said.

"These are remarkable. Why would you give them away?"

She shrugged. "I knew you had to have them."

"But you don't even know me," I said.

"I know you better than you think," she answered.

I was warm under the collar, wordless. The truth was she probably knew me as well as anybody knew me, except for Casey. The thought depressed me and thrilled me at the same time.

"Can I ask you something?" She swept her hair away from her eyes and tucked a few wisps behind her ears again. As we talked, she led me back through the barn.

"Sure."

"How *is* he?"

"I think you know as much as I do."

"You haven't noticed anything out of the ordinary?"

I shrugged, not knowing who the "ordinary" Eli was.

"All right. I'll take your word for it," she said.

"Are you two close?" I asked.

"What do you mean?"

"You seem very protective, that's all."

"I worry about him." She paused at the top of the stairs. "Why?"

She studied my face. "Like I said, I'm happy you're here, Jack. Stick it out. He's a pain in the ass, but cut him some slack. He's been through a lot."

"See what I mean—you're protecting him, without telling me why."

"I'm not gonna get involved," she said, turning away.

"Okay. I get it," I said. "But the truth is he isn't always of a clear mind these days. Maybe you could help me fill the gaps."

"Sorry. I wish I could help, but you've got the wrong person."

Downstairs, the old man shifted in his stool, which startled me. I'd forgotten he was even in the barn, let alone within earshot.

"Is it hailing?" Ivory said, his voice like a child's, high and winded.

Jenny and I descended, looking out the open barn door as we did. We watched as hail fell straight down from the clouds like marbles poured from a huge bucket.

"Yes. You're right again, Ivory," she answered, shaking her head.

"Thought so," the old man said as he settled back down into his seat.

"I better get a move on. I don't know how to thank you for this." I made sure the harmonica case was securely locked.

"How about you come to dinner soon? You do owe me."

"Sure. I could do that."

"Just so we're on the same page, it'll be a family affair. Not exactly painless."

"Oh. Okay," I said, as the blood drained from my face. Jenny hadn't struck me as a meet-the-parents type of person, but it was increasingly clear that the Jenny I held in my mind was a thin pencil drawing, waiting to be filled out. "That may count as two favors."

"Don't freak out on me," she said. "It's just Sunday dinner."

"I wasn't freaking out."

She rolled her eyes. "Yes you were."

"Usually, I like to take someone out a few times before we get to the parents."

"Knock it off." She punched me in the arm. "Consider it a welcome to Galesville dinner. Don't overthink it."

"I wouldn't dare."

She smirked. "You should go before it gets worse."

The storm hadn't let up. I ran down the path. The hail mixed with large beads of rain and beat on the back of my neck.

As I drove away, I noticed Ivory Belanger's house directly across the street from the barn. Its aluminum roof looked battered and pockmarked even from a distance. The yard and the hill were sprinkled with white pellets that lay atop the blades of grass. I couldn't help but wonder how Ivory Belanger crossed the road, on a hill, near a blind spot on the county route, which saw more traffic than most of Galesville's streets. Did someone help him? Or did he just take his chances and bolt across when it was silent?

In the middle of the violent hailstorm, I turned onto North Church and headed toward the bridge when, out of nowhere, a red light filled the shell of my car and a siren boxed my ears. Cursing, I came to a stop and killed the engine.

The cruiser parked on my bumper — so close, I expected a nudge. There was no escaping the lights. They enveloped me, penetrated my skin, and accosted me with their unpredictability. The hail rained down upon my roof and windows, a thousand pings a second on the windshield. It was impossible to see anything as the rain washed over the glass. It was as if the car was sinking into a lake. I waited. So did the trooper.

When the hail let up, a distorted uniformed figure approached in my side mirror. I recognized his swagger but was intent on keeping my cool as I rolled down my window.

"Was I speeding?"

"License and registration."

I handed them over. "What's this about?"

"Have you been drinking?" The trooper pursued his own line of questioning.

"Drinking? No," I replied. "It's one in the afternoon."

"How else do you explain the swerving?"

"I swerved?"

I leaned forward, turned my head, and peeked out the window. I was sure I was speaking with Mark Calvin, but I could see only the trooper's torso. I needed confirmation.

"The hail, the downpour," I said. "Sorry I swerved, but I was trying to stay in the lines even though I couldn't see them all that well."

"Rain doesn't excuse poor driving. You could've killed someone." He cleared his throat. "Where're you coming from?"

"Why do I think you already know?"

"Don't get smart. Answer the question."

"Belanger's."

"What were you doing there?" he asked.

"Christmas shopping."

"Listen, smart-ass," he said, raising his voice to speak over the rain. Then he bent down and popped his head in the window. "I could give you a ticket."

I couldn't stop the smile from spreading across my face. I swear I tried. He looked like he was about to arrest me for smart-assery. His shoulder and face were soaked. But then I felt a twinge of sympathy for Cal. I wasn't sure about his history with Jenny, but I suspected it was out of his control.

"I wasn't doing anything wrong," I said.

"You crossed the double line."

"Come on. What's the big deal? Can't we handle this like adults?"

"Stay here," he fumed.

The rain lightened to a mist. I watched Cal, his uniform drenched, strut back to his cruiser and slam the door. He took his sweet time, returning more than fifteen minutes later.

"Take it." He held out a ticket.

"You're really giving me a ticket?"

"Failure to keep vehicle under control. You crossed the line."

"This is ridiculous."

"Could be worse. Here." He gave me a photocopy of the New York statute on "Failure to Keep Vehicle under Control."

"How very thorough of you, Officer," I said.

"Smart-ass," he muttered as he walked away.

I rolled up my window.

Eli met me at the door.

"You look like you've just been punched in the gut," he said.

"I got a ticket."

"Calvin?"

I nodded.

"What'd you expect? You move to town, live with me, and start up with his fiancée. That's three strikes. I'd have a problem with you too."

"I didn't start up anything," I said. "And, by the way, they're not engaged."

"They were. For a long time."

"Well, they're not anymore."

"Except in his mind," Eli replied. "And trust me, sometimes that's all that counts."

After dinner, I grabbed the Hohner case from the car and carried it to my room. With that old, battered metal to my mouth, I breathed in, dragging the notes into existence, and out, expelling them into the air. As I slipped the last of the three harmonicas from its place, I saw a piece of paper wedged inside the case. I pulled it out and unfolded it. In tiny cursive letters was a message, barely legible. I stared at it until the words were blurry, and I swore it read: "Have I wasted my life?"

The wail of the alarm clock bludgeoned me, yanked me from the brightness of a dream, and plunged me into a black box, a void, somewhere between the waking and the dead. 4:30. The clock's red numbers mocked me as I stumbled across the room, reaching blindly for the wall. Finally, I found my way to the bathroom, plugged the sink, and filled its porcelain basin with cold water. I dunked my face in and held it under for as long as I could stand.

Outside, in the chill, a fog lingered.

Had I finally beaten Eli to the daybreak? Before I had time to pat myself on my back, the exterior houselights went on, catching me in their glow. I bolted behind a crab apple tree, slicing my arm just below the elbow as I crouched behind its chaotic branches. Five, seven, twelve minutes ticked away. My knees stiffened. My arm stung. The wispy fog began to lift. While I waited, the river filled my head with its constant strum.

Eli exited the house with his thick cane, the black ash, in his grip and his leather satchel strapped around his shoulder as if he were headed into the dark center of the Adirondacks or as if he'd walked out of some Hawthorne short story. "Old Goodman Page." "The Musician's Black Veil." "Eli Brand." Tig stood beside him like a bear cub, his head wide and untamed. After they reached the end of the driveway and passed through the gate, they turned left, away from the covered bridge, toward the wooded hills.

I followed, careful to keep a respectable distance. The birdsong provided some cover, but I had to soften my step to stay undetected.

The moon was pale and shy, fading minute by minute.

A few hundred feet beyond the edge of Eli's property, they disappeared. I jogged down the road to catch up, and I found a hiking path that cut through the woods. Up ahead, on the path, Eli's elusive form wove in and around trees. Then he was gone again. Hurrying my pace, I dashed up the trail, looking for any sign of him or the dog.

Eventually, the path swooped around to the far side of the River Bend property, climbing the hillside until it opened to a clearing of pigweed and brush and nettles. The river, the bridge, and Eli's house were all stretched out below. It was as if I was looking down on them from the clouds.

In the distance, I heard rustling, and I turned to see Tig, a couple dozen feet in front of me, marking a tree. I crouched down and tried to stay hidden.

"Let's go," Eli said from somewhere. Tig bounded out of the brush.

I continued through the clearing and came upon a stone foundation, which had been abandoned, forgotten. Next to the stone was the impress of an old road, and I understood that a grand house had once stood there, overlooking the river, watching the land. It had long since been erased.

Just beyond its remnants was a lookout of sorts, an outcropping bathed in sunlight. There, in the center, was Eli.

Tig jumped in and out of the woods, chasing animals no larger than his paw. As I stepped closer, a branch snapped beneath my weight and everything went quiet. Even the birds put their beaks on lockdown. There was nowhere to hide. I stepped again. In a manner of seconds, Tig was anchored to the ground next to me, his teeth bared.

"You think I'm an idiot?" Eli yelled.

"Tig, it's me. It's Jack," I said. The dog didn't budge.

"He doesn't like surprises. Neither do I."

"I'm sorry. I get it. Call him off," I pleaded.

"If you wanted to tag along, you should've asked."

"Because that's worked wonders in the past," I muttered.

"What did you say?" Eli asked in earnest. Tig growled. I thumbed the buttons on my shirt and looked down at the dog. My cheeks burned; my chest tightened.

"Call him off."

"Come. Now. Tig," Eli commanded. "You know that man. Leave him be." The dog put its teeth away and retreated to Eli's side, panting.

I waited a few seconds for my pulse to come down.

When I approached Eli, I saw the lookout for what it was—a graveyard. Grass had gathered all around the stones. Some leaned, some were chipped, others were thick, bold, unmoved. The only consistent feature was that they all faced out over the bluff, positioned to observe the sunrise.

"I don't understand," Eli said, "why you can't leave me alone."

"I was worried," I protested.

"About what?"

"I think you should see someone...a doctor. You're not...together...and coming up here...it's...well, it's not practical..."

"Shut up." He walked to the edge of the hillside.

"Also, I need to tell you something else," I continued.

"Do it. Spit it out."

"Word is that you're a person of interest."

"I've always been a person of interest."

"I'm serious."

He sighed. "What are you talkin' about?"

"Calvin. He's building a case."

"Don't be stupid. A case for what?"

"Arson. Vandalism. B and E. Maybe it's time to pay attention," I said.

"Give me a break."

"If they can account for your whereabouts, it will save you the headache. Why don't you sit down with Calvin and tell him where you've been?"

"It's none of his goddamn business, that's why."

"Just tell him you've been up here. I don't see what the big deal is."

"No. I wouldn't expect you to."

By then, the sun had fully committed to the sky, and the river below shimmered as it reflected the low-lying saffron light. I crossed my arms and kept my mouth shut. I could almost see his mood shift. He relaxed for a moment; the anger evaporated.

"Do you know the seven stages of man?" Eli asked after a few minutes.

"What?"

He stared off into the distance. "'And one man in his time plays many parts.' The infant, the whiny schoolboy, the ballad-singing lover, the quick-tempered soldier, the overripe justice, the foolish old man, and, finally, last but not least is 'second childishness and mere oblivion. Sans teeth, sans eyes, sans taste, sans everything.'"

"Exits and entrances," I responded.

Eli turned and faced me. "You do know it."

"Yes." I nodded.

"Wrote about it in one of my songs, but I can't remember the name."

"'Mad Billy Bedlam.'"

"Yeah, that's the one. After Tom O'Bedlam. See, you're that ballad-singing lover who's got no idea what it means to be the old man, the second infant."

"Maybe so. But you're gone for hours on end. You should tell one of us where you are, just to play it safe. Jenny agrees."

"You've talked to Jenny about me?"

"She asked."

"You and Jenny are conspiring now?"

"We're both worried."

"How nice. I'm glad you can bond over my 'troubles.'"

"It's not like that."

"What did she say?" he asked, overly concerned.

"Nothing."

"Now you know where I am. You can find me here, on this wall, Monday through Friday, five to one, give or take," he said as he sat down on an old stone wall that surrounded the graveyard.

"Why?"

"Why not? All I've got is time," he said.

"That's not an answer."

"It's a quiet place to collect my thoughts. I've got a lot to reflect on. Begin to hate myself. Even if it's a short journey. There's too much goin' on at the house. Impossible to concentrate," he said, rambling. "From this spot I can see everything, feel everything, hear everything. Do you understand?"

"Sure I do."

"Don't mock me."

Glancing around the plot, I counted a dozen and a half graves. Skulls with wings. Angels. Weeping willows. Names and icons long faded. "Do these all belong to the same family?" I asked, changing my line of questioning.

He nodded. "This one here"—he tapped the tall stone with his cane—"Edmond Myers. He built the first house—the one that no longer stands—with his bare hands." He motioned to the old foundation I'd stumbled on earlier. "His wife and eight of his nine children are here."

"Did they own all of the land?"

"Everything on my side of the river. His son built River Bend in eighteen oh somethin'."

Whereas most of the headstones were worn to the bone, mottled black and gray, and leaning backward or sideways, the three thick stones closest to Eli stood upright and true.

"What happened to the Myers clan?"

He shot me a deadly look. "How the fuck do I know? They probably exist in some form or another. I bought the house from a Myers, but it doesn't really matter. Nothin' is permanent. What's one thing today is another thing tomorrow. Myers, Page, Wyeth—who really cares?"

"Well, it seems that *you* care. You wouldn't spend so much time here," I said, braver by the minute, "unless it mattered."

Eli dropped his head and swung it back and forth, from shoulder to shoulder.

"Are you religious, Jack?"

"Are you asking me if I believe in God?"

"No, I asking if you believe in anything."

"I don't know how to answer," I said, suddenly exhausted.

"Sit," Eli said, pointing to the stone fence. I obeyed. "Shut your eyes and listen. Don't think. Just. Listen."

"Why?"

"Just do it."

I sat down and closed my eyes. At first, I heard the hush of the river water, the birds, the wind, Tig stepping on grass, Eli breathing—all sounds I would've expected. After a few deep breaths, my body and mind relaxed. Everything nearby went quiet and I started to hear new sounds and new thoughts, if that makes sense. It's hard to describe. Something rustled in the brush, crows cackled in the distance, leaves crashed to the ground—not a pitter-patter like the locust leafs, something different, like the scratching of a needle along a record. Music was all around

me, as ubiquitous as the nitrogen in the air, and memories flooded my consciousness, offering images of people
I hadn't thought about for years. These new thoughts had
nothing to do with the river, the landscape, the breeze.
I remembered playing at a beach in Rhode Island in red
shorts; Melanie and how she always splashed water on
the floor when taking a bath; the apartment in shambles
after Melanie and I blew up; the police arriving to pick
me up; the Housatonic, which snaked behind the Clark &
Co. mills; my mother, the dark roots of her hair bleeding
into the blond dye and her tall, slim figure withered to the
bone; my mother in her grave, knocking on the silk-lined
top of her coffin, disappointed to death in me; my father,
shaking, asking for help with his boot laces; me, as a child,
realizing I was an accomplice.

"Do you understand now?" Eli asked.

I opened my eyes. A pain rose in my chest and my
throat constricted. I breathed deep and tried to calm
myself, but I'd lost the mediation. Eli must've seen the
panic in my twisted face.

"Listen," he said, solemnly. "I come here to remember
what I don't want to forget and to forget what I don't want
to remember."

The quiet, the seclusion were catalysts for memory. I
nodded to let him know that I understood. It was a way
to connect to the past. It was an exercise to beat back the
cobwebs.

The dog snored—a freight train chugging along.

"I think you want the same thing I do," Eli said.

"What's that?"

"Forgiveness. Redemption. Absolution. But see, those are all religious words. I don't think they have the words we need without talkin' religion."

The whole world around us was overcome by a brilliant blue hue as if the sun had finally decided to shine. Eli lifted a gravestone that had fallen over and straightened it until it stayed in place.

"Am I wrong?" he asked.

"I don't really know what I want right now. Everything is broken."

"Well, maybe it's time to unbreak things."

The next morning, I went for a walk along the Battenkill. Way downstream, behind the mills where the water picks up, I was overcome with the desire to cross. I don't know what it was exactly that brought on that sudden urge, but I had to get to the other side.

As I hummed "The Water Is Wide," paying no mind to the story itself, I watched an old wooden door careen down the river, smash against rocks and a fallen oak until it wedged itself between two boulders. Without thinking, I billy-goated to the middle of the river, stood over the door, and glanced downstream. The jump between boulders was farther than I thought possible, but the door was a bridge, a happy accident, a sign. I tested it with my foot. It promptly broke free and sailed out of sight. No matter. I'd come that far, and I wasn't turning back. So I leapt.

Hours later, when I made it back to River Bend, I was still drenched from toe to top. After I warmed up, I sat in my bed, daydreaming about the door, the river, the song's lyrics. My feet dangled over the edge of the mattress; my toes grazed the warm floor. Patches of light danced across the wood and tickled my toes. The daydream faded—the details were absorbed into the plaster walls. I picked up the letters, which had fallen off the bed, stood up, and carried them to the window seat.

Then I sat down at the desk, and I began to write.

When you cross that river, there's no turnin' back
When you stretch that line, it's bound to snap
Even after all these years, you're first on my mind
And I'm lookin' for some answers, if you've got the time.

• SECOND •

It was a nervous summer. Uneasy. The humidity was persistent. Some mornings, I'd peel myself from the bedsheets and stumble outside hoping it was cooler, only to be disappointed. The heat left me clawing at my unshaved face and soaking my head in hose water. Many days, after the sun had charged the sky, an onslaught of bone-rattling cracks, lightning bursts, and gale-force winds lashed the landscape. These storms swept in and out with the taut, well-practiced efficiency of a marching band, and the atmospheric instability encouraged my storytelling. Ink splashed onto the page. Words left my fingertips and washed over the notebook. Fueled by nature and nerves, the carriage barn pulsed with a relentless energy. Anything was possible. My hand cramped; I kept writing. My eyes glazed; I wrote with my eyes closed. But there was an air of mischief, a sense of dread underneath it all. More fiction than fact, I began to piece together the unauthorized story of Eli Page.

Eli was a sleepwalker. In and out of his body, he dragged his flesh behind him like a rag doll. His once-rigid

morning schedule was riddled with contradictions, incon-
sistencies, false starts. On more than a few occasions, I
caught him slinking off midmorning or returning well
after two o'clock. I began to worry that he'd lose his way
home or that he'd be caught unprepared in one of those
surging storms.

One morning in June, Eli stumbled into the kitchen at
a quarter past ten. He stretched, let out a prolonged yawn,
and opened the junk drawer beside the stove.

"Are you headed up the hill today?" I asked.

"No." His voice popped like the static on an old record.

"Are you sick?"

"In one way or another." He rummaged through
the drawer.

"Can I help you find something?"

"A purpose," he said. "A key."

"A key?" My voice cracked. "What do you need a
key for?"

"My kingdom, my kingdom for a key."

Eventually, he gave up and left the kitchen. I didn't talk
to him again for a couple days.

Left to observe the comings and goings of a ghost, I
was forced to concede what I'd feared most—his condition had worsened. His untethered mind drifted down
the river like a runaway barge, but the subject of illness
was off-limits. We both pretended he was fine. Our denial
bound us together in some type of frail brotherhood.

Still, from time to time, I tried to crack the subject open.

"Who do you think you are?" he'd bark when I did.
"You don't know what's best for me. I've been livin' this

life for years before you, and I'll be livin' it for years after you go."

Regardless of these outbursts, the connection we formed—no matter how tenuous it seemed—was real. Amid the murky waters that surrounded our conversations, there were many bright beacons of light, moments of true friendship. Over iced tea on the front step, we philosophized about writers and artists; we talked about the garden he hoped to plant on the south end of the farm; and occasionally we even delved into the prickly topics of politics and faith, in particular how Judaism figured in his life. "I'm half Jewish, half Irish Protestant, and half American cowboy; I just don't know which two halves are gonna show up at any given time," he'd say, mostly to frustrate me, but I was secretly happy to see these glimpses of the old playful Eli.

More often than not, his sentences were broken, choppy, riddled with holes. Then, without warning or preamble, he'd go mute. Hours later, he'd be clear, coherent, and articulate. Despite my attempts to force a square peg of reason into the round hole of reality, I could discern no pattern to the madness.

Again, one morning Eli poked around in the kitchen drawers while I ate breakfast. I felt his stare boring holes in the back of my head. Afraid he might be searching for the key for a second time that week, I kept my eyes fixed on my bowl.

"You don't have any brothers or sisters, do you?" he asked.

My mouth was full of Cheerios, but I let out a perceivable "no," swallowed, and then properly responded by telling him I was an only child.

"How'd that work out?" He pulled out a small brown bag from the drawer.

"Fine, I guess."

"That's all? No great only child wisdom? No deeper thoughts on the matter? I'm disappointed." He opened the fridge, removed the bread he'd stored there, and wrestled the knot at the end of the bag. His hands were bony and curved, pulling in on themselves, which made the unknotting all the more difficult.

"Who knows if things would've been better or worse? We got along okay, my mom and me, without much help." For a fleeting moment, I thought about Casey, but I let it go. We weren't blood.

Eli ran his hand around his chin, through his thick beard, before reengaging with the bag. The knot finally gave loose, and he pulled two slices from the plastic.

I finished my cereal.

"Well, come on, let's hear it." He tossed the half loaf back in the fridge and slammed the door shut. The glass bottles rattled.

"Hear what?"

"Your father. What'd'ya have to say about him?"

"Nothing special."

"Deadbeat?"

"I don't know. Can't remember much, and what I do remember isn't all that interesting."

Spreading the mayo across the bread was an act of concentration. Eli didn't remove his focus from the job until he had covered the piece from corner to corner. Then he placed a few ribbons of ham against his bread, tossed a slice of provolone on the stack, and squeezed the sandwich together. It struck me as very mechanical, methodical.

"Do you hate your father?" he asked.

"I don't know him."

"That's not a real answer."

Still intent on his lunch prep, Eli stuffed an apple and his tin-foiled sandwich into the paper bag. He twitched as he sometimes did, and he shifted his weight from one leg to the other and then back. Finally, he stared at me. His thick eyebrows were arched along his wrinkled forehead and his eyes rolled around as if they were searching for something to steady them.

"Sometimes I hate him. Most days it's a waste of time," I said.

"That's a very mature point of view—"

"Thank you." My spine straightened.

"But it's fucked." Eli walked around the counter and sat down at the table opposite me. He studied my face. I tried to keep the jaw muscles from clenching.

"Maybe it is," I said, with the meek expression of a schoolboy.

"Then spill it, stop screwin' around. What's the deal with your father?" He wasn't giving up. I yearned for his mind to fail. If there was one time it could've work in my favor, this was it. I wondered if I could wait him out. Did lucidity have a deadline? "Let's have it."

Father, Father, Father. I remembered very little, and what I did remember, well, those images were unreliable, products of my mother's storytelling or my grandmother's ridicule. My mother's mother made a point of speaking about my father as if he was always present but at arm's length—*I heard the boy's father was picked up in Worcester, he was doing this or that or he was with blah, blah, blah.* The words leaked from her mouth like bedtime drool. I never knew whether she was telling the truth or was just shaping the conversation to belittle my mother, poke at her with a hot iron. I took it all in, absorbed it, because I was hungry for any knowledge, any information I could get. Truth or fiction. What did he look like? Did I look like him? What was he picked up for? This went on throughout my childhood, but I was unable to glean any honest information from these exchanges.

"Go ahead. Avoid it. Stuff it down deep. It'll just come back to bite you," Eli said. He was happy that he had gotten under my skin. Gleeful, even. I tried to shake the thoughts away, but it was apparent to Eli that I was lost in a self-drama that might provide him some entertainment.

In an effort to change the trajectory of the conversation, I blurted out my own line of questions: "What about you? What prompted you to leave home when you were sixteen?"

"If we're gonna do this little game, I gotta warn you—I've made a livin' dodgin' questions."

"No kidding. I know the drill."

"All right, then. Despite the myth, nothin' exciting. No carnival. No rodeo. No oil rig. None of that. Times were different," he said.

"How so?"

"I had the opportunity to go to New York and I took it. Met a guy from Ann Arbor who was headed east in a new Bonneville. Hitched a ride..."

"So what're you saying—it was fate?"

"No," he said. "Fate is a trick of the mind. We dig our own graves."

"What made you think you could make it? You weren't even writing your own songs back then. There must've been a thousand folk musicians like you."

He cleared his throat. "I was just doin' what I was doin'. Dabbled in everything, floated around, abused some contacts, got lucky. That's how a life is built."

"Which came first, the music or the protest?"

"Same thing, really. Same time."

"Okay, but why protest songs?"

"Call 'em what you want, but they're just songs. Some said I had a knack for speaking 'bout the guy on the corner who was out of work or the down-and-outer who was wrongly convicted. Civil rights, blackouts, dust storms, union riots, freedom here and in the mind—these are things to sing about. There's never a shortage of people getting screwed."

"Do you regret leaving your home?"

"Home? Never really had one of those." His face tightened and his eyes drew inward. "My family didn't much worry about me," he said. "You?"

"Clean break. And I don't regret it. It had to be done," I answered.

"That's the way it plays sometimes." He yawned again. "And we just carry on."

Before I had a chance to pursue another line of questioning, he got up and left the kitchen, abandoning his paper bag on the countertop.

I placed Dylan's *Blood on the Tracks* on the turntable and dropped the needle. (To my surprise, the old Zenith still functioned.) The fuzzy, muffled songs proved that music could exist in River Bend without the walls crashing down. Desperate for a fix, I dug through the crates and boxes for a new object, a new trinket, a new curiosity. So far, I'd collected the bundle of letters from H.M., a photograph of Eli at the Bitter End, a plaster skull ("Alas, poor Yorick"), and a stack of blank postcards from Europe. Each new find was a shot of adrenaline, but it was getting harder to keep the discoveries secret.

I hummed to myself, but every two or three minutes, I'd stick my head out of the study and listen for Eli. Always on edge, I began to suspect that Eli, despite the eccentricities of his mind, knew more than he was letting on.

Inside the rolltop desk, between two decorative columns, were built-in pigeonholes, cubbies, and small drawers. I ran my fingers along the carvings, and as I did, the right column shifted. Placing my thumb and index finger around its edge, I removed the box to reveal a hollow with an expired passport, leafs of paper, and three small tattered pictures. Yellowed by age, the scalloped-edged photos pictured a baby with a piercing glare; a toddler in the snow, cheeks red; a round-faced man with a bony young woman, holding hands and smiling for the camera. The kid had to be Eli and the young couple his parents. Nothing much was known about Eli's mother and father, but two stories were accepted into the lore: His mother left the family when Eli was eleven, and his father, a gambler, won Eli's first guitar in a game of poker outside Reno. Straight flush. Whether the stories were true or false didn't matter, they were part of the gospel. I slid the column back into place. Examining the left column, I found a cassette tape. Three words were scratched into the blond masking tape above the wheels. Faded. Illegible. I pocketed the cassette for safekeeping. Satisfied, I removed the record from the turntable.

As I left the room, I noticed that the milk crates, which were always to the left of the desk, had been moved to the opposite side of the room. A sudden fear surged through me. Quickly, I took stock of the study, trying to match up the position of boxes and crates and frames with the memory of the layout in my head. Someone had been in the room. *Eli* had been in the room.

My throat burned. I realized I'd been holding my breath while I completed my snap inventory. What did he know? Was there evidence of my trespass? If Eli knew that I had broken in, why didn't he say anything? Why didn't he call me out, confront me? After all, I had broken one of his sacred rules.

Back in the carriage barn, I placed the cassette in the window seat hideaway. As I did, my fingers brushed up against the stack of letters from H.M. Again, my pulse sped up and my chest burned. The tape, the photo, the skull—these items seemed inconsequential. He wouldn't miss them. He wouldn't even know they were gone. But the letters... the letters were different. If Eli was looking for something in the study, there was a better than average chance the something was those letters. I considered returning them, but the mere thought of giving them back made my chest tighten. Not to mention that the sudden reappearance of the bundle on the desk might be more suspicious than their disappearance in the first place.

I tried to calm myself down with maybes.

Maybe Eli wasn't looking for anything in particular.

Maybe Eli entered the study to inspect his guitar collection.

Maybe the signs of my break-in went unnoticed.

Maybe Eli had completely forgotten about the letters, and it was only my fear that sounded an irrational alarm.

The tricks we play on ourselves are almost always more damaging than the tricks others play on us.

Within the confines of the Galesville mill yard, three unadorned houses sank into a tiny island of green amid a sea of pavement. The denim blue house, the last in the triplet, was the Flynn residence.

I opened the screen door and knocked.

It'd been two and a half weeks since Jenny had invited me to the family dinner, but it felt like much longer. Our first attempt was canceled because her father wasn't feeling well at the time, and our second attempt was pushed to the following Sunday, which was the only day the Flynns shared their table with guests.

"You're late," Jenny said as she popped open the door. "Get in here and save me."

"I brought a gift," I said, handing over a bottle of red wine. "Hope that's okay." As she took the bottle, my eyes locked onto her ring finger, which carried the weight of a brilliantly cut diamond.

"Stay here for a second," she said, quickly switching the bottle to her right hand before sprinting up the staircase. I stayed put beside an old wooden telephone table with a chair built into it. On top of that monstrosity sat an enormous rotary phone with a faux-gold-plated finish—it looked more like a prop for an Elizabeth Taylor movie than a phone.

The television light flickered against the hallway wallpaper. Down the hall, in the living room, cozy and comfortable, was Cal. He sat in the glow, enthralled by long-winded pundits on the screen. What was he doing there? What had I gotten myself into? Fight or flight—my body knew by instinct that I was walking into a trap, but I took a deep breath and tried to remain calm.

A formal sitting room was to my right. I ducked in to look around. The walls were covered with framed pictures. A long slab of a couch was clean, untouched. The carpet was covered with clear plastic sheeting, which formed a pathway from the door to the furniture. I'd never seen a room so devoid of emotion.

I returned to the hallway. On the wall was an antique banjo. I wanted to pull it down, pluck it, and play "Red River Valley" to distract myself from my growing apprehension and the feeling that I was being conned. I wondered if I could pick an Eli Page song with a little Scruggsy twang.

When Jenny returned, I zeroed in on her hand. The ring was still attached.

"What's going on?"

"Let me explain." She bit her lower lip; the scar on her cheek was more pronounced.

"Go right ahead. Explain away. I won't stop you."

"It's not what you think. My father invited him without asking. He thought it would be *improper* if he wasn't here."

"Why would it be improper?"

"Because as far my father's concerned, we're still engaged."

"Really? Well, that's a critical piece of information you failed to share."

She grasped my forearm with her right hand, keeping her left hand hidden behind her back except when she adjusted the wisps of hair that fell in front of her eyes. "I have to play the part tonight, but—"

"But what? What can you possibly say?"

"You're my guest."

"This is a joke, right?"

"I'm sorry." She stopped, put her chin to her chest for a moment, and then gathered herself. "Can you just play along? I know it's a lot to ask, but I can explain it all."

"It's easier if I go."

"No. I want you to stay."

She seemed sincere, and there was no doubt that she was exasperated. It would be a lie to say that I didn't start to feel sorry for her, for the situation, whatever the situation was.

"What's my role again?" I capitulated.

"Be yourself. You're new to town, and we're welcoming you to Galesville."

"A tourist who falls for the wrong woman," I added.

She took me by the hand and led me beyond the banjo into the living room—a cramped space with a couch, a recliner, and an old box television the size of a washing machine. The box was an imposing piece of furniture—overpolished with sharp, eye-gouging corners for young kids—but it'd been retired. Cal watched a smaller television, which sat on top of the wooden unit. For a few minutes I waited for him to blink; he never did. No doubt he considered it part of his job to keep up with the latest vitriol. Without his uniform, he lacked the intimidation factor. His navy turtleneck and pleated jeans didn't have the same effect. He looked weak, undersized, easily flustered. Still, I wondered how he felt about the game we were engaged in.

"Good to see you, Cal," I said.

"Only my friends call me Cal."

Jenny shot him a look, but he didn't take his eyes from the screen to catch it.

"Fine by me, *Mark*." I clenched my jaw.

He spread his legs to make sure no one would sit near him. On the wall behind him, three circles hung in a diagonal layout—an Orion's Belt of collectible Elvis plates. At the far end of the couch, beyond Cal's bulbous head, a window overlooked the mill.

"Did you pay that ticket yet?" he asked me, pleased with his timing.

"What ticket?" I walked away as he steamed.

Jenny introduced me to her mother, Julia. A short woman, just over five feet, who held several green table mats in her thin hands. She smiled and carried on with setting the table. At first impression, Julia Flynn seemed ready to make herself so small that she'd sink into the floral wallpaper.

"Thank you for having me."

"It's our pleasure."

Jenny tugged at my hand and led me into the kitchen.

Her father stood at the stovetop, stirring the contents of a silver pot. Steam rose into the air, surrounded his head and shoulders, and then dissipated. Darkened by dirt and grime, his shirt read PHIL. He extended his hand to shake; it was very clean and white. His eyes were sunken into his shallow face, his skin so pale it was translucent.

"Jack comes from a mill family," Jenny said.

"Is that right?" Phil tried to care. "Don't know about your family's situation, but this here mill has pretty much run its course."

Cal turned up the volume of the television. I tried to ignore the commentary spewing in the background, but I wondered why they were screaming. They talked loud to talk loud. There was little conviction in their voices.

A crash in the dining room was followed by, "I'm fine. It's fine." Jenny bolted to help her mother at the table, abandoning me in an unfamiliar room with an unfamiliar face.

"There's beer in the fridge," he said.

I decided against the beer, and the silence that followed was ear-shattering.

"Smells good," I said, attempting to win back a point or two.

"Nothing fancy here. Just a little Vermont Maid and spicy mustard."

Jenny popped her head into the kitchen. "Almost ready?" she inquired.

"Give me five," her father answered.

She moved her eyes to mine. I mouthed the word *help* and she raised her eyebrows and said, "Jack, come show me where you want to sit." I slipped out of the room without disturbing the cook. The whole time I couldn't help but wonder what Phil Flynn must've been thinking.

Jenny fit and didn't fit. She went through the motions and hit all her marks, but it was an act. Truly, she was a beat ahead of everyone, anticipating their next note, their next thought so that she could make their lives easier in some way. She moved differently, talked differently, and even sighed differently from the Jenny I knew. She was more cautious, careful. She aimed for sincerity.

Jenny poured wine into two glasses, one for each of us. I was grateful for the attempt. Phil Flynn had a glass of water.

As I tucked myself in, I bumped the table legs. The settings jostled and rocked. Some of the wine breached the side of my glass. My body felt tight, wrapped together as if my arms were tied to my side. No one noticed the droplets of red on the green mats, or if they did, they didn't care.

"So, what do you do?" Mr. Flynn asked as he stuck his spoon into the mashed potatoes. "Jenny hasn't told us a thing." He didn't look at me. Apparently, the family had a habit of avoiding eye contact when speaking. My mouth was dry. I hugged my wineglass and, to buy some time, took a casual sip, which only made my mouth drier.

"I guess I'd say I'm a freelance writer and sometimes musician."

"That's nice," Julia said.

Mr. Flynn's head bobbed up and down as he chewed his food.

"'Freelance' is code for unemployed as far as I'm concerned." Cal's voice was an electric knife slicing its way into my ear.

"Why are you here in Galesville?" Mr. Flynn got right to the point.

"I help out Eli Page over at River Bend Farm."

"He's Eli Page's errand boy." Cal dug deeper. "What's he got you doing this week? Smashing windows? Filling gas cans?" Mr. Flynn's forehead wrinkled as if he had something to say but thought better of it. Cal's derision poisoned the room. "Eli-freaking-Page." He couldn't stop himself; the venom dripped from his incisors. "Can you please, please explain it to me? How does he end up in *my* town of all the places in the world?"

"He's harmless," Jenny said.

"He's dangerous," Cal rebutted.

"I don't understand," Mr. Flynn said. "I thought he was old news."

"Not for me," Cal said. "He keeps popping up in my investigation. Off the record, I'm positive he's involved in our current situation."

"Involved? Is that right?" Mr. Flynn asked. "You think he's capable of arson?"

Jenny said "no" at the same time Cal said "yes."

"You never know," Mr. Flynn continued. "I'll tell you what I told Jenny when she first started helping out that old fool—he's not going to find whatever he's looking for here. No second chances in a place like this. I'm sure he knows that by now."

"He's a burnout. All those drugs turned his brain to mush," Cal said. He laughed to himself. "I'm serious, though, he's wily. He plays dumb, but he knows more than he lets on. Can't trust him. One of these days—"

"Shut up and eat your ham," Jenny demanded.

After Jenny's correction, the room was silent.

Every few bites, I glanced across the table, but Jenny barely looked up from her plate.

Julia Flynn, who sat to my left, shared only a vague resemblance to Jenny. Her porcelain face, bright pink cheeks, egg-shaped eyes, and swanlike neck were related, but Jenny's features were tougher, hardened. Mrs. Flynn showed subtle signs of her age—hairline fractures in the shell, crow's-feet, lines of trouble slightly carved into her skin. Jenny wasn't nearly as delicate.

Phil Flynn controlled the silence, and I had a sudden flash of the old man dominating all conversations, while Jenny struggled, like her mother, to be heard.

Using his fork, Mr. Flynn pointed to Cal. "I'm sure you're aware, but Cal here's a big shot in town. Jenny's a lucky young woman." Mrs. Flynn forced a smile through her tight lips.

"Leave it alone, Phil," Cal said.

"He's respected. People want to do right by him. That's what they say."

Cal's face brightened to a near-ripe plum, as if he had been badly bruised.

"A little rough around the edges, but a good man that will give Jenny a good life." Mr. Flynn raised his eyebrows in Jenny's direction and repeated, "A good man."

Cal dropped his fork; it clanged against his plate. Mrs. Flynn jumped.

"That's enough. You're embarrassing him," Jenny said. She leaned into Cal's shoulder to sell it. I always thought it was hard to fake compassion, but I began to rethink that opinion in Galesville.

I poured myself another glass of wine and downed it in record time.

"Jenny Lee," Mr. Flynn continued. "She's a real saint, as I'm sure you're aware."

"Yes, sir," I said.

"She's very talented," Julia Flynn said.

"Patron saint of lost causes," Phil Flynn continued.

Cal placed his mitt on top of Jenny's left, ring-fingered hand. Her posture sank. Mrs. Flynn remained silent—her stare pointed inward as if in prayer.

Mr. Flynn ranted about how her sense of duty was a trait that all men should admire and how any man would be blessed to have her as a wife. "But—and here's the real problem, something that Cal is gonna have to nip in the bud—she spends too much time fixing other people. Can't worry about all those strangers once you start a family. She's got to learn to zero in that attention on what matters."

"She's a saint, all right," Cal muttered. Jenny pulled her hand away.

"She refuses to start her own life until I'm gone, but I say I'd rather have the grandkids now."

"Knock it off," Jenny mumbled.

Uncomfortable, I shuffled in my seat. I wanted out. I should've left when I saw the ring on her finger, but I didn't want to run and I was a sucker for her pleas. Everyone stared at me. I needed to say something, anything. "How'd you meet?"

"It's a small town," Jenny said matter-of-factly. "We grew up together."

Cal tossed his napkin on the table and got up. He opened his mouth to speak, but no words came out. Then he marched into the living room.

"So I don't get it," Mr. Flynn said. "I'm trying to be congenial and all, but I don't get why you're here, at my table, enjoying my food."

"Dad. Knock it off. He's my guest," Jenny said, the muscles in her face tightening.

"How do you know Jenny, again?" Mr. Flynn asked me.

"We're just friends. I'm not here to cause any problems."

Mrs. Flynn knocked her fork off the table.

"This is exactly what I mean," Mr. Flynn continued. "She hardly knows you, but she invites you to dinner. I don't know if you're a lost cause or not, but you get my point. No one else would do that. She sees a feral cat and she brings it home. It's a good thing Cal's a tolerant man."

Cal laughed from the other room.

A chair shifted. Mrs. Flynn stood up and said, "Enough with this talk. Shoo, shoo. Get out of here so I can clean off this table and we can have dessert."

We did as we were told and went into the sitting room.

Jenny cornered me between the living room and the hall.

"Please don't listen to Dad," Jenny said to me. "His head's not on straight."

"I think I'm going to go," I said.

"No. Please. My mother made dessert. She'd be crushed—"

Truth or fiction, the engagement ring and the cozying up to Cal was a lot to take. We all play our roles, and we are all damned by them.

"Will you stay for me?"

I grimaced, lips pulled back. "For a few minutes," I said, against my better judgment.

Cal leaned into the couch and crossed his legs. He appeared to offer me a seat next to him, but I had the feeling that it was only for show. Jenny kept her distance.

"What's so special about Eli Page?" Cal's nasally whine pierced through my armor like a diamond-tipped saw blade. "I want to know. It drives me through the wall that this guy is considered some sort of hero when he's out there smashing windows and setting buildings on fire."

"Give it a rest," Jenny said.

I believed like so many others that Eli was an everyman, a voice that shouted from the rooftops, a brawler for the disenfranchised. He had the answers. But there I was, in the living room of a family that had struggled to survive and was entangled in the same fallacies that Eli Page had exposed. They were caught in the fray, mired down, toes sinking into the ever-expanding mud, and they still didn't hear Eli. They listened but never actually heard him.

Cal lifted his chin and cocked his head as the talk show host welcomed a fellow pundit to his studio.

"No hard feelings," Phil Flynn said as he handed me a beer. His whole arm shook as he reached out to me. I thanked him for the can. He retreated to the kitchen.

A tape of the president rolled on the television, spliced so thoroughly that all context was lost. The fact that one inane clip would be replayed for hours and torn apart by the "analysts" sickened me, but Cal was enthralled.

Jenny retreated to the couch. I forced a smile, even as I eyed Cal, who shifted closer to the television as if our silent glance was so loud that it disturbed the intellectual discourse. Cal muttered something to himself. It was call-and-response with the host. Jenny rolled her eyes, leaned into the cushions, and was consumed by the couch. She made faces, mocking his ever-serious disposition.

I took a large gulp to stifle my laughter just as Jenny mimicked Cal's posture. I choked and beer flew out of my nose. "Son of a—"

"Are you okay?" Jenny jumped off the couch and handed me a cloth napkin. Tears filled my eyes. My sinuses fizzled.

"Will you shut up?" Cal snapped. This only made Jenny laugh harder and louder.

"What the hell is going on?" Mr. Flynn said as he reentered the living room, his breathing labored.

"Nothing. Everything's fine," Jenny told her father.

Mr. Flynn shifted his attention to the television. "Why don't you turn this shit off? It's a waste of electricity. They don't know a thing about a thing."

"Right? Exactly," Jenny said. Was she mocking her father as she mocked Cal? I couldn't tell; luckily, he couldn't either.

"They know what they're talking about," Cal said.

"Like hell they do," Phil Flynn said. "And don't you talk down to me, Mr. Big Shot. They're just trying to find more ways to line their pockets by screwing over the working man."

"If anybody's looking out for you, it's these guys. They're fair and balanced." Cal pointed to the television.

"Don't give me that shit."

Jenny and I both had the same nervous look on our faces like we both knew we were about to witness two cars collide.

Cal shook his head, dismissing Phil Flynn. Everybody in the room (even Elvis, staring down from his perch) knew the scene was about to get ugly.

"Do you have something to say?" Phil Flynn said.

"I just said it."

Jenny measured Cal and her father at the same time, both had their eyes glued to the television but argued with each other by reflection.

It all happened so fast.

"No. No. I'm over here trying to defend you, and you're all above it like you think you're better than us all. I just want to hear you say it. Go on. Say it. 'I, Mark Calvin, am better than everyone.' "

"Go to hell," Cal whispered. From the bloodless look that appeared on his face, he regretted it.

Phil Flynn tightened his grip on the beer can in his hand. Cal picked up the remote and increased the volume to an absurd level. And as Mr. Flynn took a menacing step toward the seated Cal, Jenny stepped between them. Her palm pushed against her father's thin chest. The force propelled her backward onto the couch beside Cal.

Jenny yelled, "Mom!" Should I run to get Julia Flynn from the kitchen? Should I step in? Should I yell at them both and duck for cover? I had to do something.

"Everyone calm down!" I screamed. Instinct arrived at by the perfect concoction of courage and cowardice. And sure enough, everyone turned and looked at me, frozen in a tableau, shocked.

Mrs. Flynn entered. "Who wants pie? It's apple."

The television commentary devolved into more useless filler by pundits with their canned aggression. Cal's face was pale, yet it still held a tinge of its smug and superior self. His self-worth was intact.

Once she put her father to bed, Jenny met me on the porch. We walked out into the mill's darkened lot, where we could be alone.

"All they do is fight," she said. "I'm sorry you had to witness—"

"Don't apologize."

She shook her head. "My dad's a good guy. I swear. There's just a lot going on. Too much." She pleaded with herself. I was an innocent bystander.

"Cal is nothing if not consistent," I said. We were going to talk about him whether she wanted to or not.

"Mark is always trying to prove that he's someone to somebody."

Her reaction stunned me, and for a moment I had some small form of pity for Cal. No, not pity. Empathy. After all, I too wanted to be something, someone I wasn't. We all did.

"Strange opinion to share about your fiancé," I said.

"Stop," she said as she punched me in the arm. "I called it off months ago."

"What about the ring?" I pointed to her hand. "That's a dangerous game."

"Like I said, it's for Dad's benefit," she said. "His health isn't good. We didn't want to give him something else to worry about. Believe it or not, he really likes Mark. They've always been close. He thinks of him as a son. We just didn't have the heart to let him down."

The moon embraced us within its soft light.

"You have to tell him sometime."

"When I was a kid, my dad was a different person." She glanced back at the house and the yellow porch light. "When he wasn't at the mill, he was always trying to teach me something. He had a lesson for everything, a story for every situation. He pointed out the beauty in everyday objects. He didn't want me to take it all for granted. In some ways, I think that is why I do what I do. That's why Belanger's is so special to me, but of course, now he thinks it's ridiculous, naïve. I can't win."

"The patron saint of lost causes, right?"

"Yup, and he's patient zero."

She dropped her chin to her chest and her hair fell across her face. Without thinking, my hand, controlled by the moonlight, by the gravitational pull, by something other than my head, reached out and gently brushed the hair aside so that it framed her face. As I did, she rested her head in my palm.

Cautiously, I slid my hand along her ear, the outline of her scar, and the corner of her lips. She raised herself on her toes, and our lips met for the first time. Even if her explanation wasn't wholly satisfying, even if nothing made sense, I *believed* that she had her reasons. I trusted her. And that was enough for the time being.

The next afternoon, as I went about my routine in the study, my mind was fixed on Jenny, Cal, and the Flynns. I didn't know what to make of the kiss or the fight or the ring. Jenny had explained and rationalized, but I couldn't escape the fear that I was being set up. For what? Failure? Rejection? I didn't really know. Eventually, made useless by distraction, I abandoned the study and went outside to clear my head.

I walked the line. The barbed-wire fence on the edge of the property had been trampled, pushed to the ground so that animals could come and go as they pleased. I kicked the fence post upright and lifted the rusty wire with my bare hands.

Before I returned to the house, I glanced southward, where the Battenkill swerved to hug the mills, and saw Eli sitting in the grass along the riverbank. Tig lapped at the water beside him.

As I approached, Tig popped his head out of the water and greeted me.

"Good dog." I petted him on the head. "Good dog."

"Traitor," Eli said to the dog.

"What are you doing out here?" I asked.

He opened his mouth, but no words came out. Finally, after what seemed like minutes, he gathered himself and spoke. "Actually, I don't remember."

"Doesn't matter anyhow," I said. I wanted to believe his proclamation, but it seemed too calculated, too timely.

"Take my word for it," he said, lifting his head from his hands. "The past will always catch you. Try to beat back the charging water, and it'll overwhelm you every time. You gotta deal with it. Whatever *it* is."

"And if you don't?" I asked.

"It's only gonna hurt more when it deals with you."

He stared at me for a long while, eyes scrambled, teeth locked.

"I owe you an interview," he said. "Isn't that right?"

"Yeah, you do. At a minimum."

"Prick," he mumbled. He grabbed his leather satchel and dragged it closer to him. After digging through its contents, he pulled out a sandwich and offered me half.

"I hope you don't think this counts."

"I'm happy to eat alone if you're gonna waste my time," he said.

"Fine. What would *you* like to talk about, then?"

"Let me see." He took a large bite of sandwich. "How'd last night go?"

"It was a disaster," I answered. "Honestly, I don't know how she sprang from them. They're nice enough people, but she doesn't fit."

"Well, you know," he said, mouth full, "it's probably 'cause she didn't spring from them."

"How do you mean?"

Eli squinted at me. "Oh, I'm the asshole now." His eyes darted back and forth, searching for recognition. "Forget it. Forget I said anything."

"No way. You opened it up."

"Yeah, and I'm puttin' the lid back on."

"Doesn't work that way." My patience was trumped by my fear of being excluded from some discovery or knowledge. However trivial it might be, I had to know. "Let's have it," I said.

Eli took another bite of his sandwich, obviously contemplating his escape, but there was no exit ramp in sight. His back tensed up.

"Because I feel sorry for you, I'll spill it, but I'm not happy about it." He paused before commiserating. "Phil and Julia—they aren't her real folks." He let that sink in for a moment. "Her mother up and left before she was even a month old. Can't believe she didn't tell you this. Her father was never in the picture."

"They adopted her?" I dropped my sandwich. My appetite was gone.

"Julia's her aunt. Took her in as if it was second nature, as if it was the most natural thing in the world. That's how Jenny tells it. Now you know. Don't tell her I told you."

I don't know what bothered me more, that Eli had known this secret history and neglected to tell me or that Jenny didn't think enough of me to divulge it. I felt like an outsider. "And here I thought we were getting somewhere," I said, mostly for my own benefit.

"How do you mean?"

"Apparently she doesn't trust me enough to let me in."

"Have you told her about your father?" he asked. "Or about New Haven?"

Point(s) taken. Damn that red folder.

"What did I tell you?" Eli continued. "People live behind their masks."

"This is different."

"Why?"

I had no answer.

"For fuck's sake, you're both pieces of work. Too busy lookin' over your shoulder to see what's right in front of you. You deserve each other."

"Maybe."

We sat together wordless for a while, listening to the river and birdsong. After two months at River Bend, I knew when to enjoy the silence.

"Have you spoken to Barry?" he asked, snapping the quiet.

"No," I answered. It had been two and a half weeks since I last spoke with Barry Gettleson, and I was beginning to think that the deal had fallen through. The last time we exchanged words, he wasn't happy with me. I'd pleaded for some flexibility. I needed to find a way to extend the project time line, or I needed to be cut loose. "Why?"

"No reason. I was wondering how much he knows," Eli said.

"About what?"

Eli didn't answer right away.

"Good days. Bad days. I can tell the difference, you know." Eli glanced up at the cloudy sky. "There are times when I can't...connect." He tossed what remained of our sandwiches to Tig. "This conversation, it never happened."

"You should think about getting checked out."

"Yeah. I know."

"Well, what's holding you back?"

He didn't answer, instead he switched topics.

"You'll get your interview. Soon."

"'Soon' is a four-letter word," I said.

"Now you're startin' to see the world through my eyes."

The rain began to fall. I wondered if he'd remember any of what he'd said or if by nine or ten at night, after a scotch or two, it would just fade away and be lost forever. Then again, did it matter? Memory isn't all it's cracked up to be.

The next morning, I was startled awake by a knock at the carriage barn door. I flipped over, tossed the sheet to my waist, and lifted myself onto my elbows. The noise stopped. After a moment, I relaxed back down, only to be roused by a second round of knocking. When my eyes finally adjusted to the dawning light, I recognized Eli in my doorway.

"Let's talk," he said.

I glanced over at the nightstand: 5:11. (I hated that clock and its stupid red digits.)

"What's going on?" My breath was short, my vision blurred. Was he finally going to give me an interview, in the early morning, before I was prepared? Was he going to call me out about the study, the stolen objects? The betrayal hung around my neck like a yoke, dragging me down. Did he know that I knew about H.M.? If so, spill it,

I thought, I'll deal with the aftermath. Tell me something I don't know. If I'm going to go down for the snooping, at least let me know the truth. Then I can go back to sleep.

"Something's come up," Eli said. He wasn't angry or annoyed, which only made me wonder if he was on the up-and-up or if this was another elaborate misfire.

A vein rippled in my neck.

Eli's boots scuffed the floor as he crossed the room and sat on the window seat. It creaked as the wood flexed under his weight. "You know, I used to sleep in this room," he said. "I'd sit here in this exact spot to look out over the river."

Taken aback by his nonsensical admission, I couldn't even construct a follow-up, not even a "what the hell are you talking about?" or a "run that by me again." Why would he have slept in the carriage barn?

"Listen," he said. "I've gotta go . . . for a while . . . and I've come to ask a favor. Can you take care of the dog . . . and the house . . . while I'm gone?"

"Wait, you're leaving? For how long?"

"Don't know. Few weeks. Longer," he said. "Will you look after Tig?"

"Yeah, sure, that's not a problem." I still wasn't convinced he knew what he was saying. Maybe, I thought, he ended up in the carriage barn by accident, and the whole scene was just a memory error or a cover story for something else. But his thoughts weren't fragmented; they weren't stitched together willy-nilly. He was clear-minded, as far as I could tell, and I had to assume that his decision to leave was made while lucid and sober. "Are you okay?"

"That's what I'm tryin' to find out."

"Where're you going?"

"Does it matter?"

"A little more information would be nice." The words flew out with too much attitude.

"It's somethin' I've gotta do. I've scheduled a few different tests. Understand?"

"Sure. Yeah. Of course. But for two or three weeks? Why can't you just see a doctor here or Bennington or Albany?"

"Just the way it is."

"If that's what you have to do, I'm not going to stand in your way," I said. No doubt I was glad he was considering a doctor's visit, but I had little confidence he was telling me the truth. The whole thing was strange, and my morning cloudiness gave the exchange a dreamlike quality.

"When I get back, we can go over what you need to finish up."

"When are you leaving?"

"Soon."

"Why so quickly?"

"Quick is best."

"Well, Tig will be in good hands," I said.

"You've been patient with me, Jack. Don't think I don't know that. You know as well as I do that I can't go on this way."

I nodded, knowing full well that it was wishful thinking.

He slowly made his way to the door.

"Word of advice: Let Tig think he's the boss," he said.

"Will do."

"And, Jack—try not to mess it up with Jenny." He backed out of the room, shutting the door behind him. "I meant what I said yesterday. You two deserve each other."

Groggy but distracted, I fell in and out of sleep until nearly nine o'clock. When I woke, I dialed Barry Gettleson's office.

"Would you like me to leave a message?" Gettleson's secretary asked.

"Tell him to call me. Right away. The time line will have to be pushed."

"Well, Mr. Wyeth," the young lady said. "Mr. Gettleson took the train to Rensselaer last night. I believe he was scheduled to arrive in Galesville by cab at seven thirty this morning. Don't tell him I said anything—it's not my place, but I thought you should know. Have a pleasant day."

Gettleson had already come and gone, and he'd taken Eli with him.

Soon after the first grant dollars flowed, the mural's unveiling and ribbon cutting had been inked into the mayor's planner for the Fourth of July. It was an election year, after all—front-page pictures with scissors the size of cross-country skis were more effective than endorsements or yard signs.

The *Mirror* had played it up like it was *the* event of the summer. Locals, who observed the mural-in-progress from their car windows or while walking their dogs along Main Street, were curious. I'd heard, on more than a few occasions, people on their way to the Fire Department's pancake breakfast or the Elks' contra dance or the VFW's BBQ say, "I wonder what she's doing" or "It doesn't look like much" or "I don't get it."

By the time I arrived, a crowd had already amassed. The mural itself was covered by tarps, which were tied down with three weighted ropes. Each line was held by a volunteer who would, on cue, tug until the tarp broke free.

Finally, several minutes past noon, the mayor clapped his hands together and widened his overwhite smile. Oxford shirt, starched stiff, sleeves rolled to his elbows, red tie pinned down by a gold star clasp, he was the vision of a small-town politician. He stood behind a podium, and a crisscross of red, white, and blue ribbons stretched out in front of him, from stanchion to stanchion. Jenny hid behind the mayor's left shoulder while various dignitaries stood to his right, ready for their photo op. "What did I tell you? People love a pretty face," he said to his fellow officials as they exchanged handshakes. When he leaned toward the microphone, the air buzzed with feedback and the crowd shushed.

"Folks," he began, "it is my distinct pleasure to be here with my fellow Galesvillians to unveil our newest treasure." He waited for applause. "This work of art, commissioned by the town and made possible by our friends at the Chamber as well as the generosity of the IGA" — those friends turned to the crowd, waved — "was painted by one of our very own. Jenny Lee Flynn. And she has done a masterful job. Masterful, indeed. Need I remind you folks, this is what can happen when the arts and local business come together with a common purpose. We can create beautiful things. Beautiful things, indeed."

Without warning, the mayor left the mike and placed his arm around Jenny, mugging it up for the crowd. Jenny raised her eyebrows and forced a smile, lips pulled inward. Meanwhile, the mayor gave a thumbs-up, then a double thumbs-up, and then he pointed to the crowd. The photographer snapped a dozen pictures in rapid succession.

"Now," the mayor said, returning to the mike, "before we take down these tarps and cut these shiny ribbons, I need to get serious for a moment." His face turned down. In a somber tone, he continued, "It is a blessing in trying times, like the times we live in, to see a community so bonded in friendship. A blessing, indeed. Our men and women are sacrificing their lives on the fields of battle to give others the chance to live like us — as free people. We may celebrate and have fun, yes we may, but we must remember those brave soldiers. Soldiers like our own Captain Sweet, God rest his soul. We must remember them in our hearts. On this Fourth of July, I am honored to be your mayor. This mural is meant to show our spirit, our values, and our community pride. Jenny has done a remarkable job capturing the spirit of Galesville, if I may say so myself. I'm sure Phil and Julia are both very proud. As they should be. They have raised a very *resilient* young woman. So, after we cut this thing, I invite you to have some good ol' American hot dogs, hamburgers, and potato salad. God bless Galesville."

Before the last syllable of "Galesville" was uttered, the crowd cheered and waved their miniflags in the air. I half expected a chorus of volunteers to break out into an impromptu "Star-Spangled Banner." What would Eli think about such rhetoric and empty displays of patriotism? Eli loved his country, as did I, but we shared a healthy dose of skepticism about all the red, white, and rah, rah, rah. Mark Calvin and others mistook this type of skepticism for malice.

Jenny, the mayor, and the others all grabbed their scissors, stepped up to the ribbons, and waited for their cue. The crowd counted down. "Three, two, one." Once the photographer was in place, the mayor nodded. As they sliced the ribbon, the tarps were released and the mural was revealed.

Everyone clapped politely. One or two people audibly gasped. Heads tilted, eyes squinted, and whispers filled the air.

"Now that that's over, let's eat," someone said.

A steady stream of viewers gravitated toward the refreshments. A few of them hugged Jenny, shook her hand, or gave her a high-five. Others studied the mural, curious and perplexed. It was not what they expected. They didn't know how to feel. Not yet. Not in that first instance. If I had to guess, I'd say that the audience expected a primitive landscape, a folk art mural in the style of Grandma Moses like the one a few towns south in Hoosick Falls, but Jenny offered something different. You could feel the countryside in the lush, fertile greens, the ghostly lavender hills in the background, and of course in the silver-white river, which wove its way throughout the wall, connecting the past and present, the new and old. At the same time, set on top of the opulent background, Jenny had spray-painted figures in gritty black and white, graffiti art style. It was these figures, cartoonish in a way, that drew the crowd's attention.

I stepped into line to get a closer view.

"How dare she ... ?" the woman beside me bellowed. "Look at that." She pointed to the bottom left of the brick wall.

"What? What are you looking at?" her companion, an older gentleman, asked.

"This. This right here," the woman said. "You can see it. Don't be dense." Then she reached up and put her hands all over the mural.

In the foreground, a few spray-painted figures appeared as if they'd walk right out of the wall and into the street. They carried Galesville's bounty — flowers and vegetables and farm goods — in their arms. A guitar-slung troubadour, flanked by a young girl, led the group into Galesville. They were proud, heroic figures. Bright and energetic. In contrast, on the other side of the river, off in the distance, a half dozen men and women, shoulders slumped, trudged off into the darkened background.

"Outraged. I am outraged," the woman continued. A small group flocked to her side, eager to hear her interpretation, trying to latch on to something that was concrete, literal, recognizable. What is she saying? Should we be offended? Within a few minutes, a whole team of perturbed individuals gasped, whispered, and shot dirty looks toward Jenny.

"I don't think they like it," Jenny said, when I joined her at the refreshments table.

"Mural art is never appreciated unless it pokes and prods," I joked. My attempt to lighten the situation fell flat. The mood had soured.

I studied her. Arms crossed, lips pursed, a fresh bruise on her wrist, and I wondered what was going on behind her eyes. "How're you doing?" I asked while pouring lemonade into a plastic cup.

"I'm fine," she said, not realizing that I was referring to the mark and her change in body language.

She stared at the crowd, shaking her head ever so slightly as if she knew all along what was coming. She was on guard, ready for a fight.

Meanwhile, the mayor was executing his escape plan. Despite his platitudes, it was clear that he was upset about his rally being ruined. The woman who took offense to the mural jabbered in his ear. He waved her off and slammed the door of his truck. Fed up with the mayor, she marched toward Jenny, who didn't have a truck to hide in.

"You should be ashamed of yourself," the woman said.

"I'm sorry you feel that way, Mrs. Walker." Jenny grimaced and squinted as if she was staring into the sun. "What is it that you don't like this time?"

"It's offensive. You're spitting on the fine citizens of Galesville. We're not a bunch of flower children, smoking marijuana, living in some fairy-tale world. You know what I think? I think you've been spending too much time with that Eli Page character. Thief. Traitor. He shouldn't even be up there at all. Much less depicted as some sort of leader. Especially now, with all that's going on. I demand that you change it."

"I can't do that, Mrs. Walker."

"You will do that. I will see to it."

"No. I won't," Jenny answered, flatly. "Have you ever heard of Diego Rivera? I'm sure you'd love him, Mrs. — "

"Don't condescend to me. Look at you, so high and mighty. Well, you're nothing but trash, missy. I know your story. You're not fooling anyone." She turned, head held high, and marched off with her gaggle of concerned Galesvillians.

"Miserable old woman," Jenny said. "I wish she'd crawl off and die." Despite her quip, she was visibly shaken.

I snorted. The jolt caused me to spill lemonade on my shirt.

Jenny covered her mouth as she mocked me, revealing the purple mark again.

"That bruise is pretty nasty."

"Oh, it's nothing," she said. "Maybe you should concentrate on not dying a beverage-related death on my big day. That would be a real buzz kill."

On the walk back to River Bend, I spotted a black Dodge Ram—the same make and model that had blown by Eli's several times—parked along the commons. Its owner was nowhere to be found. I was eighty percent sure it was the truck that stalked the farm, attempting to frighten or intimidate. I looked over my shoulder to double-check that I was alone. Then I investigated.

The door was locked. An empty gun rack hung in the back window, a Stewart's Shop coffee cup sat in the center console, and a newspaper was folded up on the passenger's seat. In the bed of the truck, under a packing blanket, I saw a small round gas can, a shovel, and a chain.

My fingers buzzed with the desire to break the window, dig out the registration, and ID the son of a bitch. Instead, I hung back at the gazebo on the commons and waited. I was determined to match a face to the vehicle, even if I had to sit there for hours.

Ten, fifteen minutes later, a man twice my age swaggered up to the truck. Despite the summer heat, he wore a long-sleeve green plaid shirt, a full beard, a worn-out John Deere hat. Even though I got a decent look at him (from a hundred feet away), I couldn't make out any distinguishing features. He resembled a lot of men in Galesville; in some ways, he even reminded me of Eli.

He popped open the truck's door, but before he stepped into its cab, he fixed his stare across the commons and firmly on me. I tipped my head in his direction, but he didn't return the gesture. I'd been made. His stare intensified, but I didn't look away. After what felt like a full minute of this, he flipped me off, got in the truck, and drove away.

The heap of intelligence I'd gathered in the study offered a glimpse into the hidden life of Eli Page, but only a glimpse.

In Eli's absence, I was free to explore the house without interruptions or surprises, and the process of understanding Eli began to speed up.

I spent countless hours in the study. Too many. Basically, whenever I wasn't with Jenny or walking Tig, I was in the locked room, attempting to devise some process to establish an archive.

I read H.M.'s letters three, four, five times a week, searching for a code or a clue that might open up a new line of thought. I even resurrected Eli's guitars from their dusty, cramped cases. Well past midnight, I'd break in and strum through random set lists, which consisted mostly of Eli's songs but also classics like "Where Did You Sleep Last Night," "32-20 Blues," and "House of the Rising Sun." I played until my fingertips bled or until I nodded off in his chair.

Tig barely moved. He spent hours curled up on the front doormat, waiting for Eli's return. Quiet, too quiet at times, I'd forget that he was even there until a whimper or huff reminded me to replenish his food and water or let him outside. During a few random moments each day, he'd spring up, show his teeth, and bark at the door. The low, throaty woof-crack-woof, his guard dog DNA, burst through his body, aiming its wrath at a skunk or a squirrel or a passing truck.

On one particularly humid afternoon, after hours of digging through cardboard boxes of concert memorabilia, I collapsed into the armchair and dialed Casey's cell number. An old Victor Breeze-Spreader blew hot air into my face as I waited for him to pick up, which he finally did on the fifth ring.

"What do you want?"

"Is that how you greet a friend?"

"I've got nothing to say to you."

"I know, I know. It's been really busy," I lied, getting to my feet.

"Well, then, I'm honored you found the time to call. It has to be hard to carve out time in your busy schedule for your supposed best friend—"

"Come on, cut me some slack."

"Slack?" He huffed. "Of course. The kids, the high-pressure job, the grad school thesis, the mortgage payment—it's a wonder you can function day to day." He paused, as dramatically as one can on a phone. "Oh. Wait. That's right. You have none of those responsibilities. Nothing even close. Must be really draining."

"Are you done?" I circled the room.

"Not even close."

"Well, you've made your point. You can stop at any time."

"Can I? Thanks for your permission, padre. I'll take it under advisement." He inhaled deeply and sighed. "Get to it—what do you want?"

"Advice."

"I'm fresh out," he said.

"What the hell is wrong with you?" I asked. He did not answer right away, and for a moment I thought he'd hung up. "You're more of a hothead than usual."

"Am I?" I heard the faint ticking of a computer keyboard in the background, and I got the sense that he wasn't really paying attention to the conversation.

"Eli's gone. You should drive over and chill out here for a weekend."

"I'm not really in a vacationing mood." Apparently, Cascy's anger had been stewing for some time.

"What's your problem? I called to—"

"Shut up," he said.

"Well, pissed at me or not, the offer stands."

Tig whined and threw his giant paw over his face. My pacing was making him anxious.

"I've got to go," Casey continued. "Email me. Let me know if you decide to grace us with your presence in the near future. I have to get back to work."

"You're working on a Saturday? I thought that was against your code."

"Got a meeting. Talk to you later."

He hung up.

I stuck my phone into my pocket but continued to pace. It was unlike Casey to be so impatient from the get-go—it usually took him a good five, six minutes to build up a head of steam. I considered driving to Saratoga, buying him a beer, and hashing it out, but my first responsibilities were to River Bend. Casey would have to wait.

Tig stood up and sniffed around the room, back and forth, back and forth. Was he mocking me? I took it as a sign that we both needed some fresh air.

It was hazy outside, but that did not stop Tig from bolting around the yard like he'd shed seven years (and twenty pounds) during his nap. We hiked along the border of the property and inspected the fence posts. The corner had been trampled, breached for a second time. Again, I lifted the wire fencing and fixed the posts. Then Tig and I trudged up the hillside to the graveyard.

I surveyed the area from Eli's concrete bench. Alone, apart from Galesville, above River Bend, among its dead, my mind turned inward. Despite my frustrations, a lot had happened in my short time in Galesville. I gazed out over the house, Eli's acreage, the Battenkill. The clouds drifted eastward, shifting shapes from floating fortresses to boats against a current. Where was Eli? Was he getting help? Would it matter? If he returned to River Bend a changed man, would his life be any simpler? No. He might be able to recall the past, retrieve his memories from forgotten catacombs, but he still wouldn't be able to revise history. Time and space are the graveyard's playthings.

Tig bounded up and around tree trunks and rocks. He darted back and forth in the woods, playing hopscotch with a chipmunk. I called to him.

After we returned to the house, we both collapsed in the living room. As I drifted off to sleep, it began to make sense to me. The hike, the play, the hillside—it wore you down. It allowed time to crawl, memories to resurface, fractured scenes of your life to roll like motion pictures projected in the clear sky. Up there on the hillside, it's possible to relive your regrets, it's possible to fight against the annoying persistence of time. At least a little bit.

The next morning, I found myself on the blanket trunk in the study with a guitar strapped across my shoulder. Strumming. Humming. I shifted from a C to E minor, and the skin on three of my fingers cracked, pulsed, and bled on to the neck of Eli's guitar. I winced. Then the B string snapped. I put the instrument down, picked up the phone, and dialed Jenny's number.

Jenny sat on the gazebo's steps, enveloped by the street-light's glow. Knees hugged to her chest, she rocked ever so slightly as she talked or cursed or sang—her mouth moved, but I couldn't tell what she was saying. From the edge of the commons, in the twilight, I observed Jenny like a gambler observes his table, anticipating outcomes, measuring risk. At the same time, I sensed that someone was watching *me* watching her. The curtains in lighted windows fluttered, and I imagined hidden faces peering out from behind linen to see me, the simple figure of a man, hiding in the shadows, staring at a woman in a gazebo.

A loud, piercing yap confirmed my suspicions. Something had been eyeing me. The bark-growl-bark was followed by a frantic scratch, scratch, scratch on a windowpane. I swiveled my head to locate the animal. What I found was a scruffy little terrier locked inside the house to my right. "Don't be a jerk," I said. I couldn't blame it for calling me out, but I hated its sour little face nonetheless.

Alerted by the noise, Jenny stood up, adjusted her hoodie, and tucked her hair behind her ears. Then she waved a newspaper in the air as if to signal me in from a long flight. I picked up my pace and greeted her with a hug, pretending that I'd just arrived and hadn't, in fact, been watching her for ten-plus minutes.

"Tell me the truth—I looked like a crazy person, didn't I?"

"What do you mean?"

"Talking to myself," she said. "I do that sometimes." Her cheeks reddened.

"Where do you want to go?" I asked.

"How about you buy me an ice cream?"

As we walked along the slate sidewalks, I pushed the banter aside and aimed for sincerity, if only for a moment. "How're you holding up?" I'd overheard that Helen Walker's antimural campaign was gaining momentum — it was getting more and more difficult to dismiss it out of hand.

"Have you seen the latest?" She handed me the newspaper.

Was it Thursday already? Since Eli's departure, I'd lost track. No doubt the paper still sat on the front step, unclaimed. I'd planned to tell Jenny about Eli soon after we exchanged hellos, but she was caught up in something else, and my courage waned.

"Front page," she said, attempting to appear in control of her anger, but I knew better.

A photo of the mural and its accompanying headline covered everything above the fold: "Public Art or Public Disgrace?" The caption below quoted the mayor: "'As a piece of public art, we need to make sure it does not take sides,' said Mayor Higgins, 'and this mural indeed takes sides.' Its future will be addressed at the next council meeting."

The streetlights cast the newsprint in a ghostly golden hue.

"Of course it takes sides," Jenny said. "What a stupid comment."

Inside the paper, Mrs. Helen Walker's letter to the editor was a font size larger than the other letters. Upset by the "subversive imagery" and the "anti-American sentiment," Mrs. Walker demanded the town paint over the new mural and recover any taxpayer dollars used in the creation of "this abomination." It ended with a call to boycott the IGA. At the bottom of the page, another letter writer confessed that he "didn't get it." He wrote, "Why the uproar? We have bigger things to worry about. The mural is a distraction from real issues, not the least of which is Galesville's recent, unprecedented crime spree."

"It is too easy to create a mob," I whispered.

"Either way, it doesn't look good," Jenny said.

"You yourself told me that she's a stick-in-the-mud. Cooler heads will prevail." Even as I said it, I knew that "cool" was a word—much like "reason"—rarely used in contemporary discourse. Reason was the enemy of truth and truth the enemy of reason and so on and so forth. We were all bound by the whims of the person with the loudest bullhorn.

"It's too late," Jenny answered.

"What do you mean?"

"Forget it." She took a deep breath, exhaled, and tried to smile. "Let's talk about something else."

I would've pressed her on the subject if I hadn't been distracted by the teaser on the second page: "Law Office Latest Target of Break-in." Buried on page seven, the article contained little information. As was often the case with the *Mirror*, it relied mainly on insinuation and assumptions. Basically, Tully's Law Office on Main Street had been tossed on Monday night or Tuesday morning—they weren't sure about the time frame, because the office was closed the first week of July for the holiday—and, like the Historical Society, the smoke detectors had been ripped from the wall and the files had been set on fire. I was struck by the realization (and concern) that Eli was still in town at the time of the break-in, and I couldn't vouch for his exact whereabouts.

We walked along Main Street. The air was beginning to lighten, but it was still muggy. My shirt clung to my arms. Jenny's face flushed.

From the opposite side of the road, the mural was somehow softer as if the farther away you got, the more the black and white faded and the lush, verdant backdrop took over. As I stared, I saw a dozen or so orange dots in the right-hand corner, over the artist's signature. Jenny didn't notice, and I didn't alert her, but I was sure they were paintball wounds, similar in size and color to the marks I found on the River Bend property from time to time.

Inside the Stewart's Shop, customers sat in maroon booths and cackled over milk shakes and chili dogs and scratch tickets. We made our way to the counter, and as we did, the background noise faded to sharp whispers. Jenny pretended not to notice. I ordered a sugar cone with coffee ice cream and sprinkles. She ordered black raspberry. When we turned around, everyone was glaring at us.

An old man in a reflective vest approached. "What does it mean?" he asked Jenny. "Why did you choose to paint it that way?"

"I don't know what you're talking about," she replied, staring at her cone, refusing to make eye contact with the man.

"Maybe I'm a little thick-headed, but it seems like you were picking winner and losers."

"No, that's not—"

"We're just here for some ice cream," I interrupted. "Have a good night."

The man nodded and headed back to his table.

We exited the convenience store. Moments later, laughter erupted from behind Stewart's glass window. We both continued walking, pretending that we didn't hear a thing.

"So much for cooler heads," I said.

She paused, seemingly unsure of herself. Ice cream dripped on my fingers. "Has Eli said anything?" she asked.

"Like what?"

"About the mural? About me? It's not a big deal. I just thought he would've said something at some point, but I don't know how often you two converse."

"*Converse*? We never converse." I scratched my stubble and looked away.

Jenny chomped on her cone.

"I worry about him. It's hard to explain. I feel like I need . . ." She finished chewing. "I need to shield him."

"From what?"

"From Mark, from himself, from the unexpected." It took me a moment to realize she was referring to Cal when she said "Mark."

"Why is Cal so stuck on Eli? You'd think he'd have a few theories to work by now."

"He's convinced Eli is dodgy, unpredictable. He says that he's 'two strings short.'"

"Very clever of him."

"He's proud that he came up with it." She licked the edges of her cone. "Only took him a month and a half. But he says his gut tells him Eli is trouble. He means well, in his own way, but he's always had a one-track mind."

My hands were sticky. Jenny handed me a wad of paper napkins.

"Are you sure Eli hasn't mentioned anything?" Jenny inquired again. "I know he never really leaves River Bend these days, but I thought for sure that he'd check out the mural."

I couldn't avoid the conversation any longer. "Eli's gone." My voice wavered as I spoke.

She froze and stared at me as if I'd just told her that her puppy had run away.

"What do you mean?" Her face turned from turnip red to an ashen gray as if she was going to be sick. I revised my statement.

"He took off a couple days ago. I think he went to see some doctors." Maybe someone knows why I couldn't tell her the complete truth about his "condition," but it wasn't in me.

"How long will he be away?"

"He wasn't sure. Couple weeks maybe. Or more."

"You don't know where?"

"I was half asleep when he told me. It was important."

"I'm sure it was." She tossed her half-eaten cone in a nearby trash bin.

Out in the distance, beneath the parking lot light, I saw the manager of the IGA hosing down the mural wall, washing away the paintball splatter.

"Follow me," she said.

At the Galesville Depot, an old rail station–turned-tavern, Jenny wove through the crowd to an empty booth along the trackside of the building. Passenger trains had stopped running in the 1930s, but according to Jenny, freight cars carried slate and marble from the county south to the Port of Albany until the Second World War. A man named Hawke, the leader of a short-lived motorcycle gang in way-upstate New York, reopened the Depot as a dive bar in the 1970s. For every person who referred to the bar as the Depot, there were three who referred to it as Hawke's. Jenny wanted a drink, and this was where you went in Galesville to get a drink.

Onstage, four men in old-school leather jackets and wraparound sunglasses offered up cover songs as background music. CCR, Billy Joel, the Eagles, they jumped wildly through styles and decades, but no one was really listening.

"We don't have to stay here," Jenny said.

"No. This is great. I'm glad you called."

The room was full of grunting and laughter and hot, sweaty bodies.

"This place used to have its moments," she said. "But it's changed."

I nodded, but I wondered if places like the Depot ever really changed or if it was merely the patrons who changed or grew out of it and then accused the bar of selling out.

The music died down for a moment. A middle-aged front man removed his jacket to reveal a white T-shirt. Then he started in on Springsteen's "The River."

"Let me get you a drink," I said.

Jenny didn't hear me. So I got up, squeezed into the booth beside her, and spoke into her ear. She nodded. Then she leaned her cheek into my shoulder and asked for a beer. The room was boiling. The wisps of her hair were wet as they grazed my arm.

"Sit tight. I'll be right back," I said.

On the mirror behind the bar, a sheet of paper hung by a single piece of Scotch tape. "We Will Remember." I'd seen the same picture around town on bulletin boards and in storefront windows. Captain Samuel Sweet and his wife Penny, son Sammy, and newborn baby girl Hope—dressed in their Easter bests in front of a white drop cloth—were the subjects. Captain Sweet was killed by an IED sometime around Thanksgiving. There was a glass jug on the bar, a collection for the family. I dug some change from my pocket and tossed it into the jug.

The bartender pointed at me, and I shouted my order. While she poured, I turned to watch Jenny from across the room. Alone in the booth, she stared at the table, frowning as she slid dimes and nickels across the laminate.

The guy beside me held a tray of shots. The smell of tequila tickled my nostrils. A young woman at the bar drank from a bottle of Southern Comfort and stared intently at the glass countertop. "I can't find my face," she cried. "I can't find my face." I don't know if it was the collection of those words or the smell or her blank expression, but it made me think of Eli.

"Eight dollars." The bartender slapped the counter to get my attention. "Sorry." I handed her a ten and walked away.

Back at the booth, Jenny and I drank our beers without exchanging words. Thankfully, after a mean, overrehearsed cover of "Whiskey Bar," the band finished their set and took a break. The music throbbed in my ears, bounced around my head like a persistent pessimistic thought.

"This is the life that every girl dreams of," she said.

"Old train stations and watered-down beer."

"Cheers." We clanked pint glasses.

"We could run away," I said.

"Let's do that," she replied.

Taken by our banter, I almost missed Cal's big entrance. He burst through the front door with his arm around a woman's shoulder. It took me a moment to realize it was Nikki, the cashier from the hardware store. He announced himself with a "let's do this" half holler. Everyone looked up from their conversations, saw him, and promptly returned to their drinking. I sank into the booth's padding.

"Whoa," he yelled when he saw us. "Look. At. This."

Nikki waved to Jenny; Jenny dutifully waved back. I knew next to nothing about Nikki. Apart from our brief exchange over spilled paint, we never crossed paths, but I was baffled by her relationship with Cal. He slithered away from her and sat opposite us in the booth.

"Just the man I wanted to see." Cal was pleased with himself, mocking. His breath smelled like he'd already been drinking for hours.

"Mark," Jenny interrupted. "Can you give us some space?"

"Sorry. Can't do it. I have business to discuss with Jack. You see, you probably heard there was an incident over at Tully's Law Office. Strange, isn't it?

"So what?"

"It's only a matter of time until we pick him up."

"For the love of God," I said. "You just can't let it go, can you? Since you're terrible at your job, I'll help you out. Eli is out of town."

"When did he leave exactly?" he asked.

"Tuesday morning. Early."

"Well, ain't that fucking convenient. B and E plus criminal mischief and arson over at Tully's on Monday night, and Eli Page gets out of Dodge the next morning. How stupid does he think we are?"

"Well—"

"Shut up," he said, realizing that he'd walked right into that one.

I stared at Jenny, and it was as if she had checked out; her eyes were vacant as she mindlessly slid three nickels along the table. Nikki, bored, began tapping her foot and staring at Jenny, hoping to engage her in some sort of can-you-believe-this-shit conversation.

"Let's be serious for a moment," he said, dropping the smile. "After all, I'm only interested in the truth. And justice. And law."

"You're a philosopher, are you?"

"Maybe," he said. "The question to be answered is this: Why would Eli Page break into a law office?"

"I don't know. Why?" I could play the part.

"Just so happens the perp made off with a couple files and some cash. I checked into his records—turns out that your famous musician is flat broke, going on bankrupt. Only a matter of time."

"That's ridiculous," I said. Cal was an expert at getting me wired. I didn't believe a word he said, but my hands were shaking as if I did.

"Papers were missing or set on fire. You wouldn't happen to know anything about that, would you? Important documents. Broken windows. Missing files. Careful little fingerprints everywhere. It's really a shame that it's this easy."

"What files?" Jenny asked, out of nowhere.

"Mostly files related to the Myers family and River Bend Farm. Another coincidence?" he asked with joy on his tongue. It was clear that he was getting a kick out of his little reveal.

"He has an alibi."

"Alibi? What do you think this is, *Law & Order*?"

"Fuck off."

"Hold on. This is just a casual convo between two guys. No need to lose your cool. Oh, wait—" He leaned back in the booth. "You see, I just so happened to look into you too. It's amazing what those little computers in my vehicle can pull up." He paused, and even though I tried to remain calm, I know he saw my jaw clench and my eyes glaze over. "Now that I think about it, maybe I should inquire about your whereabouts. Criminal mischief. Sounds like your MO. I always figured you for his sidekick, but maybe I underestimated you."

Jenny repositioned her spare change on the table. Her reaction was tempered, but I recognized the intensity and building anger in her neck muscles and forearms. The night had gone awry.

"I'm getting another," I said.

With two empty pint glasses in my grasp, I squeezed my way between a girl trying to drink from a shot glass in her cleavage and a man wearing a leather vest. The bartender filled two new glasses while I waited. The beer tasted like salt water, but I drank it in two large gulps that made my eyes water. Was it true? Was Eli broke? Did he break into the office? Is that why he ran when he did? For a vivid moment, my mind flashed on Eli weaving through the graves.

Cal's laughter shook me from my thoughts. He pushed his way in front of me and blocked my path. As he did, his newly acquired beer sloshed over the side of his glass and onto my sleeve. I had nowhere to go.

I glanced back at Jenny. Nikki sat next to her in the booth, talking about something that demanded wild, sweeping gestures. Jenny did not appear interested.

"What's a matter? Did I finally convince you that Eli's a pinhead?" Cal said.

"Get away from me."

"Save yourself."

Seriously? "Save yourself" was his advice to me like we were in some horrible action movie. I tried to wiggle by, but he stepped in my way. I changed course and he deliberately bumped into me. Despite my best efforts to remain calm, I lost control. I shoved him away from me, away from the bar. Beer spilled across his shirt. His face turned a shade of red rarely found in nature. I never made it back to the booth. The last images I recalled involved a Taser's teeth coming toward my neck, the sparkle of his giant class ring next to the bolt of electricity, and a yelp. Then everything went to black.

The stale scent of wet plywood was lodged in my nose. My face, damp from sweat or beer or both, was pancaked to the floor. When I opened my eyes, my world was fuzzy and distorted. All boots and chair legs. Voices. Maybe this is what it felt like, I thought, when you hit the bottom. Maybe it was this literal. Something tickled my neck and, by instinct or residual electricity, I flinched.

"Take it slow," a voice said. It took me a minute before I realized it was Jenny's hand against my neck.

There was blood on my lips. As I tried to sit up, my mind pieced together the rapid order of events to the best of its ability. Cal. Bar. Shove. Spill. Beer. Electricity. Flash. The jolt from the Taser sent me to the floor like a KO'd boxer, smashing my face into a barstool on the way down. And then nothing. Nada.

"Are you going to make it?" Jenny asked.

Cal was nowhere to be found. "What did you ever like about that guy?" I asked.

Jenny smiled, obviously relieved.

"I need an answer. So much depends on that answer," I said.

She withdrew her hand from my cheek and slipped it below my elbow to help me to my feet. The bartender and a couple dozen watery-eyed patrons looked on as I wobbled upright, and they applauded when I stood on my own.

"Let's get out of here," Jenny said.

In the night air, my mind cleared.

"That went sideways in a hurry," she said.

"Don't worry about it. Cal? Oh, he's harmless," I said. My sarcasm didn't land. I rubbed my neck again.

Jenny looked at me with her curious, off-kilter grin. She was trying to read me, to gauge my mental state, which I'd describe as astonishingly mellow after a high-voltage beat down.

"If I'd known he was going to be there . . ." she said, not completing her thought.

For some reason, I began to laugh, and then the laughter took hold of my whole body. My propensity for trouble or, more accurately, my ability to stumble into someone else's slapstick routine was unmatched. For a brief and fleeting moment, I thought of my father, drunk, tumbling into the Housatonic River. I wondered if it was nature or nurture that tagged me with this talent for the absurd.

"You're freaking me out," she said, laughing along with me.

"I should've guessed Cal would have a Taser on his belt," I said, fully aware that I must've seemed unhinged. "Next to his pager."

"He's always been a button pusher," she said, pleased. "It's a gift."

"Has he always been a fucking douche bag?"

As we entered the commons, I remembered the bruise on Jenny's wrist, and I wondered if it was Cal's work.

"Has he ever hit you?" I asked.

"What? No!" she said, genuinely surprised at the accusation.

"What about the bruise?"

"That wasn't him."

"I don't believe you."

"Why would I lie?"

"You don't always tell the whole truth. At least not to me."

"Is that so?"

"You didn't tell me about your mother," I said without thinking it through. She stopped walking and yanked my elbow so that I spun and faced her.

"What did Eli say?"

"He explained the situation. He assumed I knew."

"Situation? I don't have a 'situation,'" she said.

"I meant 'history.'"

"What's there to tell? My mother disappeared before I had a chance to know her. I don't remember much. It's personal." Maybe she was telling the truth or maybe she wasn't, but she did share it with Eli, which begged the question, why Eli and not me? We started walking again, but the space between us had widened.

"How about your father?" I asked. "Have you ever thought about finding him?"

She shrugged. "My mother never meant to get pregnant. Phil and Julia don't know who my father was, but after my mother—Lily was her name—after she realized she'd have to raise me on her own, she took off."

"I wasn't trying to pry."

"Yes you were."

As we continued up Church Street, she told me the stories she remembered about her mom—a total of four visits, which stopped when Jenny turned seven. She seemed happy to tell the stories out loud.

We entered Eli's enormous gate after midnight. The carriage barn felt so temporary all of a sudden. So empty. Forgotten. Sometime after three, we fell asleep in my tiny twin bed.

Early the next morning, before the sun rose, Jenny and I made love. Half asleep, we reached for each other in the dark. I acted on an impulse—the need to reach out, to connect. I'd promised to make her breakfast, but I was too sore to get out of bed. My neck felt as if it had been split apart with an axe. Instead, we lay beside each other for another half hour observing the quiet, the electricity pulsing through my fingers to her thigh. I reached through the silence and put my hand on her chest, over her pounding heart. She arched her back and slipped her lips to mine. I kissed her. She kissed me, and we locked into one another again in the humid, dimly lit room.

When I woke for good, the midmorning sun poured in through the front window, where Jenny, tangled in the stolen top sheet, stared at the river.

"I told you about my mother. Now tell me something about you," she said.

"What do you want to know?"

"Have you ever been in a serious relationship?"

"Actually, believe it or not, I was engaged once too. It was a disaster."

"How about your family? Tell me something about them."

I thought for a moment, too aware of our naked bodies to think straight. I wondered why she suddenly felt vulnerable. She had given me a little about her family, and I was yet to reciprocate. "When I was a kid, everyone called me Bird." She looked over her bare shoulder, smiled when I said "Bird." I slid out of the bed and tried to locate my clothes.

"How about *your* father?"

"He left when I was a kid. Just up and vanished."

"Do you know what happened to him?"

"I can guess."

"Maybe we're all orphans," she said.

"Or runaways."

Jenny sat on the kitchen counter, her feet crossed at the ankles. She twisted a dish towel in her hands and stared out the window, across the clover-covered yard, to where Eli's property met the road. When I reached around to gather the clean plates and glasses from the rack, she snapped me with the towel.

"You didn't answer my question."

"I trust you, I trust you," I said.

"Prove it."

"How?"

I carried the dry wineglasses into the dining room; they chirped like falsetto birds as I placed them side by side in the hutch, where they split my face in a thousand directions. I lingered for a moment at the image and then reentered the kitchen.

Jenny jumped off the counter, simultaneously tossing me the towel.

"Come on," she said. At that moment, she knew I'd do anything she asked.

In her Blazer, we followed the Battenkill as it cut through the foothills of the Greens, which dipped down to the river on one side while the Adirondacks rose up on the other. Every little imperfection in the road sent me up and down, in and out of my seat. Somewhere in the middle country, Jenny veered down an old road that curved back and forth up a hill. The pavement's surface was blanched white by the sun. Finally, it leveled out by a maple shack. Orange lines wove in and around the trees. Jenny pulled into a tiny dirt lot opposite the lines, alongside an old Subaru wagon.

There, in the lot, a sun-drenched woman in denim cutoffs and a bikini top sat on the hood of a car eating strawberries. Jenny got out of the Blazer, slammed the door, and waved. I followed, ready to demonstrate my trust.

"Wow. Hey, stranger. It's been like forever." The woman offered a strawberry to Jenny; she declined. "How's your mother holding up these days?"

"She's getting by."

"Who's the puppy dog?"

I leaned forward for an introduction but was ignored.

"I don't know, but he won't leave my side," Jenny said.

"The good ones will follow you anywhere," she said. "Hey, tell your parents we said hi."

"I will. Thanks," Jenny answered.

The woman nodded as she chomped on another strawberry. "Hey, be careful down there today," she said while chewing. "And if you see Ezra, can you tell him to get his ass up here already?"

"Will do." Jenny's voice was childlike, overly polite.

The river roared below us.

"Who was that?" I asked.

"Family friend."

Up ahead on the trail, a shirtless man with impressive chest hair hiked toward us.

"Ezra," Jenny said, "meet Jack."

"Dude. It's cool to meet you," he said with a sincerity I wasn't accustomed to. Then he looked me up and down. "I can tell, man. I can tell, Jen Jen." He gave Jenny a hug and continued up the path. "Have fun down there."

"A good friend?" I asked.

"He's a riot," she said, tugging me down the path.

At the trail bottom, a forty-foot waterfall poured into a small pool of water and propelled the Battenkill on toward the Hudson. The mist from the incessant splash drifted along the lower rocks like steam from a mill. The constant rush of the water overwhelmed the beauty. It was as if five thousand radios blasted static at full volume.

"High Rock Falls. Lovingly referred to as the Tombs," she said with a sly grin.

"You're not exactly inspiring confidence."

"Well, you said you trusted me."

"A horrible error in judgment—I see that now," I said. "What are we doing?"

"Just follow me and you'll be fine."

She stripped down to her underwear. I left all but my boxers on the trail. Then Jenny stepped into the river's mist and began to scale the left side of the falls.

"Pay attention and you'll be okay," she yelled over her shoulder.

My fingers dug into the smoothed natural grips. I followed like a good soldier, watching her every move, and the rush of blood in my ears began to mirror the rush of water beside me. The right side of my body was soaked. The wall, a death trap at first glance, was well worn, but it functioned as a ladder of sorts. In a few minutes, we'd climbed twenty-five feet.

Jenny reached for a small ledge, a stone slab that protruded four or five feet beyond the wall—a diving platform for teenagers, drunks, and adrenaline junkies. She pulled herself up with ease, as if she was made of feather and air, and then she held out her arm to help me conquer the final steps. My shoulders and chest ached. My pain subsided when I inhaled and took in the view, which went on forever above the path of the river. Jenny's underwear was soaked from the mist and her skin looked blue under the white cotton, her nipples purple and hard. Suddenly, as if by accident, I realized the rolling water was freezing cold.

"Are you ready for this?" she asked.

"Are you crazy?"

"The water below is deep, but go in feetfirst." She spoke loud to overcome the waterfall. "More important—jump away from the rocks to get as much space as you can. Okay? Do you understand?"

"Jump away." My chest rattled. "This is insane," I said.

"You've got to jump," she said. "There's no other way. You'll kill yourself if you try to get down the way we got up."

Jenny took my wet face into her hands and kissed me like she might never see me again. Then she let me go, turned, and dove off the ledge.

In that moment, everything slowed. The water stopped charging, my eyes widened, my lungs collapsed, and the blood rushed to my head. Her descent was a picture of beauty. After instructing me to go feetfirst, she dove head-first like an Olympian. Poetry in slow motion. The water cracked when she hit it and her splash jumped high over the pool. I waited, breathless, for her to resurface, but she'd disappeared into the dark and the mist. A few seconds felt like an hour. I panicked and screamed her name, but my voice was absorbed by the river's mouth. In the end, I did the only thing I could think to do—I jumped.

Somewhere between the rock and the water, I realized where I had gone wrong in life. "Trust" had always been a deadly word. I'd never really trusted a soul. Not my father, not my mother, not Casey, and certainly not Melanie. I knew that, sooner or later, they'd vanish and leave me.

Maybe my perspective had changed in Galesville. In the stillness of the jump, I didn't care if I lived or died, I just wanted to hold on to what I had and not let go.

I tucked my arms in and crashed into the water. It was like rocketing into an ice bath. The cold tightened its grip around my throat. I kicked furiously to reverse the downward plunge. Deeper and deeper I went until my toes tickled the river bottom. As I swam furiously to the surface, I felt as if I wasn't going to make it in time. I was drowning. The water was too high. When I finally broke through, I gulped the air. My chest heaved. I spun around, looking for Jenny. Where was she? In my oxygen-deprived haze, I almost didn't recognize her on the grass beside the beach.

"So, how long ago were you engaged?" she asked.

We lounged in the grass beside the river, recuperating from the jump. The adrenaline had faded from my body.

"A couple years," I said.

"What happened?"

"It fell apart. She wanted something different than I did. She wanted too much."

"Who called it off?" Jenny asked.

I wished that I could've exited the conversation gracefully, but there was no escaping.

Years ago, after Melanie slammed the apartment door, leaving me bloody on the floor, I shut down. The apartment was full of sweat and dust, always dark with the shades pulled tight to the casings. The sour smell of old milk rose from the sink. Once I peeled my face off the linoleum, I deposited myself on the couch for three days, listening to bootleg recordings of Eli Page on repeat. Eli at the Gaslight. His voice bounced and echoed as if it was trapped inside a claw-foot tub. Beyond the shuffle and scrapings of chairs, it was achingly beautiful. There was a faint Irish lull in the soothing high notes—the remnants of an accent, a generation removed.

Eventually, I snapped the shades to let the light in, put on clean clothes, and went for a walk. The early-winter chill hit me, and my pride began to sting (along with my nose, mouth, knuckles, and ribs). When I walked out to the wharf, it started to snow. Long Island Sound was a silver plate of glass, a wavy old mirror. I thought that if I ran in, I could make it out twenty yards before everything shattered and I drowned. In the distance, a huge freighter sank deep into the water. The wharf was an engineering marvel—a manmade shoreline. Beneath my feet were layers upon layers of compressed garbage. I was seeping into that landfill landscape like the freighter in the Sound.

I saw the police as I approached the apartment, but I had no idea they were waiting for me. Still, I resigned myself to the outcome. Sometimes I wondered if I was even there—the whole ordeal was more like an overwrought play than an actual significant, life-altering moment in my life. That wasn't me. That was some other Jack Wyeth.

Months later, after I was released from Connecticut, I'd made a conscious decision to leave that old, tired persona in New Haven. Reinvention, I thought, was the best practice. The idea was that I could start over as a new Jack Wyeth, a better Jack Wyeth, an honest Jack Wyeth. I

doubted, even then, that reinvention was possible. Reha-
bilitation was probably closer to the truth. Was a criminal
always a criminal, a slacker always a slacker, a liar always a
liar? That was what Melanie proclaimed. At first I set out
to prove her wrong, to prove that people are more complex, to prove that change is possible. After a month and a
half in Galesville, I was looking for something more than
reinvention.

Still, here I was again, thinking about that old Jack Wyeth.

"It was a mutual decision," I finally answered. Why do
we lie when we know it will end badly? I didn't have the
nerve to go into the details with Jenny. Not yet. I knew it
would change the way she looked at me. "How about you
and Cal?" I asked.

"Mark is a better man than he lets on, but it was never
going to happen."

"Then why were you engaged?"

"It's Galesville. We'd dated on and off since high
school. After I came back from college, I had these notions
about settling down. They almost convinced me he was
the man."

"They?"

"Mark and my dad. They're best buds," she answered.
"Luckily, I pulled the emergency brake."

What was going to happen between *us*? That's what
I wanted to ask, but I'd spent all of my courage earlier in
the day. In many ways, after the splash, I was new again.
I was a kid sitting next to a mysterious girl and dream-
ing about the future. The river water crashed along the

rocks, and I was content, for once, to listen and enjoy the moment without searching for its flaws.

A confession.

On more than a few occasions, I pulled out the 1949 Martin or the Gibson J-50, sat on the front step, and plucked haphazardly at their strings. My fingertips rehardened. While I played, I wondered where Eli was and whether he'd ever make it back to Galesville. Part of me feared that I'd never see him again; an equal part feared his return.

I strummed the chords to "Girl from the North Country," *Nashville Skyline* style. Then, when my mind grew quiet, I picked apart one of Eli's called "Maybe the Time's Not Right." It seemed to fit my mood—it was a song about doubting your convictions. *Doing nothin' is always easier than doin' somethin'*, it went, *and doin' somethin' almost always gets you nothin'.*

A truck revved its engine out front. Tig smashed his face into the living-room window and launched into an unbreakable series of low, menacing barks designed to alert the world of danger—each one snapped as if it were on a spring. Startled, I dropped the guitar in the grass, stood up, and watched that same Dodge Ram buzz by the gate, taunting me yet again before bursting down the road in a cloud.

"Leave it, buddy," I said to the dog, halfheartedly. He stopped barking, but the remnants of his alarm clung to the glass. I went into the kitchen to scrounge up some Windex.

At first, we slept in the carriage barn; we ate dinners at the harvest table (Eli's possessions moved to neat, orderly piles on the floor); we relaxed, linked together, on Eli's sofa; and we strolled, hand in hand, along the river like two insufferable teens. For a brief time, Eli's house was a respite for Jenny, a retreat from her familial obligations.

I buried my face in the newspaper. Jenny stood by the stove, an empty travel mug in her hand, and waited for the teapot to whistle.

"What're you thinking?" she asked when she caught me staring over the top of the paper.

"I'm wondering if this is what it would be like."

"If what would be like?" She poured the water into the mug.

"Living together. Getting hitched. You'd make tea; I'd stare aimlessly out the window. That'd be a good life, wouldn't it?"

"Maybe," she said. "Maybe." She lingered for a moment by the stove, stirring sugar into her tea. "But what makes you think I would marry a layabout like you?"

"We should do something tonight."

"Like what?"

"Go out on an actual date. Get dressed up. Go to dinner. You know, like people do on a Saturday night."

"Really?"

"Why not? We can play the part."

To my surprise, Jenny warmed to the idea.

Unfortunately, less than an hour before our reservation, I realized I had nothing to wear that would qualify as "dressed up." When Jenny arrived, I was in Eli's room, looking for clothes that would fit me, and the occasion.

"Are you ready?" she yelled from the bottom of the stairs.

"Hold on," I said as I stuffed myself into an old suit that I'd found in the closet. It was short in the arms and legs, but it would have to do. His dress shoes were worn but comfortable. The jacket smelled like mothballs and Sambuca. When I straightened my spine, I had to adjust the shoulders and found it hard to breathe.

"What's taking so long?" she asked.

"All right, all right. I'm coming down."

In the tiny second-floor bathroom, I splashed water on my face and glanced in the mirror. My eyes were bloodshot, my cheeks sagged, the beard that I'd acquired was growing wild.

At the foot of the stairs, Jenny twirled around in a green dress. Her heels clicked on the wood floor. I made my way to her side. Then, almost by force of habit, I ran my hand through her hair and tucked it behind her ear.

"Look at us," she said.

I cleared my throat, lifted my chin slightly, and opened the front door.

"Right this way, miss," I said. She took my arm and I led her to the Chevy.

When we arrived at Fiddler's Elbow—the only table-clothed joint in town—we were ushered to a window seat. A candle flame flickered, its yellow glow reflected in the glass and danced like hop clover in the wind.

"Do I look like Eli?" I asked.

"Can't say I've ever seen him in a suit," she answered.

"I feel like I'm dressed for my own funeral." My arms itched underneath the jacket. It was strange to be in Eli's clothes, as if I was cloaked in his costume, incognito. I had a horrible habit of slouching, but the jacket pulled me upright.

"What's good?" I asked, unfolding my napkin and placing it on my lap.

"It's been a while since I've dined at this fine establishment."

"Doesn't seem like a place that Cal would enjoy."

"That's the truth. He'd never step foot in here, but a friend of mine and I used to eat here whenever we were celebrating."

"Celebrating what?"

"I can't remember, exactly," she said. "School. Engagements. New adventures." Her eyes—locked on her napkin, her bread plate, her water glass—never rose to meet mine.

"You must've been close with this 'friend.'"

"Very. We were best friends."

"Were? Where is she now?"

Jenny didn't answer. I knew that I should let her off the hook.

"I'll have to introduce you to Casey," I said. "If you're ever up for a trip to Saratoga Springs. He's a bit of a jackass, but he's well-intentioned. Most of the time." Those last words were spoken more for my own benefit than Jenny's.

"Are you happy?" Jenny asked.

"Huh?"

"Happy. Are you happy, Jack?"

"Yeah, sure. Happy enough." The heat rose in my face, and I reached for my ice water.

"What does 'happy enough' mean? Are we only meant to have so much?"

"How about you? Are you happy enough?"

"I'm getting there, bit by bit," she answered, her eyes still fixed in the window.

The waiter arrived and we ordered. Soft music hummed in the air. The tune was familiar, and it bugged me. Finally, when the food arrived, I realized it had been a Muzak version of Eli's "All Keep Calm." I laughed.

"What?" Jenny asked.

I told her about the song, and she laughed too but quickly let it go.

"So, what is it with you and Eli?" I asked, acting casual.

"What do you mean?"

"How did you two become friends?"

"I wouldn't say we're friends."

"What would you say?" I asked.

Jenny stared at me. Her gaze was stern, serious. "It's not important."

"Yes, it is. You're his only real connection to what goes on outside River Bend. How did you meet? You must've made a good impression."

"The opposite, actually."

"How so?"

Again, Jenny didn't answer. Instead, she pulled inward and her face tightened.

"I'm sorry," I said, noting the change. "I didn't realize the discussion was off-limits, but sort of proves my point, doesn't it?"

"What do you want from me, Jack?" she asked.

"What do you mean? I don't want anything," I said, feeling the lie flutter and fade in my chest because I did want something, and I felt guilty about the wanting. I wanted first and foremost to know the answer to that question, and I thought it was odd that we hadn't talked about it. What was she holding back?

"I've been used before. I can see it coming."

"Hold on."

"Let's just eat."

And we did. She didn't speak to me at all during the meal.

For dessert, we shared a rhubarb crumble as we both gazed at our own reflections in the window, interrupted by the flickering candle and headlights from passing cars.

Nina Simone sang out from the speakers.

What if I stood up and grabbed Jenny by the wrist? What then? What if, by impulse or instinct or desire, I hugged her close to me and we danced? I wondered if Eli ever danced in that suit, and, if he did, who he'd danced with. I couldn't stand; the time had passed, the impulse had faded. I looked at myself in the window, and I felt as if I'd lost something precious, something I could never regain. I wondered if Jenny felt the same way.

"Let's go upstairs," I said.

"That's not a good idea." Days later, after tensions had eased, we were wrapped up in the living room, underneath a blanket, and my eyelids were garage doors, too heavy to lift. Yawning, I stretched my arms and tipped my head back until my neck crunched.

Earlier, Tig and I had hiked the trail to the graveyard and back, and before dinner, I'd spent three hours in the study, sifting through papers. By sundown, I was running on empty.

"Think of it as an adventure," I said.

"We should respect his boundaries."

"He's not here," I said, hoping that the obvious would be enough. "It's just a bed."

Back and forth we went until she gave in. "Fine. I don't care. Whatever you want to do." I stood, took her arm, and led her up the squeaky stairs. As soon as we entered Eli's room, I collapsed on the bed. She lingered.

"What are all these Post-its for?" Jenny asked before I faded.

"Cheat sheets."

"I didn't realize it had gotten that bad."

The next morning, in the bird-chirping predawn, I woke to a Jenny-less bed. Had I dreamt it all? There's nothing like the terror of confusion to unsleep your eyes. I rolled off the mattress and stumbled into the hall. A cold draft slipped across my bare ankles. Jenny stood fifteen feet in front of me, motionless in the doorway of the guest bedroom.

"What are you doing?" I asked, even though I already knew the answer. Or part of it.

I crossed the hall to be at her side. When I reached out and placed my hand on her shoulder, she pulled away, slid into the room, and ran her hands on the quilt, smoothing out the wrinkles.

"Why didn't you tell me about this?"

"What's there to tell?"

Jenny circled the room in slow motion, running her fingers across every surface, examining every drawer, exploring the closet and under the bed. The room was a shell for someone's life to fit into, hollow and abandoned. For some reason, the discovery injured Jenny.

"Come on. Let's get out of here," I said.

"Not yet," she replied softly.

"We shouldn't be in here." My nerve started to falter.

"You're the one that insisted we come upstairs," she said. In the slivers of sunlight that penetrated the room, I saw that Jenny's eyes were wet, her cheeks tear-stained.

"What's wrong?"

"Just leave me alone."

Later that day, after she shut me out for hours, Jenny returned to River Bend. Tig and I were preparing for our walk along the property line—by then, a daily routine. She joined us, but she didn't say a word for nearly a half hour.

"Look," Jenny finally spoke. She pointed to a section of the wire fence that had been clean cut for easy passage. "Proof that it's not an animal."

For a third time, I tried to fix the fence, but it was beyond repair. I'd have to dig new holes for the posts.

We started back toward the house. Tig bounded ahead on his stocky legs, leaving us alone. Jenny's pace slowed.

"Why didn't you tell me about the bedroom?" she asked.

"I didn't think it was important." She was hiding things from me. I was hiding things from her. The truth was coming out in dribs and drabs. She knew more about Eli than she was letting on, but I was accused of withholding. "It's meaningless to me," I argued. "Until you tell me otherwise, it's just another room, a doll's house."

She sighed.

"Whenever I ask you about Eli, you turn off, push me away. Why? Why can't you talk about it? It makes me think you're hiding something from me."

"He deserves his privacy. I do too," she said.

"Yes. We all do. No one is saying otherwise."

"There's just a lot going on now," she continued. "Here, at home, at the barn. It's too much. If I open the door, even just a sliver, it'll all come out. Do you understand? And I can't deal with that. Not now. Not with everything else."

"But you can trust me. You know that, right?"

Her silence said more than any words she could've uttered.

"I'm trying. As hard as I can. One of these days, I hope you can meet me halfway."

Jenny always slept on her side, in a fetal position, with her knees tucked to her chest. I slept on my back, tossed around, and often teetered on the edge of the mattress. Two or three times each night, my legs twitched, offering a warning sign that I was about to plummet to the floor. One night in late July, my twitching had me awake before the sun. I watched her sleep.

Eventually, Jenny slid off the bed and opened the window shades. The shallow light warmed my exposed feet. Naked except for her cotton underwear, sculpted tight to her flesh, she stood between Eli's heavy taupe curtains. She gazed out the window, trancelike. Her body tilted somewhat, as if one leg was longer than the other.

"I know you're awake," she said.

She'd been spending more and more time at the Flynn homestead and, consequently, less and less time at River Bend. Somehow, in the brief time we were together, we'd lost momentum.

"Are you okay?" I asked.

"Tired, I guess. I wish I could sleep." She grabbed a fistful of shirt from the floor and tucked her head through its opening. Then she pulled on her jeans.

Sure, relationships ebb and flow, but this wasn't a simple symptom of time flexing its muscles. I was holding back and she was holding back, and there was no moving forward if both of us were carrying rocks in our pockets.

I got up and put my clothes on.

After she slipped on her sandals, Jenny headed for the door. She paused.

"I wasn't honest with you, Jack," she said.

"How so?"

"I knew the girl who used to live in that room." It took me a long moment to realize she was talking about Eli's guest bedroom. "We were friends."

"I don't understand." I was confused, but of course, Jenny would've known the previous owners of the house.

"After he bought the house, Eli must've kept the room intact, or just ignored it altogether. I don't know why he would do that, but who knows why he does anything."

"This house is full of secrets," I said. She turned her head, arched her right eyebrow, and looked at me. "Let me show you something."

She followed me to the first floor, across the living room, and to the study door.

"If I show you what's behind the door," I said, "will you promise to help me?"

"Help you what?"

"Tell Eli's story."

"No. You know better."

"You don't need to protect him. Not in this way."

She glared at me. "I won't be a part of it. The Eli that lives here, under this roof, is not the man you think he is. Whatever you plan to dig up is dead and buried and not coming back."

"Are you sure about that?"

"Open the door, Jack."

I hesitated before reaching up and lifting the key from the casing.

She narrowed her eyes, waiting for my next move.

I opened the door.

She gasped as I did the first time I saw it. A pause and stutter was quickly followed by a burst of energy. Her feet were unable to stay put as she thumbed through the records in the black plastic milk crates, bounded around the room, and touched everything. She wiped the dust from the guitar strings of the Sunburst acoustic I'd propped in the corner. I remained silent, eyeing her from the doorway as she then casually wandered through the room, taking it all in.

"We shouldn't be in here," she said unconvincingly.

"Probably not, but it's too late now."

She shot me a disapproving look. I shrugged.

"This is interesting. What do you make of it?" She pointed to a small picture hung on the wall above the row of guitar cases. A crowd in a field. From the clothes and the color quality, I guessed it was from the late '60s, early '70s.

I shook my head. "Doesn't look familiar to me."

"It's the fairgrounds," she said. "Before it expanded." Letting that statement hang in the air, she picked up three boxes from the floor and began to look through the photographs.

Part of me didn't believe her. Why would Eli have a framed picture of the old Washington County Fairgrounds in his study? It didn't make sense, but at the same time, I knew Jenny was the Rosetta stone, the key that could unlock it all.

I snatched a picture frame from the desk. "What about this?" I asked, holding it up in front of her. "Any ideas?"

Jenny's focus shifted to the photograph. She reached over and took it from me.

"Be careful, the glass is broken," I said.

The black-and-white image showed Eli, maybe twenty-five, and a woman sitting on a picnic table. By the lack of shadow, I imagined it to be lunch hour on a midsummer's day. Eli sat on the tabletop, his feet planted on the bench, a guitar in one hand. The young woman sat next to him, facing away, sketching in an oversized notebook.

Jenny lifted the frame closer to her eyes as if she were analyzing the clarity of a jewel. I placed my hand on the small of her back. Her body was tense—her muscles tight, her shoulders locked. She slid the frame onto the desk and pretended the picture inside was meaningless, but I knew better.

"You know who it is, don't you?" I asked.

Jenny didn't acknowledge my question.

"The woman. What can you tell me about her?"

Her chin lifted ever so slightly as she stole a quick glance at me. Jenny's fearlessness, her self-assurance, her exuberance, all of those traits that I noticed when we first met were gone. Suddenly, she seemed as nervous and unsure of herself as I did.

"Her name is Hadley," she said.

"Hadley? Okay. That's something. I can work with that."

Jenny stared at me, seemingly unsure of what she should do or say next. Then it was as if she made the decision to jump all in.

"You've only been here a couple months, Jack."

"What does that—?"

"You're caught up in this Eli-as-cultural-hero bullshit, but that Eli doesn't exist. It's PR. It's a persona he created. It's a persona Barry Gettleson pushed and shaped for years."

"What's your point?"

"There's more to Eli Page than the spin. Maybe the *truth* you're looking for is that the man deserves his privacy."

"I'm not out to hijack his life, Jenny. I'm looking for answers."

"So you can put them in a book."

"He asked me to write the book. I'm just doing my job."

"I don't believe that," she said. "I don't believe he wants a book about his life."

"Okay. Then why does he want me here if not to ghostwrite?"

"Yes, yes. That's the right question."

We both took a moment to catch our breath.

"Tell me about Hadley," I said, wearing her down. "What's her last name?"

She opened her mouth to speak but was interrupted by a knock at the door. Tig stood up and moved his furry body from the doormat. A shrill yelp was followed by three menacing barks. Then he gave up and crumpled into a ball on the living-room rug.

Jenny moved toward the door, but I grabbed her arm. "What's her last name?"

"Let go," she said.

"I'm sorry." I gave her back her arm. What was I doing? I had lost my damn mind.

"Myers. Her last name was Myers."

More pounding.

Jenny opened the front door to find Nikki standing there, her eyeliner smudged, her shirt wrinkled.

"Nikki, what's wrong?" Jenny asked.

"I thought someone should tell you."

"Tell me what?"

"I don't want to."

Jenny shrank as if she knew what was about to be said.

"Spit it out," I said from behind the sofa. My voice was direct, annoyed.

"Someone painted over your mural," she said. "It's destroyed."

"Come on, slowpoke!" A boy in full sprint, his skinny arms dangling at his sides, his feet in white sneakers flop-flopping like they were three or four sizes too big, rammed into my knee and bounced off before continuing toward his destination.

"Sammy. Watch where you're going, for crying out loud," his mother, the slowpoke, yelled. She lunged after the boy and grabbed him by the shirt collar, all while hugging a baby wrapped to her chest. "I'm so sorry," she said to me. "Sammy. Turn around and tell this man you're sorry," she demanded.

"Why?"

"Do it."

"Sar-ree," he said. "Can we hurry now?" he asked his mother. The woman looked to me for sympathy, shook her head, and carried on down Main Street. I knew her from somewhere, but I couldn't put a name to the face.

When they reached the edge of the commons, the boy sprinted down the sidewalk and knocked into a group of peers like a bowling ball into pins—a few boys toppled and rolled around on the grass. Sammy cheered. "I don't know what to do with you," his mother said to herself. "So full of energy." The woman was my age, more or less, but the lines on her face told me she had lived twice as many years and hadn't slept in months.

Up ahead, I saw a group of a dozen or so people gathered with Helen Walker, who'd led the protest of the mural and boycott of the IGA.

Sammy and the boys screeched. The woman whipped her head around to check on her son, who tried to climb a tree but was too short to reach a critical branch. Where had we met before? As he fell to the ground, I finally remembered. Penny was her name, Penny Sweet. After the news of her husband's death, the family picture had been posted everywhere including the Depot bar, which was where I'd seen it last. For a while, the Galesville Library collected donations for the children in honor of Captain Sweet's service and his untimely death.

Sammy abandoned the tree and ran after a kid half his size. "You can run, but you can't hide." His mother ran after him. As she did, she looked over her shoulder, nodded at me, and offered a soft smile, as if to say thanks for some reason.

Jenny and I had agreed to meet at the mural, but she was nowhere to be found. I wondered if Helen Walker's little boycott had scared Jenny off, but it wasn't like Jenny to be deterred by conflict. I glanced at my phone, but there were no messages or missed calls.

The boycotters lined up along Main Street, across the road from the IGA. Mrs. Walker's irritating voice was magnified by a bullhorn. "Don't tread on us," she repeated. The action did not stop people from grocery shopping, but it did distract from the mural itself, which had been marred by vandals. A bucket of paint had been tossed on the Eli figure and his cohorts.

The makeshift protest reminded me of a photograph I'd found in Eli's study. In it, the image of a dark-haired woman, college age, in Washington Square Park; she was holding an illegible sign above her head and her mouth was open wide in midscream. Hadley. Hadley Myers. H.M. Now I knew the name.

Again, I gazed down Main Street for Jenny to no avail.

A couple of men, coming from the nearby Stewart's Shop, stopped at the mural to get a closer look.

"Of course they destroyed it," one of them said. "I would expect nothing less."

"A few rotten apples. Always the case," his companion said. His voice was raspy, mere minutes away from abandoning him. "Dangerous to speak in generalizations."

I recognized the voices from my first visit to the hardware store.

Across the street, Helen Walker raised a sign over her shoulders. It had an image of Jenny, taken from the newspaper, with a blindfold drawn on. Just then, I remembered a cartoon I had seen of Eli. I couldn't recall the caption, but a crudely drawn Eli Page had a guitar smashed over his head—it pinned his arms to his body, the snapped strings had curled in all directions. Instead of a harmonica, there was a rag in his mouth. A bump on top his head peeked out from his mop of hair. Birds danced around the bump as if they were drunk and stoned. The cartoon was from some Southern newspaper (I can't remember which) in the summer of '68.

"Why did you stop speaking out?" I once asked Eli.

"I didn't."

"You stopped showing up. I read that. Everyone was pissed."

"It wasn't somethin' I decided to do or not do. That's life."

"Not true. You made a decision to walk away."

"Do I look like a leader?" he asked. "I wasn't who they wanted me to be. And it got harder and harder as time went by to make that clear. What was I supposed to do?"

"It was your fight as much as it was theirs."

"What you start out fighting for is not necessarily what you end up fighting for."

"But you came back."

"By then, protest songs were out. Everything cut to the quick."

Those words still echoed in my head. *Everything cut to the quick.*

For a moment, coming out of that memory, I thought I saw Eli across the street, leaning against a maple. When I moved in for a closer look, I saw that it wasn't Eli at all—it was the owner of the Dodge Ram. Arms crossed, lips tight, he stared at me before slipping on sunglasses.

Sweat dripped off my forehead and stung my eyes. I tried to wipe it away, but my hands tensed up. I thought about running over there and tackling him, shaking some answers loose. Instead, I was distracted by Cal, who pulled his cruiser into the IGA parking lot. Maybe he could help put a name to the face, I thought, if he was in a giving mood.

"Not going to Tase me again, are you?" I asked as I approached, hands in the air.

"Listen, smart-ass." He paused. "I would apologize, but I'm working."

"No surprise there. Have you seen Jenny?"

"No. I have not. Have you?"

"No."

He kept his attention on the small group of boycotters. "This is a waste of time," he said, shaking his head.

"Aren't you with them?" I asked, pointing to Helen Walker and friends.

"No. I'm with the law." He spoke those words so matter-of-factly that I assumed they'd been plucked from some John Wayne movie. "Plus I didn't think the mural was half bad."

"All right, lawman. Maybe you can help me out. Can you tell me the name of that guy over there by the maple tree?" I could pretend for a moment Cal and I got along if it yielded some info.

"What guy?"

"Sinewy guy with the sunglasses," I said, nodding over my shoulder. "Drives a black Ram with a gun rack, if that helps."

"There's no one there."

I spun around, and sure enough, Cal was right. The guy had disappeared again. As I searched, a Harley's roar split the air, frightening the birds from their wires and boughs.

It was then, in the chaos of the noise, that I saw Jenny. Red hot. Jaw sharp. Eyes locked on the protestors. She did not flinch or smile or wave when she noticed me standing by Cal. Instead, she walked steadily in my direction, and as she did, I felt that she was looking right through me, to some future in the unmade distance.

"How long have you been here?" I asked.

"A few minutes."

"You look sick."

She kicked at the ground with the tip of her boots, and then quickly raised her eyes.

"I need your help with the supplies. They're in the back."

Jenny and I gathered the paint cans, tarps, and brushes and carried them to the mural.

"Do you think you can re-create it?"

She nodded, and then she went to work. Like a surgeon's assistant, I handed Jenny the tools she needed—spray cans and stencils and brushes—while she repainted in a hyperfocused state. By the time the sun set, the boycotters had left, but several hangers-on had gathered to watch Jenny in action. Each detail was reinstalled. Her version of Eli slowly came back into view. In the end, it was a near replica of the original, except that in the background she added the boycotters, their faces contorted, and their signs on fire. Then she signed it: "Summer 2010."

The next morning, when I reached across the bed to pull Jenny toward me, she was gone. To be fair, she'd warned me. "I can't stay the night," she'd said after we'd washed the paint from our hands and curled up in Eli's bed, but I didn't believe her. Attempting to ignore the cold impression left behind on the mattress, I rolled over only to be rattled by three noises in quick succession: tires on the driveway, a heavy car door slamming shut, and Barry Gettleson's voice.

I launched out of bed to peek out the open window and confirm what I already knew.

Eli was home.

A beat-up green-and-yellow cab idled in the driveway. Its Capitaland logo half caked in muck. Gettleson stepped into the grass. "What did I tell you?" he asked sharply. "Let me be clear. I. Will. Be. There. Tonight. Do you understand? I will be there tonight. Stop wasting my time with your bullshit. Are you there? Can you hear me?" It took me a moment to realize he was speaking into his cell. I leaned closer to the window screen to put a face to the name "Barry Gettleson." He was skinnier than I imagined, gangly, and his extraordinary length made his head sit like a watermelon on a stick. (A stick in a shiny suit, but nevertheless, a stick.) He held his phone in the air as if to offer it up to the sun. "I hate this fucking town," he yelled, as he wandered down the road to find service.

The car's trunk popped open. A leather-faced, button-lipped old cabman stepped out of the driver's side, proceeded to the rear of his vehicle, and lifted a large suitcase from the trunk. The rear passenger door creaked open and Eli crawled out. Frail and frazzled, as if he'd withstood hours of electroshock, he'd aged a decade in the few weeks we'd been apart. All his sharp edges had been dulled.

A breeze drifted through the open window. The curtains swayed.

When I yanked on my jeans, something pierced my thigh. "Goddamn it!" I said through my teeth. I buttoned and zipped before digging into my pocket to discover the key to Eli's study. Was the study door open? I pressed the silver key, a bird's beak with three fangs, into my palm as I tried to remember how I'd left the door.

Time was running out. I made the bed with the speed and efficiency of hotel housekeeping. My "crap, crap, crap" was followed by a louder "Where's my fucking sock?" I stuffed the key back into my pocket, smoothed out the quilt, and grabbed my shirt from the floor.

Slowly, I shut the window, watching Eli offer the driver a tip. The cabbie refused, waving him off. Gettleson returned, grabbed the bags from the driveway, and headed toward the house. I locked the window and closed the shade. Still one-socked, I barreled down the stairs, turned the corner around the banister, and threw myself into to my boots.

Tig was frantic, spinning in circles and nosing the door. "Hold on," I said as I ran to the living room, locked the study and returned the key to its hiding place, straightened the furniture, and tossed magazines into random piles. Tig snapped three times. Sharp, piercing barks—he knew what was on the other side. I rushed to the front door. Listened. Nothing. Three more barks. I tried to calm the dog, but in his mania, he scratched me twice with this front paw. The white marks on my forearm burned before they rose and turned red. "Fine. Have it your way." I opened the door. Tig sprung forward in a blur, whipping around the corner of the house and out of sight.

When I finally stepped outside and looked around, there was no sign of Eli or Gettleson. Just a big suitcase and a few bags by the carriage barn door. I followed the dog's path around the side of the house and spotted the men and the dog at the riverside. By the time I'd reached them, Gettleson had wandered off again, phone in the air. Tig sat next to Eli, panting, enjoying the attention as his companion scratched his floppy ears like he used to do.

"Welcome home," I said. "How're you feeling?"

He grunted.

"That good?"

"Dizzy. From the car ride."

"Not used to the winding roads anymore?"

"He drove like the highway was fallin' into the Hudson."

"Where'd Gettleson run off to?"

"He's around . . . around . . . he's always around."

"Good. I'll finally get to meet him in person."

"Fair warning: You aren't missin' much," Eli said. "He's a prick. Always been a prick."

I laughed—a by-product of nervous energy, relief, and confusion. The homecoming didn't seem to move Eli. I searched his face for an expression of happiness, anger, anything. If possible, he appeared more disconnected, more removed. When he spoke, his voice was garbled and wispy like smoke extinguished from a campfire.

He bent down, picked up a handful of rocks, and tossed them into the Battenkill. Underhand. A dozen little circles spread out along the water's surface, but they were quickly overrun by the river's incessant march.

"Seems high. The water. Higher than normal."

"We had a lot of rain while you were away." I swatted a team of mosquitoes from my forehead and cleared my throat. "Otherwise, we tried to keep things in order," I said. "The same as you left it."

"We?" Eli asked. He still had an uncanny ability to uncover what I so feebly hid. I shrugged. "Did you stack the wood by the mudroom?"

"I did."

"How 'bout the brush in the back?"

"Taken care of."

"The dog? Did you make sure he wasn't loafin' about feeling sorry for himself?"

"More or less."

Eli bent down to look in Tig's eyes. "You're an old one, aren't you? Me and you, facin' that abyss, and there's nothin' to be done." He scratched under the dog's jaw. Then he stood and looked back at the farm.

From the riverside, the front of the house appeared smaller than I knew it to be. The paint job had already begun to fade.

"Did you find what you were looking for?" I asked as we began to work our way back.

"Does anyone . . . ever?"

"I'm serious," I said, sick of the nonanswers.

"I saw a dozen doctors, of varying degrees of uselessness, and they all said the same thing—it's just a matter of time. It's just a matter of time."

"Was that the official diagnosis?" I asked, only half joking.

He opened the door and entered his house. Gettleson was in the kitchen, searching through the refrigerator like a teenager with the munchies. His thick gray eyebrows made him appear gruff, impatient. Despite his age (mid-sixties), he reminded me of a child. Must've been a hellion in his day. I imagined a spitfire grandmother raising him, laying out his career options early on: strip club proprietor, entertainment manager, or hit man.

"Jack of hearts," he said when he noticed my presence. "Follow me outside. I'm waiting for a call." He carried a big bottle of apple juice he'd taken from the fridge.

Behind us, Eli clunked up the staircase to his room. Tig plopped down on the stair landing. No doubt he'd stay there until Eli returned. I, on the other hand, against my better judgment, followed Gettleson. From the driveway, I glanced back at the second-floor window, wondering if my body's imprint was left on the bed. When I turned back to meet Gettleson, his pupils narrowed and his eyes appeared to darken.

"He's not well," he said. "It's now or never. No more fucking around."

"Not well how? What's the diagnosis?"

"None of your business—that's the official medical term. It's a rare condition for the celebrity types. Understand?"

"Well, maybe the book's not the best—"

"Maybe you should shut your mouth and do what I'm paying you to do. The book's the only thing, Kemosabe. Don't you forget it. We're trying to capture Eli, bottle him up, so that his legacy doesn't fade. Tell me you get this."

I stared at him, and I could feel the blood pulse through my body.

"Why are you suddenly playing hard to get?" he asked.

I listened to the river, hoping it would provide me with some direction.

He took a swig of apple juice from the bottle.

"How long are you staying?" I asked.

"A couple hours tops."

His phone rang, and he looked down at the number.

"Got to take this, Jack-off," he said.

Gettleson was a leech. What did Dylan sing in the New York sessions: "I've been double-crossed too much. At times I think I've lost my mind"? He could've been ranting about Eli and Barry Gettleson. Eli saw it, right? He did call him a prick. It wasn't as if Gettleson was fooling anyone. But if Eli knew that Gettleson was using him, what did he think about me? Was I just another hanger-on, another parasite, another thief? Eli, since the '60s, rarely met anyone who did not want something from him, and I was just another in a long line of users.

A car arrived for Gettleson before lunch. Even Tig was happy to see him go.

With Eli hidden upstairs and Gettleson on his way to the train station, I drove to Belanger's to find Jenny. After all, there was a chance that she'd stroll into the house (or bedroom) to find Eli. I had to give her a heads-up. When I arrived at the barn, Ivory lifted his head slightly and looked at me as if he could see me standing there.

"It's Jack Wyeth," I said.

"Of course it is," he said. "She's not here."

"I thought she was working today."

"Was. That's correct."

"When did she go?"

"Checked out a couple of hours ago. Had something urgent to do. I don't ask questions."

Maybe she already knew about Eli, I thought. Maybe she saw him come into town. Word gets around fast.

"Is she coming back?"

"No. I'm closing up as we speak." He didn't move.

I drove back to town, punching the gas and racing through the village center, the commons, North Church Street. As I accelerated, I eyed every inch of the street to make sure I wasn't missing the Blazer, Jenny on the sidewalk, or Cal in the speed trap. The sun beat through the windshield. Sweat gathered on my neck, soaking my collar. I flicked on the AC, but the blower was shot.

When I made it back to River Bend, I knew I was too late. Something was off. The house was wide open. Eli stood in the doorway, his body twisted like a corkscrew.

"Where'd you go?" He squinted. His eyebrows scrunched together as his voice trailed off and the words rose in the air. "I'm upstairs for a second and you're gone."

"I went looking for Jenny," I said. "Any chance she was here?"

The answer was yes; I saw it when his eyes shifted to the left. I saw it as he tried to hide in his beard. Suddenly, I had an overwhelming urge to apologize for something I had yet to put to words. He rubbed his chin as if he was contemplating punishment.

"She was here," he said.

"Was she surprised to see you?" My voice wavered. I stepped into the house beside Eli. He moved to block my path. "What did she say?"

Eli swallowed hard, and I could see that it pained him greatly to speak whatever words he had to speak.

"What did she say?" I repeated.

"She said her father was dead."

It was a science of memory as much as ceremony. Five service members stood a dozen yards from the mourners—their uniforms tight and impeccable, their faces cold as granite, their hat brims tipped to shield their eyes. To their side, a noncommissioned officer. Another uniformed man, much older, stood apart, perpendicular to the line of the clean-shaven honor guard. Whether by instinct or recollection, I knew the drill.

"Load." On command, the five men shifted to the right. "Ready." They unlocked. "Aim." They lifted their rifles to their shoulders, cranked their heads, and pointed the muzzles over the casket. I closed my eyes. "Fire." *Crack.* They returned to port arms, rifles diagonally in front of their bodies. "Aim." Up. "Fire." *Crack.* Return. "Aim." Up.

"Fire." *Crack*. Return. As each shot thundered against the clouds, my neck muscles tightened beneath Eli's borrowed tie. "Cease firing," the officer snapped.

The echoes faded. I lifted my head ever so slightly to witness the grief, which rose out of the air with the bugle's call. Alone in a crowd of headstones, the bugler was cloaked by the shadows of charcoal clouds, the distant hills his backdrop. The wailing of the instrument slowed to an excruciating pace—the spaces between the notes were filled with such longing and sorrow that my chest ached. I clamped my teeth, locking my jaw in place.

The unit removed the flag from the casket and folded it into a little triangular pillow—its white stars shimmered against the blue background, headlights in the dawn. Then the NCO presented the bundle to Mrs. Flynn like a nurse passes a newborn to its weepy-eyed mother. "In God we trust," he muttered. Julia Flynn's slouched body, an upside-down J, shook and shook as she sobbed and dug her fingers deep into the cloth.

A circle of mourners descended on Mrs. Flynn. She was the epicenter of grief, alone in time and space, floating above the casket with the rotting body inside, among the blue hue of heaven inside the flag, beyond its stars.

The crowd exhaled before dispersing through the cemetery's gravel paths. Tiny armies of mourners shuffled to their cars. I followed their lead while pinching the corners of my eyes. Car doors thumped shut, engines turned over, and wheels tracked on pea stone.

Trees swayed in the wind.

A soldier stood watch.

It never occurred to me that Phil Flynn had served in the armed forces. He was the right age for Vietnam, but one doesn't consider those things without some trigger to aid the mind—a picture, a medal, a conversation. Now I couldn't help but imagine Phil coming home from the war, going to the mill to find work, and searching for whatever order he could find.

The family lingering at the graveside. I watched them through the safety of my car window. Mrs. Flynn hadn't moved from her seat. Cal held a clump of red dirt in his fist. Blood or not, it was clear that he was family. His bond with Phil was something I never quite understood, but it was real. Jenny reached out and clutched her mother's frail shoulder. Both women were tired saplings in a windstorm. I was just another useless soul, imprisoned in my car. I pulled out into the worn, rutted path, but before I made it to the gate, Jenny crossed the field of stones, opened the passenger-side door, and jumped in.

"Go," she said. I'd been mistaken. She wasn't crying. Not an eyelash was out of place. Maybe, I thought, she was fed up with the tears, the endless nose blowing, the ongoing sob stories that accompany the first days of mourning. Or, more likely, she was like me—she pushed it all down deep for another time, a less open and vulnerable time, a private moment between herself and the bathroom mirror.

"I hate the bugle," she said, mostly to herself.

The Flynns' driveway shared its pavement with the mill's employee parking—an isthmus of tar amid a grass sea. I parked the car and turned off the engine.

"I'll only be a minute," she said.

"Are you sure you want to do this?"

"Yes. Don't you bail on me now." She stepped out.

As I waited, a steady line of cars with dim headlights pulled in around me. The crowd trampled across the Flynns' lawn, and every passerby stared at the strange man in the Chevy. I wondered what they thought of me, if anything.

Cal's cruiser, washed and waxed to such perfection that the deep blue appeared mean and arrogant, zipped by me and pulled onto the grass. I attempted to ignore Cal and his sparkling copmobile by flipping on the radio. "Sorry, I didn't realize it was the Cal show," I muttered to myself. He shot me a cold look. As I turned the dial, I saw—or saw again—that my car was equipped with a genuine, factory-installed tape deck. "Son of a bitch." It had malfunctioned so long ago that I forgot it even existed. I had to squash the urge to fly back to the carriage barn and snatch the tapes I'd discovered in Eli's desk. After all, I'd promised Jenny I wouldn't bail.

Jenny wanted out. She didn't want to be part of the wallowing. Or so she said.

The night before, at the wake, she'd solicited my help.

Before I left for the service, I mentioned Jenny's plan to Eli.

"It's a bad idea," he said. "She'll regret not bein' there."

"We'll only be gone for thirty-six hours."

"It's a mistake." He placed his plate and mug in the sink, rinsed them with cold water, and rubbed his eyes with his soapy hands as if he was tired and having problems focusing.

"She can't stand the thought of playing hostess while everyone in Galesville does their best to feel sorry for her. That's what she said. What am I supposed to do?"

"You could say no."

"I'm not sure I can," I said. "Plus, I think it sounds like a good idea."

"Of course it does. Stupidity and inspiration are siblings." He paused and put his hand to his temple. "Sometimes you've just gotta stay put and deal."

Eli winced.

"Are you okay?" I asked.

"Headache." The vowels were jumbled.

"Eli, are you gonna be all right?" I asked, but for some reason, I couldn't continue. I wanted to tell him about Cal's suspicions, about the new charges of vandalism and arson, about the mural. I wanted to ask if he was broke. But it was all too much. I couldn't risk Eli entering the blurriness of his own mind, especially as I was leaving for the weekend. He needed to remain sharp, so I let it all go. "Call me if you need anything."

"Why would I do that?" Eli poured himself a glass of water and placed it on the counter. His headache was getting the best of his attention.

"I hope you know what you're doing," I said.

"Thanks for the concern, but I'm not the one who needs direction."

"Just be careful," I repeated. "I'll be back before you know it."

"Don't run away now," he said. "Things are just getting' good and complicated."

"I'm not running." I opened the door. He stared at me so intently that his cheekbones sharpened. In that moment, I felt that I was being forced to choose between Jenny and Eli, and I didn't know what to do. "I'll be back tomorrow."

"Tell Jenny Lee I'm sorry about her father. It's a terrible thing for the living."

Cal walked arm in arm with Mrs. Flynn. His navy blue suit was as sleek and as fancy as his spiffed-up cruiser. His white shirt collar hid behind a tie I could only describe as *American Bandstand* gold. Even his sunglasses sparkled. It was a sign of respect for Phil Flynn, but it felt showy, contrived. Perhaps in Cal's mind, there was a direct correlation between how much you cared for a person and how much time and money you spent preparing for his burial. We all grieve in our own way.

Unable to sit idle any longer, I made up my mind to go inside and find Jenny, but as soon as I reached for the door handle, Jenny came out of the house with a tiny overnight bag. She brushed by Cal without even looking at him. He said something I couldn't decipher. She turned and responded, but I was too far away to translate their muffled words. Cal released Julia Flynn's arm and stepped toward Jenny. My spine straightened. Jenny turned her back to him, shrugged, and walked away. I leaned over the front seat and opened the passenger door.

"Where the hell are you off to?" Cal dropped his nice suit jacket on the ground. I locked the doors. Then, as if we were pulled over and he was on duty, he tapped my window with his bulky class ring, bent down, and glared at me.

"Get out," he said, words muffled by the glass.

I put the car in gear.

"You'll regret it, you fuckhead."

Behind him, a group of mourners shook their heads and carried on.

"Just go," Jenny said. I wasn't sure if she was speaking to me or Cal, but I hit the gas anyway, secretly hoping that I'd run over Cal's shiny leather shoes.

In my rearview mirror, I saw him fold his arms like a drill sergeant, shake his head, and bend over to retrieve his jacket. Behind him, Julia Flynn walked through the door alone, and no one was paying any attention.

The summer landscape flickered through the glass like flames from an old film reel. As we drove alongside the county fairgrounds, Jenny pivoted toward the window, and I saw two separate women—the loyal daughter, thick-skinned and responsive; and the introspective artist, sifting through the craziness all around and attempting to find order, balance, calm.

Her gaze was fixed on the fairgrounds, the adjacent fields, the borderlines of Galesville. I chose my words very carefully so as not to upset her or remind her of the heaviness of the day. She searched for something in the fields, in the trees, or in the last bend of the Battenkill. As I tried to figure out what it was, the wheels slid off the paved road and into the dirt shoulder. I quickly corrected the slip.

"Pay attention," she scolded.

"Sorry."

I slowed down.

Between the bend and the side of the road was a wooden cross staked in the ground and surrounded by flowers with bursts of brilliant summer reds. Gray, weathered wood peeked through its once-white paint. As we drove by it, Jenny held her breath.

We arrived in Saratoga Springs just before the second race post time, and it was hot. The Race Course was packed with men in wrinkled suit jackets and women in awkward, gravity-bending hats. Everyone glistened in one form or another. I confessed that I knew nothing about the program, the horses, or the betting.

"That's okay. I just want to see them run," Jenny said.

We made our way beside the railbirds. The area was jammed with bodies—tense, amped, overwrought, holding racing sheets in curled fingers, eyes hidden behind sunglasses, fixed on the track. The horses pulsated behind their little gates. Above them, the bright splash of the jerseys and colorful helmets bobbed. And then they were off, sprinting away from my line of sight, growing smaller and smaller. The audience stomped and screamed and flailed about, calling out names or numbers. "Come on four, come on four, come on number four." As they crossed the mile mark and beat down the stretch, it was as if the crowd, as one unit, conspired to achieve simultaneous coronaries. A deep sigh and a mass exodus from the rail signaled the end of the race, and the end of wishful thinking.

"Let's get out of here," Jenny said.

In town, Jenny and I walked up and down Broadway before ducking into a tiny air-conditioned restaurant on Phila Street for crepes and pommes frites. Afterward, we browsed an old bookstore, strolled around Congress Park, and tossed pennies into each fountain for luck. We barely spoke to one another, but when we did, it was as if the morning hadn't occurred. The denial was our escape.

After dinner, we entered Caffè Lena's split door and climbed its narrow stairway. Not surprisingly, the Caffè's brick walls and red curtains were still faded, its painted pine floor still scuffed and wavy. Onstage, a bluesman who called himself Mr. T. K. Tucker howled some mean old-timer acoustic blues. I'd heard him play many times, in what seemed to be a lifetime ago, but the music rattled me in new ways. As Eli professed, "The blues hurt more when you've got something to lose."

Jenny and I stood side by side at the top of the stairs, waiting to pay. I glanced around the listening room. No sign of Casey. It was unlike him to be late. Jenny squeezed my arm as a volunteer pointed us to a table near the stairs. After we'd sat down and ordered coffee, I caught Jenny staring at her hands, lost in thought. The distraction was wearing off.

Tucker's set ended, but the folkathon continued. He tipped his hat and slowly stepped down as a tiny teenage girl hopped up to keep the music flowing. No more than sixteen or seventeen, she stood confidently in the stage light. As she checked her guitar's tuning, she smiled, her teeth large and pearl gray, and made a joke about her pharmacist not filling her birth control prescription. Everyone chuckled. Tucker hobbled between tables toward the back of the room. She cleared her throat, pounded the hand-me-down guitar, and belted out Ani DiFranco's "Napoleon." There was dirt in her voice. Real anger—not some manufactured angst for the local high schoolers or undergrads. Something was happening. The roots were mounting a mighty comeback. The mood had darkened—a new climate, one of resentment and distrust, had resurfaced. The ground had cracked beneath our feet. For her second song, much to my surprise, she sang "With God on Our Side." People were listening on a whole other level. "All music is political and all politics are personal," Eli once said to me, "it just takes a while for people to hear the right notes in the right order."

Finally, Casey appeared on the stairs, looking like a sleepwalker stumbling toward the middle of a highway. I waved him over. He paid and stomped his way to our table, knocking into a few chairs along the way.

The musician missed her chord change.

"How's it going?" I slid the seat to him. He fell into it.

"Sorry I'm late," he said, humorless.

He hadn't shaved in what looked like a couple weeks, his eyes were pink and bloodshot, and his breath stank of cheap mouthwash.

He stared at Jenny, at me, back at Jenny.

"Who's this?" he asked.

"This is Jenny. Jenny, Casey." Jenny wanted nothing to do with him — that much was clear. "I told you she was coming."

"Oh, right. Jenny." Her name seemed to amuse him.

The performer finished her set, and the crowd applauded extra loud to make up for Casey's interruption. The room's impatience had ticked up a notch.

"Did you go to work like that?" I asked.

"Leave of absence, my friend. How do you like that?" He stood up, raised his arms in the air, and pronounced, "Leave of absence!" Then Casey reached across the table and lightly smacked my cheek before plopping back down in his seat. Some in the crowd snickered and shook their heads.

"What's going on with you?" I asked.

"Tough to say."

"I'm serious," I said. "What's your problem?" I moved my chair across the wood floor to be closer to him.

"Nothing really. Denise left me, man. But screw it."

"What?"

"She took off with some dildo from downstate."

"When?"

"Why the fuck does that matter? I don't know. What day is it?"

"Saturday."

"Seven weeks ago," he said. "Give or take."

"Two months? What the hell?"

"You should see this idiot she's humping," he added. He crossed his eyes and faked an overbite to give us the picture. "He kind of looks like a deranged horse."

"Do you want some water? Coffee?" I asked.

"My kid will be brought up by a breeder. A horse breeder. Did I tell you that he breeds horses? I've said too much."

Jenny asked for some water and sank into her chair. People at nearby tables eyeballed Casey as two men took the stage. One of them carried a five-string banjo and the other an old guitar. The crowd shushed us.

"I'm sorry, Case. Is there anything I can do?" I whispered.

"What're *you* going to do—annoy them to death?"

Everything went quiet before the banjo started in. Its rapid rolls were met with a heavy strumming of the guitar. The crowd stomped their feet and the room shook.

Casey looked at me. The sadness in his eyes was a shock. I'd never seen him so low, so beaten. Did I play a role in the separation? Denise was not my biggest fan.

"Looks like things are peachy with you," he said, acknowledging Jenny. "I told you," he continued, raising his voice to overcome the strings. "I told you to put it on the line, man. And look at you now. That's a W in your column." He slapped my shoulder. The music grew louder.

"I owe you."

"Damn right." He rocked his head back and forth until his neck cracked. "Now you can forget about Melanie—easy to do when you've got a new piece of ass."

I choked on my coffee.

The banjo player started in on "Worried Man Blues."

"Wait," Jenny said, hands up. She had to shout over the banjo picking. "Keep me out of this."

"Sorry. Sorry. No offense. Didn't mean it the way it came out."

"How did you mean it, then?" she pressed.

I had to do something, but I wasn't sure what. Get him out of Lena's? Sober him up at home? Knock some sense into him? I wanted to throttle him, but I felt sorry for him. And guilty. And confused. And sorry.

"Casey. Let's get you some water."

Jenny's eyes were soapy, livid. She had no time for him. As much as I feared for Jenny, I had a sinking feeling that she could destroy Casey. She didn't care about Denise. She didn't have a history with the guy. He wouldn't make it out alive.

The duo began to sing "Where Have All the Flowers Gone" a cappella like Seeger, and they held everyone's attention (even Casey's) for that minute and a half.

"Let's start over," he said to Jenny. "Where are you from?"

"Galesville," she answered. "Do you have a problem with that too?"

"No. My bad. I should've figured. I'm a dick. I apologize."

She didn't respond.

He staggered to his feet. Behind him, the manager plotted with her staff. Everyone was hoping he'd leave of his own volition, but that outcome was becoming less likely by the minute.

"Let me tell you something. What's her name again? Jules?" He breathed on me. I had to turn my head away.

"Jenny." The night was full of misery.

"Jenny. I've known this guy my whole life. Do you think he's a good guy? Well, do you? Of course you do. A stand-up dude." .

She refused to acknowledge his game.

"Let me answer," he continued. "He is. He *is* a good guy. A little distant, very needy, oddly obsessive...but I always thought he was a good egg."

"Casey. Let's go." I held up my hand to signal to the manager my intentions and my apologies.

"Explain this, then. Something that's bothered me for years—I need to get it off my chest. Why is it that he's so needy? He's got real abandonment issues. They cost him a lot, but I bet he hasn't talked about all that."

"Okay. Enough," I said.

"For the love of God, will you just leave?" a man at the adjacent table pleaded.

"Caused a lot of disruption," Casey continued. "I mean, he missed his own mother's funeral, and that's just one—"

I grabbed his arm and tried to yank him out of his chair, but he pulled away.

She'd never admit it, but I saw Jenny perk up. She was intrigued. Casey was a good lawyer, after all; he knew how to control a room. The back of my neck ached. I started to get dizzy, and when I reached for the table to steady myself, my throat closed.

"Cancer. His mother dies and he's...otherwise engaged...detained...can't get a pass to the funeral. Well, I don't know about that. I think they would've let him. I bet he didn't even ask. Shit like that is why Denise hated you, couldn't look at you. All the shit you pulled. Poor Jack. Poor Jack. Always the victim."

"Are you done?" I asked. He paused. I looked over at Jenny and shook my head as if to say, *Don't believe it*. But she did. I could see she ate up every last crumb that Casey had left for her.

"That's Jack, though," he continued. "Just the way he is. Always been too cool for school...aloof...yet always the victim...poor Jack...and Melanie, well, Denise really liked Melanie...and you go and screw it all up. It was like you're an expert in finding ways to fuck things up. Melanie didn't know what hit her."

"He doesn't know what he's talking about," I said to Jenny. In all my years, I had never experienced a drunk *and* self-loathing Casey. It was usually one or the other. Not both.

"I know about Melanie," Jenny said to Casey.

"Do you, now? I find that hard to believe. Has he told about the day she left, the fit he threw? He tormented her, like he tormented me, with his indecision and his unhappiness." Casey turned back to me. "Yeah, yeah, yeah. We get it, we get it, we get it. You're unhappy. You really want this, you really want that. But you know what? Everyone feels that way — you either do something about it or continue to get run over by the clock." He returned his attention to Jenny. "I bet he hasn't told you everything. Destroying the apartment, pushing Melanie around, getting his ass beaten to a pulp — has he told you about all that?"

The two men onstage stopped playing.

The manager was behind Casey's shoulder. "You need to leave," she said. "Now."

"That was a long time ago," I said.

"Wasn't so long ago."

"You don't know—" I started. Casey appeared to listen, but I knew better. "Doesn't matter. Things have changed." I leaned over to Jenny and apologized for the hundredth time.

"No need. This is good," she said.

Was she mocking me?

"Did you know he was locked up," Casey continued, "for assault and battery and criminal mischief?" Casey stared at Jenny; she didn't flinch. "You say you know about Melanie, but it's pretty clear you don't know a thing."

"Shut up and get out," someone in the crowd shouted.

"I'm sorry," I said again, to everyone.

The manager grabbed Casey's elbow. He pulled away.

"Stop apologizing for me," Casey screamed as I pulled him out of his seat. The audience was on edge. "You say things have changed. Have they really? The only thing you were ever passionate about was Eli Page and this stupid folk music. What's changed? Your life revolves around the guy. Now you just have someone to kill time with, someone else to take care of you."

Casey exhaled in my face. I pushed him toward the door.

"Grow some balls." He smiled.

My jaw clenched so tight that my eyes hurt.

"Are you going to hit me or what?" he asked. "Or don't you remember how?" Then he pushed me and I bumped the table. Jenny stood up. Three men from the audience joined the manager by Casey's side.

Without thinking and before anyone could stop me, I hit Casey. Immediately after, my knuckles pulsed with sharp, irregular pain. I'd managed to hit him on the side of the head, above his ear, in a very solid portion of skull. He didn't fall. Not exactly. He tripped over a chair while shouting, "Ouch." Then he stood, stared at me, and laughed. I spun around, trying to locate Jenny, but she was gone. At the same time, a mass of arms and bodies pulled us down the stairs by our shirtsleeves. "Sorry, sorry," I said, but it was too late. I winced as pain shot through my hand. I winced at the embarrassment of it all.

Outside, we stood in the dense August air and neither of us wanted to speak. I'd known Casey for so long, and from the moment I saw him walk into Lena's, I'd let him play me just like he'd always done.

"You all right?" I asked.

"I'll live."

"What the hell was that?" I was uncomfortable, sweating in the humid night air.

"I don't know." After our banishment, he was more lucid, more articulate. "I had to get it out of my system. I'm sorry I brought up—"

"I've been trying. So hard. To let it go," I said.

"It was going to catch up with you at some point."

"I couldn't go home, you know," I said. "Even if they let me."

"Forget it."

"No. I couldn't go back."

"I had to be a pallbearer in your place," he said. "She was your only family. You should've been there. They would've let you."

"Maybe," I conceded, but I was done talking about my mother. It had plagued me long enough, causing all sorts of panic and pain. "Are you sure *you're* okay?" I asked, swinging the conversation back to him. I was worried. Denise and Casey Jr. were his life. Shit happens, but all I could do was ask questions.

"I'll live to fight another day."

"What are you going to do now?"

"I don't know. I'll land on my feet as soon as I can find them." His eyes were puffy, and there was a little cut by his ear. "Do you like this girl?"

"Yeah. I do."

"And Galesville — worth it?"

"Sure," I replied. "It feels close enough to home."

"Then don't let it go." He smacked his hand against my shoulder. "It can all turn to shit. Look at us, man. Finally, you get the upper hand."

"You're drunk. Get home, drink some water. Sleep it off."

"The tables have turned. It was bound to happen." He nodded and stumbled off toward Broadway.

"Where are you going?"

"My condo." He pointed to a new building on the Saratoga skyline. "Go find her. Apologize for me."

Casey wandered out of view.

As soon as I entered Congress Park, I saw Jenny beside the enclosed carousel, peering in through the thin windows. I approached her without thinking through my response.

"Listen. This wasn't what I had in mind when I suggested Saratoga," I said when I caught up to her. "I'm really sorry."

"Don't be."

"He shouldn't have—"

"Knock it off. It's no big deal."

I shut up, relieved.

The bright, intricately carved carousel was enclosed in glass to protect it from the elements, from vandals, from drunks. Alongside the brick walkway was the Canfield Casino, a Saratoga landmark of beaux arts architecture. The park was seventeen acres of rolling green surrounding a duck-filled pond and three natural springs, with statues and monuments scattered around the grounds. As I walked beside Jenny, I couldn't help but recall the first time I'd visited Saratoga, years ago with Melanie (her parents owned one-eighth of a horse). After a nice patio dinner, we lingered by the springs. Melanie had told me that the water had healing qualities and people came because it tasted pure, youthful. "Everyone drinks it up," she said. "It's amazing."

Older men in tan fishing caps and Hawaiian print shirts crowded around the springs, filling their mugs or their blue bottles to the brims. Some sat on the curb and gulped the water. Melanie said, "Drink it, come on, drink it and see." Maybe I thought it would help. Maybe it would cure whatever was ailing me. Maybe it would heal that part of me that felt diseased, unlovable. So I drank it. I took a big sip and it burned and fizzled like rusty, yellow bile, and it made me gag and gag. Melanie laughed so hard that she had to sit down next to the old men and hold her side. Then she took my head in her hands, kissed my cheek, and apologized. "Sorry. Now you'll live forever," she'd said. "Just like me."

Did I ever really love Melanie? Did it matter?

I placed my hand on Jenny's arm.

"Let me explain," I said.

In New Haven circa 2007, I was employed by a television database company with a misleading name: Shoreline Media Services. Despite its name, Shoreline Media was housed in a giant concrete block seven miles from any water. I wanted to claim it was false advertising, but I hated starting any conversation with the VP. I had the distinct feeling that Shoreline was where creative-minded individuals went to repent for their artistic failures. Basically, when I attempted to settle down with Melanie, I abandoned music and writing to edit those handy summaries found in the "What's on Tonight" section of your local paper and digital cable pop-up menus. I'd call program directors around the country to ask what episodes of *CSI* they'd be rerunning at 7 P.M. on the East Coast or what guests were appearing on *Maury* the week of the 17th. I spent most of my nights waiting for Melanie to return from play rehearsals. Despite my mother's venom on the subject, I often wondered if my office job was any more rewarding than mill work in Stockton. At the very least, the laborers at Clark & Co. could say with pride that they made the paper that all U.S. currency was printed on. My typical introduction went like this:

Person: "Jack, what do you do?"

Me: "I work for Shoreline Media."

Person: "How interesting. And what is it you do there?"

Me: "Well, [insert any name here], it is because of me that you know what the Food Network will be showing at two A.M. on a Sunday morning."

It was only a matter of time until I cracked.

That day just happened to be Halloween. (Side note: No matter how much you want to, it's very difficult to forget the time you came to work dressed like Arlo Guthrie.)

I was having trouble with my computer when Melanie called.

"I'm going to Westport. Alone," she said. "And I'm not sure I'll be back."

"What exactly does 'I'm not sure I'll be back' mean?" I asked.

"I need to get away. You should too."

"What are you talking about?"

The line was dead.

I tossed my Arlo wig and spectacles to the floor.

Then, in a stunning display of self-restraint, I tried to let it go. In fact, I sat back down in my office chair and tried to open Shoreline's database program. That's when my computer froze. For the fourth time in an hour.

"Are you fucking kidding me?" I dreamed of picking up the box and throwing it out the second-story window. Oh, how sweet the thud on Shoreline's stamped concrete walkway would be; I could almost hear the low thunder that cracked and reverberated in all directions. I imagined the shell shattering, small plastic bits and microchips exploding across the walk and finding a home in the pots of wilting mums.

CTRL – ALT – DEL

Halfway through the reboot, that little hourglass stopped doing its job. Before I had time to cool, I reached below my desk and yanked the surge protector and network cable from the wall socket, wrapped my arms around the bulky monitor, and tugged. I couldn't get the unit to break free. So I shoved the whole bulky, worthless piece of shit off the desk. The wires snagged for a moment, and then the computer crashed to the floor. As it fell, its mouse, still connected, launched into the air and caught me across the cheekbone.

Startled by the noise, Caroline, a coworker, burst through my door. When she witnessed me among the wreckage—with a growing welt on my cheek—she gasped and covered her mouth. Her nails were sports car red. Of all things, that was what my brain centered on. Gasp. Lips. Hand. Nails. Cherry. For a moment, I wondered why I never felt foolish around Caroline.

She shook her head and asked in her soft, cautious voice, "What are you doing?"

Glancing through the open door, my fellow employees leaned back in their ergonomic chairs to examine the situation as they all pretended to talk on their phones. It was probably the most exciting thing to happen at Shoreline Media in years.

Suddenly, the room became very small. The walls pulsed and pounded on my skull. The fluorescent overhead lights dulled my senses, and my chest felt like it'd been rolled over by a front loader. As I sat down to catch my breath, a pain rose in my throat—it was as if a jagged piece of glass was being pulled out by a string.

"You look terrible," Caroline said.

Shoreline Media would fire me. That was indisputable, but it didn't matter anymore. I took a deep breath. None of it mattered. Tired of the tediousness of it all, sick of the tie, sick of the stagnant corporate air, sick of the buzzing computer with the fuzzy monitor that more times than not left me with a migraine.

I grabbed the wig from the floor. The long gray mop was heavy in my hands.

"Good for you, Jack Wyeth. You don't belong here anyway," Caroline whispered, apparently afraid that someone might overhear her sedition.

Her cheerleading made me want to vomit.

I brushed by Caroline. "I'm sorry. Take care," I said. With the wig back in place, I sauntered through the landscape of cubicles, making sure to avoid eye contact with any of my so-called coworkers. Yes, I was smug. I admit it. Why? Because, damn it, I sat in that same windowless center of the company for fifteen months before I got promoted to my new office, which had a wonderful view of the parking lot. I knew each of those poor souls was plotting to take my place. I whistled "Alice's Restaurant" as I navigated the hall.

In the faux-marble lobby, I eyed a vase of white roses by the door. Without hesitating, I grabbed it off the front desk. The receptionist rose to say something but gave up. As the glass door shut behind me, I heard Caroline explain to the others, "He's having relationship troubles."

Our apartment was in a yellow, three-story U-shaped building with five fire-engine-red doors—we were on the second floor, sandwiched between a piano teacher and a toy dog enthusiast. We'd moved in soon after we got engaged and had quickly outgrown it, but the thought of moving again was too much. I stood at the door and strategized, resisting the temptation to kick my neighbor's shoes down the steps. Armed with new ideas, flowers, and the promise of an unrealistic future, I was ready to convince her to stay. It was that easy. I opened the door.

The room had been flipped upside down, shaken, and poured back onto the polished hardwood. Books were scattered across the floor. The coffee table, futon, television, even my old Eli Page concert posters were gone. I ran across the room, nearly tripped on a lamp wire, and rummaged through the pile of useless crap on my desk, looking for the one thing that I cared about more than all of these objects. I breathed a sigh of relief when I saw it—*Up Country*, the cover signed by Eli Page. I pulled the record out of its sleeve to make sure it wasn't scratched. I ran my fingertips over the lyrics on the back cover. Then I slid it behind the desk, out of view.

Everything in the apartment was out of place, thrown across the floor or haphazardly on the few remaining pieces of furniture. My guitar case looked as if it had been punted around the room. I tightened my grip on the glass vase and slowly and quietly traveled through the living area to the hall and down to the bedroom, which, I soon saw, was in worse shape than the front of the apartment.

In the kitchen, two cardboard boxes propped open the back door, which led from the apartment to the parking lot in the rear of the complex.

I heard voices on the stairs, laughter bouncing off the walls and into the kitchen, a girlish giggle, a falsetto "stop it," a playful "I mean it." When the door was pushed open, Melanie strolled into the kitchen, her attention still over her shoulder. She spun her head around as if to demonstrate the bounce in her hair. Behind her, a heavy man in a polo shirt and dark jeans covered his teeth with his flabby mouth. Reflexively, I chucked the vase. It shattered into a thousand pieces against the wall, inches from the door. Water and roses splashed across the linoleum. Melanie screamed and covered her head; the man moved away from the site of impact. He was big, a bull of a man with horn-rimmed glasses, but his face was friendly, peaceful.

Melanie peered through her hands to see who the vase thrower was—she looked like she'd been electrocuted, her hair on end, eyes ablaze.

"What the hell is wrong with you?" she said. I had never heard her voice so low and strained—it was coarse like she was getting over a cold and in complete contrast to the giggle that had echoed in the hall moments before.

The bull acted as if he understood something Melanie and I didn't. He lifted two boxes in his soft-muscled frame and exited the apartment. The door swung shut. Melanie rushed me and started hitting me on the shoulders and neck. I could do nothing but try to block the blows by covering my head with my forearms. She stopped her assault after she realized I wasn't going to fight back. Then she began to cry. I wasn't convinced the tears were real; I could never tell if they were real.

"I thought we were being robbed," I said.

"What are you doing home?"

"I quit. To come home and talk with you."

"What the hell, Jack?"

"I thought we needed to share our disappointments, isn't that what you always say?"

"The wedding's off, but that's not really a surprise, is it?"

"I got you flowers." The words just came out.

"You threw a vase at me."

I wanted to say I was sorry, that I wasn't throwing the vase at her, and that she had done worse. We both glanced at the puddle on the floor.

"I can do better."

"Jack." She grabbed my arm. "No you can't. This was over before it started."

"That's not true."

"There's something wrong with you. I don't know what it is exactly, but no one is going to put up with it. Look at you. What the hell are you wearing?" I'd forgotten about the costume. I pulled off the wig and hat and tossed them onto the kitchen table. "It's over."

"So that's it?"

Melanie twisted the ring off her finger. She held it out in front of her; I snatched it from her with more force than I intended.

"Who's the guy?"

"His name is Victor."

"What does Vic do?"

"Victor. He's an actor—"

"Of course he is."

"And a director."

"How appropriate," I mumbled. Before she replied, my mind was back in the theater admiring her stage presence. Melanie was an actress who lived inside her roles — at least that's what she wanted everyone to believe. *Cowboy Mouth* was the most recent outlet; she was perfectly cast as Cavale, a mental and manipulative mess forcing Slim, a lanky boy in a cowboy suit, to become something he's not. (At least that's how I remember it.) Just then, as I recalled her strut onstage, I knew where I had last seen those horn-rimmed glasses. During the curtain call, the bull (aka Victor) stood off stage left, laughing, his white teeth sparkling in the spill of the stage light.

"I knew I remembered those teeth," I said.

She snorted. "Screw you, Jack. You spend more time listening to Eli Page records than you do paying attention to me. It's not like we were Tristan and Isolde or even Romeo and Juliet. More like George and Martha in *Who's Afraid of Virginia Woolf?*"

"Not this again." She always dropped references to dramatic literature texts, and it was fucking annoying.

"I'm not telling you anything you don't know. Let's just cut our losses." Melanie must've realized that the tone of her statement was harsher than she meant because her eyes swelled. Like a true actress faced with an obstacle, she tried a different tactic: "Maybe this is just better for everybody. You can find time to do whatever it is you do. You don't have to babysit me. This is a good thing. For both of us. I'll tell you what I think you should do."

"What's that?"

"Deal with your father so you can stop being so pathetic. It's not attractive. "

"Get out."

"Don't take that tone with me."

"Get out. Run back to your Daddy and his fat checkbook."

"You're an asshole." She chuckled. "Let me give you some advice. It's not the money that sets us apart; it's your attitude. You never listen."

"Get out. Get the fuck out," I yelled.

"Don't you dare—" Melanie stepped forward and pushed me with all her weight. I stumbled back against the wall. Then I lunged forward and shoved her. (I'd lost myself somewhere in that apartment. I knew it even then, but it was as if I'd been stretched so taut that I finally snapped.) Melanie, who weighed fifty pounds less than me on a bad day, shot back, tripped over a box, and slammed her head on the kitchen cabinets as she toppled. She grabbed whatever was in her reach and started chucking it at me. I swiped at the flying toaster, the plates, all the airborne objects, knocking them aside one by one like a bear swatting at bees.

Her scream woke me up. What am I doing? I thought, but it was too late. The bull entered from the hall, saw the blood on the side of Melanie's head, and pummeled me. Flatout destroyed me. Before I had a moment to plead for mercy, I was on the ground, bloodied, bruised, unable to move. In the moments before I passed out, I saw Melanie get up.

"I'm sorry it ended this way," she said as she left, leaving like a pro who had rehearsed her exit a hundred times.

Blood obscured my vision. In my haze, I remember thinking, At least she's not hurt.

Looking back, I despise the person I was that day. All of the bottled-up anger, all of the self-doubt, all of my fears rose to the surface like an infection that had been brewing underneath for too long. In the end, the blowup had little to do with her. She deserved better. Until it all fell apart, we did share something uncommon, and there were good times that I wouldn't take back. I can't blame her for pulling away. Not really. I'd done worse. If I'd been half the man I purported to be, I would've let her go long before, but instead I let our relationship fester until it was too weak to stand. I know that now, but in the moment, I was in a fever that refused to break.

After she left, I could've placed my hand on a hot stovetop and not even noticed my searing skin. I hated that she was right, and I hated myself for being such a coward. After three days of getting out of bed only to relieve myself, I showered, shaved, and went for a walk. The police were waiting for me when I returned. Charged with assault and battery as well as two counts of criminal mischief (one count related to Melanie's property and one count initiated by Shoreline Media, which didn't take kindly to the destruction of their computer and office furniture), I pleaded guilty and served nearly six months in the county jail. It was the least I could do.

My mother died while I was away. Casey was right—they would've let me go, chaperoned by two deputies, but I didn't alert family outreach. Months later, after I was released, I packed my small life into my Chevy and drove to Saratoga, hoping to apologize to Casey and start over again for the third time.

I didn't tell Jenny all of that, but I told her enough.

We wandered to the far side of Congress Park, crossed Veterans Walk, and entered an octagonal stone island. The names and ranks of Saratoga's fallen soldiers were carved into bricks along the walkway. Their legacy defined by civic grandstanding.

"I really thought the mural would work," Jenny said. "I wanted to pull people together, to show a bit of pride in how far Galesville has come, lift the community up."

"People only see what they want to see," I said. "And they tend to see their fears before good intentions."

"You don't think people can see the goodness in others?"

"People are easily duped. Myself included." My head was soaked from the weight and heat of the night air. My right hand ached from my knuckles to my wrist—Casey's noggin was a concrete globe, the wrong target for my fist.

"So, we are all at the mercy of cynics like you?"

"There's always hope," I said. "But it takes someone extraordinary to get people to believe in it. And a bit of timing."

Smack in the center of the smooth monument, staring into the darkness, we stretched out on our backs and breathed in the heavens. I felt like I was hurtling through the black sky. My fingers traced over Perseus and Andromeda. With my arms stretched as high and as far as I could physically endure, I captured a handful of nothing.

It felt good to be on my back on the stone while the humidity pressed down on my flesh. I inhaled deliberately, and my ribs vibrated. Jenny, hearing my sigh, slinked over the top of me and kissed my forehead. I reached up to touch her, to make sure she was actually there and I hadn't fallen asleep.

"I thought we'd stay with Casey. Since that didn't pan out, we should find a room before—"

She kissed me again. Her lips tingled. The pain in my hand disappeared. I didn't know it at the time, but that kiss was meant as a farewell.

The waterfowl stirred. In the dawn's periwinkle, they waddled by the monument and splashed into the pond. I sat up, took in my surroundings, and realized I was alone. Mostly. A jogger, preoccupied by the ducks, tripped on his own feet. He was gone before I could help—a spot of blood left on the pavement from his skinned knee.

I stretched, wiped the sleep from my eyes, and spied Jenny on a bench in front of the carousel. I felt unsettled, as if everything that was said the night before was about to come back to bite me. "Should we get a move on?" I asked.

"I have to return something," she said when we were at the car. "Something I stole last week while you were sleeping." She reached into her bag and pulled out a picture frame.

I refused to take it from her. Instead, I jabbed the key into the ignition switch.

"Can you slip it back into the study for me?" she asked.

"Fine."

"Do you want to see what it is?"

"I've seen them all," I said. "I've cataloged every single item in that room. I know Eli's possessions better than I know my own."

She dropped the frame on my lap. There was Hadley sitting on the grass, hands wide open, reaching for someone to help her up. The photographer's long shadow stretched out beside her. The camera captured a glimmer of fading daylight in her eyes. It also captured something else, something I'd missed—a small, rounded belly.

When I refused to pick it up, Jenny snatched the frame back, flipped it over, and ripped off the backing.

"What are you doing?"

"I'm trying to meet you halfway. Look for yourself." She removed the flimsy picture from its mount and handed it to me. On the back it read: "Galesville, '75." It was fragile in my hands.

"She was twenty-one and beautiful," Jenny said.

"What happened to the baby?" I asked with too much acid. Even now I don't know quite why I was so upset, but I remember feeling that the study was mine, as if she had no right to dig through the items as I had done.

Jenny's upper body rocked away from me. Then she turned and stared into my eyes, her expression clouded by distrust. "How did you know—?"

"Did the baby live?" A river of blood sloshed around in my head and pounded on my eardrums. Any shred of patience I had left had been supplanted by the fear that I was purposefully being left on the sidelines.

"Yes. The baby lived. Her name was Eliza. After her father."

"And Hadley?"

"Died of internal bleeding—something to do with the placenta detaching. I don't know the details. Hadley's parents took care of Eliza. Raised her."

"Why are you telling me now? You know I've been trying to stitch this story together for months, and all of a sudden you decide the time is right. Why?"

Jenny stared at the windshield, her jaw locked, her eyes wide, her mouth pursed.

"Where is Eliza now? Can you at least tell me that?"

Jenny refused to answer. I pleaded with her to tell the truth, but she was no longer listening to me. Not entirely. Finally, to shut me up, she lifted her chin. She wasn't looking directly at me, but rather at the bridge of my nose. "Jack," she said. "You come into Galesville, and you think you can figure it all out, but you can't. It's not that easy. It's not just material for the book or memoir or whatever it is that brought you here. This is a life. Many lives you're screwing with."

"Oh. That sounds like something Helen Walker would say, doesn't it?"

She recoiled. "It's not the same, and you know it."

"You're right. It's not. *This* is important," I said. I tried to take it back, but the words were full of lead. They were impossible to put back in the barrel.

We were both silent, staring straight ahead. After a few minutes, I tried to speak her name, to open the door for an apology, but she slammed it shut. "Take me home," she interrupted. Again I tried to make it right, and she refused, "Just shut up and take me home."

Besides insulting her, I was demanding more of her than she could give. Jenny had just offered an answer to the big question: Why had Eli picked Galesville? He'd come to find his daughter, a daughter he abandoned long before she even entered the world. Jenny had broken whatever contract she had with Eli and given me something. She had met me halfway.

"I'm sorry." By the time I got it out, the moment had passed. "I'm an idiot. I didn't mean—"

Jenny reached over and turned the key for me.

As I pulled out of the parking lot, the view in front of me began to peel apart. Suddenly I was dizzy with guilt, sick to my stomach. Words floated around and I tried to reach out and grab them and string a sentence or two together but everything was nonsense. I *was* sorry, but I *wanted* more.

"Are you hungry?" I asked after a half hour of insufferable silence. Jenny tucked her feet between her thighs and the seat. I could sense that she wasn't ready to return home, but she didn't want to stay with me either. "We should eat," I said. She gazed out the window, staring at the sky or the treetops or her own reflection in the glass.

I stopped at the Battenkill Diner, a tiny chrome building that signaled the line between the business section of town and the historic district. It was less than four miles from River Bend but a world apart. Three pickup trucks sat in the far corner of the lot—staging vehicles for kayakers slicing through the river. It was a coming and going place.

I opened the door and stepped out. Jenny remained seated, refusing to look at me.

"You don't have to talk to me," I said. "But I know you don't want to go home."

At first, she didn't respond, but after I attempted to bribe her with coffee and breakfast, she relented, probably just to shut me up.

At the table, we didn't speak to each other for a long time. An unbearable time. Our window overlooked the street and the old cemetery, which was where she kept her gaze.

"You have to know I'm truly sorry. I didn't mean—"

"No? What did you mean, then?"

I didn't have a good answer.

The waitress delivered our coffee.

"Why did you come to Galesville," Jenny asked, "if not to expose Eli?"

"That wasn't my plan at all."

"Then why?"

"Honestly?" I asked. She gave me a look. "I was promised a second chance."

She lifted the white-speckled coffee mug to her lips and blew across the top. Her body relaxed, and I knew her distain for me had softened.

"If it wasn't for Belanger's, I wouldn't have stayed, no matter how sick my father was," she said.

"No? Where would you go, if you had the chance?"

No answer. Again she stared at the thin diner windows. Her rosy cheeks and brilliant green eyes were faint reflections in the imperfect glass. Beyond her visage, my focus was drawn to the grime and then to the grave markers and the maple trees. The panes rattled in the breeze.

Outside, two cruisers flew by in a comic blur. The regulars at the counter craned their necks in unison to track the sirens.

The waitress returned with our food. Hungrier than I thought, I shoveled a forkful of scrambled eggs into my mouth. Jenny didn't touch her plate.

"When I was a teenager, I kept this Rand McNally atlas from 1980 on my nightstand. The cover had a winding road on it, like the river I painted on the mural. I loved that thing. Eliza and I marked it all up." Jenny seemed to be relieved when she said the name. Eliza. "We wrote notes on every page. We circled every place we wanted to hit. It would've been an epic road trip."

"You were good friends?"

"Best friends since third grade," she said, nodding.

"Didn't you want to go to Paris, Rome, Venice?"

The windows shook again, and I felt a cold front was on the way. The clouds charged through the sky at a sprinter's pace.

"No, no, no. It was a US road atlas." She sipped her coffee. "But we had big plans. Crazy Horse, the Badlands, Redwood. There's a lot to see between the oceans."

"What happened?"

"It didn't work out," she said.

"Well, it's never too late." My response burned like newspaper in a hungry fire — consumed before it had time to breathe.

Jenny's eyes quivered. I began to understand that Eliza was gone for good, and my stomach sank. Having learned my lesson, I didn't press Jenny for answers.

"Are you thinking of leaving now?"

She shrugged. "I don't know. I've been thinking about that atlas, thinking about Eliza, thinking about going back to school."

"If there's something you want to do, don't wait. Just go do it."

I could see that she was still inside her own memories. Finally, she said, "Have you ever wanted something that was so close...only to have it disappear...and then you forgot you ever wanted it in the first place?"

"All the time," I said.

"What did you want?" she asked.

"When I was a kid, I wanted to play guitar. I wanted to be in one of those families of folk singers, each generation taking over for the last, carrying on the tradition."

"Like the Partridge Family?" She smiled.

"More like the Carter Family or the Guthries. My father played, but he took off when I was young. Doesn't take a therapist to guess it was a way to connect with him."

"You do play."

"Not like that. Not like I imagined it. Touring around the country in a beat-up bus, meeting hundreds or thousands of people, hearing other musicians play those old songs—I used to stand in my room with my guitar and act the part. The whole thing. Even the banter with the crowd."

"What would you say?"

"To the crowd? I don't know. I'd tell stories."

"So you were always a storyteller?" she asked.

"At my core," I answered. "A terrific liar."

Jenny still hadn't touched her food. She caught me looking at her plate.

"It isn't what we dreamed it would be, is it?" I said.

"What?"

"Life."

"We can't all be rock stars," she said between breaths. The line made me laugh.

I pushed my plate to the center of the table, dropped my elbows on the Formica, and rested my head on my fist.

"She's dead, isn't she?"

"Yes." Jenny choked on the word. She shifted in her seat.

"Why didn't you tell me?" I asked. Jenny stared at me, defiant, suspicious. "I'm asking as your friend. Not as Eli's ghostwriter."

"He asked me, for her sake and his, to keep it private. He wanted to tell you in his own time. Do you understand? I couldn't betray his trust—not after all of this."

"It was unfair of him."

"No. It was anything but. I owed him as much."

"We should go," I said, still confused but cautious.

"Jack, you can't tell him I—"

"I won't."

I left cash on the table, and we left the diner as if we were ending a blind date.

Outside, the sky was preparing for rain. In the distance, I heard the cry of sirens locked in place, and I wondered what was causing all the commotion.

"I'm sorry," Jenny said. "I'm sorry I didn't tell you sooner. I'm sorry everything got fucked up along the way."

"Yeah. Me too." What I should have said: "You're a good person, Jenny. You were protecting him. No one can fault you for that." Instead, I barely acknowledged her apology. She stared at me, waiting for more; her face went pale and her vivid eyes were blank. Her trust was delicate. She had let me in, and I had let her down.

I climbed into the car and drove her home.

"Thank you," she said when we arrived. "For getting me out of town."

I didn't deserve it. As she crawled out of the car, I held back the questions that kept rising in my throat. Torn between the desire to know more and the fear that everything would crack and fall apart if I pushed too hard, my mind was paralyzed.

She started toward the house, turned back, and said, "Listen, I've been taking care of everybody else—Dad, Eli, Ivory, Mark—but I'm not a saint. I can't take care of you too. You should know that."

"I don't expect you to."

"Good. Then we understand each other?"

I forced a nod. Truth was that I wasn't sure if she was warning me or cutting ties.

She stepped away from the car. Then, as she stood still, I thought she was going to take it all back. She leaned into the passenger-side window, her eyes locked on mine.

"You could've told me about your past," she said. "I wouldn't have judged you."

My chest pounded again and my head began to swim.

"I could say the same to you."

"We're not so different, me and you."

"I've tried to forget it," I said. "To move on."

"Have you...forgotten?"

"No."

"Me neither."

"We have to deal with it all sooner or later," I said.

She opened her mouth to speak but must've decided against it. I held her stare.

She was waiting for me. I was waiting for her.

Lights pulsed along the river water, rippling like crimson waves downstream, before disappearing around the bend. With the sirens hushed, the lights were convulsive and threatening. *Keep away. Turn back. Don't cross us.* The Celebrity groaned as I punched the gas and blew through the covered bridge.

At Eli's property, two state cruisers expertly blocked the entrance to the driveway. There was no way around. So I parked on the side of the road, hopped the barricade, and ran toward the house.

A trooper, who stood guard at the front door, his grays starched and stiff, observed my demeanor, held out his palm, and cautioned me to stop.

"Let me in."

"Nope. Can't do it." He stiff-armed my sternum.

"I live here."

"You'll have to wait where you are." His eyes studied me, trying to anticipate my next move.

"Is Mark Calvin in there?" I asked.

"Maybe, maybe not."

"Come on. Can you at least let him know that it's Jack Wyeth?" I pleaded. "Whatever's going on inside, I can help."

He sighed extra loud for my benefit. Upon exhale, his shoulders lowered a fraction. "Wait here," he said. "I mean it. If you move, I will shoot you in the kneecap." The trooper slid away and spoke into his shoulder. Static was followed by a dampened "fine, fine, let him in." Dutifully, but with a wry smile, the trooper opened the front door and stepped aside.

"Thanks, Officer," I said, brushing by him.

He grunted a noise that sounded vaguely like "uh-huh."

The house was trashed. A random assortment of objects—papers, crates, frames, books, forks, cereal boxes—covered the living-room floor and spilled out into the hall and dining room. The furniture was tipped on its sides. Boxes were upside down. Even though it was an oppressively hot summer day, a fire roared in the fireplace. Soot and ash spread across the wood floor, a faint shadow of footprints circled the room. Everything had been torn to pieces.

Eli stood in the far corner. His eyes ablaze, he held a guitar like a baseball bat and muttered, "You're gonna come in here? Just try it. Go ahead. Go ahead. Try." No doubt he would swing away if I got too close. I straddled the threshold that separated living room from hall.

Inside the room, Cal leaned against the window sash. With his arms crossed, eyebrows pointed up, mouth stretched in an I-told-you-this-would-happen manner, the scene was evidence that he was right about everything in the world. Every. Single. Thing.

"What the hell is going on?" I asked.

"Neighbors called," Cal said. "They were worried."

"What neighbors? The closest house is a quarter mile away."

Cal shrugged. "We got a call from a concerned citizen."

"Is that right?"

"Are you questioning the veracity of my statement?" Cal asked.

I stepped toward the center of the room, between the two men. Eli's knuckles whitened.

"Eli." I tried to remain calm and collected, but I ended up sounding like a hostage negotiator on his first job. "It's Jack. Remember me?"

"Shut up! I know who you are. I'm not a fuckin' child!"

Cal huffed and looked down at his watch.

"I know, I know. Can you put the guitar down?"

Eli lowered the guitar—the '49 Martin—for a brief moment. My eyes were wet from staring. The moment I blinked and turned my attention to Cal, Eli let loose and smashed the guitar into the mantel. It burst into pieces as he pounded and pounded the instrument into the marble until the splintered neck was all that remained. Cal's spine straightened when he realized, as I did, that the jagged pieces of wood were potential weapons.

"Put it down, Mr. Page. Don't make me get physical," Cal said. His typical authoritative tone had zero effect on the situation.

"Eli. You need to calm down," I said.

"Shut your mouth!" Eli waved the guitar neck like a saber.

"He's been like this since I got here. I don't know what set him off," Cal whispered to me. "But if you don't do something soon, I'll have to subdue him."

"Just wait," I said over my shoulder.

I took another step toward Eli. He froze.

"What happened?" I asked as I tried to get a clear accounting of the damage. Everything was shattered, broken, in pieces as if the place had been ransacked. Books and magazines were thrown off their shelves. Boxes were spilling their contents. Papers and undefined objects were used as fuel for the spitting fire.

My head ached—a mild thumping in the back of my ears and around my temples, which were wet from the heat. I wished for two aspirin and a glass of water. It was then, in that instant, that I realized that the boxes, the papers, the posters, the glass, the books, the guitar, the records, the frames, the scattered photographs, every damn thing that was strewn across the living room belonged in the study. I looked across the room, and there, in front of me, I saw that the door was wide open.

"I haven't got all day," Cal chimed in, ever helpful.

"Eli, tell me what's wrong," I said.

"What's wrong? *What's wrong?* Always with questions. Always bug, bug, bug. There's nothin' you can say to fix it. Nothing."

"Fix what, Eli? I'm just trying to help."

"Don't feed me that line. Don't try and trick me. You know what you did. You know why I had to turn this place out."

"No. I don't. Tell me," I said. My stomach sank into the abyss. I think I did know, but I wasn't going to say it aloud.

His eyes sharpened. "Something very important to me"—he spoke deliberately and he directed all of his words at me—"was missin'. I had to find it." Eli dropped what remained of the guitar neck. It crashed into the floor.

"Let me help."

"You've done enough," he said.

"What have I done exactly? Tell me." I stared around the room, at all the destruction and disorder, and I couldn't help but think of my New Haven apartment.

"Officer?" he said, suddenly composed.

"I'm a New York State trooper," Cal corrected him.

"I don't care," Eli replied. "I'd like to report a crime."

"Really? Of course you would." Cal turned his head, stared at me for a moment, and shook his head.

"Someone"—he glared at me—"has stolen some of my possessions."

"Why don't you tell me what's missing?" Cal asked.

"Personal items."

"Okay."

"And my dog," Eli continued. "My dog is missing."

"Tig is gone?" I asked.

"Where is the dog, Mr. Page?"

"I told you—missing."

"When did you see him last?" Cal asked.

"I don't know."

"Did you kill your dog, Mr. Page?"

"No." Eli was defeated, confused. The accusation startled him.

"Eli, what happened to Tig?" I asked, struck by a panic in my chest, the clutching at my breastbone. "Tell me what you know."

Eli shrugged and leaned against the wall.

A third trooper entered and called Cal over to the hallway. They discussed something important through whispers and nods. When Cal returned, he asked, "Mr. Page. Do you own a gun? A twenty-two-caliber rifle?"

"No, he doesn't," I said.

"Yes. I keep it behind the pantry door, but it was gone this morning."

"Any idea where it ran off to?"

"I don't know. It must've been taken with the other things."

"Well, that's convenient, isn't it?" Cal snarked.

"What's going on here?" I asked.

"We have reports of a man fitting Mr. Page's description threatening some citizens with a deadly weapon. Also, we believe that this same individual, whoever he may be, took target practice on the *Galesville Mirror*'s window just after midnight. I don't have to tell you, Mr. Page, that those are both serious crimes. Can you account for your whereabouts last night?"

"That's what this is about?" I interrupted. "So, can I assume the neighbors didn't call?"

"Closest house is a quarter mile away." Cal smiled. "Mr. Page, answer the question."

"Eli," I said, "tell him where you were last night."

"Fuck off. Both of you."

"I can take you in," Cal said. "This is a courtesy. I don't need your statement."

"I was here," Eli said. "I was right here."

"Can *you* vouch for that?" Cal stared at me knowingly.

"No." I shook my head. "I was out of town."

"Very convenient."

"Wait," Eli said. He clawed at his beard. "It's the prom date. He's setting me up."

"Who?" Cal and I said in unison.

"I don't remember his name." Eli described a strange man who followed him around Galesville, but the details were vague—average height, blue jeans, "hair like mine." That man was to blame, he pleaded. "He's trying to make me look insane."

"Well, he's doing a crack-up job," Cal joked.

"It's true." Eli dug through the boxes and papers on the floor. "I'll find it."

"Is he a fan? A stalker?" Cal asked, unmoved.

"No. I don't know. He stares at me through the windows. He hides in the trees. I may be losing it, but I wouldn't hurt anyone. You'll see. He doesn't like me. He's never liked me."

Cal grunted and then scratched something into a notebook.

I rubbed my forehead. The headache had exploded.

"There has been someone on the property," I said.

Cal took me aside and whispered, "You're actually buying this crap?"

"Did you check out the guy with the black Ram?"

"Yeah, and maybe I'll check out every cockamamie story drummed by a delusional senior and his sidekick," he said.

"See for yourself. The barbed-wire fence has been cut," I added.

"I'll get right on that."

"How 'bout you do your fucking job?"

"My job? What do you know about my job?" Cal stepped toward me, gritting his teeth and pointing at my face. "Shut your mouth or I'll haul you in for being an accessory to the freak show. Or better yet, I'll Tase you again. How's that sound?" When I didn't respond to his threat, Cal turned his attention back to Eli.

"You wouldn't happen to have a name, would you?" he asked.

"No. I can't remember." He kept digging.

Cal glanced back at me and shook his head.

I waited for some help—the hand of God to come down and pluck me up and out of this place or at least deliver a divine backhand to knock me clear across the living room, the hallway, through the kitchen, and out into the driveway.

"Keep him right here," Cal ordered. "Or I'll have Wayne shoot you both." As he left to investigate the fence and the pantry, the young trooper from the front entered; straddled the door, half in and half out; and watched us.

I stepped toward Eli.

"What're you looking for?" I asked. "Maybe I can help."

"You've done enough." He kicked the stuff on the floor in my direction. In the pile before me, I saw a picture of Hadley, torn in half. Then he pulled a stack of letters from his coat pocket. I knew what they were before he removed the band, and I felt sick. "How hard is it to follow three simple rules?"

"It's not what you think."

He held the bundle of letters in his fist, and he visibly shook with terror and anger and sadness in a way that I can't quite explain.

"I knew you were going in there. I'm not stupid," he continued. "But what made you think you could take — ?"

"Eli. I know I broke the rules, but — " As I said those words, my shoulders sank. What a fucking mess I'd made of it all.

"This is my life. My personal property . . . my . . ."

"I'm sorry."

"No. No. You're not. I wish I'd burned them. I wish they never existed at all. And for you to come into my house . . . to be invited into my home . . . and then to do this . . . it's fucked is what it is. It's underhanded." His sentences were clearer, more lucid, as if he'd been revving up and replenishing his energy at the same time.

"You brought me here to write your book." I measured my words. "How was I supposed to know? I had no idea where it all would take me."

There was a long moment of silence.

"Maybe I should've given you the interview you wanted. Maybe. But my failures don't justify your actions." Eli tucked the letters back into his pocket.

"For what it's worth, I *am* sorry," I repeated.

As if I hadn't said a word, he scooped up a pile of papers and photos and posters from his floor, brushed past me, and tossed them into the fire.

"What are you doing?" Pushing Eli aside, I rescued several pieces from the fireplace. My fingers grazed something plastic, and I realized it was the cassette I'd reclaimed. Blindly, I stuffed it into my pocket as he shoveled more material in. There was only so much I could salvage.

"Do you think I just picked you out of a crowd? Do you? Do you still think it was some random act that brought us together for a half-assed memoir project? I'm not in the habit of takin' in clueless buskers for life lessons. Didn't you think it was strange?"

"You're not making sense."

"Despite his problems, your father...he was a good man...he cared for you, Jack. I said I'd do it and I did it. I did. That counts for somethin'. But I didn't expect this. It wasn't part of the deal." He stepped around me, continuing to fill the fire.

"What are you talking about?" My voice was higher than usual, overtuned. I couldn't move. "What are you saying?"

"I know...this...isn't easy." Eli tripped over the words.

"Spit it out."

"But it's not about me. Never was. It's about you." Eli shook his head, slowly, as if he was disappointed in me, as if he was heartbroken, as if he couldn't believe it had come to this. "You don't know what you want. You're lookin' for somethin' to fill a gap? You're lookin' for me to step into some role, but I'm not your father, Jack. I've tried, but I can't be that guy."

"You're lecturing me about playing roles and filling gaps? Let's not go down this road, Eli, unless you're willing to talk about Hadley and Eliza," I said, my voice booming. "Because if anyone is playing games and looking to fill holes in their life, it's you. So save me the lecture."

"Get out!" he said. His whole body shook. The fire raged. The Eli I knew was absent. The man in front of me had damage in his eyes. "I can't have you here anymore. I don't trust you. Why did you go and make me not trust you?"

"Give me a break. I'm not buying the act. Tell me why you're bringing up my father now."

"No. Get out. I have nothing more to say." He bent down and grabbed the broken guitar neck, which he swung wildly back and forth. Then he poked at me like I was an animal. For a moment, I believed that he just might impale me with the makeshift wooden spear, and I just might deserve it.

"You owe me an explanation."

"We're done," he said. "Get out. Get out of my house. Now."

When you cross that river, there's no turnin' back
When you stretch that line, it's bound to snap
Even after all these years, you're first on my mind
And I'm lookin' for forgiveness, if you've got the time.

• THIRD •

John James Wyeth was all-around handsome even if he was thin as a nylon pick. Refusing to lose himself in the usual trends that occupied the '80s, he rocked a rugged bohemian look that would've impressed Jack Kerouac, if Jack Kerouac could've been impressed by such things. Until he took the job at the mill, he was a blue-collar guitar-for-hire straight out of Mr. Kerouac's Lowell, Massachusetts. He was wounded, but he kept up appearances. His bushy beard and dark eyes gave strangers the impression that he was brooding, distant, troubled. As a boy, I loved him all the more for it.

Some nights after dinner, he'd kneel down on the kitchen floor and let me barrel into him at full speed. I'd laugh uncontrollably as he crumpled to the floor, or I'd sit on his chest and declare myself the king of the house. He called me "kiddo" and "little man" and "banana bread." Sometimes he'd chase me around, hands like skeleton bones; when he caught me, he'd carry me through the room by my ankles until my mother told him to put me down or until I was purple. On his best days, he'd drop the needle on a record, lift me up, and dance with me in his arms. His aftershave was the Wild West—blood and heat and oak barrels. My mother always stood in the doorway with her arms crossed and her eyes fixed on him. He called her "the sheriff" as in "don't let the sheriff shut us down" or "look out, the sheriff doesn't approve." She didn't enjoy the nickname.

Two memories are more vivid, more clearly lodged in my temporal lobe than all the others. In one of them, I am four, and I'm sitting in the middle of the stairs, toes grasping at the new carpet, ears focused on a low cry reverberating from the kitchen like the whirring of a power drill. I never saw tears, but I was shaken by the sobs and the sharp intakes of breath that filled the air. The whole house sighed. After I gathered the courage to investigate, I jumped from stair to stair and called out, "Daddy, are you down here?" just to warn him of my presence. The sobbing stopped. I knew enough, even then at such a young age, to let him come to me. And he did, after a few minutes.

"What the hell are you doing up, little man? It's late." He straddled the kitchen and living room, keeping his face in the shadows.

"I can't sleep. It's too hot," I said. Fibbing always came easy.

"Open your window."

"I did, but it's still hot."

"I don't know what to do with you, Bird." He rubbed his eyes.

"Are you going to work now?" I asked.

"I'm running a little late. Maybe you can help me out," he said, slipping into the kitchen. A moment later, he returned with his work boots in his bony arms. While he carried the shoes, those arms shook like he was having a seizure from the shoulders down. "What do you think? Can you help me get these things on?"

I nodded. He passed me the boots, which were so unexpectedly heavy that they immediately dropped through my tiny hands and thumped to the floor. He lowered himself to the bottom stair. Employing a bear hug, I picked up the steel toes and brought them to his side. He stuck out his right foot. I pushed. It slipped on easily. "Remember that everything's backward," he said as I tried the laces, even though I couldn't tie a knot. When I glanced up to admit defeat, his bloodshot eyes balanced themselves, and I could tell he was trying to control the tremors. After strapping on his left boot, he bent forward, stuck the limp laces into his sock, kissed me on the head, and said, "Be good, be good." Then he left for work. I always tried my best to do as I was told.

The second memory was formed three days later as I celebrated my fifth birthday at a tricked-out McDonald's Playland. Cousins and preschool friends and nameless family members frolicked around while my mother sat in the corner with Grandma Kathleen. Both of their necks were tight as they talked; my mother's arms flailed around like Rock'em Sock'em Robots. My stomach spiraled from excitement and orange drink as I slid down the tube slide and jumped into a pool of plastic balls.

When it was time for presents, I ripped the paper off the biggest box first to discover a guitar. "Look Mom, look

Mom—it's just like Daddy's," I shouted, jumping up and down. "Is he here? Did he come back?" Then I ran in circles, staring at each face, trying to find the one person I wanted more than any other. I ran through the play area, the McDonald's, the men's restroom. Nothing. When I ran back to my mother, she whispered, "Don't be rude. Open the rest of your presents." Her eyes were focused on my forehead. "Where is he?" I asked. I still remember the vibrations on my lips when I spoke, and I remember the silence in the room that followed, everyone staring at the birthday boy, waiting for a meltdown.

"He'll be here," she said.

I never saw him again. Worse, in some ways, was that I never knew why. Why did he go? I asked my mother, but she never answered directly. She led me to assume that he was a deadbeat, a runaway, a half man who was afraid of reality. The more time slid by, the less connection I felt to him—memories were fluid, malleable, corruptible. Soon enough everything was distorted by the weight of time. John James Wyeth was an idea, a waking dream; there was nothing left to do but turn him into a villain. So that's what happened. Although it would be less than honest to pretend that I gave up hope for a reunion (and an adequate explanation). A kid never loses hope. That happens much later.

When Eli, in his theater of madness, brought up my father, it was just another attempt to confuse me, stifle me, stop me from prodding him. I provoked him, and he wanted to hurt me the way my betrayal hurt him. I got that. It made a certain amount of sense. Though it was madness, there was method in it.

Did he actually know my father, or was his confession some kind of power play? Maybe it was a delusion conjured by dementia. I wanted to give Eli the benefit of the doubt, but he had rattled me so deeply that I grew light-headed. I couldn't think straight. As I drove away from River Bend Farm, I told myself that Eli was—and always had been—completely and utterly unreliable. Was it possible that their paths intersected? Yes, of course. Anything was *possible*. Especially given my father's history. But it was highly unlikely and too damn convenient. Maybe, I thought, Eli had been prepared all along to rebuke me with this story, or maybe, on the other hand, it was true and the whole thing had been a setup.

It was then that I finally saw my own actions for what they were, and I knew I had no one to blame but myself. Yes, Eli and Gettleson had pointed the way, but I had willfully wandered down this path without a clear exit plan. I was always going to betray Eli's trust. He knew it; I knew it. But I didn't have to go so far.

My car listed to the passenger side as I pulled into the motel's gravel lot. Cut and run or stay the course? The green lights on the dash offered no guidance. The speedometer was broken, the AC didn't work, and the idling engine wheezed. The old Jack Wyeth might've run away to another city, but now I felt I had too much to lose. Eli wanted to bust my nose, Jenny needed space, and the ghostwriting gig had fallen to pieces, but I wasn't going anywhere. Not without plucking a speck of truth from Eli's tangled web of nonsense. Not before I apologized. Not before I set things right.

As I turned the dial on the car radio, I remembered the tape, the goddamn cassette tape. Struck by my own absurdity and dumb luck, I dug the cassette out of my bag and pushed it into the car's player. The factory deck gurgled and whined. "No, no, no," I yelped as I pounded my fist on the dash and jabbed at the stereo's face. I hit the eject button, but it refused to cooperate. Eject. Play. Eject. Rewind. Play. I hit every button on the console. Finally, as if the Celebrity was calling out "stop it," a tooth caught the wheel and the spool began to move.

Static was followed by laughter and then a man's voice: "What are you waiting for? Let's knock 'em out. Let's hear 'em. We can futz over the details later." The voice belonged to a young Barry Gettleson.

Chairs shuffled.

Eli's whiskey-soaked voice replied, "Fine. Let's get on with it. I'll set them down if you'll get off my case."

"Well, stop talking about it and do it, then. We don't have all day."

Eli began to strum a simple A-D-E, which could've been one of a million different ballads, but one I recognized as his variation on "The Water Is Wide," which I'd heard him do only once before, on the night that I first met him at the PAC. The strumming was dampened, muted by the heel of his hand, and at times a second guitar entered and picked apart the chords to provide texture and a sort of forcefulness and momentum. Together, there was a haunting give-and-take to the instruments as if one guitar was stifled while the other bloomed. Throughout the narrative, Eli's voice wavered, and his words were slow but deliberate. The last note hung in the air for an all-too-brief moment before Gettleson burst in, unsuspending my disbelief.

"Do it again, you know, for good measure?" There was a long and painful pause on the tape as Gettleson waited for Eli's response. "Okay. Guess we're moving on, then," Gettleson finally said. "Whenever you're ready, chief."

"I'm ready now."

"Then go for it."

Eli continued with another traditional: "I Ain't Got No Home."

I ain't got no home, I'm just a-roamin' around
Just a worker wandrin', I go from town to town
And the police make it hard wherever I may go
And I ain't got no home in this world anymore.

Eli's voice, thirty years younger, was tired and gloomy. These songs, massaged and molded by Pete Seeger and Woody Guthrie decades ago, weighed on his spirit. From all that I had read about Eli, I knew that these folk standards called to him, inspired him, led him to the footpath he'd eventually take from humble beginnings to voice of a generation. But this tape was made much later (late '70s by my guess), and I wondered why he felt compelled to record them at that time, so far along in his comeback. Where were *his* songs? Where was the new material? Then, as if he'd heard my line of inquiry, Eli changed course. Seemingly on the edge of exhaustion, he introduced a third song: "This one is called 'Let Go the River.'"

Let me be clear—I own every song Eli's ever released. In fact, I own 391 tracks in total on vinyl, on tape, and on CD. I'm sure there are Eli Page fans who have more material than I do, but no one had the music on this tape. No one.

The song's refrain was as low and forlorn as the earlier covers, but it was uniquely Eli's. Even the casual music fan, if asked, could've identified the authorship without deliberation.

This river's gonna ruin your life.
Let it go. Let it go. Let it go.

There was a distinct difference between Eli's previously released work and the stuff on this tape. He had cast aside his old journalistic tendencies and offered up something that was more confessional, personal, and intimate. Maybe it was just a snapshot in time, but it was as if Eli was drawing a line in wet cement. Even if it was mostly for his own benefit, he was announcing a shift.

"That song's not half bad," an unidentified voice said.

"Maybe not, but—"

"But we're moving on," Gettleson interjected, finishing Eli's thought.

"That's right. Doin' one more," Eli said. "Let's call it 'If You've Got the Time.'"

There was no playfulness, no political posturing. There was only the slow, throbbing sadness of his voice. The song was wrist-out, blood-drippingly honest. That's the only word that works: honest. Eli had come out of the '60s, out of reclusion, out of some hidden relationship, and he entered the mid-'70s on a different note. The finger pointed inward.

Whereas "Let Go the River" was unabashedly about the shadow of regret, "If You've Got the Time" was a shade or two darker. Eli's voice flickered as the sound quality went in and out. The intake of breath, how he dropped the lyrics at the end of each verse, the wavering—it was as if he was not sure the song should exist. No doubt it was deeply personal. Given what I knew now, I saw it for what it was—an unaddressed letter to Hadley and Eliza, confessing his regret and flirting with forgiveness, the type of forgiveness that he'd never be granted.

"Are we done? Because I'm getting' hungry," the unidentified voice said as the tape reached its end. The third man in the room. The second guitar. The voice didn't belong to Gettleson or Eli, so who was it? In my ragged and distorted mind, it sounded to me a lot like John James Wyeth.

"This is all we got," the owner said. "This or nothing."

"It'll do," I assured him.

He shoved a clipboard toward me. I accepted.

"You ain't gonna skip on me, are you?"

"Nope. I'm not going anywhere."

"Uh-huh. Well, sign here." He tapped the top sheet with his meaty finger. I printed and signed my name in two separate little boxes. "You gonna pay cash, or do you want me to hold on to your card for you?"

I dug some folded bills out of my pants pocket and paid the man.

"That'll buy you a week," he said. Then he turned and walked away. The silver key still hung in the door. The orange plastic dangling from its chain read UNIT #9.

The Sunshine Inn was a rest stop for outcasts, drifters, and the near divorced, but it maintained a certain country charm. A relic of a bygone era of roadside convenience, it was a place to rest your eyes before defeating the next four hundred miles. As I'd soon learn, my motel unit was pinned between a friendly group of bikers (who just needed to crash for a few days) and a mousy guy named Dale, who spent the evenings slap-boxing the vending machine until a packet of stale Cheez-Its let loose.

I dropped my stuff on the shag, locked the door, and fell onto the bed. The stiff, scratchy comforter looked as if it had been stolen from an off-color British B and B. As a bonus, it felt like low-grit sandpaper on exposed skin. I stared for an hour or more at the water-stained ceiling panels before finally falling asleep with one thought in front of all others in the queue: No matter how much I wanted something, how much I was willing to fight for it, some things were just out of my reach.

After midnight, I was roused from sleep by the roar of three hogs. A tangerine glow from the exterior light penetrated the room. I willed myself out of bed. As I pulled back the window blinds, I watched as a huge bike plowed into a utility pole with enough force to (1) toss its rider ten yards to the left and (2) bring down a set of power lines. The motel unit went black. Flickers of blue and yellow lit the parking lot like a carnival sky as shadowy figures scurried across the road.

"Don't be a fool. We're all here for one thing," Eli once told me, "to find a live connection and hold on to it until it bucks us off."

With no prospect of electricity, I returned to bed and pretended to sleep through the ambulance, the power company trucks, and the blackout party in Unit 8.

The next morning, when all was restored, I scrunched into the motel bathroom, splashed water on my face, and studied the man in the mirror. The form in front of me wasn't familiar. *His* scruff had finally become a full-fledged beard. When *he* stripped down, he could see the outline of his ribs. *He* counted every one and stuck his fingers between the curved bones. Then *he* got into the shower and let his skin absorb the hard water. *He* didn't know what to make of this new self. Strange how much can change in just a few short months.

Borrowing time, I watched a blurry HBO show on the old set, ordered food from the House of Pizza, and contemplated my strategy (or, more accurately, lack of strategy) to right the ship. I decided to give Jenny a few days of peace before I pleaded my case. With Eli, my move was more tenuous and time sensitive. There was no walking away. He'd strung barbed wire between us, but he needed me as much as I needed him. I couldn't hop over the fence with a white flag, call for a truce, and shake hands, but I had to do something.

Even in his condition, Eli was a gifted actor, as cunning as he was quick-witted—he pretended that he was all tuned up, but it was an act that couldn't hold. Isolated by his own stubborn design, Jenny and I had been the ropes that secured him to the dock. Without us, sooner or later, he'd float away and be forever lost in the whitecaps of his wandering mind.

Who, plagued by a guilty conscience, could stay still in a motel surrounded by cold pizza and question marks? Inaction was the same as failure, I told myself. I got up and drove into the village.

Halfway between the motel and River Bend Farm, the Celebrity sputtered and choked. I tapped the gas, but it didn't respond. So I coasted into the lot behind the library and parked the death trap all by its lonesome on the far side, under a small tree. In a final act of mercy, I left the doors unlocked and the key in the ignition.

As dusk settled in, I crossed through the covered bridge and spied Eli in the living room's light. He paced around the room, window to window, picking up the mess. He tossed objects into cardboard boxes, mouthed words to himself, and stacked books and magazines on top of each other beside the fireplace. As I lifted my arm to massage my aching neck, Eli paused and looked at the window. I pivoted behind a tree, waiting a few minutes before peeking around its trunk. He was gone. I considered going in for a closer look, but just then he returned to the room and began to unpack the boxes he'd just packed.

I wondered if Cal had arrested Eli the night I was thrown out. I wished I'd been there to see how it all played out. I thought about contacting Cal, but I knew it would be a waste of time.

A twig snapped in the field. "Who's out there?" I said. A rustle and crunch of grass followed my words as if some animal had bolted at the sound of my voice. A deer? A dog? Tig? Over my shoulder, I watched a moonlit shadow slide across the open field, through the broken corner of the fence wire, and along River Bend Road. I pursued it, knowing it was proof that Eli wasn't paranoid—someone was out there. But there was too much distance between us. When the moon fell behind the clouds, the figure was gone. I listened for footfalls, but my own heavy panting distracted me.

Suddenly, I was sick to my stomach. Sick that I had come this far and blown it all. Sick that my actions had unraveled Eli. Sick that I was in the dark. Sick that our whole relationship was predicated on a lie, that I let it slip away, that I couldn't protect him from whatever lurked outside. I turned and threw up on the unkempt lawn. When I finished, I wiped my mouth and walked away, spinning back once to see Eli staring into darkness on the other side of the window.

Every time I dialed Jenny's number, it was busy. Off the hook or disconnected, it didn't matter, I was shut out. No one picked up at Belanger's Barn either. So it was on the first Sunday morning after she went her way and I mine that I found myself standing on the Flynns' porch, knocking on the aluminum storm door. When no one answered, I sat on the front step and waited for her to return. I couldn't think of anything else to do.

The shade on the porch cooled the back of my neck.

The dead mill beside me was a hulking dull red slab of bricks and darkened windows. No activity. No trucks in and out, no smoke rising from the stack, no workers lingering on the loading dock. Again, it made me think of my hometown, how far I'd come, and how misguided I'd been. What if I'd stayed? Where would I be? Who would I be? It was a tad unsettling to consider how every decision influences the next and next. On and on it goes. Good news: Most times, it's easier to right a wrong than wrong a right.

Behind me, metal hinges squealed and the door wobbled like a Foley artist's thunder sheet. Jenny's mother (or aunt, I suppose), dressed in blue jeans and a maroon shirt that together resembled a large bruise, loomed over me, a half-tied silk scarf unraveling over her shoulders. Her pale face grazed the sunlight and retreated. Her eyes were red and heavy, as if she'd been sleeping or knocking back Jim Beam, but her hair was perfect—not a strand out of line. For a moment, a brief moment, I saw Jenny; not in physical resemblance per se, but in the way she held her body—her right hip tilted up ever so slightly so that her spine curved like a lazy creek; her hand rested on the higher hip in contemplation.

"I'm sorry." Those were the first words that came out of my mouth. "I didn't mean to bother you. I was looking for Jenny."

"You're sitting on my step," she said flatly.

"Only for a moment."

"Come inside." Julia Flynn was quiet natured; when she spoke I had to lean in to hear the soft words.

The heart of the house was a disaster. Piles of newspapers and glossy inserts leaned along the baseboards, old clothes were draped over the couch, an army of empty glasses covered the coffee table, and half-full boxes of knickknacks and decorations and picture frames obscured the rug. Covered with nails and discolored patches in rectangular and trapezoidal shapes, the walls were hardly recognizable. The Elvis plates were down; the banjo was gone. The dining room table was covered in stacks of gold-trimmed china and ironstone pitchers and serving plates—they rattled in time with our footsteps.

Once in the kitchen, she invited me to sit at the small Formica table, which was pushed against the wall and flanked by three chairs. The fourth was beside the refrigerator—its red seat cover worn and cracked at the center like a diner's stool. A jagged piece of metal stuck out from the corner of the table. I winced as it jabbed the fleshy inside of my thigh. Julia Flynn filled the teapot with tap water and placed it on the burner. She moved in slow motion, dragging her body alongside her. She leaned on the counter by the stove and did not speak for some time. By default, I zeroed in on the buzz of the refrigerator and a nearby clock with a persistent second hand tick, *wait... don't... go...*

"Tea," she said, leaving off the question mark. Her back was to me.

"Sure."

She reached into the cabinet and pulled out two mugs, dropped the tea bags in, and slid the sugar container between them. Then she removed two spoons from the silverware drawer and placed them to each side. Spoon, mug, sugar, mug, spoon. Strange to see the order in the way she prepared for the tea, especially after walking through a house in shambles.

"I don't know when Jenny will be back," she said.

"Do you know where she is?"

"Belanger's. She's been living up there."

"I tried calling—"

"You shouldn't take offense. She's not answering my calls either."

"Oh. Okay. I'll try to catch her there, I guess," I said, but I couldn't leave. Not yet. Not after I offered her some company.

Julia Flynn gathered herself with a deep, sorrowful breath.

"Still smells of death in here," she said. "I hope you'll forgive the mess. I haven't gotten the motivation to clean. They're kicking me out, you know."

"No. I didn't know."

"Well, you understand."

I nodded. I did understand. The mill owned the house, and with Phil Flynn gone, it was time for her to find a different arrangement. Soon after she moved, the mill owners would tear down the last of the houses and pave over the lots.

She was right, I could still smell the wake—the distinct smell of the prepared dead, old suits and furniture polish, a musky lemon smell that singed my nose hairs. I remembered Cal standing over the body, mouthing a prayer or curse or something indecipherable. Embarrassed, I'd pulled my eyes away to let him have his private moment. The wake crept along. Jenny spent the better part of two hours sitting on the stairs like a kid. I moved in and out, from Jenny's stairs to the dining room, where a group of old men told stories to keep their minds from the corpse in front of them. (Or perhaps to keep their minds on the corpse.) I read somewhere that after thirty minutes the brain can no longer focus on the intensity of grief required for such situations, so it relents and allows another emotion to take over. Julia Flynn's thirty minutes were up days before, but grief nudged itself into every corner of the house.

Another memory, which replayed a thousand times behind my eyelids, was of Cal and the pallbearers struggling to get the casket out through the narrow front door. I'd never been to a traditional wake before, so the labor was etched in my mind, partly because of my curiosity and partly because of the awful suspense created when Cal tripped on the doormat and stumbled, losing his grip on the casket's gold handle. His eyes were wide open in fear, punctuated by an audible gasp by the crowd as the other pallbearers, grunting and straining, adjusted to keep the casket right side up.

I blinked and tried to distance these thoughts. I felt bad for all involved.

"Is Jenny okay?" I asked Mrs. Flynn.

"I haven't seen her ... a moment here, a moment there ... I haven't been very aware ... you can understand, right?" Julia Flynn poured the hot water into the mugs, carried both of them to the table, and sat down opposite me. When she leaned back, she seemed to disappear. I shifted in my seat to face the empty kitchen like my host.

"It's too bad," she said. "Too much to take…for me…for her…she's seen too much of this…experienced too much."

I stared at her and listened, trying to maintain my calm. I knew, from the few interviews I'd conducted, that if you give people enough dead air they will almost always choose to fill the silence with their stories, damning or not. (Of course, it wasn't true of Eli, but Eli was the anomaly of all anomalies.)

"When we took her in, we wanted one thing—to give her a happy life." Julia Flynn's voice cracked as she spoke.

"Haven't you?" I asked.

"It's been hard. It gets harder every day." She cleared her throat and sipped her tea. "I never met her father, and I won't talk about someone I haven't met. I will say that my sister…well…she wasn't in a position to deal with a newborn."

"Jenny was lucky to have you," I said.

"I wonder."

What could I say to that? It was a lot of information to absorb between the ticks of the clock. *Please…don't…go…*

"It's too much. Life just seems to pile on, but she's a big girl now. Even if I still think of her as a kid. Tell me, what does she say about it all to you?" She glared at me and her pupils vibrated. It was as if her whole being was searching for something unnameable, intangible, and I had to be the bearer of bad news. There was nothing I could say or do to ease her fear.

"She hasn't said much to me about any of it," I answered.

"Oh…I was hoping…"

"She's a strong person. Smart. Deliberate." This addition to the conversation was like purporting that someone was in a "better place" after he or she died. It was meaningless, false because it was a standard, impersonal response used to exit an uncomfortable situation, but what was I to do?

"Eliza was such a good friend…a tragedy, really…to this day, it breaks my heart to think about it…they were inseparable, those two. It was a rare thing…friendship like that."

A creaking noise from the front room startled us both.

"Hello?" Julia called out.

We waited for someone to enter and join us, but no one came in. I shifted in my chair to peek into the hall. No Jenny. Nothing but boxes and the house settling underneath them.

"She was a beautiful child. If it was Jenny, I—" she stopped. She had such a measured tone in her voice when she said those words that I grew anxious.

"Yes." I swallowed the word as I said it.

"She feels guilty and so do I."

Silence.

"What happened exactly?" I asked.

"She hasn't told you?"

"No."

"Oh, dear. Well, the car upended in the river. Jenny was thrown. Amazing that she walked away with only a few stitches to the face and a broken wrist. Poor Eliza was trapped inside. She drowned. Jenny never had a chance to get to her." Mrs. Flynn paused. "I'm rambling. It was a long time ago. You shouldn't listen to me."

"I wish she'd told me."

"It's a small town. Everybody knows that story," she continued. "Maybe there's a reason you don't know. Did you ever think that maybe that's why you're so special to her?"

The tea was bitter and too hot for a summer day. We drank in silence, backs against the wall.

"I like you," she said, moving on. "My husband was very fond of Mark. He couldn't understand that it wasn't going to work out. But I like you."

"I'm sure he wanted what was best," I said.

"Best for Mark, for some reason. Phil never could see what she sacrificed for this family."

"School?"

"Everything. College included. She took some time after the accident, but she stayed to help care for him. And he could be a mean son of a bitch. Especially after he got sick. And Mark was always a sore spot in their relationship."

"How so?"

"When Jenny finally told him she was done with Mark, Phil grabbed her wrists and yelled at her. I think he just wanted... security. But he even bruised her. If he wasn't a sick man, I would've..." She shook her head.

"It must've been tough."

"I shouldn't speak ill. No. I like you. And I think you want what's best for Jenny. She deserves that. After all of this, she's earned the right to be happy."

I nodded.

"Try Belanger's," she said. "And, if you see her, tell her we need bread."

A gray fog hovered on the skyline, and a pungent, sickening smell hung in the air as if someone nearby was burning plastic. I stopped for a moment to wipe the sweat from my forehead, and I swear I heard someone shout.

Imagining the guilt that Jenny must've held inside, I no longer felt as if I was beating back the charging water. Instead it was as if the water was heating up all around me, and I was drifting downriver with no end in sight. I wondered if Jenny felt the same way.

Car tires squealed. The volunteer alarm wound up and wailed. Three pickups sped by me, their flashing lights cutting through the post-alarm silence. Off in the distance, the commotion grew louder. Voices yelled, buzzed, cried out.

Another fire?

As I climbed the hill, I saw Belanger's, engulfed. Thick black plumes of smoke pushed through the sky, an orange glow flickered and reflected off the truck windows, wild flames roared out of the barn's doors.

I ran toward the barn, joining a group of spectators by a thin line of yellow caution tape. Behind it, volunteer teams scrambled. James, the teenager employed by the IGA and deliverer of groceries to River Bend, darted back and forth. He wore a shirt with GFD on its chest. I grabbed him by the forearm and asked if he had any information.

"Back off, man," he shouted, yanking his arm from my grasp.

"Was anyone inside?"

"Just let us do our job." As he spoke, I saw a flash of recognition behind his eyes. He remembered me. Maybe he wanted to help me out, but he couldn't. Maybe he was just too scared or too powerless or too young to do anything. "That tape's there for a reason," he added, before joining his crew of ragtag young volunteers for traffic control.

More sirens howled. Lights flashed. Another hose truck entered the scene.

The cruel heat and smoke made it difficult to breathe. Each rumble and crack that echoed across the landscape made my body flex. Radios fuzzed and chirped. As the emergency personnel trudged up from the dirt staging area to the barn, the fire whistled and long flames lashed out of the open spaces.

Across the lot, far from the barn, I spotted Jenny's Blazer. Ivory Belanger sat on the SUV's bumper. Skirting the tape, I ran toward him.

"Ivory, are you okay? Did you get caught inside? Is Jenny in there?" I asked when I reached him, out of breath. He cupped his head in his hands, curled his torso toward his knees, and rocked. "Why?" he cried. "Why?" Even though he couldn't see the barn folding in on itself, he could hear all of the cracks and whines and rumbles, all the frantic shouts, and he could feel the intense heat, which seemingly melted the air between us. Despite the pangs of sadness I felt for him—and I did feel a tremendous sorrow—I was more concerned with answers.

"Ivory!" I grabbed him and shook him, but his expression didn't change.

The fire grew. I left Ivory at the Blazer and circled around the barn, knocking over garden gnomes and weaving through pillars and fences and brass bed frames. In the labyrinthine side yard, I dashed through the sculpture garden. Smoke poured out of the barn's charred gable vents.

"Jenny?" I yelled, but her name was absorbed by the firewall.

Julia Flynn had been careful to divulge only a piece of Jenny's story. A glimmer of light. When I left the house, I couldn't help but think about Jenny's abandonment and adoption, her dreams, the drowning, the confession to Eli, her father's affinity for Cal, her father's death, and of course the overwhelming and unfair demands that were laid upon her. In many ways, every single person carries around a tapestry of tragedy and pain, love and ecstasy. It was Jenny's capacity for love, her innate empathy, her resilience, her self-inflicted pangs of guilt that kept her terrible burden from consuming her like the mad fire was consuming the barn.

"Jenny?" I called out again.

The inferno created its own weather system, and the storm began to resemble a ravaged sail. After twenty minutes, the barn started to sink into the ground. I made my way around back, among the tall grass and hunks of metal, away from the weary eyes of the volunteers.

Reconstructing the time line in my head, I finally understood why Jenny had left UVM — why she had to leave. Her life had gone awry. And as my throat burned from the smoke, I felt like a selfish, sniveling fool for complaining to her about Eli, about Melanie, about my pathetic, petty problems. She'd endured far worse and with far more grace.

I rounded the corner of the barn, and the heat from the fire singed my hair. As I turned away from the burn, I saw Jenny standing in the field beside a row of concrete angels. Alone. Frozen. Her face sweaty and blackened with soot. I shouted, but she didn't notice. Even from a hundred feet away I saw the panic in her eyes.

I sprinted through the field to be by her side. As I grasped her and pulled her toward me, her stare remained fixed on the barn.

"I thought—" I said, unable to finish.

The fire roared, beams cracked, and the upper floor slammed through the furniture, the Library Room, the antique clocks, all of her creations. A few spectators screamed as a wall of dust and smoke blew toward them. James and the GFD volunteers pushed people back.

I was soaked in fear and perspiration.

"Are you okay? Do you need an EMT?" I asked.

Her face was quiet. The look, her body language, her silence said that she didn't need comfort, she didn't need a hug, and she didn't need someone to check her over. What she needed was plain and simple—someone to stand there and watch with her as the barn was swallowed into the fire and forever lost. And that's what we did. We watched it all disintegrate into embers and ash. We watched it all flicker away.

Thirty minutes, sixty minutes, ninety minutes—it seemed like a lifetime.

Off in the mob of emergency workers, Cal stood, arms folded, in the flashing lights. At first, I thought he'd let us be, but after a few minutes, he approached with a wicked purpose in his stride.

"Were you in the damn building? Were you? Were you in there?" Cal yelled.

She didn't answer or even acknowledge his presence except, perhaps, in the slightest squeeze of my hand when he began to bark.

"Were you inside?" he continued. "He could've killed you."

"Who?" I asked. "Do you know who did this?"

"Shut up," he said, refusing to look at me.

Cal reached out and tilted Jenny's chin with his hand so that they were looking eye to eye, unlocking her from the shock for a moment.

"Were you inside?" he asked her again.

She nodded and pulled her chin from his grip.

Flaming bits and pieces of barn floated through the air, higher and higher until they joined the clouds. "It happened so fast. Ivory smelled smoke coming from the second floor. I ran up to check and saw the flames. By the time I led him out, it was too late."

"Did you hear anything else? See anything out of the ordinary?"

"No," she said.

Another crash. The north side of the barn was gone.

"Where's your pal now?" Cal addressed me like a suspect. It took me a moment to realize what he was insinuating.

"Why?"

"Why do you think, genius?" he said.

"I don't know. You know he kicked me out. Haven't seen him since."

Cal sighed. Jenny stared at me, eyebrows bent.

"I warned you. Don't say I didn't warn you."

"Don't be an idiot, Mark. Eli didn't do this," Jenny said.

"I told you before," I said. "There's someone else involved. Did you look into that black Dodge I told you about? I saw someone—"

"Do you know how many black Rams are registered in Galesville?" he asked. Then a voice on his radio blurted out some code. "See those two guys over there?" Cal pointed to a pair of men next to his cruiser. "Do you know what they said to me as soon as I arrived?"

"No. What did they say?"

"They swear that they saw a skinny old guy with a beard and a black walking stick outside the barn. Just hanging around. They said he hobbled into the woods not twenty minutes before this fire began."

"That's ridiculous," I said, but I'm sure he saw doubt flash across my face.

"No. Eyewitnesses, that's what it is. Am I supposed to look the other way because you say so?"

"No," I said. "Just do your fucking job."

"That's the plan. You know as well as I do that I need to pick him up."

"This is all a mistake. Eli didn't do anything," Jenny said. But if I had to guess, in that instant, I'd say she had the same unnerving thought I had: Could Eli have done this?

Cal turned and walked away.

The volunteers shouted back and forth. The barn was down and the yard was on fire. Flames surrounded the stone angels. Everything—rock, wood, plastic, metal—was changing into a different form. All of the magic was gone; only a strange, sorrowful alchemy was left.

After Cal's cruiser took off, Jenny pulled me across the dirt path to the parking lot. It was then that I remembered Ivory, and I slowed down.

"What's wrong?" Jenny asked, noting my pause.

"I left Ivory here when I went to find you. He wasn't in good shape."

"Someone probably scooped him up," she said, but I could see the question in her eyes. Should she help Eli or Ivory?

"You're probably right," I conceded, as I jumped into the Blazer.

Before I had time to shut the door, Jenny drove up over the grass and the sidewalk until she hit the paved road. Then she pointed the vehicle toward River Bend. A horrible orange glow filled the Blazer.

As we left, I spotted Ivory, stumbling across the road to his home, body jerking up and down as if the ground was shaking. I felt then, at that moment, as if not one but many generations had been burned and buried that night.

By the time we arrived at River Bend Farm, the village police had already barricaded the driveway. Jenny parked up the road on the far side of the property, so that we could duck through the cut wire fence. "Stay back! Stay back!" someone shouted when we entered the yard. Who was it? I couldn't tell. All of my attention zeroed in on Cal and the young cop next to him, who looked like he had just swallowed a bug. They both had their guns drawn.

Without thinking it through, I dug my toes in and sprinted toward the house. Jenny wasn't far behind.

"Mark!" she yelled. Cal pounded his fist three times on Eli's solid wooden door. He spoke into the wood. When no one answered, Cal banged again, harder, more insistent. Then he stepped back and glanced at his fellow officer, who nodded in agreement, before kicking the door open, splintering the frame.

I kept running.

Suddenly, an intense pain split my side. My feet were in the air beside me—I was weightless, floating over the lawn. A millisecond later, I was drilled into the ground and the wind was ripped from my lungs. I must've known on some level that the cop had tackled me, but I felt as if I'd been struck by a runaway truck. Grass and dirt clung to the left side of my face. I struggled to keep consciousness.

"I warned you," a local officer said as he cuffed my wrists. I sat in the lawn, arms behind my back, catching my breath, helpless as Cal tore through the guts of Eli's house. Another young trooper pulled Jenny back toward the stone fence, instructing her to be cooperative.

At that moment, Tig darted out of the trees with a speed I'd never seen in him before. He made a beeline for the uniformed officers, panic in his eyes. I called out his name, but he would not be distracted. A few feet from the front step, Tig planted his feet and bared his teeth, growling in between ear-piercing barks. If Cal tried to enter the house, Tig would take his arm off—I was sure of it.

"Get that goddamn dog away from me," Cal instructed.

One of the troopers tried to sweet-talk the animal, to no avail. Then he took two sticks and smashed them together to startle the dog, but Tig was locked on.

After a few failed attempts, the trooper turned to Cal and shrugged. Cal stepped forward, raised his gun in the air, and fired a warning shot. Tig whimpered and retreated into the woods.

Cal turned his attention back to the entrance.

I saw Eli before the pride of officers did. He emerged from behind the carriage barn with a rifle in his left hand and a red gas can in his right. I stared at him, silently pleading for him to turn around and go back into the woods or wherever he came from. "Eli," Jenny called out, probably believing, as I did, that the worst was about to happen. "It's okay. It's okay," Jenny said, and I didn't know if her words were directed toward Eli or Cal or some unnamed entity. Her pleas caught the attention of the officers, who spun around to see what Jenny and I had already seen. Cal stepped out of the house, eyes like quarters. Before I could blink, four different guns were drawn and aimed.

"Drop the weapon," they demanded, almost in unison.

"You've got to let me see her," Eli said. "I've come a long way."

"See who?"

"Don't play dumb."

"I don't know what you're talking about," Cal said.

"I know she's here. Try and say she's not."

"Mr. Page." Cal tried to calm his voice, but it wavered. "You're confused."

"Facts are facts. She's my child. My blood. Don't try to deny it." He paused. We were all watching him come undone. "It's terrible what happened to Hadley, but you can't keep me from my own daughter."

"No one's daughter is here," Cal said.

"It didn't have to come to this," Eli said, looking down at his hands. His fingers tightened. At the same time, I thought I saw a glimmer of recognition form behind his eyes as if he was waking to a new day.

"Eli," I shouted. "Can you put the rifle on the ground?"

"What?"

"Put the rifle down," Cal and I said at the same time.

"This? Found both of 'em out back. Someone left 'em there." He raised the rifle a fraction. At the same time, the troopers and the village police aimed. "Don't think it even works anymore." He dropped both the can and the rifle by his feet.

Cal rushed him, slammed him to the ground, and slapped the cuffs on his thin wrists. Shouts and curses and codes and radios buzzing—I couldn't decipher what anyone said in the cloud of noise. The officers secured the items as Cal dragged Eli to his feet and marched him to the state cruiser. Eli's chin and shirt collar were full of dirt. With a blank expression on his face and a bloodied nose, he slumped in the backseat, and he glanced around the car like a child on a ride-along. Cal shut the door, took a deep breath, and exhaled. I saw his body relax, his neck muscles let go, before he turned his attention to me.

"That was a stupid move," he said.

"He's not well," I said loudly. "You saw it. He has no idea what's going on."

"How do you know it's not an act? Everybody plays dumb when they get caught."

Jenny, stunned, appeared introspective. "You saw the same as we did."

Cal looked over my shoulder at her and pulled back his bravado. "I did. But I have to take him in."

"He didn't do it," she countered.

"That will all work itself out," he said.

"Will it?" I asked.

Jenny spun away from Cal and walked over to the cruiser. She tried to get Eli's attention by knocking on the window, but he refused to turn his head.

"The truth will come out," Cal said, and he believed it.

I struggled to my feet. He unlocked me. My wrists were bright red from the metal clamps.

"Are you happy now?" I asked.

"Not even close."

"You do realize he's sick, don't you? He doesn't think clearly."

"By the smell, I think he's drunk, but I wouldn't care if he was blind and bedridden, he had a gun and a gas can. I think he has to answer some questions."

"What do we do now?" Jenny asked as Cal drove away, but I had already dialed Barry Gettleson's number. It was Sunday, so I left a message, noting that it was an emergency. Gettleson called back less than three minutes later.

"Eli's been arrested," I said.

"For what?"

"Arson, I guess."

"That's ridiculous. What the hell is going on in that fucking town? Who's in charge? Heads will roll, I'll tell you that. Heads will fucking roll." His voice faded. "Where are they taking him?"

"I'm not sure. The village station."

"I'll send someone."

As we walked down the road toward the Blazer, I couldn't help but ask myself, How did it come to this? I'd arrived in Galesville as a ghostwriter, and life had gotten in the way. One morning I woke up and I was no longer the man I thought I was. All of those inventions and reinventions were pointless. Even though I was embarrassed to say it out loud, Eli and Jenny were all I had.

"When did he kick you out?" Jenny asked. The Blazer's interior smelled like a campfire, which turned my mind to Belanger's, still smoldering in the distance. As she accelerated through the village, windows down, she shouted at me to be heard.

"Last week, after I dropped you off," I answered.

"How was he then?"

"Not good. I tried to talk him down, but it didn't go well. We exchanged words."

"You should've called."

"I *did* call." The taste of smoke burned in my throat. I coughed as I tried to explain.

Jenny parked in the shaded lot behind the police station.

"Isn't that your car?" she asked.

"We've parted ways," I answered.

GPD was located in the basement of Middle Block. Its rear entrance was concealed by a group of overgrown, low-hanging trees, but the path in was marked by a small blue-and-white sign that read GALESVILLE POLICE DEPARTMENT in huge block letters and *To Protect & Serve the Citizens of Galesville* in a small, fanciful script.

"This is a joke, right? They can't hold him."

"I was inside once for a middle school field trip," Jenny explained. "There're three old jail cells below that window." She pointed to a small rectangle about seven feet up the back wall, which looked more like a vent than a window. "Two of the top bars in the right-hand cell were bent inward by a football player. Roid rage. That's the story they tell during the tour. It's not something you forget."

We waited a long time for something to happen. Nothing did. Eventually, dusk settled in. I crammed myself between the seat and the door, attempting to find some relief for my stiff neck and aching wrists. Jenny cranked her seat back and rested on her side, her legs folded so that her knees pointed toward me. Whenever a bright pair of car lights cut through the window, I'd lift my head and hope for reinforcements.

I don't remember when it was that I fell asleep, but the dawn's light woke me as it warmed the side of my face and filled the inside of the Blazer. I got out, stretched, and pissed in a withering shrub. A few minutes later, as I stumbled back to the vehicle, Cal arrived — smug, starched, and pressed. I slammed the door, waking Jenny.

"Sorry," I said.

"What's going on?" she asked.

I tipped my head in Cal's direction. Quickly she sat up and wiped the sleep from her eyes. Her cheeks and forehead were smudged with dirt and grime. We both still smelled like fire.

I stared at the small window and tried to picture Eli and imagine what it was like for him. It wasn't so much the physical space that worried me; it was the possibility that he might not even know where he was. Given his confusion, he could place himself in an empty box, a cage, or a coffin with equal ease.

Two more hours dragged on. My left leg bounced uncontrollably. I massaged my neck to ease the tension. What's going on in there? Had Eli slept? Was he clearheaded enough to keep his mouth shut? Jenny wondered aloud if Eli would be transferred to the Washington County Correctional Facility in Fort Edward. Eli certainly had a knack for taking a bad situation and making it worse, and that was when he was lucid. Jenny reached over and placed her hand on my knee. I relaxed for a moment. Innocent or not, it could all go so wrong.

At a quarter to ten, a glossy red Audi zipped into the lot. I straightened my back to ease the horrible kink in my neck. Gettleson's head-roller had arrived. Jenny perked up. I stepped out of the Blazer, crossed the gravel, and greeted the man with a handshake.

"You must be Jack," he said as he folded the driver's seat and reached in the back of his car for his suit jacket. He was younger than I was, clean-cut and red eyed. His breath smelled like espresso.

"Thanks for coming."

"Don't thank me yet," he said, slipping on his jacket and adjusting the knot of his tie. He grabbed a briefcase from the backseat. "He's been here all night? Is that correct?"

"Yes. Since yesterday afternoon." My head rocked up and down in a perpetual nod.

"Any activity in or out?"

"Not really."

"Not really? What does that mean? Who's inside?"

"The local guys...and a state trooper...Mark Calvin." Whatever version of calm I was trying to portray had abandoned me.

"That's the one with a hard-on for Mr. Page?"

"Yeah. So, what's the plan?"

"The plan? What is this, *MacGyver*? You wait here. That's the plan," he said, pointing to the gravel under my feet. His finger was bony and obnoxious.

The young lawyer made Gettleson look about as intimidating as Jimmy Stewart. He entered the station like a man of privilege, armed with a check and shit-eating grin, to retrieve his son from the vice principal's office. That wouldn't play in Galesville. Or so I thought.

I leaned against the rear bumper.

Less than a half hour later, Cal emerged from the station, his shirt wrinkled. The scowl on his face was evidence of some small victory for Eli. He scuffed his boots in the dirt, got into his cruiser, and slammed the door. He didn't turn the car over right away. Instead, he sat there, staring straight ahead. Jenny took a step toward him. Almost simultaneously, he turned the key, shifted into drive, and punched the gas. As he drove by, he flipped me off.

Jenny didn't see the finger. I shook my head in amusement, and she stared at me quizzically like the whole exchange was my fault. I suppose we all forgive people who should, by all objective measures, remain unforgivable. The dynamic that existed between Jenny and Cal was not something I could easily crack open and read. They had grown up together, shared each other's losses, and watched each other turn into adults. I got that. It was a bond that I'd never truly understand, and one that drove me to an undiscovered level of irrationality, but I got it.

Jenny joined me on the bumper.

"Where did you go after?" she asked.

"After what?" The temperature of my face rose.

"After Eli kicked you out. Where are you living now?"

"The Sunshine Inn."

"I wish I'd known, I would've—"

"I like it there. It fits."

We were both quiet for a few minutes, watching the police station door, waiting for a sign.

"It's not like him. To just throw you out. What did you do?"

"It's never one thing, is it?" I said. "He knew I'd been in the study and that I knew about Hadley." She nodded as if it all made sense to her. "It didn't go over well."

"You didn't tell him that I—?"

I shook my head.

"He wasn't himself. He flipped out and muttered something about my father. Implied that he knew him. They were friends. They made some sort of deal. What do you make of that?"

"Stranger things have happened," she said.

I was struck by the fact that she didn't dismiss it outright.

"Do you think it's true?"

"It wouldn't surprise me," she said knowingly.

Suddenly, I was filled with the sinking suspicion that she'd known about the supposed connection all along. I wanted to be angry, but it didn't take.

My head yelped. With each minute that ticked by, the stone building in front of me became more and more abstract. Did Eli know that we were there? Did he, locked up, hear that same sickening slip of reality? If he did, I was sure he would've laughed us off and told us to get on with our lives.

"Jack. I love you, but I don't think you're comfortable in your own skin. Until you come to terms with who you are and where you come from, it'll all be an act, won't it? Maybe Eli's confession will help you get there."

The door opened and Eli emerged with his lawyer. Even with his head down, it was easy to see that he hadn't slept and was more than likely on the verge of a complete mental collapse. From my perspective, he didn't appear to know what was going on, where he was, or why the young man in the suit tugged on his arm. Kept awake for hours, the last twig of his mind might have finally snapped. He didn't look at us; he didn't acknowledge us at all. The head-roller opened the passenger door of his Audi, stuffed Eli in, and then shut it like he was spiking a football in celebration. Eli disappeared completely behind the tint.

Jenny and I walked in unison toward the car.

"Bottom line," the lawyer said. "He's released pending an evaluation, and I'm sure your trooper friend Calvin will keep an eye on him, if you get my meaning."

"Thanks for your help," Jenny said.

"He's not a well man," he added, slipping into his car.

A car's engine gurgled outside the motel unit's window, drowning out the sound of the AC and the television. I parted the curtains to see who was making the racket, and sure enough, baking in the sun, I recognized the vehicle. Eli's '66 Mustang. Nightmist blue. Pristine.

I opened the door. Outside, the air smelled gasoline rich. He shut off the engine and stepped out of the car. To my surprise, he was clean shaven.

"How'd you know I was here?" I asked.

"Jenny told me. It's the last place I woulda looked."

"So the old thing still runs?"

"Yeah. It just needed some attention." The whitewall tires gleamed in the sun.

"Come on in."

Eli had been released from custody three days earlier. Without the facial hair and within the confines of the motel unit, he was somehow shorter, smaller in stature, as if he was slowly fading into the ether. He pulled a wooden chair from the table under the window and slowly eased down into a comfortable position.

I sat on the corner of my bed, folded my arms, and leaned against the wall.

"Nice digs."

"What happened to your beard?"

"Shaving accident," he said. "Lawyer said it made me look crazed. Told me to cut it off. That was his advice. You think he'd offer somethin' a little deeper for a grand an hour."

"Well, you do look better than the last time I saw you."

"Sleep helps, I'm my best self in the mornin'. Things fall apart after lunch."

"So why are you wasting good time with me?"

He cleared his throat and straightened his back. It was odd to see his naked face. Without the protection of the beard, his expressions were more exposed, open to interpretation. His wild, electric hair was matted down as if he'd actually attempted to comb it for the first time in decades.

"I promised you an interview," he said. "I'm here to deliver."

"Why now?"

"Fair is fair. Come on, I gotta get it off my chest."

"Okay. First thing. Be honest," I said. "Was there ever going to be a book?"

"Not if I had anythin' to do with it."

"So it *was* all just a big waste of time."

"Was it? That's up to you."

"You know what I mean."

"Gettleson made the deal. He said we needed the advance. Money issues, cash flow, or whatever nonsense he shouts about on a daily basis. Figured I'd die before they'd come lookin' for the money back."

"Then why hire me?"

"Listen. I'm sorry it came out the way it did." He paused. It seemed as if he wanted to continue but couldn't construct the sentences. He bowed his head before restarting. "I promised a friend I'd look out for you," he said slowly, deliberately. "That's the truth."

"That's what you meant, the other day, when you brought up my father?" Muscles I didn't know I had wrenched my neck into a bowline knot.

"Yes."

"Well, I call bullshit."

"I'm sorry," he said. "I am. It wasn't supposed to be like this."

"Well, if you two were so chummy, why don't you tell me what he looked like then?"

"Okay, I can do that," he said, thinking for a moment. "Tall. Skinny as a post. Black Irish. He had long fingers, which made him one hell of a guitar player. Eyes and chin like yours, but he had a deep scar on his chin from smacking his face on the ice that time he fell into the river. You and I wouldn't be sitting here —"

"Stop," I said. "Just stop."

He waited a moment, but he was determined to get it out.

"He showed up in Woodstock, where I was recording. We'd played together dozens of times before, but I couldn't help him. Not that time. He was a good guy, a great guitar man."

"Was?" I asked.

"Yeah. Unfortunately."

"How did it happen?"

"His bad habits came to collect on their debt. He was pretty strung out."

At first, I thought that this new information would be a revelation, and I was puzzled by my lack of reaction. Call it shock or whatever, but I was numb to the news as if I'd known it all along. Maybe I'd moved on. Maybe nothing had really changed.

"I never saw any of it around the house," I said.

"We've got an amazing ability to hide things we want hidden," Eli answered.

"What am I supposed to do with that information? You come in here to tell me my father is dead and you were somehow appointed my guardian angel?"

"I'm no guardian angel. I'm just tryin' to give you some perspective," he said. "When I sent him away, he made me promise to check in on you from time to time . . . to make sure you didn't end up like him. I had no intention of doing that, by the way. None. Then I met you back-stage at UMass—well, I figured it for a sign. I'd already made enough mistakes by ignoring promises, you know? He would've had a good laugh about that whole gig, the chancellor, that house manager. He would've loved to have seen that. I've kept tabs on you since. Or . . . Gettleson has." He took a deep breath. "Listen. I don't have much to offer. Never did. But I've made more than my fair share of bad decisions in my day . . . maybe I can . . . you know . . . so ask what you're gonna ask. That's what I've got to give."

I could almost feel my mind slip backward through time, but I refused to wallow in memory's nettles. I needed to change the subject.

"Anything?"

"Yeah. Anything. Go for it."

"Did you love her?" I asked.

"You're gonna have to be more specific."

"Hadley." I choked on her name.

"Yeah, I did."

"Well, then, what happened?"

"I fucked it up. It's that simple."

"She was from Galesville, right? So how'd you meet?"

"Sounds like you've found out some answers on your own." He cleared his throat. "Met her in the Village. I'd seen her around. Sketchin' during gigs. Givin' me the eye. One night I ran into her at Gerde's. I asked her to hang with me. She did. We kept it quiet, though. Right from the start."

"Did she know who you were?"

"Sure. Yeah." He rolled his head back. "Not that she really cared."

"How'd you hook up?"

"Hook up? I guess that's what it was. You know what's funny? I remember all of it as if I'd lived it a dozen times, but I don't . . . I don't know how I got here . . . with you . . . I don't know what I had for breakfast . . . but I remember Gerde's and meetin' her for the first time."

"How'd it happen?"

"You don't need the details—I'll keep those between myself and whatever's left of my mind, but it was serious. Know that. I was serious. So serious, I quit the scene. The Village was packin' up anyway. Everyone was moving up the Hudson or out west. It was crazy. It felt like it was all done. We lived together for a while in a third-floor walk-up. Gettleson knew what was going on. He kept it quiet. I think he wanted me to have a chance at whatever it was I was doin'. Then she got pregnant."

"You knew she was pregnant?"

"It's why we came north. Talked about it for a long time, but when we got the news...we...you know...left for greener pastures."

"Did you plan on getting married?"

"Damn right."

"You lived here? In Galesville? There's no record—"

"Nobody cared to know."

"Then why did you leave?" I asked.

"After a while I grew restless. I was never one for stayin' put. Soon as I got here, I was writin' new songs, and some of them weren't half bad. When that second wave came in, I wanted to ride it. I had to get goin' again. It's hard to explain, but she understood."

"What about her letters? Why did you ignore them?"

It was the first time I'd acknowledged the letters. He shifted his gaze and clamped his teeth. Suddenly, his face was blank. A minute or two passed. I could've let him off the hook. I could've asked another question, but instead I decided to wait it out. Finally, he came back to life. "What?"

"The letters?"

"Yeah, I read them," he said. "A better man would've come home; a better man would've called. That wasn't me. Too selfish, too obsessed, too cowardly. And you've gotta understand—everyone wanted somethin' from me. Do this. Say that. The tour was larger than one man. That new album was larger than one man, larger than anything I'd done before. People counted on me."

"She counted on you," I said, surprising myself. "How could you just cut her loose?"

"Don't know, but as soon as I did, I wanted her back." He rocked as he spoke, unable to get comfortable at all.

"But you didn't write. Why?"

"There's no excuse. I kill myself tryin' to walk it back, but what's the use."

"You couldn't've known it would end the way it did," I interrupted. His crooked smirk said he appreciated the attempt, but he had thought about it endlessly and had come to a different conclusion.

"It's somethin' I've tried to forgive myself for, and it just doesn't take."

"When did you find out . . . that she had died?"

"The one call I made. On the due date. She had been dead for two weeks. I had a couple shows left, and I called to check in and tell her I was coming back. Her mother answered, and she tore my fuckin' head off." The veins in his neck pulsed. He swallowed hard. "I was just sittin' there thinkin' I should hang up on this woman, but I knew I deserved every word she threw at me. She would've butchered me into tiny pieces and fed me to the pigs if I wasn't halfway across the world."

"That's why your last two gigs were canceled." I remembered reading about the strange conclusion to the European tour, but I (like everyone else) assumed it was drugs and the requisite detox. "Did she tell you about Eliza?"

"No. She told me to stay away from Galesville. She said the child had died, but I could hear a baby wailin' in the background. Little girl had my lungs. I tried to imagine what that screamin' baby looked like, but I couldn't even paint that picture in my mind." He paused. "You know, I drove to Galesville in '85. Spied on them. Saw this little girl with long black hair in the yard—looked like the ghost of her mother, even so young. I heard them say her name, and I knew it was true. That's all I had of my daughter. The name." He brought his hand to his eyes and pinched away the tears.

"Eliza is a good name."

"Hadley wanted it. Bet the Myerses hated it, but they kept it. That's somethin', isn't it?"

"Did you try to talk to her?" I asked.

"No. They would've shot me dead in the street if they saw me. No one would've thought twice." He cleared his throat. "Harold died of a stroke in '99. Deb put the house up for sale a couple years later. I had Gettleson buy it for Eliza. Planned to give it to her when she was ready."

"How'd you find out about the accident?"

"Gettleson told me the news, but it was Jenny Lee who filled in the details. She came asking for my forgiveness, and she answered all of my questions."

"Did you forgive her?"

He nodded. Then he lurched out of the chair and opened the door. "I need some air."

Convinced he'd leave, I watched him through the window as he paced on the broken sidewalk in front of the motel unit. After a few minutes, he reentered, but he didn't sit down.

"You okay?" I asked. He looked like a mine worker after an explosion and a ride up the rescue tube. He stood in the doorway for what seemed like forever, eyes blank, arms and legs motionless. Then his chest heaved and he snapped back to life.

"How sick are you?" I asked as he started to walk away.

"Sick enough to know I've come to an end."

"What's that mean?"

"There's no way forward, Jack. There's only behind."

I opened my mouth, but I was at a loss.

"Let me give you some advice. I don't know what's going on between you and Jenny, but figure it out. Don't do anything stupid. If my words can stop you from that . . . well . . . maybe I'll feel like I've done somethin' for you."

I nodded.

"One last thing for free."

"What's that?"

"Watch out for the prom date. He's gunning for us all. Know what I mean?"

"No. Do you remember the name?"

Eli shook his head. "Hadley's old boyfriend. He's had it in for me for years. Check the boxes when you get back; you'll understand."

"Back?"

He tossed a set of keys on the bed. "When you're ready," he said. "This place smells like stale coffee and 409 cleaner."

I took the offering. It was the least that I could do.

On my way to Eli's, I stopped to admire Jenny's mural. I couldn't help but focus on the river, carving its serpentine path through the land, connecting the old and the new, the right and the left, the top and the bottom. It doesn't matter if it's tragedy or coincidence that guides us, we're all headed toward the falls.

After Belanger's burned to the ground, the *Mirror* reported on the increased police presence in the village and newly imposed rules. Large gatherings were discouraged. In fact, any group of three or more people was stopped and questioned. An informal curfew had been implemented, and townsfolk were asked to be "vigilant." In most ways, the mural controversy had spread into something harder to contain. Anger and distrust smoldered just below the surface. Many were scared and suffering in silence. They believed that the shape of their future was in doubt. Who could blame them? Television pundits declared that the situation was dire, the country was on the brink, we were at a tipping point. When Belanger's was consumed, both sides cast an empathetic eye on their neighbors for a moment, but there was too much acid to dilute, too many people fueling the fire for personal gain, too much cynicism. Astonishingly, Jenny had captured the tension in her mural, anticipating the derision.

As I approached the farm, I saw Tig, lying in the grass by the door, waiting to be let in. His fur was matted down, muddy, as if he'd been scrapping around outside for days. I refilled his water and food bowls and called to him, but he didn't answer. Peeking around the corner, I saw him collapse on his pillow, relieved to be back, if only for a moment. I was relieved that he was still alive. He was a fighter. Despite the wear and tear, he was going out on his own terms.

The house was in shambles. The study had been emptied of two-thirds of its belongings. Piles were stacked waist high in random spots throughout the living area. As I walked through the living room toward the dining room, the wide planks creaked with menace. There was even a slight echo as I crossed into the dining room.

Two mysterious boxes labeled OLD – H FOR ATTIC sat on the harvest table. They weren't from the study. In all my snooping and investigating, I'd never come across these boxes. Inside were hardbound albums, simple framed pictures, and thin photographs. I sat down and thumbed through each item, finding many pictures of Hadley and Eliza. Eli was right — it was striking just how much Eliza looked like her mother; the two decades that separated them didn't even warrant a change in hairstyle or clothes. I examined the outside of the box again. The label, scribbled in black marker on all four sides, wasn't in Eli's handwriting. If these boxes didn't belong to him, my guess was that they'd been left behind in the attic by the Myerses.

For so long, I'd wanted to stand in Eli's shoes, to live inside his life, to be him in every possible way, but I finally saw what he'd been trying to show me. Like rushing water, the past had washed over him and pulled him under. Sorrow was too weak an emotion for what I felt for Eli, pity too short and sweet. He'd spent his entire adult life pretending to be something he wasn't. I mourned for the Eli Page who never had a chance to exist.

A second handful of photos showed a young Hadley, a Hadley I hadn't been aware of a few weeks prior, but one who seemed so vivid and alive in my hands at that moment. Two framed photographs stood out from the pile. In both of them Hadley was with a doughy boy with short-cropped hair. The boy's beaming face filled the frame while Hadley's gaze was detached, bored, and rueful. I flipped the frames over and popped them out of their cardboard just as Jenny would've done. The first one said, "Hadley & Todd, Prom 1971," and the second said, "Engagement Party."

"The prom date," I muttered, remembering Eli's phrasing. These pictures, unleashed from the attic, must've triggered the warning, but who was this guy?

As I looked through the box for more images of Todd, there was a pounding at the front door. I ignored it, choosing to continue digging. Footsteps creaked through the hall, through the living room, and into the dining room until the intruder was right behind me. I spun around quickly and found Jenny, her hair matted down by the soft, almost imperceptible rain.

"Jack?" The question sounded like a curse. "You surprised me."

"What're you doing here?" I asked.

"I was going to ask you the same," she said. "Have you seen Eli?"

"Not today," I answered. "He's probably at the graveyard."

She stepped to the windows, looked out over the barns, the field, the rock piles, and the hills. "I was just up there," she said. "There was no trace of him. I'm beginning to worry."

"I'm sure everything is fine." Just saying those words conjured the memory of the first night I'd met Eli, at college, after he'd gone missing before the show.

"Have you checked upstairs?" she asked, already on her way. As she climbed the staircase, her Wellies on the wood planks were so loud that I could tell which room she was in just by the clomping.

She walked down the hall, turned around, and hurried back down the stairs.

"Any luck?"

"No." Her eyes fell on my bag, which lay on the floor next to the table.

I explained Eli's visit to the motel. "He was driving his Mustang."

Jenny crossed through the mudroom and opened the door to the garage. "It's gone too," she reported.

"I'm sure he's fine," I said, but her worry worried me. Something was off. "Stay here with me. He'll show up sooner or later."

"What are these?" she asked, pulling back the cardboard flap on a box to peer inside.

"I'm not exactly sure. Eli had them out," I answered. "He must've been looking at all this stuff before he left."

Jenny snatched a handful of photos out of the box. Suddenly, she let out a brief but forceful laugh. "That's me on the right," she said, pointing to a little girl with braces and bubble bangs. "Eliza's grandmother and I packed this stuff up the winter after the accident. That's her handwriting on the box."

I pulled out a piece of folded newspaper. Jenny froze as I unfolded the gray pages, which had been saved from the *Galesville Mirror*. Eliza's obituary. Centered on the thin leaf. But behind the obit was an earlier article from the *Post-Star*. As I read the article to myself, Jenny turned away.

Woman, 21, Killed in Galesville Car Accident

GALESVILLE, NY—Authorities are investigating a car crash on the Batten Kill that took the life of a 21-year-old woman from Galesville.

The accident happened in Holland field, just west of the town line, at around 10:30 p.m. on Sunday, June 26.

Authorities say Jenny Lee Flynn of Galesville was driving a maroon Volkswagen Jetta westbound on route 29 at about 25 to 35 miles per hour when she swerved off the road into the river.

Flynn was thrown from the car, authorities said.

Eliza Myers drowned in the river after sustaining serious injuries during the crash and becoming lodged in the car's cabin. She was pronounced dead on the scene.

Myers's grandmother told WNYT her granddaughter was an artist and was set to begin her senior year at NYU in the fall.

Flynn received minor injuries, including lacerations and a broken wrist.

The cause of the crash is now under investigation.

A memorial service for Eliza Myers will be held at 11 a.m. Saturday at St. Joseph's Catholic Church, located at 196 Church Street in Galesville.

Scrawled in the corner, in Eli's hand, were two words, fresh with ink: "Forgive Yourself."

I slid the frames I'd handled earlier toward Jenny. "I found these too," I said, intentionally interrupting Jenny's descent into memory and guilt. "Do you know this guy?" I pointed to the first frame, which pictured Hadley and her date on prom night. "It says his name is Todd."

She stared at it for a long time and then handed it back to me. "Yeah, sure, it's Todd Decker. Lives down the street," she said, wiping two errant tears from the side of her nose. "You've got to picture him with a beard and without the baby fat."

"Tell me he drives a black pickup."

"How'd you know that?"

All along I'd wondered if Eli's paranoia was a symptom of dementia, but my doubts were unwarranted. Eli knew exactly what was going on. He just couldn't always articulate it.

"Eliza used to complain about him all the time," Jenny continued. "He was creepy. He always checked up on her. She called him the stalker. Joking, of course."

"Apparently, Hadley was engaged to him." I showed her the other frame.

"For two seconds," she said, unmoved. "It was never going to work."

"You knew about this?"

"It's old news. Eliza and I laughed it off years ago."

"It must've been serious."

"No. I don't think so. Wishful thinking by the Myerses. He was drafted to Vietnam about the same time Hadley left for New York. Since coming home, he's lived alone in that trailer down the road."

Rummaging through the detritus on the table, I searched for an answer to Eli's whereabouts. Bills, magazines, letters, bags, prescriptions, and last week's issue of the *Mirror*. I spun the paper right side up and unfolded it, hoping to find a note from Eli in the margins, but there was only a huge black-and-white photo of a Ferris wheel.

"I think I know where he is," I said, feeling a sinking sense of urgency.

Jenny stared at me. I looked at the clock. It was almost four thirty. Still no Eli, but it wasn't Eli I was worried about at that moment; it was Todd Decker.

Jenny tightened her grip on the steering wheel, punched the gas, and called out the numbers. I entered the digits and handed her the phone, which she cradled between her right shoulder and ear. "He'll listen to me," she said more than once, trying to convince me that Cal was a person we could trust.

The Blazer bucked as she shifted into fourth gear. The cell popped out of place. She reached up and adjusted it. "No answer," she said before leaving the voice mail: "Mark. It's Jenny. It's important. Please call me back at this number. We're on our way to the fairgrounds. We need you. *I* need you." She pocketed my phone, powered through an ungodly row of potholes, and turned toward the fair's parking. "Maybe he's already inside," she said.

"Maybe," I answered, still stung by "I need you." Did she need me like she needed Cal? Had she ever really needed me that way?

"Let's split up," Jenny said. "You go toward the lights." She pointed to the midway. "I'll meet you at the Ferris wheel in fifteen." Before I could respond in the positive or negative, she was off into the crowd.

Thunder rolled over the mountains. All the treetops leaned to the east.

Whole masses of people brushed by me—farmers, agri-salesmen, young families, politicians, vendors, retirees, teachers, nurses, doctors, lawyers, mechanics, young professionals, old professionals, volunteer firemen, and everyone else I had observed in my short time in town. I knew none of them and all of them at the same time. I smelled the tension in the air, a mix of manure and sweat and sun-crinkled hay.

Oblivious of the simmering heat, the kids I followed wove through the crowd like skilled running backs sliding through their offensive line, yet they slowed down at each food booth—the 4-H Pancake Shack, Jim's Fish Fry, the Galesville Fire Department (hot dogs and hamburgers)—to see if they knew anybody at the picnic tables. Eventually, they split off in different directions. I continued on the paved walkway, which was jam-packed with sweaty bodies and strollers and giant stuffed monkeys and balloons and animals crossing from barn to barn.

Along with the chatter of conversation, a whir of electricity filled the air, interrupted for a brief moment by distant chanting: "U.S.A, U.S.A, U.S.A." I stepped over a mass of cords, which was pinned to the muddy ground by plywood strips. Then I circled around the Tilt-A-Whirl, the Bullet, and the Round-Up. The machines were run-down, greasy, rusted. The Tilt-A-Whirl's clunky red buckets struggled to spin; the massive chain that spun the arm of the Bullet ticked like the cocking of a gun. Laughter. Screams. Shouts. Cheers. Hair band rock poured out of nearby speakers. Quiet Riot. Too old for this crap, the teens riding the Rock 'n' Rollercoaster wore bored expressions.

In all the chaos, there was no sign of Eli.

In front of me, toddlers tossed Ping-Pong balls into tiny fishbowls and clinked plastic rings off the necks of beer bottles. My head filled with the rapid fire of pellet guns and the bells and whistles of the water cannon race. A pale man with a red mustache and a torn blue tank yelled at me. "You!" he said. "You. I'm talking to you." I ignored him at first. "Throw a ball, win a prize. Throw a ball, win a prize. Toss the ball," he said. "Lots of prizes. Come on, my man. You look like you need to feel good about yourself."

"No, thanks."

He smiled. His teeth were an unnatural shade of white.

"Three shots for five bucks. Can't beat that with a stick."

I waved him off.

"Don't tease me, bro," he said. "You're really gonna walk away?"

I did.

"Chump."

A balloon popped to my side, pierced by a dull dart. Flanked by two boys in peewee football jerseys, a young father spun the darts in his fingers. The boys cheered when the second balloon popped. The man lined up the third dart, steady in his eye, elbow ninety degrees, and he let it fly—it hit a green balloon directly in its bulbous center and bounced off.

"Oh, that's rigged!"

"Try again?" the carny said. The man shook his head. "What kind of father are you? You gonna let your kids down?" I viewed the prizes that were hung around the booth—glass pictures of a Siberian tiger, Tupac, Kim Kardashian, Eminem, and one with a skull and crossbones that read BAD TO THE BONE. Still, the kids sulked as they walked away.

I circled around the sea of lights to the Ferris wheel. Jenny hadn't resurfaced.

The storm drew closer. The air was heavy.

The faces in the crowd all started to look the same. Angry. Hot. Sweaty. Swindled.

It would've been thirty-five or thirty-six years ago that Eli and Hadley were at the fairgrounds. I wondered how the fair must've looked then. I imagined agricultural products and 4-H crafts and livestock. Other than the Ferris wheel, the rides were most likely of a different variety—the carnival had become a traveling theater of unholy crap. The flashing lights and the bombardment of noises made you think that life was exciting, but it induced seizures and chest pains, and kids left with giant poorly made stuffed aliens and glass paintings of faded pop culture heroes. This is where icons came to die, I thought, as I passed by a blond-haired boy vomiting behind a barn.

On my return to the Ferris wheel, someone yelled my name. I turned around to find the owner of the voice—Nikki.

"Hey, I thought that was you," she said.

"Have you seen Eli?"

"Did you lose him?" she yelled over the noise.

"Not exactly."

Jenny entered behind Nikki, out of breath, chest heaving. The two of them exchanged glances and offered hellos without the necessity of words.

Just then, amid Jenny's soft wheezing and the crowd's buzz and the onslaught of noise, I could make out the faint moan of a fiddle. I spun around, trying to locate the music.

"I don't think he's here," Jenny said, her voice sad and lonesome.

"He's here." I walked toward the fiddle and spotted the old bandstand. "Did you find Cal?" I asked.

"He said he's not going to waste his only day off thinking about Eli Page."

"Not surprised," I muttered. Word was that he'd been warned to stay away from Eli while there was a case pending.

"I asked him to keep an eye out for Todd Decker," Jenny said. "He nodded, for what it's worth."

"You guys looking for Todd?" Nikki asked. "'Cause I saw him about an hour ago—"

"Where?" Jenny and I interrupted together.

"Over by the bandstand."

The rain came and went and came back again. Thunder rumbled above the clouds, and the wind swirled around the barns and through the booths and bleachers.

"Go back to Cal," I said. "Tell him to get over here. Tell him I found Eli. Drag him by his neck if you have to."

Trusting me fully, Jenny bolted without uttering another question. I followed Nikki, who'd agreed to lead the way to Decker.

In the bandstand, a hefty mustachioed man with a banjo stood next to a woman in an emerald dress. Even in the gray, lightless sky, the dress shimmered like bioluminescent plankton in the night sea, and her long amber hair curled and whispered in the breeze. The fiddle rested under her chin as her bow swooped back and forth.

"He's gone," Nikki said. "I swear he was right here."

I scanned the faces, but I didn't see Todd Decker. The fiddler smiled, moved her elbow forward, and burst into a windstorm of slides as her feet moved side to side and her body swayed. "I'll Fly Away." The audience stood up and bobbed their heads in time with the music, which made my job all the more difficult.

When I die, Hallelujah, by and by.
I'll fly away (I'll fly away).

I closed my eyes for a moment, drifting into reverie. It wasn't hard to imagine Eli and Hadley sitting together in 1974 or 1975, taking in the music, the smell of livestock, the bone-dry air. Eli and Hadley abandoned New York City to find some peace, and he found a sliver of it in her upstate town, but he quickly grew restless. I guess we're all forced to make decisions—some of them pan out, others don't. Who knows which ones we will regret?

The band didn't let the rain slow them down. I cast an eye over the stage. There, to the right, beside the speakers, a ghostly figure stood alone, arms folded. I stepped forward, daring the figure to vanish. It didn't. He didn't.

Dressed in dark jeans with a large silver belt buckle, a blue plaid shirt, and a wool cap, Eli was preparing to do something he hadn't done in years—perform. He looked the part, except that his leather bag hung by his hip. I wondered if he'd forgotten to set it down. At that moment he was a watcher too, waiting for something.

During the limbo that was my life between the Melanie debacle and my arrival in Galesville, I'd worked security for a few Bob Dylan concerts. My job was simple: Guard the ramp that led to his trailer. One time, as I stood at the aluminum rail, listening to the raw and bluesy music of Steve Earle, Dylan exited the trailer and brushed by me. I watched him stroll behind the stage and around the grass outfield, free from an audience or from his manager or the road crew or the other musicians. A dog ran up to him. He knelt down to pet it. Then he tossed a stick out into center field and waited for the dog to bring it back. The animal grabbed the stick and ran off. I couldn't help but think of that moment as I pondered Eli's next move.

"Is that him?" Nikki asked as we bumped shoulders. I didn't answer her. Instead, I asked, "Any sign of Decker?"

"No."

Eli hung his head and rolled it back and forth. Finally, he stepped forward to steal a portion of the stage light. At first, the woman in the emerald dress didn't notice or didn't care. The banjo player and the bassist carried on, also unmoved by this strange man entering their space. Suddenly a thunderous buzz filled that tiny corner of the fairgrounds. Eli lifted a guitar from the rack. One by one the musicians stopped playing, leaving only the fiddler, who finished with a zip of the bow. No one recognized him without the beard. Not at first. Not until he spoke.

"Thank you." Eli lifted the guitar strap over his head; it sat on his shoulder on top of the satchel's strap. "I wasn't gonna come back up tonight, but I couldn't leave without givin' you good folks an encore." He checked the action on the guitar, retuned. "So that's what I'll do—give you an encore."

Realizing that something was amiss, the crowd began to mutter. Eventually resentment gave way to recognition and then confusion. A few "boos" rang out. Someone yelled, "Get off the stage, old man."

Eli was oblivious to the heckling. "You might know this one," he said. He picked the intro to Dylan's "You're a Big Girl Now." The strings rattled and buzzed. No doubt his fingertips were soft and tender, no longer trained to hold the wires down.

The band looked around for some guidance. The woman in the emerald dress shrugged, resigned to the moment. She picked up her bow and joined Eli. The others followed. Some in the crowd stepped to the front of the bandstand for a closer look; others exchanged confused glances. Most pulled out their phones and began to record. By the third verse, the audience had doubled in size.

"What's he doing?" Nikki asked me.

"I don't know."

I was locked in time and space. It was miraculous to see him up there again, but I was stuck between watching this glorious event and scanning the faces in the crowd. When the song ended, I waited for Eli to leave the stage, but he stayed put.

He moved to the microphone. "Been on tour awhile now," he said. "But it feels good to be here again. It always does. Good folks here." An air of concern rose from the crowd. Of course, it manifested itself through the force of a hundred cell phones raised in the air, taking photos and filming video. "Thought I'd play one more song for you tonight before I close it down," Eli continued. "Now, this is a song I don't do in public, but this is a special occasion. A homecoming." A rumble rolled through the crowd. There was a commotion to my left. People were pushing and pulling. Eli turned his attention toward the stirring and caught me, dead in the eye. I held his stare. "When I was much younger, I met a girl from Galesville. We had a life. For a few months. We had a life. We came here, to these fairgrounds, thirty-somethin' years ago, but then I left for a tour and she didn't make it. This is for her. And for our baby girl."

Eli picked a few notes and began to play "If You've Got the Time." The agony in his face, the wavering in his voice, were almost too much to bear. Deep sorrow and anger and longing were on display for everyone to see. The faces in the crowd turned to each other. Whispers were silenced by the storm. He was a thin man, wrapped in a guitar just like he'd been that first time I saw him at the PAC, and I was hit with a sudden sadness that I cannot fully describe here with words. It stretched far and wide and reached out to every corner of Galesville from the Battenkill to the Green Mountains.

Thunder cracked and everyone looked to the sky. Unfazed, Eli stood at the very edge of the stage and finished his song.

Maybe I screwed up early on
Didn't know which way to turn
Maybe I got caught in the dawn
Lookin' for a new trail to burn
But there's nothing I can do to make it up to you
There's nothing I can say to make it go away
When you cross that river, there's no turnin' back
When you stretch that line, it's bound to snap
Even after all these years, you're first on my mind
And I'm lookin' for a miracle, if you've got the time.

I'm hopin' for a miracle, if you've got the time.
Yeah, I'm hopin' for a miracle, if you've got the time.

For a moment, wrapped up in all that I was witnessing, everything was perfect and everything was perfectly broken, and I understood that no matter how hard you try, there are just some things that you cannot put back together again. Sometimes the water catches up and overwhelms and there's nothing to do but let go.

When it all happened, it did so in slow motion.

Three shots shattered the air. *Crack. Crack, Crack.*

Eli stumbled back, fell to the stage floor, and flattened.

After a moment of blood-curdling silence, the crowd rushed for cover, trampling anything in their path. Jenny was swept up in the surge, beating through the retreating bodies, swimming against the current. She and I were the only people moving toward the noise, toward the stage, toward Eli. Her face was screwed up as if she was bellowing against the wind, but I couldn't hear a word. When I reached the platform, I planted my palm on the lip and hurled myself onto the stage. Eli was silent, but he was conscious, staring at the bandstand's ceiling, blinking repeatedly. I must've called to him, but I can't remember. My memory is contorted. I remember I wanted to get him some privacy. So I dragged him upstage, behind a row of speakers, out of sight.

He propped himself up on his forearms. I removed the leather satchel that was strapped to his shoulder, and I patted his body, searching for blood, wounds, and bullet holes. There was nothing. "Are you hurt?" I asked two, maybe five, times. "Were you hit?"

Eli's face was cauliflower pale. He didn't recognize who I was. Not at first. His pupils were nickel-size and clouded by confusion, but he was breathing.

"We should get you checked out," I said

"No. No need. I don't need help." He grabbed my wrist.

"Let me get someone."

"I don't need an EMT. If you want to help, get Jenny Lee. I need to tell her something."

"Now?"

"Tell her it's not her fault; it's mine. She needs to hear it. Will you tell her?"

"Hold on. I'll get her." Against my better judgment, I did what he asked. It took me a second or two, but I found Jenny at the foot of the stage. She raised her arms above her head. I reached out, grabbed her hands and wrists, and pulled her up. From the bandstand, we both looked back over the bleachers and the field and the scene of the crime.

"Is he okay? Was he shot?" she asked.

"He's fine," I said. "He asked me to get you."

She didn't move right away. "You were right. It was him," she said, voice shaking in tandem with her hands. "All of it. This whole time, it was him."

"Go," I managed to say, despite not having full control of my senses. My mind was scattershot, but as she brushed by me, I thought about the newspaper page that Eli had left on the harvest table. *Forgive Yourself.* Those two words, which he'd inked in the margin, were meant for all of us in our own way.

From the stage, I watched the remainder of the crowd thin out to reveal Cal standing tall over Todd Decker's dead body. A body cloaked in Eli's clothes—the same jeans, the same sun-washed canvas shirt, the same type of wool cap. Decker's gun was in the mud. Slowly, Cal turned to look at me, and he tipped his head. I nodded back. Above him, the sky was dark and brooding. Sirens wailed. We were all wet and wired and shocked and out of words or gestures. Cal's gun was reholstered, but before I turned away, I saw that his right hand was still shaking.

First responders flooded the area.

Thunder rolled.

Jenny shouted, "Jack. He's not here."

"I left him upstage, behind the speakers," I said, somehow doubting her ability to see him prostrate right in front of her. Then I ran to the spot where I'd last seen Eli and discovered it was empty. She was right. Nothing. No body. Even his satchel was gone. All that remained on the stage floor above the speakers were three tiny drops of blood.

I spun around, searching for any sign of him. A bolt of lightning lit up the field behind the stage for a split second. In the flash, I thought I saw someone. I jumped off the back of the bandstand and ran toward the figure.

"Eli." I called his name again and again.

Lightning flashed, and I kept running. Thunder shook the ground. It was right on top of us. I stood still in the field under the wild sky and felt the vibrations rise through my feet to my knees. I was ready for whatever would come.

When the sky flashed again three times in rapid succession, I saw Eli—or something that looked like Eli—within the strobe. He turned to me and nodded, water pouring off the rim of his cap. Everything went black. My eyes were slow to readjust, and when they did there was nothing in the field but mud puddles. The sky opened up and the rain came down heavier than it had ever come down in my lifetime.

I stared into the empty space and then behind me at Jenny, who was sprinting in my direction, then back at where I'd last seen Eli.

But he was gone.

Jenny tugged on my arm, spinning me to face her. From top to bottom, she was soaked, her hair stuck to her forehead, her clothes sealed to her body. Wonder filled her eyes, but it was quietly supplanted by worry.

"Did you see him?" she asked.

"No. Wasn't him."

The thunder was pulling away, following the old troubadour down the road. The flood was just beginning. It would rain for several more hours. It would rain for days. In some ways, it has never stopped raining.

"Come on," she said. "Let's get out of this field." She ran for cover. I turned and followed.

That was the last time I ever saw Eli Page. As the rain swirled and the sky roared, I ran back toward the stage, toward Jenny, toward Galesville, and toward whatever life we'd choose to pursue in Eli's wake.

When you cross that river, there's no turnin' back
When you stretch that line, it's bound to snap
Even after all these years, you're first on my mind
And I'm lookin' for a miracle, if you've got the time.

• OUTRO •

B arry Gettleson called this morning.

"Do you have anything we can use?" he asked. "Anything at all?"

"Nothing," I lied. What he doesn't know won't kill him, and he certainly doesn't know what I've been up to for the last few weeks. My story, typed hastily on this old Underwood, is not the one Barry wanted me to write. It's something far different, far more personal. This "book," the story of Eli Page and how he gave me so much, is a song for Eli, but I think I'll keep it under lock and key. At least for a while. Maybe one day I'll share it or burn it or publish it or chain it to a cinder block and sink it into the deepest section of the Battenkill. I don't know where it will end up, but I know it had to be written.

The last time Gettleson and I saw each other, he was less than pleased. He showed up at my door, carrying a large envelope. "We need to strike while the iron's hot," he said. Eli had been missing for less than a month, and Gettleson was already working the angles.

Inside the envelope was a file folder that contained a one-of-a-kind handwritten interview: "Everything You Ever Wanted to Know about Eli Page but Were Afraid to Ask." Gettleson explained that Eli had written the piece when traveling to see doctors, but he'd sealed it and demanded Barry deliver it to me if anything were to happen.

Gettleson was optimistic. He believed that this piece could be the key to the book or, at the very least, something that *Rolling Stone* would be interested in. "The prospect of this work is the only thing that's kept me sane," he proclaimed. "So open it up."

I ripped open the envelope and pulled out the document. Its yellow pages were loaded with questions, followed by three possible one-word answers: "yes," "no," and "maybe." In a makeshift multiple-choice format, one of those words was circled underneath each question, but I wasn't sure I could trust the answers to be real. In fact, I knew they were all lies, which triggered a fit of laughter.

Gettleson, on the other hand, wasn't amused. The envelope was his last best hope.

"There are no shortcuts," I told him as he stormed out.

In addition to his role as trickster, Eli, at least in the few months that I'd known him, was a creature of habit. Besides comfort and self-reflection (often opposing needs), there was a starkness, a nakedness to his pattern making that offered a flicker of insight into his life. Or so I learned over time.

After Eli's disappearance, I too fell into a routine. I got up at dawn and Tig and I visited the river before hiking to the graveyard, sitting on the stone bench, and looking out over the land. Eventually, writing this book became part of my routine. Certainly, without a doubt, it has helped me cope, helped me grieve, but somewhere along the line, the routine began to feel passive, almost indifferent. I started to wonder if it was just an obsessive tendency with no prospect of meaningful return. Was I just wasting time?

That's just the long way of saying that I'm done. Cooked. Moving on. So this morning, for the first time in a long time, I didn't go to the river or the graveyard, and honestly, it felt like the manacles had come undone. Whatever I needed a month ago or two months ago or one year ago is no longer needed today. Now I need to get on with my life while I've got the time.

So this is it—my last few thoughts.

River Bend Farm, which had been home to Hadley and Eliza and Eli, is a canoe, a shallow boat that drifts slowly through time, picking up debris and slogging through memory. One day it may reach its destination, but that remains to be determined.

According to Gettleson, Eli wanted me to have the farm (or half of it). Sometime before his arrest, Eli had updated his will, splitting what was left of his "estate" and bequeathing it—along with custody of Tig—to his "two loyal friends, who deserve to duke it out": Jenny Lee Flynn and John "Jack" Wyeth. One last laugh before he exited the stage for good. (I have to hand it to him—it worked. Jenny and I are both holding on to that live wire until it bucks us off.)

Eli would've turned seventy this week. The day will pass as it's always done. Right now, as I type, Jenny is waiting for me. She's home from school for the long weekend, and guests have begun to arrive. The last time we saw each other (a few weekends ago), we agreed to resurrect Eli's barn concert as a way to celebrate his birthday. So tonight, thirty or forty people will take over the old barn with music, food, and storytelling. Musicians have traveled from all over to pay respects, to cover Eli's songs in Eli's barn, and to celebrate his life. With or without him physically present.

Not surprisingly, everyone is listening to Eli's music again. The blurry videos of his final concert went viral, picked up and shared by millions. Now his older fans listen to the songs side by side with their children or grandchildren—they share something, connect in ways that weren't possible before, hear things they didn't hear before. The younger generation trades bootlegs of Eli's concerts online, downloads the albums for their iPod playlists, and wears hipster T-shirts with Eli's profile screen-printed over their chests. There are websites and discussion boards devoted to Eli, YouTube covers, tribute albums, and too many blog posts to count (a few are bold enough to claim that he's still alive, living off the grid, deep in the Adirondacks). And, in an absurd twist, Eli Page even has a Facebook account and a Twitter handle. The mask has a life of its own.

There were always two Elis, and two Elis remain. One is embedded in the public's consciousness; the other is elusive, personal. Only a few of us knew them both, yet every single one of us was charmed by the myth as much as we were charmed by the man. Sometimes myth can be more powerful than truth.

Eli's story is not my story to tell or reappropriate or co-opt, but it is the only story that I have, the only story that matters, for it is the story that changed my life's trajectory. I interrupted him; he interrupted me. Our histories are scratched into the same vinyl, burned into the same disc, archived on the same digital tapestry (even if I'm but one note for his two hundred thousand). But make no mistake, what you see here, on this stack of paper, is my story. Eli just helped me play the right notes in the right order.

People come up to me all the time, just as Eli predicted they would when I first arrived in Galesville, and ask: Who was the real Eli Page? What was he like? Was he a genius? I can only say to them that Eli was my friend, and he was a man like any other—flawed and hurting and grasping for answers.

Galesville, 2010

ACKOWLEDGMENTS

I'm grateful for the many wonderful teachers who have instructed, guided, and inspired me along the way, including Sarah Schulman, Richard Panek, Matthew Zapruder, Kirby Farrell, Carol Frost, Robert Bensen, Duncan Smith, Ken Golden, Robert Bresnick, David Cody, Terry Fitz-Henry, Kim Noling, and Jim Duquette.

I owe an oversized thank you to everyone at Other Press, but especially to Judith Gurewich, who believed in the book and took a chance on an unknown writer. Keenan, Marjorie, Yvonne, Charlotte, Terrie, Jeff, and the rest of the team who championed this novel along the way (and those who continue to champion it today) thank you for your expertise, your enthusiasm, and your hard work.

For my agent, Christopher Rhodes, who shepherded the book through the ups and downs, never wavering in his belief and his support, I am so grateful. Your dedication, your reassurance, and your tenacity meant a lot to me throughout the process, and they mean a lot to me now as we look ahead. Thank you for lifting me out of the pile and putting me on the right path.

Thank you to past, present, and future readers, as well as past, present, and future folk music lovers, especially those who continue to support clubs and coffeehouses like Caffè Lena. Speaking of the Caffè, thank you to Sarah, Dianne, Stanley, and the rest of the board who keep the Caffè alive and kicking. Also, on a somewhat similar note, thanks to Sue and Jeff at Beehive Productions and to M. R. (Mike) Poulpoulous for their generosity, time, and talent—I feel very lucky to have worked with you all, and I hope you had fun.

I'd also like to acknowledge the bookstores that are my lifeline and where I've spent so much time—Northshire Bookstore (Saratoga Springs, NY, and Manchester, VT), Battenkill Books (Cambridge, NY), and Market Block Books (Troy, NY); the organizations that have recharged and motivated me on multiple occasions, including the New York State Writers Institute, Grub Street, the Frequency North reading series, and the now-defunct Inkberry; and the spaces in between including MASS MoCA, Caffè Lena, and Sage. Thank you all.

For my family and friends, who have heard me talk about the writing, the book, and the process ad nauseum for years without the opportunity to see what I was up to, thank you for your patience, your occasional eye rolls, and your encouragement.

Most important, thank you to Kate, Finn, and Molly, who make it all worthwhile.

W. B. BELCHER grew up in western Massachusetts and earned his MFA from Goddard College. He lives along the Battenkill River in upstate New York with his wife and two children. *Lay Down Your Weary Tune* is his first novel.

◫ OTHER PRESS

You might also enjoy these titles from our list:

BROKEN SLEEP by Bruce Bauman

Spanning 1940s to 2020s America, a Pynchon-esque saga about rock music, art, politics, and the elusive nature of love

"Vibrant, captivating, and touching...*Broken Sleep* is brimming with colorful characters, fascinating dialogue, and beautiful yet tragic relationships, making it easy to read and hard to forget." —*PopMatters*

WHISPER HOLLOW by Chris Cander

Set in a small coal-mining town, a debut novel full of secrets, love, betrayal, and suspicious accidents, where two courageous women make choices that will challenge our own moral convictions

"*Whisper Hollow* is wonderful. It's carefully written, unpredictable, sexy when it should be, and scary when it has to be...Reminiscent of D. H. Lawrence." —*Houston Chronicle*

STALEMATE by Icchokas Meras

A classic of Holocaust literature from "one of the great masters of the short novel." —*The New Yorker*

This is a moving story of a father and a son who shame their cruel perpetrator with their dignity, spirit, and extraordinary courage. As a parable that gives voice to the unspeakable, *Stalemate* is an antidote to despair.

"Gripping...a truly memorable work." —*Booklist*